P9-CDF-704

F
Pella   Pella, Judith.

             Homeward my heart.

DATE			

Seneca Falls Library
47 Cayuga Street
Seneca Falls, NY 13148

3/05
BAKER & TAYLOR

Seneca Falls Library
47 Cayuga Street
Seneca Falls, NY 13148

Presented by

Grace E. Cafolla

In memory of

Rose C. Sinicropi

Homeward My Heart

Books by Judith Pella

Beloved Stranger
*The Stonewycke Trilogy**
*The Stonewycke Legacy**
Texas Angel / Heaven's Road

DAUGHTERS OF FORTUNE
Written on the Wind
Somewhere a Song
Toward the Sunrise
Homeward My Heart

RIBBONS OF STEEL†
Distant Dreams
A Hope Beyond
A Promise for Tomorrow

RIBBONS WEST†
Westward the Dream
Separate Roads
Ties That Bind

THE RUSSIANS
*The Crown and the Crucible**
*A House Divided**
*Travail and Triumph**
Heirs of the Motherland
Dawning of Deliverance
White Nights, Red Morning
Passage Into Light

*with Michael Phillips †with Tracie Peterson

JUDITH PELLA

Homeward My Heart

BETHANYHOUSE
PUBLISHERS
MINNEAPOLIS, MINNESOTA

Homeward My Heart
Copyright © 2004
Judith Pella

Cover design by Dan Thornberg

All rights reserved. No part of this publication may be reproduced, stored in a retrieval system, or transmitted in any form or by any means—electronic, mechanical, photocopying, recording, or otherwise—without the prior written permission of the publisher and copyright owners.

Published by Bethany House Publishers
11400 Hampshire Avenue South
Bloomington, Minnesota 55438
www.bethanyhouse.com

Bethany House Publishers is a division of
Baker Publishing Group, Grand Rapids, Michigan.

Printed in the United States of America

ISBN 0-7642-2424-7 (Trade Paper)
ISBN 0-7642-2848-X (Hardcover)
ISBN 0-7642-2847-1 (Large Print)

Library of Congress Cataloging-in-Publication Data

Pella, Judith.
    Homeward my heart / by Judith Pella.
        p.   cm. — (Daughters of fortune ; 4)
    ISBN 0-7642-2848-X (alk. paper)
    ISBN 0-7642-2424-7 (pbk.)
    ISBN 0-7642-2847-1 (large print pbk.)
        1. Americans—Soviet Union—Fiction. 2. Missing persons—Fiction. 3. Soviet
Union—Fiction. 4. Stepbrothers—Fiction. 5. Cold War—Fiction. 6. Sisters—Fiction.
I. Title II. Series: Pella, Judith. Daughters of fortune ; 4.
    PS3566.E415H655   2004
    813'.54—dc22   2004012914

Fic.

Seneca Falls Library
47 Cayuga Street
Seneca Falls, N.Y. 13148

About the Author

Judith Pella is the author of several historical fiction series, both on her own and in collaboration with Michael Phillips and Tracie Peterson. The extraordinary seven-book series THE RUSSIANS, the first three written with Phillips, showcases her creativity and skill as a historian as well as a fiction writer. A Bachelor of Arts degree in social studies, along with a career in nursing and teaching, lends depth to her storytelling abilities, providing readers with memorable novels in a variety of genres. She and her husband make their home in Oregon.

Visit Judith's Web site:
www.judithpella.com

PART I

"From Stettin in the Baltic to Trieste in the
Adriatic an iron curtain has descended
across the continent."

WINSTON CHURCHILL, FULTON, MISSOURI
March 5, 1946

* * *

"There is no doubt
that Mr. Churchill's speech
is a call to war with the Soviet Union."

JOSEF STALIN, *PRAVDA*
March 13, 1946

1

Germany
April 1946

CANDLELIGHT MADE odd shapes on the pure white tablecloth, flickering patterns of light and dark. Cameron stared at the fluttering hues, transfixed. She tried to keep her gaze averted from the empty chair across the table from her, but there was nowhere else to rest her eyes, nowhere that didn't make her heart clench as if a fist had grasped it.

But she and Alex had promised each other they would do this, would perform this ritual that now seemed both silly and poignant. For that reason she had requested the hotel's best china, silver, and crystal for two settings. A young man had delivered the things and assisted in setting the table. He'd given her a little wink, assuming she was arranging for a romantic rendezvous. He was still grinning when, just a half hour ago, he'd wheeled in a cart with an elegant meal for two. The boy was no more than eighteen or nineteen, blond and fresh faced. He could have been one of Hitler's Youth, for all Cameron knew. By his appearance you could not have discerned that barely a year previously his country had suffered a devastating military defeat. He looked more like a kid wanting a bit of fun. Cameron tipped him well so that he could take his girl to dinner and a movie. There ought to be at least one romantic interlude for someone that night.

9

It would not be here in room 214 of the Schmidt Hotel in Nuremburg, Germany. Cameron had known even as the meal cart had been delivered that she would have no appetite for the roasted beef, au gratin potatoes, and sautéed carrots. It was all purely symbolic, as were the candlelight and the elegant place settings. This was how she and Alex had imagined they would spend the first anniversary of their marriage had they actually been together. Alex had predicted they might not be able to do so in a physical sense, but it might take the sting out of the separation if they could arrange a spiritual connection of sorts. In the few letters they had exchanged, thanks to Robert Wood at the U.S. embassy in Moscow, who had been acting as a conduit for the illicit communication, Alex and Cameron had even arranged the time of their meal. Because Cameron had known by then she'd be in Germany, they had chosen seven o'clock in the evening Berlin time, which would be nine o'clock in Moscow.

At this very moment in Moscow Alex would be sitting at a table, probably in his small apartment, with candlelight and as fine a meal as he could manage in a country that had not yet recovered from wartime shortages. What was on their plates did not matter, whether it be borscht and bread or chateaubriand. Alex was there also staring across a table at an empty place setting.

Were they simply gluttons for punishment? Was this the most morbid ritual ever devised?

Tears welled up in Cameron's eyes. Oh, how she hated to cry! And she'd always had little sympathy for people who felt sorry for themselves. But she couldn't easily shake off her melancholy. She'd known on her wedding day that they were entering into a seemingly impossible situation. She'd *known*, but on some level she hadn't truly *believed*. She remembered what she had told Alex when she had proposed to him. . . .

"Alex, there is a power in the marriage bond. I know it! A deep spiritual power but also another kind of power, one that I know in my heart will bring us back together in the future."

Now she realized that when she had used the word *future*,

she'd been thinking weeks or months. Not a year . . . and counting! They had both been so full of hope back then, such that they had eschewed the idea of running away together and forcing Alex to become a fugitive, a deserter from the army with a death sentence on his head. Looking back, she wondered if the risk might not have been worth it. The world was big, with many hiding places. But neither of them was built for hiding, and Alex had tried running away once from his troubles in America, and he knew from experience that running solved nothing.

Besides, running and hiding seemed to discount their faith in God's care. Cameron needed to believe that God was exercising control over their lives. Perhaps if she'd been in charge, she would have done things differently, but she had to believe that God's way was better, no matter what it appeared on the surface.

With stoic determination she lifted the silver lid from the serving platter. The fragrance of beef in a rich wine sauce rose to her nose. She'd been in Germany long enough since the war's end to know better than to waste food, regardless of her melancholy. For that reason, symbolism aside, she'd requested a small portion of food. She spooned the beef, then some potatoes and carrots onto her plate. She left the one across from her empty. She thought of Alex as she took a bite of the meat, of their first meeting in the Moscow bomb shelter, how Cameron had convinced him to go with her to the roof of the building to see what was going on during the bombing. He'd thought she was crazy. She smiled. He probably considered most of her antics after that crazy, as well. Still, he'd fallen in love with her. And she had probably first begun to fall in love with him there on the roof, when she had compared him with her friend and sometime lover Johnny Shanahan and had perceived a depth in Alex, a many-layered character that had been lacking in Johnny and so many other men of her acquaintance.

She attempted to conjure a picture of Alex in her mind, his tall strong form, his light wavy hair, and those incredible blue eyes. But the image in her head was blurry. The eyes that reflected emotion like a pool reflects a crisp, clear summer's day were . . . dull.

Both panic and anger twisted inside her. It wasn't fair that she had only a fading image to comfort her.

"No, I wasn't going to go in that direction!" she reminded herself.

She jumped up and went to the bedside table, where she found the Bible her mother had given her before she left the States for this German assignment. Tucked within the pages of Psalms were the photos her friend Edna had taken at her wedding. They were black and white and small, except for one that she'd had one of the *Journal*'s photographers enlarge. Her heart actually skipped a beat as she gazed at the happy couple standing before the altar of the Lutheran church in the German village where she and Alex had married. In the background bomb damage could be seen—a stained-glass window partially destroyed and a corner of the roof open to sunlight. But that was no more discordant than the couple themselves holding hands and gazing into each other's eyes. They were hardly dressed for a wedding— Cameron in her Army fatigues, and Alex in ill-fitting secondhand clothes bought from some of the villagers.

In a moment of uncharacteristic sentimentality, Cameron kissed the tip of her finger and touched Alex's image in the photo.

"I love you, Alex," she murmured.

And, in an odd way she could not explain, she felt certain he was at that very moment saying the very same thing.

I love you, Camrushka . . . the silent expression traveled to her over the nearly one thousand miles that separated them.

Alex had been right. This ritual was a good thing. But please, God, she prayed, this isn't how I want to spend our *second* anniversary!

2

THE METRO TEEMED with humanity even at this time of day, but many were still working long hours even though the war had ended. As Alex bumped shoulders with a hurrying passerby, he glanced at his wristwatch. Eight o'clock. He shook his head, bemoaning once again that this had been the only time the man he was to meet could make contact with him. In an hour he was to have his symbolic anniversary dinner. He was barely going to make it.

"I'm sorry, Cameron," he said silently. But of course she knew he was always late.

However, this time it was not going to be due to his notoriously frantic medical schedule. Yet perhaps she'd be just as forgiving of this lapse. In a way it was for her, for them, that he was making this rendezvous in the metro. Though he still questioned its wisdom. Perhaps he should have questioned it more two weeks ago when he had agreed to do this thing.

It was then that a friend who attended Alex's underground church had shared that his son was being watched by the MVD, a new appellation for the secret police previously called the NKVD. The young man was almost certain to be arrested soon. The father wanted to help his son escape the country but had no idea how to begin such a process or who to approach to obtain false papers. It might have been prudent for Alex to remain silent despite the fact that he knew a person in the business of making such documents. Several years ago he had aided Cameron in the failed attempt to help Sophia's husband escape. Alex's part had been to act as go-between with the printer of Oleg's false papers. He'd contacted the man who did the work—he wasn't certain how Cameron had come by the fellow's name, though he thought someone at the American embassy had come up with it.

Regardless, Alex had information that now might help his friend, if the person was still in business. Alex had offered to look into it. He still had a fair amount of free movement because of his occupation. He could easily explain a visit to a stranger with the excuse of making a house call. Though his reason for agreeing wasn't entirely altruistic.

He had not been patiently watching the year slip away since his marriage. Indeed, he was becoming more desperate as each day passed with no prospect in sight of reuniting with Cameron. He had hounded the Emigration Bureau until he sensed that to do so again would surely bring him under police scrutiny, if it hadn't already. So with legal means of leaving Russia seemingly exhausted, he was thinking more and more of other means. By contacting the illicit printer for his friend, he was also exploring some possibilities for himself.

Was it a risk he was ready to take? Was he truly that desperate? If it backfired, as in Oleg's case, it would be the end for him and Cameron. Poor Sophia had heard nothing from her husband since his arrest and wasn't even sure if he was still alive. Alex wouldn't put Cameron through that.

Still, the words *nothing ventured, nothing gained* popped into his head. That would no doubt be Cameron's response.

He smiled as he thought of his dear wife. And his heart ached for them to be together, to have a real life with each other at last.

And toward that end, whether he was ready or not, he forced his concentration onto the task at hand. He gazed about the platform casually. A train sped into the station with a loud roar. Many of the crowd surged forward. Alex made sure the copy of

Pravda tucked under his arm was visible. It wasn't a very good means of recognition, since every other person had a newspaper in hand. But he and his contact had met once before, so they knew each other's faces. Still, the fellow seemed to enjoy playing the spy game, for he had given yet another means of recognition. Alex was to stand beneath the mosaic of the strong Russian peasant woman with a fat, healthy baby in her arms. He did as instructed, but unfortunately it wasn't as crowded here. He realized now that crowds could be a blessing. He felt vulnerable. Yes, his contact could see him more easily but so could the police. He concentrated on appearing nonchalant.

There he was!

The same middle-aged man with thinning brown hair and thick spectacles that Alex had met with a week ago and had arranged for the papers to be made. The same man who had prepared the documents for Oleg. Alex only knew his first name, Pytor.

He strolled casually toward Alex, though he never once appeared to even see Alex. He had obviously done this many times before. Alex shifted his gaze from the man and waited.

Suddenly the man stopped a couple of paces from Alex and bent down, apparently to tie his shoe.

"Third phone stall from left at exit," he voiced, just loud enough for Alex to hear. Then he rose and sauntered away.

Alex waited till the man was out of sight, then ambled away himself. He took the up escalator and located the row of phone stalls near the exit. The printer was there with the phone receiver held to his ear, but he quickly hung up the phone and walked away, never acknowledging Alex. Alex took a coin from his pocket when he reached the stall, lifted the receiver, and dialed a number, his hospital's number, though it really didn't matter what number, but he thought it would look better if he actually made a call. As he did so, he saw the envelope tucked on the small tray beneath the phone and laid his newspaper on the envelope. His hand was trembling. He'd performed delicate surgery in the midst of heavy bombing with a steadier hand. He simply was not cut out for this cloak-and-dagger business!

When the hospital operator answered, he made some innocuous request about visiting hours, hung up, then gathered up his newspaper with the envelope tucked inside and walked away. He held his breath, his heart pounding. He felt at any moment the police would jump out at him.

He was still a jangle of nerves a half hour later when he climbed the stairs to his apartment. He'd lost his old place because of his absence during the war, and now with shortages of living space as well as everything else, he was fortunate to have found a room to rent in the home of a family. It was not a spacious apartment to begin with, and the family consisted of Mr. and Mrs. Rimsky, along with her aged parents and four or five children—they came and went in so many different directions that Alex was never able to get a clear count, but they ranged in age from about ten to sixteen. The place was always noisy, and Mr. Rimsky drank to excess and was unpleasant when drunk. But they didn't mind Alex's erratic work schedule, so Alex tried not to mind theirs.

His room was at the back, about a hundred and twenty square feet. It was barely large enough for essential furnishings, and now, with only a half hour before his "rendezvous" with Cameron, he began to wonder about the logistics of this dinner. He'd been thinking of this event for days, anticipating the moment almost as if it were a real meeting, foolish though it might seem. But he'd been thinking only of the spiritual and emotional elements, not the practical. What was he going to do for food? This was *supposed* to be a dinner. Had he not been so shaken by his meeting in the metro, he might have thought to pick up something at a market on his way home.

He turned around and headed toward the kitchen, happy to find Mrs. Rimsky still there washing up after her family's dinner.

"Well, you're home early, now, aren't you?" she said in a congenial tone. She was forty, dumpy and drab in dress and appearance. She looked older than her years, and no wonder with having to work full time at a munitions factory in addition to caring for her household. But the worst toll had been the loss of a brother and her oldest son in the war.

"I was able to get away early for a change," he said. "But since I usually eat at the hospital, I completely forgot my dinner. Do you suppose I could buy a bit from you? Just some bread and tea would be marvelous."

"Och! Just some bread and tea," she scoffed. "And how's a strapping young fellow like you expected to function on that? Sit you down. I have some soup left from our dinner to go with the bread. And keep your money. I'll not have it said I sold food to a veteran and hero of Russia!"

Alex hadn't considered such an invitation and suddenly felt awkward. How could he decline and not appear rude? He certainly couldn't easily explain the real reason he wanted to eat alone in his room.

"That's very kind of you, Mrs. Rimsky, but I was thinking I would eat while I did paper work from the hospital."

"That's simply not good for digestion."

"I know. But it is the only way I'll have time for everything." He hated lying, especially in the face of her kindness. So he added, "Mrs. Rimsky, I'm afraid I've told you a little fib. There's another reason why I want to eat alone, but it will probably seem silly to you. You see, this is an anniversary . . . mine and a young woman I care for. She doesn't live in Moscow, and we couldn't be together today."

"Someone you met in the war, yes?"

"Yes. We thought that if we performed this mock dinner, we might feel closer."

"That's not silly. It's romantic. I've always wondered why a handsome young fellow like yourself is alone. You poor dear. Let me—"

Just then one of the Rimsky children burst into the kitchen.

"Mama, there's a man at the door, a stranger. He wants the doctor!" The boy was flushed and excited. Visits by strangers were not commonplace, even in this busy household.

"You go and see what it's about, Doctor," Mrs. Rimsky said.

17

"I'll fix you something for your . . . dinner."

"Thank you." Alex rose and followed the child down the hall to the front door. He was filled with misgiving. He had never had a visitor since coming here. He felt for the envelope he'd picked up in the metro, which was now tucked into his inside coat pocket. It pressed like a burning, accusing hand upon him.

His misgiving eased only a little when he saw the figure of his old friend Anatoly Bogorodsk standing in the open doorway. Anatoly was a friend, but he was also a high official in the MVD.

"Hello, old friend," Bogorodsk said with a warmth in his tone that helped ease Alex's worry. The MVD agent glanced over Alex's shoulder. The Rimsky boy was lingering in the hall, no doubt hoping for a bit of entertainment. "Can we speak privately?"

Alex nodded, the gravity in Anatoly's final words causing the knot in his stomach to tighten once again. "My room, if you don't mind. It's small but private."

"You have only a room in this place?" asked Anatoly as he walked beside Alex.

"It's all I need. As usual, I don't spend much time at home."

"Nothing has changed, even with the war's end, eh?"

"There are shortages of medical personnel, as with everything else," Alex replied. "Too many were killed in the war." They reached the door to Alex's room, and he opened it. It was never locked. He had nothing of value and little to hide. Only the letters from Cameron, which he kept hidden under a loose floorboard.

He offered Anatoly the only chair in the room, while he sat on the edge of the bed. The agent's huge form all but dwarfed the small wooden chair. He'd always been a hulk of a man, not overly tall but all muscle. He still was, even though since the war he had risen in importance in the police organization.

"It is always good to see you, Anatoly," Alex said, "but I have a feeling this isn't a social visit."

"It is too bad that the only time we seem to see each other is for business." Anatoly shifted and the chair creaked. "My Vera

18

has asked after you. And Stephan tells me he wants to be a doctor like you. This makes me very pleased. I surely don't want him to follow in *my* footsteps! A doctor is a far more honorable profession. He makes top grades in school and will have no trouble getting into the university."

"I'm glad to hear that." Several years ago, before the war, young Stephan had been Alex's patient. He'd been seriously injured in an automobile accident and near death. The boy had survived, and Anatoly attributed his son's recovery solely to Alex's skill. Alex always chafed a bit under the man's praise. "But, Anatoly," he said now, "if anyone brings honor to your profession, it is you. You have always been fair and just."

Anatoly shook his head dismally. "It is a nasty business I'm in and no denying it, though I do appreciate your sentiment. I try to be fair, and that is why I have come to you this evening." He shifted again, and Alex hoped the chair would survive the man's obvious distress.

"What's going on, then?"

"I am usually made aware when citizens apply for emigration papers—especially multiple applications. It seems you have done so at least a half dozen times."

Alex gave a sheepish nod.

"Aleksei, my friend . . ." sighed the agent. "Do you think that is wise? You must not believe that being a veteran and hero of our Great Patriotic War will protect you. And to request emigration to America! Oh, Aleksei, that is not good."

"America was our friend and ally. Why should that be a problem?"

"Perhaps you have your head buried in your hospital too much to see that the political climate is changing. Tensions are growing between us and our one-time ally. Someone in your particular position should be playing *down* your past ties to America, not doing what you can to shed light upon them."

"But I still have those ties. There are family and friends still in America I would like to see."

"I thought you had accepted the fact that your ties with your family were broken when you came here."

"But there has been a war. I would like to see with my own eyes that they are all right."

"Your mother and father are dead, yes?"

"But there are others—"

"None important enough to risk your freedom over," Anatoly interjected firmly.

"Well, it is a moot point in any case. I've already realized the mistake in my applications. There will be no more."

"I'm glad to hear it."

"I am being watched, then?" Alex ventured.

"No." There was no hesitation in his voice. "As I said, this information came to me in a routine way. We have better things to do than watch a man who has done nothing but serve his country with honor. Yet if another besides myself had been in the position to intercept your applications, you might well be considered more of a risk." Anatoly smiled. "Under no circumstances would I wish my son's hero, and perhaps mentor, placed in a compromising position."

"I appreciate that," Alex replied but felt again the pressure from the envelope of illegal papers. They were an affront to the friendship Anatoly offered. Yet it would only compound his foolishness to mention them. "And, Anatoly, I would be pleased to help Stephan in his studies," he added sincerely.

"That will make him happy." Anatoly rose.

Alex joined him, opening the door.

Pausing, Anatoly added, "I can see myself out. You look tired, Aleksei. You don't get enough rest."

Alex shrugged.

"Vera wants to fix dinner for you. Come see us. How is Friday for you?"

That was several days away, and Alex had no idea what the day would hold, but he said, "I'd like that."

When the door closed behind the agent, Alex sank down on the bed, not knowing what to think of the visit. At least it reaffirmed that he still had an ally with the police. Anatoly had come to his rescue on a couple of dicey occasions. He would not want to do anything to bring trouble to his friend. Yet now knowing for certain that his fears about legal means of emigration were valid, he had no choice but to seek more dangerous methods. Nevertheless, he intended to do his best to separate himself from Anatoly, thus protecting his friend. He'd have to find some way to get out of that dinner with the agent's family.

A soft knock came to his door. It was Mrs. Rimsky bearing a tray loaded with good-smelling things.

"I saw your visitor leave, so I thought you might be ready for this," she said with a somewhat conspiratorial smile.

"Look at this! You have truly outdone yourself." He momentarily forgot his present troubles. There on the tray were a loaf of bread, a pot of tea and two cups, and two steaming bowls of soup. And in the middle of the tray a slightly used taper in a pottery candlestick.

Mrs. Rimsky set the tray on the desk, then struck a match and lit the candle. "When I was young and having a romantic dinner, candlelight was always important." She grinned.

"Thank you so much!"

"Enjoy!" she replied, then scurried from the room.

Alex glanced at his watch. It was a quarter past nine. Not too bad. Not for him at least.

"But, Cameron," he murmured, "I am going to work on this flaw so that when we are truly together, I will be more punctual."

Then he was struck with the significance of this ritual. At this very moment Cameron was seated somewhere at a table, thinking of him. He had no doubt she would remember. Knowing her and her practical nature, she had probably put together a truly romantic dinner.

"Ah, my Camrushka, I love you so!"

Dear God, let her feel my love now; let it travel over the miles to her. Let her know it is real and eternal.

3

Los Angeles, California

THE DINING ROOM was filled with the low buzz of voices in many intimate conversations. The light was low, as well, enough to be romantic, but still bright enough to know you were in an elegant restaurant. White tablecloths, a rosebud on each table, good china, silver, and stemware. Jackie was dressed for the occasion in a burgundy crepe dress, knee-length and trimmed in velvet around the neck and the cuffs of the sheer long sleeves, so it would have been appropriate for a far more formal event.

The outfit was too much, she was sure. But she had been told to dress for a nice place. And while she and her mother were shopping, Cecilia had raved over the dress, and Jackie had been caught up in the excitement too much to wonder where she would ever wear such an ensemble. She wished now she had saved it for a more special occasion, yet part of her seriously wondered if there ever would be such a time.

"I've been told I'm a born salesman," the man seated across from her was saying. "I get it from my father. He has one of the top insurance brokerages in the city, you know."

"And didn't you say you work for him?" Jackie tried to show some interest in the conversation. It amazed her how one could drone on for so long about insurance.

"Technically I do, but even he says I am the company's

strongest asset." He chuckled in an attempt to appear modest—not a very successful attempt, Jackie thought.

Jackie tried to think of a clever response, but she hated small talk and wasn't good at it. She nodded, but Bradley Williams didn't really seem to need her for encouragement.

"My dad says I could sell eyeglasses to a blind man. It just comes naturally, I guess. But enough about me. Tell me about yourself, Jackie. My cousin didn't say much when she set this date up."

Nor did Marcy say much about her cousin when she'd encouraged Jackie to go out with the man just once. She had said he was good-looking—and he was. Maybe Marcy hadn't realized how self-absorbed the man was. Maybe she was too concerned about Bradley liking Jackie to think that Jackie might not care for this fine specimen of American manhood. Marcy meant well, Jackie supposed. Her friend knew that most of the young men of Jackie's acquaintance had shied away from her, especially after they found out about Emi. Simply having a daughter was considered a strike against her, but that the child was half Japanese—that was usually the whole ball game. Mentioning Emi was the quickest way to lose a man. Marcy had suggested that Jackie let the men get to know her a little before telling them about Emi. But Jackie hated the subterfuge.

"I have a daughter, you know," Jackie said. Well, the man wanted her to tell him about herself!

"Do you?"

"She's three and a half. Her father was killed in the war. She's—"

"I'm sorry to hear that—about her father, I mean." He wasn't very good at hiding his sudden awkwardness. He hurried on, "You know, I can set you up with a very nice life insurance policy. You would want the child cared for should something happen to you. These are sad realities, but we must be prepared."

Jackie smiled benignly.

"Oh, there I go! I tell you, it's in the blood. But part of it is that I just can't hold back when I know I can help others. Marcy tells me your father is an important man, publisher of the *Journal*, right? But these days a woman likes to be independent. However, I bet I could even set your father up nicely. Few people have enough life insurance."

Jackie wanted to scream. He'd been going on like this throughout dinner. She didn't think she could make it through dessert. If only he would talk about something besides insurance. Anything—sports, cars, fishing—anything!

Then, without her even noticing the transition, he *was* talking about cars.

"It won't be long before I can afford a Cadillac. I've got a nice little Ford coupe now, nearly new, too. One of the first autos off the postwar assembly lines. But of course, you knew that." He chuckled. "We drove over in it. A good little car. I've got a nice comprehensive policy for it. You can't be too careful. . . ."

Was she being too critical? That's what both her mother and her mother-in-law told her. They both felt it was time for her to remarry and move on with her life. Even Mrs. Okuda! Why, the woman had even tried to set her up with some young Japanese men she knew. Yet they were no more eager to marry a white woman than white men were eager to be with a woman who had, in their minds at least, been befouled by sleeping with a Jap. Oh, they weren't all so rampantly racist. One fellow had been refreshingly decent and honest.

"I admire you," he had told her, "for having the courage to marry the man you loved no matter what. I don't think I could have that kind of courage." He never called her again.

After a year and a half Jackie still missed Sam terribly. Part of her believed it was too soon to have feelings for another man, yet she could not deny that part of her was lonely, too. Because of her wonderful relationship with Sam, she longed for that once again. She yearned for someone like Sam to share her life with. Unfortunately, it seemed the only way to find that perfect someone was to wade through all the Bradleys of the world.

"I had a jalopy when I was in high school, and even that was insured. People laughed at me until I got into an accident that wasn't my fault and all the expenses were paid for. I had the last laugh then. Are your father's vehicles insured? I could get him a good rate. Why don't you give him my card—"

Jackie broke in as he was reaching into his jacket pocket for his business card. "My daughter is Japanese."

"Huh?" he said, and for the first time that evening the man was speechless. His hand, now holding the card, hung in midair.

"Emi is half Japanese," Jackie reiterated. Okay, maybe it was a challenge, as well.

"Y-you adopted her?" he asked hopefully.

"No, Bradley, I got her the old-fashioned way. My husband was Japanese."

"Oh . . . my . . ."

Just then the waiter arrived with the chocolate cake Bradley had ordered. She hadn't ordered dessert because she was full from her meal. Now he simply stared at the cake, obviously having lost his appetite. In spite of herself, Jackie felt sorry for the man.

"I shouldn't have been so blunt," she said.

"It was rather a shock. You could have handled it with a bit more diplomacy."

Her sympathy for him was quickly waning. "Could I?" she said tightly.

"You should have said something right at the outset. Does Marcy know?"

"Oh yes, she knows."

"Well, that's hardly fair, then."

Jackie dropped her napkin on the table and pushed out her chair. "I think I'll go home."

"I'll have them bring the car around—"

"I can take a taxi."

"I am not the kind of man to take a woman out and not see her home properly," he said with affront. "Even if she was false with me."

"I am not the kind of woman to go home with a cad!" Jackie countered, rising.

He rose, too, then noted he was still holding his business card. "You wouldn't care to pass this on to your father . . . ah, would you?"

She glared at him in response, then strode away.

————

Back at her apartment building in West Hollywood, Jackie paid the cabby and then went inside. She took the elevator to the third floor and unlocked the door to her apartment.

"Hi, Peggy," she said softly, so as not to startle her baby-sitter or wake Emi, who would be asleep. It was eight-thirty, much earlier than she had expected to be home.

"Oh, Jackie, I didn't expect you this early." Peggy Parker rose from the sofa, where she had been reading a copy of *Life* magazine.

Jackie smiled ruefully. "Nor did I."

"You didn't have a good evening, then, dear?"

"Probably the worst."

"I don't have to run off if you want to talk about it." Peggy was Jackie's mother's age, and when Jackie had moved here to her own apartment six months ago, the woman had become a friend. They always chatted a bit when she baby-sat or if they met in the hall—Peggy lived two doors down.

Jackie plopped down on one end of the sofa, laying aside her pocketbook and kicking off her shoes. The baby-sitter took that as an invitation and resumed her seat on the other end of the sofa.

First Jackie asked, "Everything go okay with Emi?"

"Yes, and she was sound asleep the last time I checked. What a sweetie! How she loves me to read to her. I think you've got a scholar on your hands."

"She's like her daddy," sighed Jackie. "Oh, Peggy, maybe I am being too picky, as everyone tells me. I am trying to meet other men, but in the case with my date tonight, I'm certain it wasn't just me. The man was a bore, in more ways than one."

"Can you really be too picky, Jackie? I wonder."

27

"I don't know. Mom certainly thinks so. She tells me all the time I'm too picky."

"Well, I certainly don't want to contradict your mother. I've only met her a couple of times, but she seems a fine woman. . . ." Peggy paused.

And because it seemed she had come just short of saying it, Jackie added, "But . . ."

Peggy smiled. For a fifty-year-old woman who was on the plump side, she was quite pretty, with smooth skin and long brown hair that showed little gray. Jackie suspected she touched it up, but it looked fairly natural. Her hair was gathered in a single braid at the back, which Jackie's mother thought rather immature for a woman of her age. She also dressed fashionably, though a bit flamboyantly, or as Jackie's mother put it, "bohemian." She often wore slacks and brightly colored blouses and shawls. Jackie supposed that was because she was an artist, which was why she worked at home and was often available for baby-sitting.

"Okay, I admit it," Peggy said, "I do disagree with Mrs. Hayes. My own life has made me see another side of it."

"Would you tell me about it?" Jackie gazed with interest at the woman. "I'm desperate to know if I'm doing the right thing or not."

"Everyone is different. I'll tell you how it was for me so you can see there are other ways. I've had two husbands, both passed on now. My first, Henry—oh, we were so much in love! And besides being the love of my life he was also my best friend."

"Just like Sam and me."

"Yes, I'll bet it was . . ." Peggy got a rather dreamy look on her face. "We married and right off had two children. Then the Great War came."

"He wasn't killed in the war, was he?"

"No, but as you well know how it is, I worried terribly when he went to France. Maybe fearing his death then prepared me for what came later. But maybe not, because we had ten wonderful years after the war, and by the time he was killed in the auto crash, I had forgotten my earlier fears. I didn't feel prepared at all. It took some time for me to get on my feet again. I admire you, Jackie. You are so strong after only a year and a half."

"I'm only strong on the outside," Jackie admitted. "Inside, I don't always know. Emi helps."

"Yes, my children helped pull me back to life, as well. Thank the Lord for children at such times! But once the worst of the grieving was over, friends and family began nagging me about remarrying. Then the Depression hit and times were hard, especially for a single woman with two children. Everyone told me I needed to get a husband. Sometimes I felt desperate to marry, just to have a man to take care of me. But I couldn't find someone I loved. My mother said to forget love, that I would never love anyone like Henry again. I should be happy to find a man who would care for me and my children and who didn't beat me. But I couldn't settle for that. I was accused of being unfair to my children. Oh, the hurtful things people said. But I wanted what I'd had with Henry. I didn't care if the man was *like* Henry, but just . . . I don't know how to describe it."

"I think I know exactly what you mean," said Jackie enthusiastically. "You wanted the same connection of your hearts."

"That's it."

"And did you find it?"

"In 1933, nearly five years after Henry's passing, I met George. What a love we had!"

"Was it love at first sight?"

Peggy chuckled. "Hardly. He was a clerk in the grocery store where I shopped. I didn't even notice him at first. He was ten years older than I and not nearly as handsome as Henry. He was quiet, where Henry was always full of fun and laughter. He asked me out, and I only went because my mother practically forced me. She thought George was the bottom of the barrel but that I was at the point where I better take what I could get. I was willing to give the man a chance, as I had with many other men over the years. Well, there was something so dear and genuine about him that I gave him two chances. On the second date he relaxed and opened up a little, and I saw into his heart. Then I fell in love. I truly knew he was the right man when I saw him fall in love with my children and they with him. That was very important. But it was the connection between us that made me accept his marriage proposal. The ten years I had with him were every bit as wonderful as those with Henry."

"What a fantastic story!"

"Never believe anyone who tells you that you can only have one true love in your life. I had two! Maybe there's a third out there—who knows." She giggled.

"Peggy, thank you so much. Your story encourages me. I want to believe it can happen to me, too. I refuse to marry anyone like Bradley Williams."

"He must have been awful," commiserated Peggy. "At least you're not financially desperate."

"My teaching job makes ends meet. I don't have to depend on my parents, and I am thankful for that. No, it isn't the money. But I do get lonely for what Sam and I had. Did you feel that way?"

"Yes, I did. I still miss my George. It's only been two years since his heart attack."

Jackie reached over and grasped Peggy's hand. "It hasn't been very long for you, either."

"The bond I had with each of my husbands made it hard to lose them, but I think it also made it easier, because at least I have good memories to sustain me. Imagine what I'd have if I had settled for someone like your Bradley."

"Not *my* Bradley, please!" Jackie gave a mock shudder. "At least you would have had some good life insurance." Jackie could giggle now, too. "And a Cadillac—also with very good insurance coverage!"

"George had no life insurance," Peggy mused.

"But I think he had *life*."

"Yes, and that is worth far more." Peggy rose. "I best be on my way, Jackie. And any time you need a sitter for Emi, call. She is such a dear."

Jackie walked her friend to the door. "Thank you again, Peggy, for everything."

Jackie closed the door, then went to Emi's room and quietly tiptoed inside. Emi was curled into a little sleeping ball on her bed. The cover had slipped off, and Jackie tenderly pulled it up over the child.

"Oh, Emi, sweetheart," she breathed softly. "We're doing all right, aren't we?"

Her job teaching second grade at a local public school did pay the bills. And though Jackie hated leaving Emi to go to work, she knew her daughter was well cared for between her two grandmas and Peggy Parker. In fact, she thought Emi would be devastated if she couldn't see these women on a regular basis.

No, they didn't need the care of a man, not really. But it was true what Jackie had told Peggy. She was lonely at times, but not for mere companionship. She missed the depth, on so many different levels, that she'd had with Sam.

But was she ready to find that with another man? She was sure part of her would feel disloyal. Perhaps there was more to it than her being too picky. Yes, there was a lot more to it. The worst of it was that the one person she could talk this over with, the one person she knew would understand, even if he didn't have the answers, was gone. Peggy had been helpful, but only Sam would truly understand.

She bent down and gave Emi a kiss. The child stirred, gave a sigh, then settled back to sleep.

Jackie returned to the living room, curled up once again on the sofa, and as she did so, glanced at the framed photo of Sam on the end table. There were two photos, actually, hinged together, one of him in his uniform, and one of both of them on their wedding day, which she'd had enlarged from a snapshot. Her heart clenched. A temptation stole over her to put the photos away. Sometimes they hurt too much. Then she remembered what Peggy had said about good memories sustaining her. She thought back to her wedding day and the joy of that time when the minister of the little Albuquerque church had married them.

Though all had been against them, they had known what they were doing was right and good. So good.

"Will I have that again with another?"

Did she want it?

Yes, she did. She knew that, but only if it felt equally right and good. But it wasn't going to appear out of nowhere. She no doubt would have to endure more Bradleys to find it.

She gave a shudder. "Help me, Lord. I don't want to do this alone."

And that was another assurance she had, that she really wasn't alone.

4

Washington, D.C.

MOST OF THE GUESTS had left. Blair caught a glimpse out of the corner of her eye of Gary escorting a couple to the door. She should be there with him, but a small group of women had cornered her.

"Blair, you throw a marvelous party," said Mrs. Enid Townsend, a senator's wife.

"Why, your soirées are sure to become the most popular in town," added Mrs. Linda Harper, wife of a congressman.

"I hardly believe that!" demurred Blair. "I have been to parties both of you have given, and they were wonderful."

"But you have a certain flair for this sort of thing, Blair. That is quite evident," Ruth McDowell said. Her husband was an aide to the army chief of staff and one of Gary's immediate superiors.

"Thank you so much," said Blair, hoping that would put an end to the rather embarrassing praise.

"Is it true that you did all the cooking tonight yourself?" asked Enid. "It was positively gourmet."

"She did indeed," Ruth answered for Blair. "And this from a woman who before the war couldn't even boil water!"

"I decided that after all the awful stuff I had to fix for Gary in the Philippines, I should try to make up for it somehow. So I taught myself how to cook." Blair smiled.

"You are a fabulous teacher."

"I really enjoy cooking. More than I ever thought."

"Speaking of the Philippines," interjected Ruth, "when are you going to speak to our women's club? You promised you would."

Blair cringed inwardly. Yes, she had promised when she and Gary had first arrived in Washington three months ago. General McDowell was his boss, and she couldn't very well refuse the invitation the first day of his new assignment. So she had simply procrastinated, hoping the woman would eventually forget.

She decided to be honest. "Well, Ruth, I may have been premature in that promise. I really don't see what I have to say that would be interesting. It is all so unpleasant, I can't imagine anyone caring to hear about it."

"Are you kidding!" "I'd want to hear!" "It's positively fascinating!" All three women chimed in at once.

Blair stifled a groan. "You're only three," she said lamely.

"Blair, everyone wants to hear from real war heroes, and that you are a woman makes it even more desirable. I guarantee I could pack the auditorium," Ruth said.

"I just don't see it." Blair truly didn't. How could anyone want to hear about all the miseries she'd experienced?

But Ruth McDowell had a response that Blair hadn't really considered. "Blair, I don't want to pressure you. I expect your experiences may still be too painfully fresh, and if that is the case, I will say no more. But beyond that, I must dispel the notion that you have nothing to offer others. What you went through and the strength and courage you displayed would be a true inspiration to all women—men, too, for that matter. This could be a way for you to turn what I am certain was an awful time into something that can truly help others."

"Perhaps you are simply shy to speak in front of a crowd," offered Linda.

Blair had to smile ruefully. "I can't honestly claim that."

"Yes," said Enid, "you were quite a performer before the war, weren't you? I heard you were in a movie."

Blair shrugged, growing embarrassed again. "I was."

"Oh, I see Richard waving at me," Ruth said. "I must go. But please, Blair, give what I have said serious thought. And in the meantime, thank you so much for having us tonight. It was a marvelous party." Ruth clasped both of Blair's hands warmly.

The other women took this as their cue to depart, as well.

"You must get me the recipe for that dip," said Linda. "Who would ever have thought peanut butter and avocado would make such a tasty appetizer."

Blair walked with them to the door, where Gary met them with an armload of coats. Before long he closed the door behind the last guest.

Gary breathed a sigh of relief and grasped Blair's hand. "Well, we survived hosting our first Washington party."

"You doubted!" laughed Blair.

"I must admit when you insisted on making it a dinner party, I quaked a bit. I mean, the dinners you've fixed for me lately haven't been bad, but a formal dinner for twelve!"

"I cooked for more than that at the guerilla camp."

He laughed. "But monkey soup wasn't on the menu tonight."

"If it makes you feel any better, I had my doubts, too. I was so afraid the ham would be too dry. I had to call my mother twice. Half the time she just worried over the expense of the long-distance calls."

"It turned out perfectly."

"It really did, didn't it? And you know something, Gary? I actually enjoyed it. The cooking, the planning, fixing the fancy canapés—it was fun."

"Come here, my beautiful chef!" He grasped her hand and swung her around so that she gracefully flowed into his arms. He kissed her thoroughly, then continued to hold her.

How she loved the feel of his strong arms around her! There was a fervency in his touch that assured her that he needed her as much as she needed him. The separations and uncertainties of the Philippines were still very fresh. They were, for all practical purposes, newlyweds, though they had been officially married nearly five years. She still felt an electric thrill when she'd catch an unexpected glimpse of him. And the intensity of love glowing in his dark eyes, often like hot coals, was almost always evident when he gazed upon her.

"This is what I enjoy most," she murmured. "Your holding me. What could be better?"

"Yes," he purred, kissing her pale hair. "Can we forget the dirty dishes?"

"Oh," she said petulantly, hating to be reminded of practical things. "I have an appointment first thing in the morning. I don't think there will be time in the morning, and by the time I get home, everything will be dried on and horrible to wash."

"I wish I could afford a maid for you every day."

"I don't expect that. I'm a housewife now, and I certainly can handle it myself. And honestly, I'd feel like such a sluggard to leave the mess. Do you mind terribly?"

"No, and to prove it, I will help." With reluctance he released her but not before placing a final kiss on her forehead. "That's a rain check for later," he added with a grin.

Together they moved through the spacious living room gathering up glasses, used ashtrays, napkins, and other things left behind by the guests, placing the items on a tray Blair found. Blair thought she should scold Gary for his comment about affording a maid. They were, in fact, quite well set up financially. Their rented home, a lovely old Georgetown townhouse, was beautiful and very roomy for two people. With the more than ten thousand dollars in back pay Gary had received for his years serving as a guerilla in the Philippines, Blair had been able to furnish the place elegantly. Of course, she hadn't used all the money, far from it. Most they had been able to invest, especially since the position at the Pentagon had opened up to Gary so quickly after the end of the war. His salary now provided very comfortably for them, enabling him to keep the promise he'd made to her during the war—to spoil her lavishly once they got home. Truly Blair did not want for anything. Her years of privation had taught her to appreciate a more simple life, yet she still enjoyed fashionable clothes and other nice things. That Gary enjoyed such luxuries, too, surprised her. She seldom had seen him out of uniform in the past, so when she went with him shopping in New York for civilian clothes, she was a little taken aback when he headed for Saks Fifth Avenue rather than Sears. But why not? Especially when he looked so stunning in the fine duds. But he would have looked fine in Sears clothing, as well. He was back up to his prewar weight now and had pretty much recovered from the tropical diseases that had plagued him in the islands, though they both had recurrent bouts with malaria. Except for his slight limp from a bullet wound received near the end of the war, he was every bit the devastatingly handsome man who had first beguiled her five years ago at her father's fiftieth birthday party.

And Gary often told her she was just as beautiful as the woman who had won his heart at that same party. She wasn't sure about that. She was still too thin, and the tropical sun had not been good for her skin or her hair. At least she looked better now than she had six months ago, and her doctor assured her the effects of her ordeal would not be permanent.

Well, not all the effects. The doctor was extremely reticent to deliver a prognosis about the most important matter. Sometimes she felt that he was stringing her along, afraid to pronounce the truth, afraid to further wound her already deeply scarred heart. But she didn't press him. In fact, she dreaded hearing the words she feared were sure to come soon.

"I'm sorry, Mrs. Hobart, but all our tests indicate you will never be able to have more children."

Never, never, never! The words haunted her worst nightmares, the ones that were even more terrible than those in which she relived the nightmare of the Philippines. How many times had she awoken, shaking and in tears, when even Gary's tender touch couldn't comfort her? If Gary didn't have his own share of nightmares, she would have felt she was truly going insane. She only hoped her touch when he needed her sustained him. She suspected they both put on a bit of a performance in donning a normal face each day.

She liked to think, however, that it was more the sustenance of their Lord than a performance. Their faith was still strong and real, the core of their love and their lives.

She also wanted to think that God would somehow help her accept the news she was certain would come any day.

"Blair, are you okay?" Gary's voice broke into her reverie. "You've been holding that glass for a couple of minutes now."

"Oh." She chuckled nervously. "My mind was wandering."

He nodded with understanding. That happened all too often to them both.

He put a couple of dessert plates on the tray that was nearly full of dirty dishes. "What is it you are going to do in the morning, Blair? You hadn't mentioned an appointment before."

"Just something . . ." She shrugged as if that would end it. But she had sworn to herself that she would never lie to Gary. With a resolved sigh, she added, "It's with Dr. Benson."

"Why didn't you tell me?"

"I don't know. I suppose it's because if you are there when he tells me what I most fear, it will be more real."

"And if you are alone, it won't be real?" He cocked a skeptical brow.

"Maybe I could ignore it?" she said wanly.

"You couldn't ignore it even if you wanted to, and I think you know that." His tone was slightly censorious. "We're in this together, Blair."

"But it is my fault that we have to face this at all—"

"Don't you ever say that again," he cut in sharply. Then he recanted by coming to her, placing an arm around her, and drawing her close. "Please, Blair, we have been through this so many times. But you know I don't, and never have, blamed you for what happened to Edward."

Edward . . . would that name ever be spoken without it being a knife to her heart? The son they had lost in the Philippines. The son who had died minutes after his birth, which had followed the murderous interrogation she'd received from the Japs.

"Okay, then I blame the Japs," she said almost flippantly.

"Does it help to assign blame?"

"No, it doesn't, not really," she admitted reluctantly. She could be convinced the death of their son wasn't her fault, but she didn't think she'd ever believe it wasn't the true fault of the Japanese. "Maybe if we could have another baby, it would take away all the pain."

"And we will, Blair. We mustn't give up."

"But what if it never happens? Will you still—?" She cut herself off. It was a foolish fear, too ridiculous to even voice.

He assured her anyway. "I will always love you, Blair. I didn't marry you for your womb. Yes, I would love to have children, but we can always adopt. My love for you is not conditional upon your bearing children. How many times do I have to tell you that?"

"I guess a lot, more than I deserve, probably."

"I won't tire of telling you, then."

"That opens up another of my insecurities. How did I ever deserve a husband like you?"

"You were just lucky, I guess," he replied with a playful smirk. "Shall I go with you tomorrow?"

"Yes, I would like that."

Gary carried the tray into the kitchen, and Blair followed with a handful of other things. Unloading these, she got her apron from a hook and began filling the sink with soapy water. She smiled at the simple pleasure of clean water that didn't have to be boiled, and soap, especially soap that smelled good and was smooth and gentle. She hoped she never ceased to appreciate the conveniences of life.

"You know, Gary, we do have almost as perfect a life as anyone could ask for."

"Almost?" He gave her a mock frown, then grinned.

"I only say almost because if I admitted how perfect it is, I might not be able to maintain any humility at all." She scooped the dirty dishes into the water. "Even if we didn't have an abundance of material things, we have each other. I think of Cameron and Jackie and feel so bad for them."

"At least Cameron has a hope of reuniting with her Russian doctor." Gary dipped the clean dishes into the rinse water and set them into the drainer.

"Last I heard, there was absolutely no response to her many visa applications."

"It won't get easier," Gary said. "Tensions are mounting between us and the Russians. They fear their former allies will turn on them. They are worried about the bomb. They are worried there will be no repatriations expected from Germany. And they are worried about America's determination to reestablish European democracies, and to convert those that weren't before into democracies."

"Well, Churchill didn't help with that speech of his about an iron curtain descending over Europe, dividing it into a Communist and a Democratic bloc. It was certainly no surprise Stalin took it as a threat of war against the Soviets." When Gary smiled, she added, "I do pay a little attention to politics, especially where I know it has a personal effect. And living here in Washington, I have to be better informed if I am to run in your circles, you know."

"I appreciate it, honey. I truly do." He rubbed his chin thoughtfully. "You know, perhaps your sister is going about her attempts to get into Russia all wrong. It's not likely Stalin will be very welcoming of Western journalists in his country, and Cameron's other problems with the government can't help her. Perhaps she ought to try to get in as a member of the embassy staff—a secretary or something."

"You mean like a cover?"

"You've watched too many spy movies, my dear. She might just get a temporary assignment with the embassy. Your father has contacts in the State Department."

"My father isn't exactly eager to see her get into the country, not for matters of love. I have a feeling that if he really wanted her in, he'd have been able to make it happen."

"I'll bet Cameron would be furious if she suspected that. Do you suppose I should look into it? I hate to get on your father's bad side, but my heart goes out to your sister. I know what it's like being separated from the one you love."

"No one expects you to do that," Blair replied, inwardly pleased at his motives and his willingness. "I doubt it has ever occurred to Cameron to ask that of you. But if you could, oh, it would be wonderful, wouldn't it?"

"I can at least look into it. I don't have that much influence around here. I still haven't had any luck with getting Claudette and Mateo over here."

"You've only been here three months. And part of their trouble is that Claudette and Mateo want to have enough money to get a good start once they come." But Blair still had high hopes that her dear friends would soon be able to come to America to live. It should be easier than helping Cameron. Blair longed to see Claudette, who now wanted to be called by her given name, Aquilina. Blair was getting to know ladies here, but she had so little in common with them she had doubts she would make any deep friendships. She'd always had trouble making friends. Aquilina had been the first real girl friend Blair had ever had, despite the fact that she was almost ten years younger than Blair.

Both Aquilina and Mateo wanted to come to America, for they had no family left in the Philippines. Mateo's father, the dear Reverend Sanchez, had been killed by the Japanese during an interrogation, and his older brother, it was now confirmed, had died during the terrible Death March of Bataan. Aquilina had been an orphan before the war. Blair and Gary were the closest they had to family now.

The only other true friend Blair had was Meg Doyle, the missionary who had helped her so many times and had been instrumental in Blair's finding God. Meg's husband, Conway, had died in a prisoner-of-war camp in the Philippines. News had come two months ago that Meg was finally reunited with her two daughters. After the war she had stayed in the area, hoping to find them. They had become separated from their mother during the evacuation to Corregidor in April of 1942, just before Bataan fell. The girls, Patience and Hope, also dear friends of Blair's, had never made it to Corregidor but had managed to escape capture by the Japanese by hiding out in the mountains with some of the people who had been members of the Doyles' mission church. Mother and daughters were now back in the States, in Minnesota, where Meg was from. Meg and the girls wrote to Blair regularly, but she missed them. These women, along with Aquilina, were probably closer to Blair than her own sisters. Perhaps one day soon they would all have a grand reunion.

Finally the last dish was washed and put away. Blair felt better after being reassured of Gary's love and support. Thinking of her friends bolstered her, as well. Yes, she missed them, but to have such strong bonds with friends was something she would never take for granted. And the notion of somehow helping Cameron added to Blair's elevated mood. No matter what the doctor said tomorrow, she did have a good life. She inwardly thanked God for that as Gary took her hand and they went upstairs together.

5

THE RAIN AND wind pelting the windows of the apartment did not affect the warmth emanating from within. Sometimes Alex found the effort expended to get to these underground church meetings almost daunting. But always they were worth it.

Today, two hours before he had planned to leave, an auto accident victim had been brought to the hospital and required extensive surgery. Alex was an hour late for the meeting, but the patient would survive. He had toyed with the idea of forgetting the meeting, going home, and getting some much-needed sleep. But it had been three weeks since the last one, as it was getting more and more difficult for the group to find safe gathering places.

Alex had missed the Bible teaching given by one of the members but was able to participate in most of the prayer time. Now, as the folks visited after the meeting, he felt refreshed, not at all as if he had spent the previous three hours on his feet with his hands delicately reattaching severed blood vessels and patching damaged organs.

"I am so glad you made it, Alex," said Vassily Turkin, coming up beside Alex.

"So am I. When I saw how late I'd be, I almost went home instead, but I reminded myself that it is always worth it to make the effort." Alex lifted the cup from the saucer he held and sipped his tea. "Besides, who can tell when the next meeting will be."

"It is wonderful that fact acts as an encouragement to you. Not so in many cases. I am afraid all the caution required is demoralizing to some," Turkin said. "I look around and see so many old friends missing. One or two have been arrested, but most are understandably wary. You have probably noticed we have not met at my flat for several months. Marie and I seldom come together any longer. It is simply too risky."

"I didn't realize you have been under such heavy surveillance."

Turkin nodded, fiddling almost nervously with the handle of his cup. "I was hoping you'd be here for more reasons than just social, Alex."

"Is something wrong, Vassily?"

"I am very reluctant to approach you with what I have." Giving a silent gesture, Turkin nudged Alex to a place apart from the others where they could not be easily overheard.

Alex quaked inside. The last time he'd heard similar words, he had been drawn into the dangerous business of helping someone escape Russia. An attempt he'd learned later had been thwarted. Apparently the documents had been of poor quality and had fooled no one.

But Vassily was a friend. True, they never saw each other except at these meetings and seldom spoke of personal matters, but Alex felt a connection with the man. Certainly it was the spiritual bond between them, but he thought it also had to do with the fact that Turkin had known Cameron and both he and his wife thought highly of her.

"Tell me what's on your mind," Alex said with conviction.

Turkin took a deep resigned breath. "Besides not liking to draw you into this, I hate tainting these meetings with political intrigues. But Marie and I have discussed this from every angle, and this seems the best approach—that is, if you are willing to help." Pausing, he gave his head a little shake. "Excuse me, Alex, I am not expressing myself coherently. I've always done better with numbers than with verbal dissertation. That is Marie's strong point, not mine. But it is my talent with numbers and equations that's gotten me into trouble."

"I don't understand." Alex tried to remember if he knew the meaning of the reference to numbers but was only reminded once more about how little personal information Turkin had exchanged in the past. Was that just Turkin? Surely others had spoken of their professions and of their families. Everyone knew Alex was a doctor, and most knew of his sojourn in the States. But the more he thought of it, the more he realized Turkin spoke little of himself, yet he never gave the impression of reserve. He was a warmhearted man, if at times a bit bumbling and absent-minded.

"Let me see if I can be more clear," Turkin said, raising a hand to adjust his horn-rimmed glasses and nearly knocking his cup off its saucer in the process. He grabbed it before a mishap occurred. Clearing his throat, he began again. "Before the war, and during, I daresay, I was a professor at Moscow University."

"I don't think I ever knew that," Alex said.

"No . . . I don't suppose I spoke of it much. Most people find physics quite boring."

"Physics?"

"Hard to believe, yes?" He gave a self-deprecating smile. "I have never been too adept socially, but when it comes to science, I am quite the genius, they tell me. And I have always enjoyed it, especially teaching. Shortly before the end of the war I was called upon to join a project headed by none other than Stalin's right-hand man, Beria himself. We were to study the feasibility of constructing an atomic weapon. In my mind it was always mere speculation until the United States actually exploded an atomic bomb on Japan. After that, as you can imagine, Stalin's paranoia grew enormously. He made it a top priority for the Soviet Union to develop its own bomb. We on the atomic project have been driven relentlessly toward this end."

Alex only realized his jaw was hanging open and he was

listening in stunned silence when his own cup nearly toppled from his hand.

Turkin smiled, though without much humor. "It is all rather astonishing, isn't it? I can hardly believe it myself. The worst of it is, Alex, that what I am telling you could probably get us both shot. I will stop now if you say the word, and there will be no hard feelings."

"I don't wish to get shot, Vassily," said Alex dryly, "but I don't think you would have said anything at all unless it was very important. Go on."

"I am not in the top echelon of authority in the project, by any means," Turkin continued. "I should not know what I am about to tell you—only two or three at the very top have this information. I came upon it by sheer accident. It is simply that much of our recent knowledge of the workings of an atomic bomb has come to us from American sources—some of it very detailed information. I don't know the sources, but I have suspected for a long time that our current information could not have come except from outside of Russia. This was confirmed when I chanced upon some files that were accidentally left out. In any case, we are much closer to having a bomb than I believe the West suspects. On one level I feel it would probably be to the good for us to have this weapon and thus restore the balance of power to the world. But this is a political question that could be argued till we drop, not to mention all the spiritual dimensions of it. All that aside, only one element is forcing me to do what I am about to do, and that is the fact that such a weapon in the hands of a man like Stalin would be disastrous. It may be too late to prevent that, but I feel I must do something, and the only thing I can think to do at this stage is to attempt to inform Russia's opponents about how close we are and to perhaps reveal that there are leaks in their own security."

"This is extremely big, Vassily. It could indeed get us shot." Alex wished it wasn't as hard as it was to add his next words. "What do you want of me?"

"You mentioned to me once that you have exchanged communications with Cameron. Wisely, you did not reveal the route of this communication, and I still don't want to know it." He paused. This was obviously a difficult request to make, as well it should be. "I thought perhaps you could get my communication out of the country."

"Vassily, have you truly weighed the risks against the value of your information? As you said, it may not stop Stalin."

"Alex, I must do this. I have wrestled with the ethical dilemma of my work for years. But our government has ways of keeping its citizens at their jobs—"

"They have threatened Marie?"

"They arrested my son a year ago. You may recall my asking for prayer for him from time to time. I felt it best not to offer details." He shrugged, a look of bewilderment emphasizing the wrinkles around his eyes and mouth. "He did nothing to warrant this, of course. It was done in order to keep me in line."

"Doesn't that make the risk greater, Vassily?"

"He managed to smuggle a note out of his prison a few weeks ago in which he begged me not to compromise my principles on his account. Despite his courage, I still cannot sacrifice him by quitting the project. Thus I have chosen the route I suggested to you. I may protect him and still do something to salve my conscience. I suppose I don't have the courage of my son."

"I don't think that for a minute," Alex assured. "I'll do what I can to help you. The riskiest part will be getting your information to my contact. I'll have to walk the straight and narrow until then so I don't attract unwanted attention."

"I could take it to this person myself," offered Turkin.

"Thank you, Vassily, but I would prefer to protect this route as much as I can. If anything happened to cut off the little communication from Cameron, I don't know what I'd do."

"I understand."

"When will I get this information of yours?"

"I have it with me. I had hoped to see you tonight. Can your source get it to someone high in the American State Department?"

"If it is as important as you claim, I expect the president himself might want to see it."

Turkin took an envelope from his coat pocket and held it out. Alex took it and quickly slipped it into his own pocket. He barely glanced at it. He did not want to know what was inside.

Nor did he really wish to give it to Sophia the next day. There were already too many people being endangered by this. But she was the only person he knew, and whom he trusted, who could get into the American embassy without causing suspicion. Since the war Sophia had obtained a position as a Russian language teacher to staff at the embassy and had been able to get correspondence out to Cameron via an embassy official whom Cameron had befriended and who had helped in the affair with Sophia's husband, Oleg. Alex did not know the official's name and did not *want* to know his name.

When he told Sophia what the letter contained, she said she would make the delivery. He never believed she'd do otherwise. She, too, knew and respected the Turkins. Sophia would send the material to Cameron in the usual way. Cameron would know what to do with it after that.

Alex relaxed when he later saw Sophia and she said she had delivered the envelope to the embassy man without a hitch. Then he all but forgot about it.

6

ROBERT WOOD positioned his racquet as his opponent sent the tennis ball flying over the net. With racquet in the backhand position, he smoothly returned the ball, which his opponent, George Stires, Robert's assistant, just barely made contact with for a return volley. Unfortunately for Stires, his maneuver was a lob that Robert easily slammed back. Stires was not able to raise his racquet in time to connect with the ball and could only sidestep to prevent the speeding missile from hitting his shoulder.

"Your game," Stires said. "Again."

"I warned you," Robert replied.

"High school state champ. Yes, I was warned." George shook his head. "But that was a few years ago."

"I've managed to keep in practice when I can."

Both men jogged to the sidelines and grabbed their towels.

"I should have known you were a ringer when you knew exactly where to find an indoor tennis court in the middle of Moscow," said George.

"Well, I hope there will be a rematch. It's hard to find good opponents around here." Robert blotted sweat from his brow, then slung the towel around his neck.

"Now at least I'm forewarned, Bob." George's gaze lifted to beyond Robert's left shoulder.

Robert turned and saw a man in a suit approach. He looked vaguely familiar, someone from the embassy security detail. The two waited until the newcomer came up to them.

"Mr. Wood, I'd like to talk with you." The man, only a couple inches taller than Robert's five-foot-eight-inch height but built like a brick wall, had, in fact, the demeanor of that same wall. "I'm Larry Marquet with embassy security."

"Yes, I've seen you around. Is there a problem?" Robert knew he was with embassy security but had suspected he was more.

Marquet glanced at George, who quickly took the hint.

"I've got to run, Bob. Thanks for the game," he said and took off toward the locker room.

Robert wiped away another stream of sweat with his towel. "Look," he said. "I'd like to clean up. Can this wait a few moments?"

"We shouldn't talk here anyway. I'll meet you outside in . . . is fifteen minutes enough time?"

"Sure."

Robert went to the locker room. George was still there dressing and casually asked about Marquet, but Robert could not appease his assistant's curiosity. As he showered, he wondered what this could be about. He guessed it must be something sensitive since Marquet had chosen a place outside the embassy to discuss it. Everyone at the embassy naturally had to assume that all walls and telephones were bugged and that all Russian personnel were agents of the Soviet secret police. Just to be on the safe side, officials were in the habit of carrying on important conversations outdoors, where even the canny Russians couldn't plant a bug.

Robert still marveled that, with all the frustrating restraints on foreigners in Russia, he was still here himself. He had been promoted to second vice-counsel, complete with his own office, name engraved on the door—*Robert* now, which he'd always preferred anyway, because the ambassador felt it sounded more distinguished than Bob. Because of the war and his expertise with the language, his superiors had bent the rules to have him stay far longer than the usual two-year tour for embassy officials. He had gone home for a while after the war, and in many ways that experience had been the catalyst for his return to Russia.

The war had changed him even though he'd never faced combat or any real danger. That was another struggle he had faced—having to sit out the war in the safety of the embassy. He'd been told his work had been vital to the war effort, and he'd tried to accept that. But the far greater effect of the war on him was having to deal with what was coming to be called the Holocaust—Hitler's wholesale massacre of millions of Jews.

His first inkling of this horrible crime had come via Cameron Hayes and the Russian soldier she'd brought to him who had witnessed one such massacre. They had been unsuccessful in doing anything about the soldier's story; however, it was likely that even if they had been able to get him out of the country, his story, as fantastic as it was, might not have been believed. Even now, with the ghastly evidence of the death camps such as Dachau and Auschwitz, there were those who wanted to deny the truth.

Those events had forced Robert Wood to face another more personal truth. For three generations his family had succeeded in hiding their Jewish origins. His great-grandfather, Jacob Grunwald, had changed the family name to Wood in order to get a job. That had been many years ago when he had migrated to America from Germany. Robert's paternal grandparents, both Jewish, had adopted the name, as had Robert's father. Robert's mother was a Gentile and still did not know her husband was Jewish. Robert found out by accident, at the age of eighteen, when he uncovered some papers in his grandfather's attic. He questioned his father, who finally told him but begged his son to keep the secret.

"You have been given a gift," Howard Wood had told his son. "It has enabled you to go further in this world than you ever could have without it."

Robert had managed to push the whole thing from his mind for many years, but he knew that was why he was now thirty-four years old and had not yet married. He could never do what his father had done and deceive the woman he loved. Nevertheless, he couldn't tell the truth, either, for it could destroy his family.

What a terrible dichotomy he had lived all those years! A Christian man, whose faith meant something to him, perpetuating such a lie. Not to mention the many other dilemmas this posed to his Christian faith.

Robert stepped out of the shower and shook his head, sending a spray of water into the air. He wished he could as easily shake these conundrums from his head. He felt a small twinge of fear that the reason for Marquet's visit was that he'd been found out.

When he had gone home after the war, Robert had been determined to convince his father to reclaim the family heritage, but his father still pleaded with him to remain silent. For Robert, keeping silent now was nearly impossible. He'd been ashamed of his lie when Cameron had confronted him about the murder of a few thousand Jews. The death of millions took him far beyond shame.

By lying about his heritage, he felt he was condoning Hitler's reasons for the Holocaust. It made it appear that there must be something wrong with being Jewish if one must hide that fact.

Yet still he had not found the courage to betray his family by embracing his heritage. There were many complexities to consider. But he knew he could not cover up his lineage much longer.

Larry Marquet could know nothing of this. That definitely could not be why he wanted to speak with Robert. Probably just something to do with the motor pool or some other trivial matter.

Robert dressed, put on his woolen overcoat, slipped a wool hat over his damp hair, then exited the building. Parts of the world were still lulling in a comfortable fall, but here in Moscow, the chill of approaching winter was already in the air. Despite the fact that it was ten o'clock in the morning and the sun was painted against a blue sky, the air was quite crisp.

Marquet joined him, and they walked casually down the

street. It was a long walk back to Mokhavaya House, where the American embassy was located on the other side of a broad plaza facing the Kremlin. Robert had planned to take the metro back. It was too chilly for a leisurely stroll.

"So, Marquet, what is on your mind?" Robert initiated the conversation, hoping to speed it along. Each breath was accompanied by a thick puff of steam.

"I'll be direct, Mr. Wood. I know you are a busy man," Marquet replied. "Several weeks ago I made quite a disturbing discovery. I observed you having what appeared to be a clandestine meeting with one of the Russian embassy employees. Documents were exchanged, and as you might guess, this roused my curiosity. I intercepted these items after you dropped them into the mail."

"You what?" Robert retorted, aghast. The diplomatic pouch was supposed to be sacred.

"I felt the circumstances warranted investigation." There was not even a hint of defensiveness in the man's tone. He obviously felt his actions were justified.

"I am a senior embassy officer," Robert said, an edge of affront in his voice despite the fact that he had technically been using his position for questionable purposes.

"How was I to know you were not involved in some Soviet spy ring?"

"Sending information *out* of the country?"

"I was in the OSS during the war and have been in the intelligence field since," Marquet said, confirming Robert's suspicions that he was involved in more than embassy security. He continued, "It is in my nature to be suspicious. That's what makes me good at my job."

Robert had the power to send him packing in disgrace back to the States, but despite this Marquet acted as if he was in complete control. Robert wondered how much of that was due to his own boyish looks. He had been told many times he looked more like a college student than an embassy official, a senior one at that. He therefore had to work harder than some in order to be taken seriously.

"So, you ferreted out the fact that I am covertly sending love letters to America?" Robert said smugly.

"I will give you the benefit of the doubt that the material I read at that time was what it appeared. Personal letters. There was no code within them."

"Thank you very much!"

"These letters were to be delivered to one Cameron Hayes, who I have since learned is a reporter for the *Los Angeles Journal*. They were not from you. The handwriting didn't match yours."

"No, they weren't." Robert saw no reason not to tell him the truth. He'd probably already found it out. "If you must know, Miss Hayes fell in love with a Russian citizen when she was here as a war correspondent. I agreed to help them keep in touch with each other."

"Playing Cupid?"

Robert shrugged. "Cupid had in fact already done his work. I was merely helping. What I would like to know, Marquet, is why you waited this long to confront me."

"I merely wanted to make sure this was all it was about."

"Now you are sure?" Robert had a feeling otherwise. Nervously, he pushed at his wire-rimmed glasses, which had a tendency to slip down his nose.

"You met with the Russian girl again two days ago, and another post was sent."

"Which you confiscated."

"And which was a far cry from being your usual love letter."

Robert didn't like the man's smug smirk. "I don't understand." Robert had never inspected the sealed envelopes. Had that been a mistake? No. He trusted Cameron implicitly.

"Do you ever read the letters the Russian girl gives you?"

"Never. They are quite personal and none of my business. I trust these people, or I wouldn't have agreed to send the letters."

"That's what I thought." Marquet removed a glove from his

right hand, removed an envelope from his pocket, then quickly replaced the glove. "I believe you are being used, Mr. Wood." Marquet handed Robert the envelope.

"In what way?" he asked, taking the envelope. Awkwardly, because he didn't remove his gloves, Robert withdrew the pages that were inside. One was folded separately and read:

Dearest,
 I am loath to do this, using our precious lifeline for such a purpose, but I felt I had to aid a mutual friend in this way. You will know what to do with this information. I will write more later, but I wanted to get this off my hands as quickly as possible.

Robert's stomach knotted. When Marquet had first implied that his friends were using him, he'd felt anger at Cameron and her lover. He had trusted them. Now, upon reading the note, he didn't know what to feel except tension. Something bad was going to come of this he feared. He opened the other pages and read the most astonishing dissertation. When he finished, he glanced up at his companion.

"I had no idea this was in the post," Robert said, all affront now absent from his tone. "I do believe, however, that this is the first time this manner of information was sent by this route."

"I'm going to agree with you for now. Nevertheless, before this message can be delivered to the proper agency in the States, I have to verify its reliability." He held out his hand, and Robert gladly returned the letter to him. "I must investigate the source of this information."

"These are Russian citizens. You know how dicey that can be." Not only for Marquet, Robert thought, but for the Russians in question. His initial ire at having been used had dulled a bit. He would bet that Cameron was perfectly innocent and that her Russian lover had been desperate—foolish but desperate.

"There is more to it than what this letter contains," Marquet said. "Without a doubt our government will be happy to learn these things. As you well know, Russia has been all but closed to us. We in the intelligence community call it the *denied* country. The Eastern European nations now under Soviet influence are far easier for us to penetrate. We know next to nothing about Russia itself. The few defectors and escapees there are give us only crumbs, and the borders have tightened considerably in the year and a half since the war. Most of what we do know is years old."

Robert couldn't deny the truth of the man's statement. Foreigners, perhaps especially diplomats, were in such a closed-off world in Russia that they saw only what the Soviet government wanted them to see. They could not travel more than sixty miles beyond Moscow except with special permits, which were seldom given. Even an embassy staffer such as Marquet, who it appeared was also a spy of sorts, had his hands tied.

"If this information is reliable," Marquet continued, "you can see that its value goes far beyond what it actually says. We now possibly have two Russian citizens willing to aid the West."

"I would guess this is a one-time thing," suggested Robert.

"Oh, I think we could convince them to do more."

Robert didn't like the sound of Marquet's voice. Cameron would never forgive Robert if he did something that would cause her Russian to get into trouble. Never mind that the man had already put his foot into it by attempting to get this information out of the country.

"You would be placing them in terrible danger," Robert said.

"The world is full of danger. Remember, these are Russians. It is dangerous for them to read the wrong book, to talk to the wrong person, even to take a deep breath. They may be willing to aid us given the right enticement. Take the Hayes woman's lover. Wouldn't he like to see her? He could work for us for a period of time in exchange for our assistance in escape. We've done this for residents of East Germany, Hungary, and other Communist countries."

"But you said yourself that Russia is different. *Denied* is the word you used."

"He would be highly motivated."

"It is far too risky."

"Why not let the subject in question decide? I would at least like the opportunity to talk with him."

Robert felt a strong check within. Obviously Marquet had no sense of dealing with human beings. The 'subject in question' indeed! No matter what the Russian fellow had done in trying to use the diplomatic pouch for such nefarious purposes—love letters were one thing, but scientific intelligence was quite another!—Robert felt protective of the man. For Cameron's sake. Beyond that, he just didn't like Larry Marquet. He seemed an opportunistic dolt.

"I have never met the man," Robert replied. "I don't even know his name."

"The Russian girl would know."

Quickly Robert tried to think this through. He had a loyalty to Cameron and thus wanted to protect her lover. But supposing this was the only chance for him to get out of the country . . . Yes, there would be danger, but if it was his only chance, he might be willing to take it.

"I will try to make contact with him," Robert said resignedly.

"This isn't your game, Mr. Wood. I have to do it."

"No. Only the Russian girl knows the man. She trusts me and won't talk to anyone else. If she cooperates and identifies the man, I will make the first contact with him. If he wants to meet with you, then we will set something up." There was no way he would throw Cameron's Russian to the wolves unless he was willing.

"I don't like it."

"It is the only way this can happen without scaring the wits out of everyone. Take it or leave it." Robert spoke with a steely unflinching gaze. He hoped he looked more like a force to be reckoned with than a petulant boy.

"All right. But get this straight, Mr. Wood. You may be a senior embassy official, but in this matter I will call the shots."

Robert wasn't sure what the man meant except that he most likely felt the need to instill some fear into the bumbling embassy official. But Robert already felt enough fear for all of them.

7

MEETING IN A public restaurant did not seem wise. This was a crowded second-rate place where foreigners seldom ventured. It was more like the diners in the States frequented by truck drivers. Its one advantage was that, at this hour, it was crowded with workers stopping for a beer before going home.

When Robert had come to Russia in 1941, he'd been warned of Soviet restrictions. He would not be able to travel freely nor make Russian friends. It would be impossible to obtain official information or visit many institutions. It had all proved true enough, but the war had brought a loosening of many restrictions that had continued in the immediate postwar months. Yet a subtle change had come over the country in the last year, even in the last six months.

In 1941 he had been able to rub shoulders with many Russian citizens—at the theater, shopping, or simply strolling down a street. He had spoken to them on many occasions, for his Russian was quite good, and they had not run away from him. On the contrary, they had been eager to talk. Not so now. He had heard of an alarming increase in arrests of people who even casually mingled with foreigners. There were frequent arrests of Russians who were authorized to work for foreigners. Every embassy had experienced at least one such arrest in the last year.

Thus it had always been with great trepidation that he had met with Sophia Gorbenko, one of the Russian language instructors at the embassy. He was a little surprised that she had not already fallen afoul of the Soviet police, with all the letters she had passed to him since the war. Once he had questioned her about the risks she took.

"I feel I must do this for my friends," she had said. "And I know God will protect me as long as He wills it."

As a man who loved and trusted God—at least *tried* to trust—he understood her reasoning. He did worry about the girl, though, and hoped God understood, also.

With these restraints it had been no easy task to communicate to her his desire to meet with Cameron's Russian boyfriend. It took about three days after that for her to relay the information to the man and bring back his positive response. Then there had been the meeting to arrange. By the time it was all finished, Robert knew why the United States had so little intelligence about the Soviet Union. The effort and danger accompanying even the simplest encounter with a Russian were simply counterproductive.

When the Gorbenko girl had told him where the meeting would take place, he had been skeptical. She had been confident it would succeed.

He dressed in casual clothes rather than his usual three-piece suit so that he might fit in better with the patrons, though now that he was nestled at a table in the midst of the working-class clientele, he saw how futile that attempt was. He stood out clearly as a foreigner.

He ordered a pot of tea despite the fact that it probably made him stand out even more, but he could not stomach the sweet Russian beer most of the other patrons were drinking. Spooning a teaspoon of sugar into his mug of steaming brew, he sat back and listened to the many conversations around him. His Russian was fair enough so that he could follow much of what was being said.

Within about ten minutes a tall light-haired man approached his table and sat down. It was customary for strangers to share tables, especially in such a crowded situation. Soon a waiter brought him a mug of tea, which he must have ordered at the counter before seating himself.

"May I use your sugar?" he asked in Russian.

"Of course," Robert replied, also in Russian, as he pushed the bowl the short distance across the small table.

"You are not Russian."

"No. American."

"I thought I recognized the accent, but you manage very well."

"Thank you." Robert felt almost certain this was not a chance encounter. He wished he had worked out with Sophia some recognition phrases to exchange, but he was a novice in such covert operations. One other foray into this realm, the situation with Oleg Gorbenko, had been a complete failure. He said in a leading way, "I have a very good teacher at the embassy where I work."

The man took a heaping spoonful of sugar from the bowl and stirred it into his tea. As he did so, he casually glanced around the room. Apparently satisfied there was no one close listening, he said, "May I look at your papers?"

Robert took his identity papers from his coat pocket and slid them across the table.

Looking them over carefully, the man said, "Robert Wood. I have heard that name from a mutual friend. Cameron."

That seemed enough confirmation to Robert. "Do you wish to give your name?"

"Aleksei Rostovscikov—that is, Alex Rostov. Has Cameron told you much of me?"

"Only in general terms. You are a doctor, are you not?"

"Yes, I am," Rostov answered.

As Dr. Rostov sipped his tea, Robert studied him and saw how Cameron could have fallen so hard for the fellow. He was the type women found extremely attractive. Wavy blond hair, vivid blue eyes, the look of a Nordic rather than a Tartar, invader. Robert, with what he considered his nondescript looks and rather smallish frame, had always found himself in the shadow of such men.

"Are you sure it is safe for us to talk here?" Robert asked. They continued to converse in Russian, for though it could more easily be understood by those around them, it drew far less attention than English would have.

"You were followed, of course," Rostov replied. "I have been here for about twenty minutes waiting, so your observer did not see me enter. This is by all appearances a chance encounter. They will believe that you came here merely to improve your Russian."

Robert nodded. "I have always let it be known that I am quite anxious to practice the language and have made it a habit to frequent as many places as possible where common Russians are found."

"Yes. Sophia knew this, and that is why we thought this place would work."

The doctor took a packet from his pocket and opened it to reveal slices of bread and a few sausages. "Do you mind if I eat? This is the only chance I will have."

"By all means do so."

"Tell me why you wanted to meet me, Mr. Wood. Sophia told me Cameron is all right. So what else is it?" He broke off a piece of bread and popped it into his mouth.

"I thought you might have guessed, Dr. Rostov. Because it would hardly appear a coincidence that this meeting has come only a week after you attempted to get some very sensitive material out of the country."

Rostov swallowed quickly. He was quiet for a moment, then said with what Robert judged to be complete sincerity, "I am sorry, Mr. Wood. I did not like using your generous assistance for Cameron and me in that way."

"I guessed that, but why did you do it? It could have caused a lot of trouble."

"Could have?"

"Perhaps it already has. I'm not completely sure."

Rostov had a bite of sausage, chewed, and swallowed. "Be

assured, Cameron knew nothing of this. I was simply approached by a friend who was plagued by his conscience and felt he had to do what he did. This man has helped me much in my life, and I could not refuse him."

"Well, so far no harm has been done."

"But . . . ?"

Robert was impressed by the man's perception in guessing that wasn't exactly the end of it.

"Your letter was intercepted by an agent of my country's intelligence service," Robert said. "He now has it in his mind that he could use you as some kind of *agent provocateur*."

Rostov's hand froze midair with a chunk of bread halfway to his mouth. His brow arched. "A spy?" he said, his voice pitched low. He looked all about him again, as though even his whispered words were dangerous.

"We cannot talk here long, so I will try to be concise." Robert paused for a drink of his tea. He didn't like what he must say. He considered this spy business a necessary evil and was reluctant to draw what he considered innocent people into it. He had to remind himself, however, that Rostov had opened himself up to this. Also, he had to give the man a chance to decide for himself. He put down his mug. "Our country is desperate for information about Russia. Many fear another war in a few years, and as things stand now we are at a distinct disadvantage. Our government would be willing to offer in exchange for your services the wherewithal to flee Russia if you so choose. This agent I mentioned would like to meet with you and discuss the details of what he intends."

"You are asking me to betray my country."

"No, Doctor, I believe what it boils down to is betraying an evil regime. Stalin is a madman, without a doubt as perverse as Hitler. But I don't feel comfortable trying to twist your arm. My only purpose is to lay this offer before you. Before I reveal your identity to our agent, I want to be sure you are willing to at least hear his offer. I doubt I'd be able to look Cameron in the eye if I had shut this door without first presenting it to you." He paused and silence followed for several moments.

Finally Dr. Rostov spoke. "Russia is dying, its heart and soul. You know only part of the terror that is killing this nation."

"What will you do then?" Robert ventured.

"I won't couch my actions in pure altruism," Rostov replied. "I am ready to do almost anything to escape, to be with my . . . Cameron. Yet I consider Russia my mother country. She took me in and gave me a home when I had no other. I love Russia, but I hate Stalin's regime and have no qualms about doing what I must to bring it down."

"There are great risks."

"I know."

Rostov's voice held resignation but also a subtler undertone of . . . was it hope? There had to be a certain desperation in his actions, but that was not all that drove him. And now Robert recalled a brief conversation with Cameron shortly before she left Russia. They had been talking of the Oleg Gorbenko affair.

"I think if it happened now, it might have succeeded," she had mused. "I am a bit more savvy about eluding the NKVD."

"How's that?" Robert had asked.

"I've been going to church more."

"And that has taught you to be devious?"

She smiled wryly. "It is not so much the fact of church attendance but rather the kind of church."

"Is this a riddle, Cameron?"

"I'm sorry, Robert." She paused, as if wondering whether to reveal a great secret. "Okay, I know you can be trusted. I've been going to an underground church."

"With Russians?" He wasn't as surprised as he should have been about this. Cameron had proven herself quite resourceful. But then the true import of her statement struck him. "I didn't think you were much of a religious person. Is this for research?"

"For my own personal benefit." A slight blush colored her cheeks. Apparently this was new for her. "I've had what you might call a rebirth here in darkest Russia. A certain doctor of my acquaintance has helped me find the path toward faith in God."

"I'll be!" he breathed. That did surprise him. "I admire you, Cameron, for taking such a risk in order to follow your new faith. You're an inspiration."

"Goodness! That's a bit heady!"

"You know something of my history, how my family spurned Judaism and now are practicing Presbyterians," he said somewhat shyly. It was hard for him to talk of these things, but he'd known instinctively that Cameron was the right person to open up to. "But it has always been more than that for me. I gave my heart to Jesus Christ when I was thirteen years old and have tried to walk with Him since. I've let my church attendance slide since coming to Russia because I couldn't find anything that speaks to my heart here. I wonder now if I just haven't tried hard enough."

"Would you like to come with me sometime?"

"As an embassy official, I think that might be pushing it too far. But . . ." he rubbed his chin. "There must be a way around this. I do need something. Throw in this whole business of my Jewish roots, and I have been quite disconcerted lately."

"Why don't you initiate services in the embassy?" Cameron suggested. "Nothing to disrupt what might already be in place, but something extra, more personal."

"Yes, like the midweek prayer service my church back home had." He'd experienced a rush of excitement over this prospect.

"I would come."

As it happened, a couple days after that conversation Cameron had gone on a tour of the Stalingrad Front and shortly after her return to Moscow had been forced to leave the country. Robert had gone ahead with starting a Wednesday night prayer service for the embassy staff. The attendance, however, had never been great and had soon dwindled to only a couple of people. Robert did not have the gift to lead this sort of thing, and he was too confused about other issues in his life to inspire others toward faith. So eventually there were no more meetings.

In any case, he now realized that Cameron's doctor was also

a man of faith. He had guided Cameron toward giving her heart to God. This must be what Robert sensed in him now. Only faith could help a man to find hope in the midst of desperate circumstances.

How Robert longed to ask Rostov to take him to the underground church. But the risks and danger in going to such a place now were many times greater than they had been a few years ago when Cameron had ventured there. Robert understood how the risks Cameron had taken a few years ago might be inspiring, whereas those he might take now would simply be foolish. Yet he felt a strong urge to talk with this man, to share his confusion about the conflict between two faiths, two heritages. Something told him Dr. Rostov could guide him as he had guided Cameron.

Yet Rostov was a complete stranger who had enough of his own personal issues to deal with, and Robert's natural reserve held him in check. Besides, it was simply dangerous to prolong this meeting further.

Rostov must have felt the same because he said in a conclusive tone, "Tell your man that I will meet with him."

They discussed a plan for the meeting, then Rostov left. Robert waited fifteen more minutes, then also departed the restaurant.

———

A week later Alex met Larry Marquet in the back room of a friend's bakery. They could not meet in a public place because they needed to converse in English, which would have drawn attention in public. Alex's English had become quite rusty over the years with disuse, but Marquet spoke no Russian at all.

After exchanging prearranged recognition phrases, Alex said, "The owner of the bakery is very nervous, so we cannot talk long. You are certain you were not followed?"

"I know what I am doing," Marquet said.

Alex responded with an arched brow. Such arrogance worried him more than outright stupidity. "What do you want of me?" he asked.

"We would like you to act as an agent-in-place for us," said Marquet rather casually.

He was asking Alex to be a spy almost as offhandedly as he would request a cup of tea! "Mr. Wood mentioned some recompense for my services."

"Yes, of course. The means to escape Russia. We can arrange that." Again his tone was nonchalant. He was offering Alex his life, but it seemed to mean little to Marquet.

"What do I have to do?"

"For openers I want more details from your physicist friend."

"What he gave me was a one-time thing. It would be very dangerous for him to relay more information. They have his son under arrest to keep him in line."

"We would like details on exactly what German technicians and equipment were evacuated here after the war," Marquet asked, apparently not having heard or choosing to ignore Alex's statement. "We need details of Soviet military readiness—"

"Maybe I have given you the wrong idea." Alex cut in with difficulty because Marquet was highly intent on his own agenda. "I have no way of getting such information. I am only a doctor. I have no connections in government."

"I'm sure you'll find a way."

"I am beginning to think this arrangement is a mistake." Alex had never felt completely confident in what he had agreed to do. Yet time pressed upon him like a vise. Time away from the woman he loved.

"Okay, okay, settle down." Marquet spoke as if soothing a child. "My eagerness just got the best of me. You don't know how hard it has been for us to penetrate this country. Did I mention we are also in a position to reinstate your medical license once you reach America?"

Alex's heart leaped. They truly did have his life in their hands. He had to forcefully remind himself that his life was only in God's hands.

"I don't know if I have the power to give you what you want," Alex said.

"You are a Russian citizen. That fact alone gives you more leverage than we could hope for. I am sure we can work together on this. What do you feel comfortable with?"

Alex wanted to say, "Nothing." For as much as he opposed the Stalinist government, he wasn't so sure he much liked this representative of the other side of the fence.

Instead, because he knew this was a chance that might not come along again, he said, "I am a doctor. It is only by chance that I know a physicist. I can only do what I can do."

"Sure . . . of course." Marquet seemed to ruminate upon this. "You just work the physicist as much as you can for now and keep your eyes and ears open. That's as much as I can ask. But there is something else. We need some Russian identity papers—you know, originals that we can copy. Without these it has been impossible for us to get agents into the country. This also may in the future benefit you."

"How would I get these?"

"You are a doctor, aren't you? Good as you may be, I'll bet you have a patient die on you occasionally. Easy enough to pick the man's pocket after he is dead. Won't hurt him if he is discovered by the authorities to be without proper papers."

Alex gaped at the man, appalled at such an idea. But what disturbed him almost as much was just how unsuited he himself was for the undertaking he was now committing himself to. Hounding his friends, picking pockets, snooping around.

Well, he would either escape Russia or be strung up by his thumbs in a gulag. The least he could do was to try to ensure his chances of the former. The time had come for him to put action behind his hope, as he had once told Cameron he would do. Recent experience had proved to Alex that it was as difficult for Russians to get *out* of the country as it was for foreign agents to get *in*. If this American somehow had the means to help him, he could not refuse him.

"I will work for you for six months," he said firmly. "At that time, and not a moment later, you will effect my escape." He resisted the temptation of putting it in the form of a question.

But true to his character, Marquet took it in that form anyway. "We'll just base it on the quality of your work."

Alex reminded himself of that lonely anniversary celebration four months ago. The prospect of yet another lonely dinner was nearly unbearable. He had not lost hope. In fact, what he was going to do indicated that he still had some hope. The six-month cutoff date would come just before his and Cameron's second anniversary. He was determined they would spend it together.

Oh, God, I pray this is the right thing! Help me in this. Keep me in your hands.

PART II

*"I believe that we must assist free peoples
to work out their own destinies
in their own way."*

HARRY S. TRUMAN
March 1947

8

West Berlin, Germany
April 1947

THEORETICALLY, CAMERON could not complain too strenuously about twists of fate and ironies of life. Often such things had worked to her advantage. Many times in her life she had been "in the right place at the right time," and according to Johnny Shanahan, that was often what made great journalists, more so than excellence in writing.

But that wasn't the case now.

Here she was in Berlin—West Berlin, as it must be called these days. Set in the midst of Soviet-occupied Germany, she was as close to Russia as one could hope to get these days, and certainly she was in the middle of one of the hottest spots on the globe. Nevertheless, she desperately wanted to be someplace else.

Russia.

But that was nothing new. She had been wanting and trying to get into Russia for two years. And now that her second wedding anniversary loomed only three weeks away, her desperation was even more acute. What made the situation ironic, or perhaps downright pathetic, was that this morning the Foreign Minister's Conference in Moscow had ended. She should have been there for that event, if for no other reason. As a journalist she was the most qualified observer. She'd had high hopes that by now her troubles with the Soviets would be forgotten—but *she* had forgotten just how long Russian memories were.

Grabbing her coat and purse, she determined to do some-thing—anything—to get her mind off her disappointment and headed down to the hotel lobby. She was crossing the lobby's shabby carpet when she heard her name. Turning, she saw an old friend.

"Why, Lev, is that really you?" She grinned, surprised at how genuinely glad she was to see her old colleague Carl Levinson. He was a reminder of happier times, though they had been times of war and danger.

She recalled how she and Carl and Johnny had raced through Yugoslavia and Greece at the beginning of the war just one step ahead of the invading Germans. Even more fondly, she remem-bered how Levinson had once offered his friendship as a kind of replacement for the loss of Johnny.

"How are ya doing, Cameron?" He eyed her up and down with an appreciative glint in his eyes. There had never been any romantic interest between them, and she knew he was just trying to be funny when he gave a low whistle. "Still the most beautiful hack on the beat, honey."

"Are you on your way back from Moscow?"

"That iceberg? Hardly. I left there three months ago and have no regrets about missing the conference. From what I hear it was a big joke anyway."

She had a strong urge to touch him because he'd so recently been in the place she longed to be.

"I'm surprised you weren't there, though," he said.

"I'm still paying for that kiss in the hospital in Leninsk," she replied dismally.

"Those Ruskies," he lamented. "Hey, where are you heading? Want to grab some lunch and talk old times?"

"Sure."

There was a little café around the corner where the foreign press often gathered. It was one of the few places in the bombed-out city where they could be certain of getting decent food, but mostly where, surrounded by their own kind, they felt most comfortable. As they entered, there were many greetings and invitations to join other groups, but Cameron was happy when Carl suggested they sit alone. She hadn't seen him since she had been forced to leave Russia four years ago. They had a lot of catching up to do, and she had many questions for him about the shape of things in Russia.

"Okay," he said after they had ordered, "I'll lay odds you want to know what's going on in Russia since the war. But first, tell me what you've been up to."

"Nothing too exciting—"

"Peacetime is a dull beat," he agreed heartily.

"I hate to think that, or we are in big trouble, as journalists and as a world." She paused as her coffee arrived and took a sip of the steaming brew, pleased to taste the real stuff. That was one reason the foreign press came to this particular café. "I guess I am just getting tired of looking at rubble. And how many ways can you write about refugees and bleak, hopeless faces?"

"You won't find it any different in Russia, believe me," he commented, lighting a cigarette and setting it to his lips.

"True, but at least there . . ." She let her words trail away. She was too self-conscious of appearing the silly, romantic girl.

"You can't still be pining for that doctor?"

She had never realized that Lev could be as incisive as Shanahan himself. "We got married, Lev."

"What!" He inhaled too much smoke in his shock and started coughing.

While he recovered, she quickly recounted the story of how she had found Alex in Torgau, where the American Army had met the Russians in Germany.

"And he returned to Russia after that?" asked Levinson, still aghast.

"Honor, you know."

"He should have run while he had the chance."

"The Americans had agreed with the Soviets to repatriate deserters, POWs, dissidents, and others who tried to find asylum with them. It was too risky. Besides, we both believed the war would bring change to Russia, that Stalin would reward his people with more freedom."

"And you call yourself an expert on Russia?"

"Maybe it was wishful thinking on our part." She shrugged. "But we lost the opportunity, and now he can't get out and I can't get in. Tell me, Lev, is it as bad there as we hear?"

"Stalin is more paranoid than ever." He took a thoughtful puff of his cigarette. "I suppose I shouldn't be too hard on your judgment of postwar events. Everyone thought Stalin would let up and there would be better relations with the Allies. Blame the bomb, at least for what has happened regarding foreigners, especially Americans. You should read the venomous attacks on America in *Pravda*. You would think we lynch Negroes on a daily basis and that Truman is the next Hitler. Things might have been different if FDR hadn't died. I always thought he was just a shade or two away from being red himself."

"Lev, you accused your grandmother of being a Communist when you saw her reading *Grapes of Wrath*."

Levinson grinned sheepishly. "Reading *and* enjoying it, I might add!" He chuckled but made no apologies for his decidedly anti-Communist views. Well, Cameron was no proponent of Communism, either, but she had a feeling Lev had always considered her a bit too pink for comfort, also. "Truman's biggest mistake is overestimating Russian might. Russia is simply too weak now to be much of a threat. Living standards there are worse than they were at the end of the war. The harvest of '46 was a failure. Besides drought and hunger, the government must do something about rebuilding the nation's infrastructure. It will take years for Stalin to have the wherewithal to start another war."

"I heard one American diplomat predict a war in 1949," Cameron said.

"Then again, we better not *under*estimate them like Hitler did," Levinson said dryly. He went on, "With things as they presently stand, I left Russia knowing the chances of returning were slim. Soviet borders are tighter than ever, especially to journalists.

I know you don't want to hear that."

"I want to know the truth."

"Well, that's it in a nutshell. My perspective, at least. You're gonna need a miracle to get into that country."

"Lev, have I told you that I have a greater respect for miracles than I once did?" Her heart started pounding. It was never easy to tell her friends about her spiritual convictions, especially dyed-in-the-wool cynics like Lev. "I am going to put my trust in God, not Stalin. Somehow, some way, He will get Alex and me back together."

"I wish you the best, Cameron, I truly do. And if you do succeed, let me know. I've curried a couple of sources there that might be useful to you."

"Thanks, Lev, I'll do that."

After lunch Cameron returned to her hotel. Her mind was full of what Levinson had revealed. Some she had already known; most she at least had an inkling of from the trickle of information that had come out of Russia since the war. All of it worked to undermine her hope, but she kept reminding herself of what she had told her friend. Somehow God would get her and Alex together. The two of them had felt certain of this from the beginning. God was stronger than Stalin!

She was striding past the front desk of the hotel on her way to the elevator when the clerk called her.

"Fraulein Hayes! You have a message."

She returned to the desk and the clerk handed her a telegram. Normally she received wires with trepidation, an old and totally irrational fear of them always bearing bad news. But this time she thought differently. Wouldn't it be just like God, after Lev's dismal report, to send the long-awaited visa to Russia?

She tore open the envelope as she strode to the elevator. Her emotions scattered more than ever as she saw it was from her father.

CAMERON STOP YOUR MOTHER ILL STOP WILL
HAVE SURGERY IN A WEEK STOP BE GOOD IF YOU

WERE HERE STOP HAVE WIRED TRAVEL FUNDS TO
PAPER'S BERLIN BANK STOP YOUR FATHER END

The arrival of the elevator barely penetrated her suddenly
numb senses.

She hardly heard the operator's question. "Fraulein, you wish
the elevator?"

Glancing up, she nodded vaguely and stepped inside, mum-
bling her floor number. As the car jerked into motion, she tried
to pull herself together. All of the horrors of war and separation
from the man she loved paled in view of the words she had just
read. Her father hadn't needed to say this was serious. The fact
that he had notified her and, in his subdued way, asked her to
come home was enough.

Reaching her room, she hurried inside, made a call to the airline she commonly used, then pulled out her suitcase and began
packing. She'd been able to get a flight out in the morning.

9

Los Angeles, California

HE WAS A HANDSOME young man. For most of the last thirty years Cecilia had thought of her son as a cherubic toddler with a mop of curly caramel-colored hair and big, round dark eyes. But this photo that had been sent to Cameron two years ago dispelled that former image. Sometimes Cecilia wondered if it wouldn't have been better to maintain the picture of the ageless child. He hadn't been as real then, more like a fantasy she had conjured out of a distant dream.

Cecilia ran a finger along the strong jawline, firm, yet with enough roundness to hint of the baby from long ago. There was still a striking resemblance to his father. His hair, though crammed under the Red Army cap, was still curly. That much was clear even if most of it had been cropped off per military regulations. But the uniform reminded her that he had been through a war. Cecilia had read all of Cameron's articles reporting on the war in Russia, and she had listened to her daughter's verbal stories. She knew it had been a horrible ordeal. If Semyon had been in the Army, then he surely had suffered much, and it was a sheer miracle that he had survived.

Even if the years were not clearly evident, the experience of war had surely made a man of the lad.

"Dear God, I pray that he is not scarred too terribly much. It seems he has already suffered enough with the tragedies of his childhood."

She could not help but think again of the child, deserted by his mother soon after birth, then torn from the arms of his father at the tender age of five. Regret poured over Cecilia. In thirty years she had never been entirely certain she had done the right thing. She knew God had forgiven her for her mistake, for the illicit affair with Yakov Luban, and even for deserting her son. Yet how could God forgive her for her lies regarding these things when she still perpetuated them?

She had almost convinced herself that the lies were for everyone's good. The truth certainly wouldn't help Semyon, and it would almost certainly destroy her marriage. She wasn't lying to protect herself, not entirely. How many times had she tried to estimate the cost of the truth? Each time it had come out lacking.

But there were times, especially lately when she and Keagan were getting along so well, that she could believe it would not be so bad to reveal the truth. He was a more sensitive man than he had been. At least he had come to accept his own vulnerability a bit more, and in so doing he was more forgiving of the weaknesses of others.

"Cecilia, where are you?"

Cecilia's heart leaped, and in a panic she gathered up the photos, letters, and book that had been spread out on her secretary. She pulled some stationery on top of the items, but that didn't provide enough cover, so she yanked open a drawer and began shoving the things in.

As the door to her sitting room sprang open, she slammed the drawer shut. Her heart was hammering as Keagan's big shoulders and shaggy gray-red head poked into the room.

"I swear, woman, I'm going to tie a bell around your neck so I can keep track of you."

"Yes, it is easy to get lost in this big rambling house." Her voice was a bit too high-pitched and nervous.

"You look white. Are you okay?"

"Yes, I'm fine. You startled me, that's all."

She saw him glance toward the drawer and braced herself for his questions. When no question came, oddly, she didn't feel relieved. Perhaps she was like a criminal who wanted to be discovered.

"Well, pretty soon this house won't feel so rambling and empty," he said. "Jackie will soon be here from the airport with Cameron, and Blair is coming tomorrow."

"I still wish you hadn't called them, not until we knew more."

"You are going for surgery in a few days. You think they'd rather not know? If I hadn't told them, they'd never speak to me again. And this is the first time in years I can remember being on friendly terms with all my children at the same time."

Cecilia smiled. "Yes, it is rather a nice feeling, isn't it?"

"Except I keep waiting for the other shoe to fall, as they say."

Cecilia thought of the things in the drawer. There lay the means not only to make a shoe fall but to make it pound Keagan soundly in the head.

Yes, things were going well between them, but that was also an argument for keeping her secret. These last couple of years had been the best ever in their marriage, not only because of the good relations with their daughters, but also because there was a new closeness between them as husband and wife. Part of that, Cecilia knew, was because they finally had something in common in the precious gift of their granddaughter. Emi Colleen, or just Colleen, as Keagan insisted upon calling her, was truly the light of both of their lives. Now that she was walking and talking and more little girl than baby, Keagan delighted in taking her on outings. He often missed work so that he and Cecilia could take her to the zoo or the park or shopping. He had insisted on planning her fourth birthday party himself. He had a friend with a ranch in the San Gabriel Mountains who had opened it up to Colleen and her little friends for a day featuring pony rides, picnicking, and a small rodeo with real cowboys. Cecilia had thought the child might be too young for such an event, but Keagan was determined. Cecilia hadn't been at all sure that she and Keagan weren't too old to be herding around a bunch of four- and five-year-olds, but there had been several parents to help. And Keagan, so out of character, had been totally involved. If the predominantly white families had had any reservations about their children befriending the half-Japanese girl, they had been greatly mollified by the wonderful success of the party. Thanks, at least in part to Keagan, Emi would have no want of little friends.

It just didn't seem right to spoil life with the truth. Weren't some things best left alone?

"No shoes are going to fall, Keagan," she said finally, but her tone lacked a certain resolve. "Now, why were you searching the house for me?"

"I just wanted to tell you I have to run to the office for a short bit. There's a problem with an article we hoped to run in tomorrow's edition, and I have to speak with our lawyers."

"I didn't even hear the phone ring."

"I called the office to check in," he replied just a little defensively. He'd promised to be home to greet Cameron and spend the day with them.

"You are not getting sued, are you?" she asked, only mildly alarmed. No sense mentioning his promise. She couldn't expect too much from him.

"That's what I need to find out from the lawyers. That is, if running the article will get us sued. Cameron will understand if I am not here when she arrives. I'll only be an hour or so."

"We'll manage without you, dear, but Josey has planned a special dinner for four. You know how hard it is to get a good cook, and she is new, so we don't want to get off on the wrong foot with her."

"You'd think the woman was a brain surgeon or something," Keagan huffed. But he had been the one who had insisted on hiring more help around the house since Cecilia had become ill, and he had seen firsthand how difficult hiring and keeping household help was. "I'll be home well before dinner."

He gave Cecilia a quick kiss on the forehead, then turned and left.

Cecilia leaned back in her chair, torn apart all over again by the secrets that assailed her. In years past she had more easily been able to shove them to the back of her mind, hardly giving them much conscious thought. The war and her revelation to Cameron had brought the matter to the surface, especially as she worried for the physical safety of her son.

Now, hardly a day or an hour went by that she didn't think of Semyon and the secret she kept from her husband. Being faced with her mortality had that effect. She had a deadly disease and knew, though neither she nor Keagan had ever verbalized the word, that cancer was all but a death sentence. The doctor said he believed they had caught it early and that surgery might cleanly remove the tumor. But the awful word that no one even dared speak of was not to be taken lightly. Cecilia's mother had died of cancer, and Cecilia had been old enough to retain vivid memories of her mother wracked with pain and wasting away. True, that had been forty years ago. Medical science had come far since then.

Still, fear gripped Cecilia.

Could she die with the secrets locked inside her? She knew Cameron would never tell anyone without her permission—anyone in the family, that is. She realized a few others in Russia had had to be let in on the secret in order to help find Semyon. Thus Cecilia's death, for all practical reasons, would bring an end to that part of her life. Keagan would never have to be shattered with the revelation of his wife's infidelity, that her unfaithfulness had produced a son, Keagan's dearest desire and most crushing failure.

But if she died, it would also ensure that her son would never know he had a mother who had always loved him. The ache of that possibility was deeper than she could have imagined. There was no reason for him to think that his mother had heartlessly tossed him aside. Yakov was a good man and perhaps had tried to put her in a good light, but he and Semyon had been separated when the boy was only five. Cecilia knew from her experience with Emi that understanding was very limited before the age of five. Emi didn't really know why her father was gone, or even that there was something unusual in his being gone. Sad to say, she hardly remembered what it meant to have a father. True understanding and true pain of Sam's absence would come later when she was old enough to realize that a huge part of her life was missing. But Emi would have Jacqueline and other family members to keep Sam's image alive for her when the time came. Poor Semyon would have had no one. His adoptive family had cut him off completely from any prior memories. And there was a hint that the trauma of his early years had stunted Semyon's own memories. All he would have left would be some vague sense that he had been deserted. There might be resentments and bitterness to go with this.

She didn't want her son to hate her, even if his hatred was directed only at some vague image.

One other thought occurred to Cecilia. Perhaps she could reveal the truth to Semyon without doing so to Keagan. Cameron was trying to get back into Russia, mostly, of course, to be with her husband. Yet, she would, if asked, contact Semyon and tell him about Cecilia. It didn't have to go further than that.

Then she thought once more of Keagan. Doubts and confusion closed in around her again. There was no simple solution.

Well, Cameron wasn't going to get into Russia any time soon. And Cecilia did not have the heart to say anything to Keagan before her surgery—she needed him too much now for that. But when she was well again, she'd think seriously about it.

10

KEAGAN HATED hospitals. He'd chafed the entire time he'd been in with his heart attack. But this was worse. This time it was Cecilia in the hospital, and the depth of fear and concern he was feeling was quite astounding. He wasn't the heartless beast everyone made him out to be. He did have emotions, and thirty-three years with the woman only strengthened them. Not that they had all been rosy years. He knew that. And he knew that he was probably the cause of most of the strife.

Regardless, Cecilia had always stood by his side. He realized now, however, that she more than stood there—she had been a pillar upon which he had leaned without even knowing it. Pity he was only seeing that now. The thought of her being gone made him feel shaky, inside and out.

"Keagan, I want to thank you for being here with me," Cecilia said, drawing his thoughts from his woolgathering back to her bedside.

"What else would I do, Cecilia? You are going to have surgery in a couple of hours. I'll not leave the hospital until I know all is well." But he knew her gratitude was not totally off base. He had not been there for her at the birth of any of their daughters. There had always been something urgent for him to tend to at the paper. And he certainly hadn't nursed her during any minor illnesses.

He gave his wife a shrug and a sheepish smile. "This time I will be here for you. I promise," he added, because it had to be said.

"I know and I appreciate it. I have to admit I am a little afraid." She lifted her hand from where it rested on the bed-covers. "Hold my hand for a moment, won't you, dear?"

He reached over and grasped her slim hand in his big fleshy paw. He wondered now why he had treated her as he had over the years. He had neglected her terribly, especially in the early part of their marriage. He hadn't been blind to how desperate and lonely she had been in Russia. But then, as at other times, he had convinced himself that his devotion to work was as much for her and their daughters as it was for him. He'd convinced himself of a lot of foolishness. But it wasn't only his emotional distance and harsh words he regretted. There had been other women, as well. None he ever cared about. He didn't know why he'd strayed. His wife was a lovely, caring woman. Always true to him, always treating him with love and respect.

Well, there had been that time when she had stood up to him regarding Jacqueline's marriage to that Jap . . . to Sam. Keagan reminded himself that the man was little Colleen's father and, if for no other reason, deserved Keagan's respect. Sam had turned out to be a good man and had died a true war hero, with medals to prove it. But Cecilia hadn't needed medals to know the man's worth long before he'd gone off to war. When Keagan was deter-mined to blindly forbid the marriage, Cecilia had actually told him to shut up.

A little smile played upon his lips. Maybe that's when he had first realized the true substance of his wife.

"Why are you smiling, Keagan?"

"Huh? Oh, nothing . . ." Why not tell her? "I was just think-ing of that time in our living room when Sam came to ask for our daughter's hand in marriage."

"Don't remind me! I'm still embarrassed over my behavior."

"You have no reason to be ashamed. You were marvelous."

She started at him, wonder in her eyes. "My, my!" she

breathed and her hand tightened around his.

Silence ensued for several moments. He shifted uneasily in his chair as the silence grew uncomfortably long. Another reason he hated hospitals—as a visitor or even as a patient receiving visitors, you always felt there must be a steady stream of conversation.

"I do hope Blair gets here," he said finally, mostly to fill the void.

"You did tell her she didn't have to come?"

"I did, but she insisted." Shortly before she had been scheduled to leave Washington, Blair had suffered a malaria attack. She had scheduled a later flight, but her parents thought she was pushing herself too much.

"I know it is selfish, but I am glad she is coming," Cecilia said. "I just hope I get to see her before I am taken into surgery. What time is it?"

Glancing at his wristwatch, Keagan replied, "Nine o'clock. You have two more hours to wait. Blair will get here. Jackie is picking her up as we speak."

"I wanted to see all of them before I go. I wish I could see Emi, as well—"

"You can see them all you want *after* your surgery," he cut in firmly. He knew what she was getting at, and he refused to entertain or encourage any morbid thoughts.

"Keagan, we must be prepared for all eventualities. This is a serious surgery."

"Bah! You won't be operated on by witch doctors, you know. Your surgeon is one of the best in the state—in the country for that matter. You have nothing to fear."

"It is hard not to think of what . . . of what could happen."

"Well, don't. That's an order." His tone was gruff. It was the only way he himself could deal with what was ahead.

"I want to tell you something." She turned her head to fully face him. He could not read that look in her large brown eyes. Her lip trembled. She seemed to hesitate before finally speaking. "I love you, Keagan!"

Something inside his chest tightened. Words of love were seldom exchanged between them, almost never by him.

"And I you," he replied. He could not help himself. The specific word *love* just could not seem to get past his lips.

She squeezed his hand again and smiled. Did she understand? Of course, she always understood.

"Keagan, I would like to see Cameron for a few moments alone. Why don't you get yourself a cup of coffee. It's going to be a long wait."

He was glad for the release and didn't wait to be asked twice. It wasn't that he didn't care, but this was too much like a deathbed scene for him to desire more of it.

———

Nothing wrenched at Cameron's heart more than the sight of her mother in the hospital bed looking so pale and helpless. It wasn't that Cecilia hadn't always been a rather frail-appearing woman, soft-spoken, even insubstantial at times. Yet Cameron had come to realize that her mother was truly the mortar of their family. Everyone relied on her to some degree. She did not look like a rock or a pillar of strength, but she was all of that.

"Cameron, did you bring what I asked?" Cecilia said, barely waiting for Cameron to close the door to her room.

"Yes, Mom, I have it here." Cameron held out a black Bible. She went to the bedside and handed the Bible to her mother.

Cecilia opened the book to the middle, where a photo was tucked. "I just wanted to see him one more time."

Cameron cringed inwardly, feeling once more the weight of her failure while in Russia to somehow bring Semyon and her mother together. Cameron knew such an actual meeting was all but impossible, yet she felt she should have done more.

As if reading her thoughts and wanting to assure her daughter, Cecilia said, "Cameron, I can never fully express how thankful I am for this photo. I never dreamed when I told you about him that you would be able to bring him to me in this way."

"I'm glad," Cameron replied lamely.

"Your father was just here."

"Yes, I know. He told me to come in."

"I have never seen him so concerned and attentive." Cecilia's eyes flicked once to the photo, then back to Cameron. "We have become close lately. Well, closer than ever before."

"Mom . . ." Cameron sensed what her mother was leading to and wanted her to stop, but she didn't have to heart to cut her off too harshly.

"I know," her mother sighed. "It would be foolhardy. Yet I hate having this secret between us. I feel I am betraying him more now than when I had that affair with Yakov. I fear the secret is far worse than the act it seeks to hide."

"Mother, I can't keep you from telling Father, but I implore you to wait until the surgery is over and you are stronger." In case he physically attacks you or tosses you out on the street, she thought but had the sense not to verbalize.

"I know. I need him now. But what if I should die—"

"Mother—"

"Let me speak of this, Cameron." Her tone was quite vigorous, and color was rising to her pale complexion. "Everyone is dancing around this issue, but I must express my feelings to someone. I can't speak to your father about the possibility of my death, for he is far too vulnerable right now." The idea of her father being vulnerable seemed ridiculous, yet Cecilia had always been a good judge of others. She went on, "Cameron, I am afraid that for now, you are the only one I can talk to."

Cameron pulled the chair close to the bed and sat down with resolution. "Go on, Mom. I'll listen."

"Thank you, dear. I know it isn't easy for you. But I need to say that if I die today, or for that matter, when I die in the future, I don't hold you to the secret. I want you to tell your father and your sisters."

"Okay, Mom, sure."

Cecilia eyed her dubiously, and Cameron knew she had spoken too quickly and too glibly to be believed. She was about to tell her mother that she thought the secret should go to both of their graves when the door creaked open.

"Mom?" came a familiar voice.

"Blair, is that you?" Cecilia said.

"Yes, Mom." The door flew open all the way and in strode Blair, with Jackie not far behind. She came up to the side of the bed opposite Cameron.

Cameron glanced toward her mother. Cecilia jerked her hand as if to close the Bible, but then she stopped and kept the book open, leaving the photo lying in clear view. Cameron groaned inwardly.

Blair leaned down, hugged her mother, then kissed her on the cheek. "I'm so glad I got here before you went to surgery. But you look quite in the pink, Mom. Hardly sick at all. I am so relieved."

"I don't feel too bad, really. Just a bit tired."

"I won't be long then."

"No. I am glad you are here." Cecilia gazed at each of her daughters. "I am happy that all my daughters are here. I love each of you so!"

Jackie, coming up beside Cameron, patted the covers over her mother. "We'll have a grand time when you are out of the hospital, Mom. Blair can stay for at least a couple of weeks, and Cameron is working at the *Journal* again. We'll shop and have lunch and play with Emi."

Blair kissed her mother again. "Yes, all four of us!"

No one mentioned that with Emi it would make five. Cameron hoped it was simply poor mathematics on Blair's part.

Then Blair added, "Mom, who is that photo of? I've never seen him—oh, wait, it's Cameron's doctor. That's a Red Army uniform, isn't it?"

Cameron was ready to jump up and declare that it was indeed Alex.

But Jackie, leaning in for a closer look, spoke first. "That's not Alex. Don't you remember the picture Cameron showed us? This definitely isn't him."

"The light hair, the uniform . . . are you sure? Who else could it be?" Blair asked.

"It isn't Alex," Cecilia said, glancing at Cameron. "I know you won't tell them, Cameron. It should come from me, anyway."

"What are you two talking about?" asked Blair.

"This photo is of a young Russian man named Semyon Luban," said Cecilia. "He is your half brother."

On reflex Cameron glanced toward the door and, to her horror, saw that it hadn't shut completely when her sisters had entered. She sprang to her feet and fairly leaped toward the door, closing it firmly, though not before taking a quick glance into the corridor. Her father was nowhere to be seen. She returned to the bed but was too agitated to sit.

"Mom, what are you saying?" asked Jackie, then turned to Cameron. "Have they medicated her yet for surgery?"

Cameron shook her head.

"I am not out of my mind, Jacqueline." Indeed, Cecilia looked as clear eyed and sane as she ever had. "I'm too tired to go into all the details now, but Cameron can fill you in later and answer your questions."

"You knew about this, Cameron?" queried Blair.

"I told her about Semyon when she went to Russia," Cecilia answered. "I had a hope that she might be able to find him for me. Let me tell you about it before you say anything more, all right?" She smiled the smile that all the girls knew was her sweet way of telling them to obey or else. "It happened when your father and I were in Russia during the Great War. I had many reasons, many excuses. There just isn't time to go into it all now. I'm sure the nurse will be coming in soon with my medication. Simply put, I was lonely and friendless in a strange country, and your father was gone a lot. I met Yakov and he filled a void in me. What I did was wrong, terribly wrong."

"But, Mom," interjected Blair, always finding it hard to obey her mother, "what did Dad do about it?"

"He didn't know."

"But—?"

"Like I said, Cameron will explain everything. But it did happen." Cecilia paused, seeming to struggle, then continued. "I . . . had an affair and became with child." The strain of making the difficult confession was evident on her face, making creases that even her illness hadn't produced. "I managed to get to Sweden and had Semyon there. I decided for the sake of my marriage the best thing was to leave him to the care of his father. I have regretted and second-guessed that decision for the last thirty years. I returned home to America as soon as I could after the birth. Yakov wrote to me afterward to keep me informed about Semyon. Then in the chaos of the Revolution and the Civil War that followed, I lost track of them. I did not know if Semyon was alive or dead until Cameron finally tracked him down."

"You have met him, Cameron?" asked Jackie.

"No. I got close to finding him before I left Russia, but it was my friends in Russia who finally located him and somehow contrived to get this photo. I never met him," she repeated regretfully. "I don't know if we ever will."

A stunned silence descended over the room. Cameron could not look at her sisters or her mother. Again she was filled with that sense of failure. Beyond that she didn't know what to think or expect. No one would argue that each of her sisters was far different from her and would react to this shocking news in her own manner.

"I am glad I told you," Cecilia finally said. "I hope you don't feel less of me, or at least you can forgive me."

"Of course we don't," Jackie said quickly. "We have all made enough mistakes in our lives to know we are only human, even you. It's pretty shocking, that's all. To hear that we have a brother."

"It makes me realize that we were all too hard on Dad," Blair said. "I mean, it is surprising that he's stood by you despite this. I wouldn't have expected it of him."

"I thought you understood, Blair. Your father still does not know about this."

"And he must never know," added Cameron. She couldn't help herself.

"You have kept this from him all these years?"

Cameron found it surprising that Blair seemed to be having a hard time with this. She more than anyone should understand about secrets, but then perhaps that's what made her more sensitive to this aspect of the news.

"I fear it would destroy him," Cecilia said. "I know it would destroy our marriage."

"Secrets are what destroy, Mom," said Blair.

"You said it yourself, Blair," Cameron said, "when you voiced your surprise over how well Dad took the news. You know as well as anyone what would happen if he knew. He'd explode like an atomic bomb."

"But it doesn't seem right that we are not even giving him a chance. Dad has changed."

"That much?" Cameron arched a brow at her sister.

Cecilia's voice cut through the mounting tension. "Blair, I think you may be right. When I am over this surgery and strong again, I think I will tell him. I think it is the best thing."

"We can discuss all this later," Jackie put in. "This is no time for such a debate. Mom, thank you for telling us. I love you dearly, and this changes nothing. You need to rest now."

A few moments later a nurse came in, and Cameron was relieved. This was far too volatile of a subject to have opened up only an hour before major surgery. Cameron supposed she understood her mother's need to do so, but she didn't understand Blair's need to raise a debate at this time. Yet Cameron couldn't think too harshly of her sister, either. After all, Cecilia's news was a bombshell, which, added to her precarious health, was enough to push one's emotions to the edge.

Nevertheless, when Cecilia returned the Bible and photo to Cameron—it was far too dangerous to leave it lying about—she wished her pocketbook were large enough to hold it. It felt like a neon light in her hand. What if her father asked about it? What if she dropped it and the photo tumbled out at her father's feet? She tightly gripped the Bible, though it seemed to burn her hand.

11

WHEN THEY EXITED Cecilia's room, a nurse showed them to a waiting room at the end of the corridor. Keagan was there with Emi perched on his knee.

"You brought Emi," Cameron commented.

"Mom wanted to see her, so I got special permission from the hospital," Jackie replied.

Cameron gave her niece a kiss.

"Aunt Camern," Emi said, not quite able to get the name entirely right, for she'd had only a couple of days to get reacquainted with her aunt. "I have two aunts!" she declared, holding out two fingers.

"She is so proud of herself." Jackie beamed, obviously proud, as well. "She's been working on her counting. She can count to ten."

"Aunt Bear, kiss!" Emi scooted off her grandfather's lap and scrambled to her other aunt.

Everyone laughed at Emi's rendition of Blair's name. Blair was certain no one noticed her tension as she bent and lightly brushed the child's head with a perfunctory kiss or that she ignored Emi's uplifted arms. Emi didn't seem to notice, either, and was quickly off haranguing her grandfather once more.

Blair knew she was a horrible person, but she just couldn't

warm up to the child. It had been terribly awkward when she had been expected to hold Emi on the drive to the hospital from the airport. There had been no way to avoid it because the child refused to sit alone in the backseat or to sit by herself between her mother and aunt.

How could Blair long to hold her own child but feel only tension bordering on revulsion when she had the opportunity to hold her niece? Well, she knew the answer to that question. The real question was how to get over it. Babies were supposed to be the great equalizer of social differences. Perhaps she should talk to her father about it. He had no love for the Japanese and had not approved of Jackie's marriage. Yet he had found a way to accept Emi.

A nurse came to the door of the waiting room. "You can bring the child in to see her grandmother now. But only for a few minutes."

Jackie gathered up Emi and, with Keagan, left. Blair relaxed a bit and sat next to Cameron.

"How have you been doing, Blair?" asked Cameron with a touch of formality in her voice.

They had not seen or spoken to each other since last Christmas when they had both flown home for a brief visit. Neither was very diligent about letter writing, though Blair suspected some of the present tension might have more to do with the scene in their mother's hospital room. Blair was still in shock, but she didn't want to talk about it right now and guessed Cameron felt the same.

"Fine, thank you."

"You are over the malaria, then?"

"Malaria . . . ? Oh yes, that. For now I am. It never completely goes away, they say."

"How do you find Washington?"

"I like it. Gary has a good job, and we've found a lovely home to rent. I enjoy the social scene." That wasn't entirely true. There was a time in her past when she would have enjoyed it far more. But she didn't feel comfortable going into the feeling of detachment toward life that she had been feeling since leaving the Philippines. She wasn't certain if she and her sister were on that level of intimacy any longer.

"I'm happy for you."

The silence that followed lasted only a few moments before Blair remembered to keep up her end of the conversation. "And you, Cameron? How was Europe?"

"You can't imagine the destruction. Berlin is all but leveled. You have to wonder how they will recover—that is, without help from America."

Blair was surprised to realize how distasteful this superficial exchange was to her. She and Cameron had never been chums, yet she'd felt that since the war there was more to their relationship than this. The months they had been in Los Angeles together right after the war had fostered a closeness between them. And now, after the superficialities of the Washington scene, Blair longed more than ever for a real friendship. Could Cameron be such a friend? She supposed it was up to her to take the first step if she was to learn the answer to that question.

"Cameron, there's something I should have mentioned when I saw you at Christmas, but at that time I didn't know if anything would come of it."

"You've got me curious. What is it?" Cameron asked, a bit more warmth in her voice.

"Some time ago now, Gary and I were talking about your getting into Russia. He suggested trying a different approach. Instead of going as a journalist, you could try to go as a member of the U.S. embassy staff—as a secretary or something."

"That is a different approach." Cameron rubbed her chin thoughtfully, a new glint in her eyes. "But they don't give those jobs away. I'll scrub floors or wash dishes if I have to."

"Gary doesn't have a lot of influence, so nothing much came of his idea until he discovered recently he has friend, a West Point classmate, who actually works in Moscow as an Army attaché. Gary wrote to him, just to see the lay of the land, as it were. One thing he did learn was that they don't have American servants at the embassy. They're all Russian. Something about food shortages. But there are other positions, and if one becomes open . . . well, he'll keep you posted if you are interested."

"It would be a long shot."

"I suppose you're right," Blair replied, unable to mask her sense of dejection. "I guess I didn't think it through—"

Quickly Cameron laid a hand on Blair's arm. "It's a marvelous idea. You know how I always look at the negative side of things. I have to pray constantly for God to curb that tendency."

Blair smiled. "I am glad I am not the only one with a nagging flaw. Only I have more than just one."

"I have one or two others, as well," Cameron said wryly. "At least we are not alone with our flaws."

"Do you ever wonder how you managed without God in your life?"

"Constantly."

Blair was encouraged to take yet another risk. "Speaking of flaws, I am sorry for not being . . . I don't know, I guess not being as sweet as Jackie was about what Mom told us. I don't want to cause strife between us."

"Don't give it a thought. You acted wonderfully considering the shock of it all."

"We'll all talk about it soon. Okay?"

"But not now."

"Later, when we are not so worried about Mom." Blair paused as she felt sudden tears fill her eyes. "She will be all right, won't she, Cameron?"

"The doctor was very positive."

"I'm not ready to let go of her." Blair's voice trembled.

Cameron grasped her hand. "I'm not, either. I think the older we get, the more we need her."

Blair saw tears well up in her big sister's eyes. It was oddly refreshing and comforting to see that Cameron felt close enough to reveal some of her emotion.

———

Jackie came into the waiting room carrying a tray with four paper cups of coffee. She had left to take Emi to her grandmother Okuda's. Cecilia had now been in surgery two hours.

"Jackie, you read my mind," Cameron said. "I was about to head to the cafeteria myself."

"I thought since I was out already, I would save you all a trip."

Jackie offered the coffee to her father and sisters, then took a seat next to her father. The other vacant seat was next to Cameron, but Jackie felt a tad cowardly sitting there instead of by her father. Even as she settled into the chair beside him, she wanted to avoid him. She could hardly look at him because her mind was still buzzing with what her mother had told her that morning. Just thinking of those things seemed a betrayal to her father.

Yet no amount of inner fortitude could force those thoughts from her mind. She had a brother, the illegitimate offspring of an affair her mother had had with a Russian.

It was incomprehensible!

Although Jackie had tried to assure her mother that she didn't hold this deed against her, she knew that her acceptance was only intellectual. Jackie hadn't specifically asked her mother, but she knew Cecilia must have long ago sought and received forgiveness from God, and she herself could do no less than what God had done. Intellectually, that is.

In her heart she was appalled, horrified, staggered. She was going to have to pray long and hard to get her heart and head to agree.

She wondered what Blair and Cameron were thinking. Of course Cameron had had years to come to grips with all of this. They were all going to have to talk eventually. But not now.

Keagan shifted in his chair, and Jackie started, feeling the heat of embarrassment rising to her cheeks. Her father's not knowing about this wasn't right. And her mother's keeping such a huge secret from him wasn't right. Jackie didn't want to appear self-righteous, but she would never have kept such a secret from Sam.

But then she couldn't imagine ever being in a position to have such a secret, not with Sam.

Her father, however, was a totally different person. Cecilia was afraid of him—everyone, including Jackie and her sisters, was afraid of him. Well, Cameron wasn't afraid of him, but Keagan had fostered fear in others, and Jackie thought he probably enjoyed it. So from that standpoint, Jackie could understand the need for secrecy. Keagan had mellowed a bit in the last few years, but not *that* much. There was no telling what his reaction would be. Certainly not a good one.

Still, here he was, faithfully waiting at the hospital for his wife's surgery. Jackie had seen the lines of concern on his face. Even now the fingers of one hand were drumming nervously on his leg. Jackie was sure he did love Cecilia, though he seldom took the opportunity to show any outward sign of it.

And Cecilia loved Keagan. She must, to have stayed with him all these years. Of course, for her mother's generation divorce was considered far more taboo than it was today. Yet Jackie had to believe it was more than fear that had kept her mother in the marriage. And she had to believe that it was more than fear that had kept Cecilia silent about Semyon all these years.

Semyon, I have a brother named Semyon. . . . No, I cannot think of him, especially not fondly, not with Daddy right here.

Incomprehensible. Unthinkable. Amazing!

————

The surgery was taking far longer than the doctor said it would. Almost four hours. Something was wrong, terribly wrong. Keagan drained his sixth cup of coffee. Horrible stuff. He wondered if the hospital was still using one of those terrible ersatz brews some had served during wartime rationing.

He crushed the paper cup in his hand, then glanced up at the big clock over the waiting room door.

Cecilia was dead. Those cowardly doctors just hadn't found the nerve to tell him yet.

"Daddy, are you okay?" Blair's voice came from beside him.

Seneca Falls Library
100
47 Cayuga Street
Seneca Falls, N.Y. 13148

"Yes, of course." But he realized his knuckles were white as they gripped the cup with a stranglehold.

He lurched to his feet, strode to the wastebasket, and dumped the cup into it. He had long since stripped off his suit coat and loosened his collar, but he pulled his necktie even looser. It was suddenly very warm in the room, claustrophobic. He remembered the day he'd had his heart attack. It hadn't felt much different than this. No pain shooting down his left arm this time at least. He paced around the room, not for the first time that day.

As he drew near the door, it burst open, nearly smacking him in the face. Only a quick sidestep spared him. A man clad in hospital green with a matching surgical cap on his head entered.

"She's dead!" Keagan gasped.

"No, far from it," said the doctor. "I know, the surgery took longer than we expected. To be honest, I wasn't at all certain that I wouldn't open her up only to close immediately, unable to do anything. It took long because I was able to remove the tumor—all of it, I am fairly certain."

"You mean all the cancer is gone?" Cameron asked, rising and coming up next to her father. Keagan was rather shocked his daughter had used *that* word. The word he had been so studiously avoiding for weeks since its discovery in his wife.

"We can't say exactly, but I believe it is, and we saw no signs of metastasis."

"That means it hasn't spread?" queried Cameron.

Keagan found it easy to stand back and let his daughter assail the doctor, who deserved no less for making them wait so long. Besides, he wasn't certain if he could form any coherent questions quite yet. He was still rather embarrassed by his initial outburst. He would never be quite comfortable with the doting husband persona.

"Yes," answered the doctor. "I expect a routine recovery."

"What do you mean by that?" Cameron rejoined. "What can we expect?"

A smile nearly bent Keagan's lips. That's my girl! he thought. But he made himself listen to the doctor because he didn't want to show himself a fool by having to ask the same questions all over again.

The gist of it was that Cecilia would be in the hospital for at least two weeks. When she was released, she would have to take things very slowly. It would be two or three months before she was fully recovered, and even then she'd have to curb most of her normal activities for some time.

When the doctor left, Keagan looked at Cameron. The other girls were now standing with them.

"She's going to be okay," he said. He had to hear the words from his own lips.

Cameron threw her arms around him.

"Yes, Dad!" She actually kissed his cheek.

Blair and Jackie encircled him with their arms, as well. The two younger girls were crying, but he expected that of them. He was truly shocked to see tears in Cameron's eyes, too. How many times had he told her that newspapermen don't cry?

Only then did he realize his own eyes were moist.

12

BLAIR FOUGHT hard against her natural inclination toward self-ishness. Here her mother was upstairs, home from the hospital only a day, recovering from a serious operation, still with the possibility of a dangerous disease hanging over her head, and Blair was thinking of herself.

Would it ever grow easier to watch her sister and niece playing together? And there was her father playing with the child, too. This time Blair was determined to talk to her father about how he had been able to accept his half-Japanese grandchild.

The phone rang, and a few moments later the housekeeper came into the living room.

"Mr. Hayes, you have a call," she announced.

"I'll take it in my study," Keagan said.

"I really ought to be going, Dad," Jackie said. "I have lessons to prepare for Monday." She turned to her daughter. "Emi, say good-bye to Grandpa."

Emi jumped up and ran to her grandpa, arms upraised. "Bye-bye, Grandpa!"

Keagan picked her up, kissing her chubby cheek. "You come back to see me later."

"Okeydokey, Grandpa!" She grinned at her mastery of the word Keagan had taught her that morning.

Laughing, Keagan kissed her again, then set her on her feet and took his leave.

Jackie got Emi's jacket and began slipping it on the child. "Blair, can you tell Mom I'll be back later? She wanted us here for dinner, but I have to get some work done first. I only hope Emi cooperates by taking her nap when we get home."

Blair wondered if that was a subtle hint for an offer to baby-sit. Surely anyone else would have jumped in and made the offer, but certainly Jackie didn't expect that of Blair. Though nothing had been said, they both knew how things were.

"Okay, I'll tell her," said Blair.

"Kiss, Aunt Bear," said Emi. Unfortunately, the child had not a clue how things were.

Blair bussed Emi's cheek with a quick simulation of a kiss that seemed to satisfy the child. She made a mental note that if she ever had a child of her own, she would teach her not to throw her affections at everyone she saw. Emi had to kiss everybody. It was disgusting.

No, Blair, it is you who are truly disgusting.

After Jackie departed, Blair made her way to her father's study. Through the closed door, she heard him still talking on the telephone. She waited until there were a long few moments of silence, then knocked on the door.

"Come in," Keagan called.

"Hi, Dad," Blair said, opening the door. "Do you have a few minutes?"

"Of course. Take a seat."

His lack of hesitation gave her courage to go on. "Dad, I've got to talk to someone, and I think you will understand best what I want to say." She took a breath. It still wasn't easy to make the admission, even to her father. "Can you tell me how you manage to . . . I don't know, to be so accepting of Emi?"

"Yes, I can see where I would be the best person to talk to regarding that," he responded. She detected a hint of irony in his tone. "Because I am the least likely to be accepting—"

"I don't mean to insult you," Blair put in quickly. "I admire the way you are, I truly do! I wish I could be that way."

"Blair, I don't believe anyone holds your reluctance against you. We understand what you went through at the hands of the Japs—" He paused as if he might amend the term *Jap*, but then seemed to discard the idea before continuing. "I've no love for them, either, as a nation and perhaps even as a people. I am not sure I would call myself a racist, though I have been called that. However, I never believed in the mingling of the races, and for that reason I opposed your sister's marriage."

"But you seem to have accepted Emi," Blair prompted.

"The little imp got under my skin," he replied wryly. "It's difficult to explain. I just don't see the slanted eyes and Oriental features. And for some reason I'll never be able to fathom, that child likes me. She *wants* to be with me, to hold my hand and sit in my lap. That's enough to make me blind to her shortcomings."

"When I was little, Dad, I wanted to sit in your lap and hold your hand," Blair said sadly.

"I know . . ." For a moment he looked uncomfortable, but there was resolve in his tone when he added, "I know that now. Maybe I hope to make up for my past mistakes with Emi. But, Blair, all I can say to you is not to expect too much from yourself. You don't see Emi on a regular basis, so it may take time before you can accept her for herself."

"Until then I know it must hurt Jackie."

"If you'd like, I'll talk with Jackie, tell her how you feel, how hard you are trying."

"You would do that?"

"It might be better for there to be a middleman, so to speak, to help you both over this."

Blair gazed at her father for a long moment, that big bear of a man with shaggy red-gray hair and piercing green eyes. It was hard for her to fully grasp that such words of understanding were coming from this indomitable, intimidating man. He still looked so fearsome. He had been fearsome for as long as Blair could remember.

She found herself voicing the new perception she sensed.

"Dad, we have really misjudged you."

"No, you haven't."

"Then you have changed."

He nodded slightly. "People do change, I suppose. There has been a great deal of water under the bridge these last few years—a flood, if the truth be told."

"I'm sure you are right."

She knew for a fact that she had changed, and perhaps for that reason she had a better insight into certain matters than Cameron had, or even her mother. Oh, they had changed, too, but she was sure not to the dramatic extent that Blair or Keagan had. That day in their mother's hospital room Cameron had shown that she still feared her father. She simply had not perceived the depth of Keagan's transformation. And as for her mother . . . Blair couldn't say why she remained reticent with Keagan. She said she planned to tell Keagan about her indiscretion, yet Blair had the feeling since then that Cecilia would be content to leave things as they were, to not rock her marriage with the truth.

Blair continued to disagree with that, now more than ever. It wasn't right to so underestimate Keagan, to negate all his positive gains by distrusting him. More than that, it just wasn't right that there should be secrets kept from him. Blair knew the destructive power of lies and deceit. She believed that only good could come of telling the truth.

"Dad, I think there is something you should know," she began, ignoring the sudden tightness of her throat. This was the right thing to do. "Mom and Cameron may think their motives are right, but they are wrong to keep secrets."

"What are you talking about, Blair?" The sharpness in his tone should have warned her to stop. He was still Keagan Hayes, still a man to be reckoned with.

But she continued. "When you were in Russia during the First World War, Mom had an affair."

"Who told you this?"

"Mom did, right before her surgery. Jackie and Cameron wanted it kept quiet, but—"

"You decided to tell all?"

"You have a right to know, don't you? I felt so, at least. But there is more to it. She had a child, but since you were away at the Front, she was able to keep it all a secret by going to Sweden. I don't have all the details."

She paused, her heart racing as she waited for the explosion Cameron had said would come. But there was only silence. His face was red. His eyes lacked expression except for an icy cast. She kept telling herself she had done the right thing. This would all come out for good, and her mother and Cameron would thank her.

Finally, after the longest two minutes of silence Blair had ever experienced, Keagan said, "I am ashamed of you, Blair."

She opened her mouth, expecting to respond to something else, perhaps his gratitude, but when the full import of his words stuck her, she snapped her mouth shut.

Keagan continued. "I did not raise you to be a talebearer, or even worse, a betrayer of confidences."

"M-me?" she finally stammered.

"What did you think? You would somehow curry favor with me by revealing this thing?"

"I . . . I . . . don't know. . . ." She shook her head and tried to make herself deal with the awful turn of events. "Why are you saying these things to me? What about what they did—lying to you? Or what Mom did? I've done nothing wrong. Please, I just meant—"

"Quit your whining, girl!" he snapped. Suddenly he was the old Keagan, the man who had always inspired nothing but loathing, disdain, fear, and rebellion within her. "I have never been more disappointed in you."

"But, Dad—"

"Leave me now before you embarrass yourself further."

Tears were spilling from her eyes as she stumbled from his office. She was a little girl again, rejected by her daddy. She ran to her room, flung herself on the bed, and wept as she had so many times in the past after feeling the sting of her father's rejection.

Had she been trying to curry his favor?

In her heart she truly didn't feel so, but she had not been expecting *this*. What was going to happen now? Her stomach clenched into a tight knot as she imagined the outcome of the encounter with her father. He would tell her mother, and she would know Blair had betrayed her. That would be even worse than her father's disdain.

As the door shut Keagan gulped in a shuddering breath. He was shaking inside and out, though he couldn't identify the emotions assailing him. He did know the anger he'd displayed at Blair had been a smokescreen. Not that he hadn't found what she had done deplorable—it had been. But he had lashed out at her only to hide the reality, the truth of the matter—his anger stemmed from the fact that this secret was finally revealed. His anger really should be directed at Cecilia, for weakening and telling their daughters. But she had feared she might die, so who could blame her for wanting to confess?

But this thing should have gone with her to her grave. Keagan had never wanted to know about it. He'd always guessed there was a secret, a huge secret. He'd suspected that Cecilia had had an affair, though no one had ever told him. Cecilia had been afraid, and rightly so. She feared he might kick her out of his house. It wouldn't matter that he was guilty of the same sinful behavior. Everyone knew it was far worse for a woman to betray her husband. That imbalanced concept was pure rubbish, of course, but that was exactly why he had not reacted as everyone feared. He couldn't live with the humiliation of everyone knowing of his wife's infidelity.

Now his daughters knew, and no doubt soon Cecilia would find the courage to confess to him. If he did not respond by harshly castigating his wife, they would lose all respect for him. If he forgave her and they tried to go on, everyone would simply pity him. It occurred vaguely to him that they might think him more of a man for an act of forgiveness. But he wasn't sure he could forgive her, especially after Blair revealed that Cecilia's affair had produced a child. He was almost certain it had been a boy. Suddenly a communication he'd received several years ago became clear.

Keagan took a key from under the blotter on his desktop, unlocked the bottom drawer, and withdrew a letter. It had come to him via a most circuitous route, as all sensitive mail from the Soviet Union must follow. Keagan still wasn't certain exactly how the letter had come, but it had somehow fallen into the hands of a Russian immigrant on the East Coast who had then mailed it to Keagan.

My old friend,

At least I hope a meeting of the minds over your best bottle of Scotch whiskey counts as friendship and continues to stand after twenty years. I am writing this out of concern for your daughter, whom I have had the pleasure of reacquainting myself with recently. I must add that I can write with some freedom because the letter bearer can be trusted implicitly.

So, as I was saying, Cameron is a delightful girl. If she has any faults at all, it is her curious nature and her concern for others. She asked my assistance in her search for two Russian citizens who she said were old friends of your family and with whom you lost touch shortly after the Revolution. Yakov and Semyon Luban were the names she gave. Not long after this inquiry, she came to me regarding the husband of her interpreter, who had been arrested. I am afraid I was not able to fully impart to her the danger of involving herself in the affairs of Russian citizens. I thought that perhaps as her father you might have more influence with her. She must be made to understand the danger and desist from these activities. In deference to our friendship I will do what I can to protect her, but I must admit, that may not be enough.

Your old friend and drinking crony,
B.

Keagan remembered his Russian acquaintance Boris Tiulenev, who, back in Tsarist times when they had met, had been the son of an important manufacturing family and a secret Bolshevik. Keagan had interviewed him for an article, and indeed they had come to a meeting of the minds on several occasions over drinks. Keagan also had known the name Yakov Luban. While in Russia during the Great War, Keagan had not been the most attentive of husbands. But when his wife had begun receiving packages from an English bookstore in Leningrad, or Petrograd, as it had been called at the time, he investigated. The packages were only books, and Luban had seemed but a harmless shopkeeper. Keagan had felt just a bit too guilty about his neglect of his wife and his dalliances with other women to look into the matter any further. His wife had finally found a pastime with which to amuse herself and to lift her somewhat from her persistent melancholy. He hadn't believed his sweet, innocent wife could be involved in anything more sinister than discussing literature. And if he'd had the tiniest inkling otherwise, he found it quite easy to ignore.

He still felt it best to ignore this thing. If only it were possible. If Blair was shamed enough to say no more of what her mother had told her. If Cecilia's fear of her husband, or at least her own desire to maintain the status quo, remained intact.

———

Blair left for Washington two days after that disastrous talk with her father. Absolutely nothing more had been said of Cecilia's secret. Blair did not know if her father had said anything to her mother, but because everything seemed relatively peaceful, she guessed he hadn't.

She only weakened once herself when Cameron had hugged her shortly before her departure.

"This has been a great visit, hasn't it?" Cameron said.

"We've all behaved like a normal family," Blair agreed.

"It really is for the best that we have been quiet about . . . you know what."

Blair hated herself for her perfidy, but she simply could not bring herself to confess. Maybe it was for the best, especially if Keagan was keeping it quiet, as well. Maybe God was giving her a second chance after her lapse in judgment.

13

SPRING WAS COMING to Russia in fits and starts. There had been a snowstorm on April Fool's Day, but now, two weeks later, this particular day was unseasonably warm. It was perfect for the errand Alex was set upon. He was glad to be out-of-doors. He seldom had the opportunity for something as simple as a pleasant stroll. He had never attended a football game.

The Dynamo Stadium was packed with at least eighty thousand spectators, all gathered to watch the Red Army play against the MVD—formerly the NKVD—team. Alex jostled his way to his seat halfway up the rows of bleachers. He found it occupied. He checked his ticket again.

"That is my seat," he said to the occupant.

"What? It can't be—"

"This is the number on my ticket." He held it out for the man to see.

This was no uncommon circumstance. All around people were having similar problems in claiming their seats. Usual Russian efficiency! Some of the arguments reached dangerous levels, but the fellow in Alex's seat gave it up fairly easily, which was a relief. This was no time to be drawing undue attention to himself. The seat next to Alex was occupied by a middle-aged woman. It was supposed to be a man. But Alex said nothing, since he was

113

not supposed to know the person next to him.

A din of garish music competed with the roar of human voices. Then the voices seemed to merge into one as a thundering cheer broke forth. The teams were jogging onto the field. Dozens of young women jumped the barriers, surging to the field with bouquets of flowers, some huge and spectacular, others simple and small, for the players. The burly players took the flowers with grins, some kissing the girls or hugging them. They waved the flowers in triumph over their heads until a group of boys came to gather up the bouquets and take them away.

Alex had once been fond of watching sporting events, but since coming to Russia there had been no time for such leisure. In America there was no football except for a game they *called* football, and it was vastly different from the game played here in the Soviet Union. But Alex had come to enjoy the American variety while he had been in college.

He wished he could enjoy this game.

But he wasn't here to watch football.

The opening kick sent the ball flying through a breech in the MVD line. The Red Army took possession and maneuvered the ball to within scoring distance. The crowd rose to its feet, cheering hysterically. Most favored the Red Army, which seemed only natural since they were lauded as war heroes. But there were more than enough voices urging the MVD goalie to block the attempt to score. Russians did love their football. It was perhaps one of the rare times they could let down their guard. No one was going to arrest them for not cheering for the police.

Ten minutes into the game a newcomer began threading his way down the row of seats. Everyone nearby yelled at him for blocking the view. He paused by the woman next to Alex. Alex did not recognize him.

"That's my seat," he informed the woman. Alex noted his Russian was unaccented. He might be a Russian.

"You can't make me leave after the game has started!" she retorted.

They argued for a few moments until finally the woman

yielded, though not happily. As she angrily exited the row, she tromped on Alex's toe with no apology. The newcomer settled into the seat.

"I like the Red Army goalie, Andropov," said the fellow.

Alex tensed inside but said as casually as he could, "MVD's goalie is better. He won last week's game easily."

"I heard he injured his knee in that game."

The recognition phrases were all in order. This was the reason Alex was at the game.

Suddenly the crowd was on its feet again, roaring. A player was down. Though Alex and his companion had also risen, he could not tell who the player was beyond that he was MVD. There was now a shouting match on the field between the players and the referee. The audience was trying to join in.

"What do you have for me?" asked the contact. Such was the din, they did not have to worry about being heard.

Alex had tucked into a newspaper the papers that the Americans had been hounding him about for months. He'd finally been able to acquire a couple of identity documents. It hadn't been as easy as Marquet had indicated, for usually by the time Alex got to a patient, he had already been undressed and his belongings put into a locker. If the patient died, it was not always possible to get to the papers before the authorities did. Alex had been able to lift only two of the usual four documents Russian men were required to carry. In the newspaper was the standard ID document and an internal passport. For some reason the deceased did not have the others—a labor book, in which was recorded employment, and a military status book. There was also a fifth document, one that Alex carried but not all Russians were required to have—a Party membership book. The Americans would want all five but would have to be happy with what they got.

"I'll leave the newspaper on the seat," Alex said. He would sit on the paper when the crowd sat down and leave it behind when he made his exit.

The game resumed, and most of the spectators took their

seats once more. Alex waited until the cheering reached another raucous crescendo before speaking again.

"Tell Marquet my six months are up. I expect him to fulfill his end of the bargain."

"Don't use names, you fool!"

Alex could not remember what the man's code name was. "Just tell him that."

"I'm to give you instructions for your next assignment."

"All right, but I want to meet with Mar—" he racked his brain until the code name finally came to him—"with Tchaikovsky." He rolled his eyes at the ridiculous choice of name, but then this whole game was ridiculous, when it wasn't totally terrifying. "Tell him to have in order what he promised."

"I'll tell him," the contact said without much conviction that it would matter. He then gave Alex his next assignment and instructions for the next meeting.

Alex waited until half time before he left in the general exodus of spectators taking advantage of the break to stretch or refresh themselves. He didn't have the heart to watch more of the game anyway. It would have been rather fun to be just a spectator and cheer his team with an undivided glee. It would be nice to live a normal life. And that was the reason he had not told the contact to bug off and never bother him again. This man's superiors held the carrot that drew Alex on. He knew he would never have that normal life, and certainly not a complete life, until he was out of Russia and with Cameron.

A couple of weeks still remained before their anniversary. Maybe if he did one more assignment, they would give him his freedom.

———

Alex made his way from bed to bed in the postoperative ward. He checked heart rates, listened to lungs with his stethoscope, and looked at dressings to make sure they were being changed as ordered and not soaked with blood. He spoke with each patient for a few moments, assessing his needs. He was still very busy since the war, but the pace was manageable. At least now he had time to look at the faces of his patients, to actually get acquainted with them. Though the lion's share of the hospital's trauma cases were shunted his way because of his wartime experience, he was not inundated with the constant barrage of horrors the war had brought to his surgical table. Sometimes he felt that if the war had lasted another month and he'd not his faith to sustain him, he would have gone insane with those pressures.

"Doc, I can't eat this mush another day," complained one patient, an auto accident victim who'd had several perforations in his bowel repaired.

Alex flipped through the pages of the man's chart. "It's been a week. We can try some solid food." He jotted a note in the chart.

A nurse came up beside him. "Doctor, there is someone to see you in examination room five."

"I am not finished with rounds."

"He indicated it was important."

"Who is it?"

"Colonel Bogorodsk," she replied with an edge to her voice. The mere fact that Anatoly was a police agent was enough to instill fear.

Alex cringed inside, as well. "All right." He handed her the chart he'd been holding. "I'll be back in fifteen minutes."

Alex headed toward the examination room on the next floor down. He took the stairs so he could have a moment to mentally prepare himself. He knew this could not be a social visit. The dinner invitation proffered a year ago, which Alex had managed to avoid, had not been repeated. And Alex had not seen Anatoly in all that time. There was no doubt that the MVD agent also saw the wisdom in distancing himself from the risky doctor.

As Alex trod heavily down the back stairwell, he could only think that his covert activities had been discovered. Momentarily he toyed with the idea of not stopping at the next floor but instead walking out of the hospital. Perhaps he could demand asylum at the American embassy. Yet he knew that if this was to be an arrest, all hospital exits would be watched and he would get no further than the sidewalk outside. He dashed the thought of running from his mind. Hope was strong within him. Anatoly might just be here with yet another warning. How many warnings did the man have left in him? Certainly he had paid many times over for the life of his son.

Alex reached the examination room and gripped the doorknob. His hand was steady even though he was quaking inside. He'd learned the combat surgeon's trick of steadying one's hands despite terrifying bombardment. He was thankful this time it worked; that wasn't always so.

"Anatoly," he said in greeting as he shut the door behind him.

"There is a Russian proverb that says, 'Pity the fool who rescues his nose from the mud only to find his legs stuck; then pulls out his legs just to find his nose stuck once more.'"

"I have not heard that one." Alex remained standing, though Anatoly was seated on a chair.

"I've always liked it." The agent shifted in the chair, which seemed barely sturdy enough for his muscular bulk. "Please sit. This will not take long, but we may as well be comfortable." There was a sinister edge to his voice, giving no hint of friendship.

"How is your family, Anatoly?" Alex asked, hoping to remind him of what had bonded them in the past.

"They are well. I am sorry a dinner invitation has not transpired. But we are both busy men, yes?" Still there was a chill to his tone. "However, I am happy you have found time for some leisure. 'All work and no play makes Jack a dull boy.' An American proverb, I believe. But I did not know you had an interest in football, Aleksei. I can get very good seats because of my position. You could have come with me sometime."

"That's very kind of you."

"But you did have a companion during your recent excursion."

"I don't understand. I went by myself."

"You were not with the spectator seated to your right?"

"I was alone."

"You spoke with him."

"Yes, we did exchange some words, now that you mention it. I tried to impress upon him the merits of the MVD team."

"Ah, loyal to a fault, my friend." Anatoly's eyes were narrow and cold. For a rare moment Alex was harshly reminded that this man was a high-ranking member of the most feared secret police force in the world. He had not attained that place by being a teddy bear even though Alex had often deluded himself into thinking just that of this man.

"I was being followed, then?"

"In matter of fact, you were not. . . ." With a significant pause he added, "Having reaped the benefits of a friend in high places. My men were following your companion—"

"He was not my companion."

"Be that as it may . . ." Anatoly paused again. "It is a coincidence that of eighty thousand spectators, he happened to sit beside you."

"I don't know what to say. I went to the game alone. I left alone. I did not know the man before he took the seat next to mine." Alex was dancing like a Cossack around the truth. He did not want to lie outright to his friend. He sensed that Anatoly's cold attitude stemmed from the man's feeling he had been betrayed. The peculiar friendship between them had meant something to Anatoly. Alex realized it meant something to him, as well.

"He is a foreigner," the MVD agent explained, "an American businessman who has been in Russia for a few years. We became suspicious of his activities and began following him—"

"I thought you were suspicious of all foreigners and followed them all."

"True, but we were more intent regarding this one."

"Well, it was rotten luck that he took a seat next to mine, then."

"Yes . . . rotten."

"I don't know what else to say, Anatoly."

Suddenly the MVD agent let down his icy wall. "I want to believe what you say. I will believe you." This, Alex could tell, was a decision rather than a conviction.

"The man in your proverb, Anatoly," Alex said with sudden understanding, "the man caught in the mud and unable to extradite himself—that man is you not me, is it not?"

"Perhaps both of us," the agent said thoughtfully. "But I will tell you I am feeling as helpless as he. Aleksei, my friend, I am not all-powerful. I am but one man holding back a deluge with a single hand. I cannot do this any longer. It is my great shame that I cannot repay my debt to you in full."

"How much more would you have done, Anatoly?" Alex asked. "What is left but for you to sacrifice your life?"

"I would have done that for the life of my son—"

"But I don't want that. I never asked for that!" Yet Alex knew that by accepting Anatoly's aid over the years, he had tacitly acknowledged the idea of a debt being owed him in the first place. The shame was his, not his friend's. "Please! No more. I want no more." He needed it now more than ever, but honor kept him silent about that need.

"If it were only my life at stake, I would gladly give it." Miserably, Anatoly shook his head. "But this is Russia. There are ways of getting to a man without touching the man himself. This is the system I have supported. Now I am its victim."

"If ever there was a debt, it is fulfilled," Alex said firmly.

Anatoly lurched to his feet. He made no response to Alex's statement. The MVD agent lived by the kind of code that would never free him from the obligations he placed upon himself.

He walked to the door, then paused. "Please, stay out of trouble, Aleksei."

"I can't, and I think you know why."

"If I could help you—"

"Don't help me!" Alex jumped to his feet, strode to the door, and flung it open. "Get out of my life! Now!"

A small smile twitched the agent's lips. "You are a poor actor.

But I understand. And that is what must be, to my great regret."

Alex, full of his own regrets, watched Anatoly's lumbering figure walk away. With that was also a deep sense of vulnerability. That hulk of an agent had been a shield, a protector. Alex was on his own now. And it was too late to hide from what lay ahead. He had set in motion a path that he must follow no matter what. If he backed away now, he feared he might never see Cameron again.

But he wasn't about to take the blame for what had just happened entirely upon himself. Some of it the American intelligence agent would bear. Thus it wasn't hard for him to maintain his anger at their carelessness until his next meeting with him.

He wasn't surprised it was Larry Marquet who met him in the back of a small bookstore in the Arbat. He had figured his words to the agent at the stadium would draw the boss, or at least the one Alex considered in authority in Moscow.

Alex was certain he had not been followed. Perhaps Anatoly had managed one more reprieve. In any case, Alex did not enter the bookstore directly but rather by way of an apartment of a friend living in the same row of buildings. There was a little-known warren of corridors in the row, and one of them connected the apartment to the back room of the bookstore. Both the apartment and the bookstore were occupied by members of the underground church. Ordinarily Alex would not have asked to use this remarkable arrangement, but he knew this meeting must be totally private.

He was seated on an upturned crate in the dim recesses of the store's storeroom. It had the musty fragrance of old books and dust, with an unlikely hint of cabbage filtering in from the apartments. He was there a half hour before Marquet arrived.

"You were not followed?" Alex asked peremptorily, foregoing the banality of greetings.

"And hello to you, too, Doctor," sneered Marquet. "I trust this finds you in good health."

"Your man at Dynamo Stadium was being followed," retorted Alex. For the last week since his talk with Anatoly, he'd become angry every time he thought of the fiasco at the stadium, nonetheless, it surprised him that he could so quickly conjure up ire now.

"Is that so?" He seemed truly surprised by this but in no way humbled. "These things happen, Doctor."

"This has been pushed as far as it can go," Alex said.

"I'll be the judge of that."

"While the rest of us are tossed in a gulag?"

"You knew there would be risks."

"I also knew there would be an end—"

"I can't authorize that at this time."

"You made a deal."

"Don't be naïve, Doctor."

"So you think you can string me along forever?"

Marquet shrugged. "Pretty soon we will be able to claim many more of what we refer to as *agents-in-place*. But for now, we have precious few. You are one of our most important, and I simply can't let you go for now."

"Then your word means nothing?"

The American agent laughed. "Of course it means nothing. I am a spy."

Alex almost physically recoiled from this man and hated that his fate was so tied up with him. He thought of Anatoly, who also was, in essence, a spy, yet there was a world of difference between the two men.

Alex knew he must take a different approach. "I won't be of value to you if I am arrested."

"We will take better care next time, Alex." Marquet's use of Alex's given name made Alex feel sick.

But that was not the only cause for the physical nausea that assailed him. The words *next time* rang harshly in his ears. He was caught in a web of his own making. He struggled to hold on to hope like a fly being wrapped in deadly gossamer. There had been times during the war when he had felt the same way, walking the precarious razor's edge between hope and despair.

14

MOSCOW WAS WELL into June when staggering news reached Alex, making him decide to cut off his relations with American intelligence. His friends Vassily and Marie Turkin had been arrested. He had no idea if it had anything to do with the information Vassily had given to Alex on a couple of occasions, but regardless, it would make Alex's position shaky if they broke under interrogation and implicated him.

He kept yet another scheduled meeting with Marquet because he naïvely hoped this time the man might finally have the documents Alex would need to escape Russia. Since the fiasco at Dynamo Stadium, Alex had done another assignment for the Americans, hoping it would be the last, only to be teased along by the fact that the Americans had been unable to properly duplicate travel papers.

This time he again met with Marquet in the back of the bookshop—another reason for ending this business. It was hard to find safe meeting places, and it was dangerous to meet in the same place twice.

Alex told him flatly, "I cannot work for you again. It's become too dangerous. Turkin has been arrested."

"That's terrible," Marquet replied in a distressingly perfunctory manner.

Alex was certain the man was looking at the news only from the standpoint of how it would affect his flow of information.

"But you have come so far, Alex. You can't quit now, when you are so close to your goal."

"Am I close, Marquet?" Alex asked sharply. "I don't believe that. You can't get me out of the country. I should have realized that months ago."

"Well, I'll admit it wasn't as easy as we thought it would be when we began." When Alex eyed him skeptically, Marquet added in an almost wounded tone, "Honestly. Russia is a hard nut to crack. Too much documentation is required for movement throughout the country, and each province is different. The papers you gave us are a start but hardly enough."

Alex knew all that. And he realized with surety that the Americans had no magic key to his escape.

"We need you, Alex, for one more assignment—"

"You expect me to work for you again when you yourself admit you cannot follow through on your agreement?" Alex asked, stunned at the man's gall even though he should have expected no less.

"I didn't say we can't or won't. I just said it was hard. I've got your documents, Alex."

Alex gaped at him in disbelief.

Marquet pulled an envelope from his pocket. Alex took it and opened it to find Swedish citizenship papers and passport, a Soviet visa allowing entry into Leningrad, and exit documents.

"We discovered it was easier to make you a Swedish business-man with interests in Russia rather than getting you out of the country as a Russian."

"But these will only be good in Leningrad."

"That's the best we could do. However, we have figured out a way you could get to Leningrad. Have you heard of the Soviet Symposium of Medical and Surgical Advancement?"

"It's a biannual convention, though it was suspended during the war. It was last held in Yalta. I attended." Alex then added with less than eager enthusiasm, for he realized he was about to be asked to take the greatest risk of his "career" with American intelligence. "It will be held in Leningrad this year in two weeks."

"That's right."

"Well," said Alex, "your wealth of information lacks one important detail. This symposium is by invitation only, and I have not been invited." It was, in fact, considered quite prestigious to attend the symposium. Alex recalled that his invitation in 1940 had caused hard feelings among some of his colleagues because at that time he had been in the country only a short time and was, for all practical purposes, a foreigner. Yuri had wrangled the invitation for him. He felt the exposure would be an excellent way for him to make a smooth transition from American to Soviet medicine.

"This is Russia, isn't it?" Marquet smiled wryly. "Surely all you have to do is grease the right palms to get in. This is big, Alex. There is a Russian Naval officer who wants to deal with us. But he can't leave Leningrad. Look, I wouldn't push this except we have been waiting weeks for the perfect opportunity to reach this man. The medical convention offers us that prospect." When Alex didn't respond at once, Marquet added, "Those papers in your hand are your guarantee that this will be the last thing you have to do for us." Alex already knew what the man's word was worth, but the documents were at least tangible evidence that this time he meant business.

"What would prevent me from taking these"—he gave the envelope a jerk—"and forgetting about your Naval officer?"

"I believe you are a man of honor, Doctor." Marquet neatly plucked the envelope from Alex's hand. "But I will hold these in safekeeping until you leave for the convention."

Alex smiled humorlessly. Yes, he was a man of honor, but the temptation to slip away as soon as possible would have been beyond imagining. It was hardly fair he was being asked to take his greatest risk ever even if it was for the greatest reward.

"Why shouldn't I simply avoid your officer after I get to Leningrad?" he asked.

"I doubt you will do that for the same reason."

"Do you understand what a great risk this task will be? I will be watched far more vigilantly once I leave Moscow."

"Just keep telling yourself that it will soon be over."

"Thanks for the advice, but it doesn't help."

"Listen, it is all very simple," Marquet replied in a reassuring tone. "You just meet the man, and he hands over his information. You've done this many times before. Then you hop on the train for Sweden, and *voila*! You are home free. Simple."

"It can't be that simple," Alex said.

"Sure it can. We're not building atom bombs . . . we're only making sure they are never used."

"That's what this is all about?"

"Yeah. Maintaining world peace. What else?"

Sometimes it was easy to lose sight of that simple fact. Yet it did surprise Alex that Marquet had not. Maybe he had misjudged the man.

"I can see how you are leery." Marquet added, "I mean, when do things always go sour in the movies? The last job, eh? Well, this isn't the movies." He grinned. "This is better."

Alex didn't agree but opted not to press the issue. As long as this was indeed the last job, he would comply.

Shortly after that meeting with Marquet, Alex casually mentioned the conference to his friend Yuri Fedorcenko, who was surprised Alex hadn't been invited. Yuri knew nothing of Alex's avocation as agent-in-place for the American government, and Alex thought it best that it remained that way. The easiest way to get in trouble with the Soviet police was to know too much. Alex already knew enough for both of them. And if his trip to Leningrad was approved, Alex realized he would no doubt never see his friend again, nor would he even be able to tell him a proper good-bye.

Within three days Alex had received his invitation. Yuri told him the board had already been considering him for the fifth slot of Moscow representatives, but there had been some snag with his paper work, which Yuri had helped expedite. This worried Alex, for after he disappeared, it might seem as if Yuri was involved. But he soon forgot that with the other ominous news Yuri brought.

"Sophia has quit her job at the embassy," he said. "She was warned by a friend that she was being watched and might soon be arrested. She hoped distancing herself from the embassy might help. She used as a very real excuse that she had to be home to care for her ailing grandmother."

"Anna Yevnovona?" Alex asked. When Yuri nodded, Alex continued, "I didn't realize. Not serious, I hope."

"She is eighty-seven, so I suppose at that age any illness is serious. It is congestive heart disease, and having a cardiac specialist for a son cannot even help her. There is little to be done besides limiting her activities, keeping her on a special diet, and seeing that she takes her digitalis. She can be a rather stubborn patient. Sophia's main task is to see that she stays in bed."

"Is she up for visitors?" Suddenly Alex knew he must visit the dear old woman before he left. Perhaps he couldn't say good-bye in so many words, but he knew for a certainty he would not see her again in this life.

"She would enjoy seeing you, Alex. Perhaps when you return from—"

"I have some free time tomorrow," Alex said quickly.

"That would be fine." But Yuri's brow knit, for he had read something altogether different into Alex's urgency. "But she is not at death's door, honestly."

Alex went to the Fedorcenko flat the next evening. Yuri and his wife, Katya, were at a meeting, but Sophia met him at the door.

"Grandmama is so thrilled you have come to see her."

"I have been terribly remiss lately in maintaining important friendships," Alex said.

"Did Papa tell you about my job at the embassy?"

"Yes, Sophia. I am sorry. I know how much you enjoyed it."

As she walked with him down the corridor, she said, "But you know what else that means, don't you?"

Yes, he knew all too well what it meant to him, but he hoped it would not matter in a few days.

"I have cut off the way to get letters to and from Cameron," she answered her own question, dismay in her tone.

"You couldn't help it," he assured. "Please don't blame yourself. It could not have lasted forever. We both knew that."

They paused before the door to Anna Yevnovona's room. Sophia said sadly, "Alex, don't be too shocked when you see her. She's lost weight she could ill afford to lose, and her breathing is labored at times."

"Your father indicated she was not serious, certainly not in the last stages of her disease."

She laid a hand on Alex's arm, and tears welled in her eyes. "You and I know Papa is one of the best doctors in Russia, certainly the best cardiac specialist, but he has a bit of a blind spot where his mother is concerned. He still wants to believe that his brother and sister will see her once more before she passes. But one look will tell you that that will not happen, even if she lives a month or six months. I am no doctor, but I doubt she has a month."

"Then I am all the more glad I've come." Alex realized that if all went as planned, he would not only be with Cameron in a month, but he would be able to see Yuri's brother, Andrei, who was a close friend. He could also see their sister, Mariana, whom Alex didn't know as well, but in America he'd be able to go where he wished. He could tell them both of their mother's last days.

Sophia opened the door. "Grandmama, look who's come to see you."

The lighting in the room was dim. There was only one small window, and it was a gray day outside. The room was small, the bed, an old mahogany four-poster, dominating the cramped space. The slight figure of Anna Yevnovona was all but lost within the covers and pillows on the bed. Alex was glad Sophia had forewarned him of her physical state. She had always been a petite titan, rosy with health and energy. Now she seemed shrunken and wrinkled, pale with a bluish tinge around her lips.

"My eyesight is poor these days," came a soft voice from the bed, "but I know only one such handsome yellow-haired young man. Alex, what a joy to see you."

"Anna Yevnovona, forgive me for not coming to see you more often."

"I had no expectations." She smiled, a gentle gesture that seemed to make her wrinkled, pale face shine. "But it pleases me nonetheless. I am bored silly since my son insisted I take to my bed a week ago. I suppose it is both a blessing and a curse to have a doctor in the family." She paused thoughtfully, then added, "No, never a curse."

"Shall I fix tea, Grandmama?" Sophia asked.

"Yes, that would be nice. You can stay for a bit, can't you, Alex?"

"I'd like that." When Anna gestured toward the chair by the bed, Alex seated himself. Reflex made him grasp her wrist in order to feel her pulse. Before he jerked his hand away, slightly embarrassed, he'd noted her heartbeat was thready and irregular.

"So, Doctor, will I live?" she asked wryly.

"You've got some fight left in you yet," he hedged. "But you must follow your doctor's regimen to the letter."

"I suppose I must," she sighed, "but I do hate it. I feel like such a lazy slug lying about in bed all day. But let's not bore ourselves talking about my illness. Yuri tells me you are on your way to Leningrad."

"In a few days."

"It has been so many years since I was last there. I shudder whenever I think of what the war must have done to the city and its people. But I have many good memories of my life there. When I was a girl of sixteen setting bewildered eyes on it for the first time, I would never have guessed it would steal such a large part of my life and my heart. Did you know I went there to be a maid in the home of a prince? I ended up with the esteemed position of personal maid to his daughter."

"Where you fell in love with a prince." Alex smiled. He never tired of hearing Anna's stories of that time in her life.

Anna laughed. "Just like an old woman to oft repeat herself."

"I don't mind at all," Alex assured. "I enjoy the stories, and they help me to have some insight into what it was like for my parents, who lived there at the same time."

"That's right. You are St. Petersburg-born yourself. I will never get used to its present name. I know the tsar did many bad things, but I am not sure Lenin and his gang were much better. Did I ever tell you that I once actually saw the tsar up close? Alexander the Second. My princess was visiting at the Winter Palace and sent me on an errand. I got lost. . . ." Pausing, she tittered lightly. "Oh, forgive me, Alex. I suppose the closer one gets to death, the more one ponders one's youth."

"You have some wonderful stories," Alex said. "It was a far more idyllic time then, I'm sure."

"Don't fool yourself, Alex. There were difficult times then, too."

"I suppose . . ."

"Something is troubling you, dear." Her brow knit together as she reached out toward him.

As her thin arthritic fingers grasped his larger, more fleshy hand, he was shocked to feel sudden tears well in his eyes. At first he didn't know why he should feel so melancholy. In a few days his dreams would be realized, and he would finally be with Cameron. Yet now he was struck fully with the realization he'd sensed earlier with Yuri. He must part from friends he knew he would never see again. He must part from a country he had grown to love. His tears sprang from sadness but also from anger at the injustice of it all.

To Anna he said, "I don't want to burden you with my problems."

"Alex, my heart is weak," she said, "that is, the muscle that beats within my chest. My true heart is still strong enough to listen to a friend."

"I will not return from Leningrad," he said flatly. "Please don't tell anyone. It could be dangerous information, but I had to tell someone. I doubt the government could hurt you, Anna."

"That is true, Alex. But why the pain? You will soon be with your Cameron, yes?"

"You of all people should understand that."

"Ah yes. It is a cruel reality of our world, isn't it?" Thirty years ago, two of Anna's children had been forced to flee Russia, and she had not seen them since.

"Anna, you and all the Fedorcenko clan have truly been like family to me—the only thing even close to family I have now. I hate having to choose between you and Cameron. It is so unjust."

"Poor dear Alex." She gripped his hand tighter, then smiled softly. "Always know, my dear, you are as a grandson to me. And everyone in this house considers you as our own. But there is one thing. Don't forget there are Fedorcenkos in America. You were like a son to Andrei once."

"I look forward to seeing him again."

"And you will have another family, too, when you and Cameron marry."

He wanted to tell her that he and Cameron were already married but reasoned that one shock in an evening was enough for the fragile woman.

Instead, he followed another tack he had been thinking of. "Anna, is there anything you wish me to tell Andrei and Talia? I can see Mariana, as well."

"I suppose they already know the important things, that I love them and have always been proud of them. I pray for them every day. And if I have any regrets in this life, it is that I could not have seen them one more time and that I never saw my grandchildren and great-grandchildren in America. I have treasured the photographs of them you brought with you, Alex, when you came to Russia."

Alex thought that what he was doing for Marquet might help bring an end to such injustices as an old woman not being able to hold her grandchildren in her lap. Yet thinking of Marquet also brought back to the surface his fears and confusion about what lay ahead.

"Anna, I don't know why I can't be exhilarated about the

prospect of being with Cameron and not consider the negative aspects—oh, I forgot! I am Russian." He tried to smile to lighten his mood but could only manage a quirk of his lips. "But it is more than that."

"What you are about to do is very dangerous, yes?"

"I believe it will be. And I am not always sure I'm doing the right thing."

"You have prayed about this?"

"Yes, I have."

"Have you heard the Scripture in Psalms that says, 'The steps of a good man are ordered by the Lord: and he delighteth in his way. Though he fall, he shall not be utterly cast down: for the Lord upholdeth him with his hand'?" She smiled wistfully and mused, "Funny, sometimes I can't recall what happened yesterday, but a Scripture I learned years ago comes to me with ease. That verse has often encouraged me over the years. Alex, you are a man of God, and you must trust He is with you in all things."

Now Alex knew why he had felt an urging to see Anna before leaving Moscow. "I need to be reminded far too often of that."

"We all do." She patted his hand, then added, "May I pray with you?"

"Yes. I know now that's why I came."

He bowed his head over their grasped hands, and she lifted her other hand and laid it gently on his head. He felt a stirring of peace even before she uttered her prayer. God had indeed led Alex's steps to Anna's bedside.

Perhaps Sophia had purposefully let them have an extended time alone. He thought he'd heard the door creak open then quietly close at one point. Soon after Anna and Alex finished praying, Sophia came in with the tea. They all visited together for another hour.

Just as Alex rose from his chair, he heard voices in the hallway outside the door. Yuri and Katya had returned. He bid Anna good-night, then he and Sophia exited into the corridor.

"Perfect timing!" said Yuri as he hung his and Katya's coats on the hooks by the door.

"Can you stay a bit longer?" Katya asked.

"I'd like that," Alex responded without hesitation. He would prolong this final visit with his friends as long as possible.

There were a dozen moments in the next hour in which Alex wanted to tell them about Leningrad, but he knew it would be selfish of him to do so. As it was, just his disappearance might well bring all his friends and acquaintances under suspicion. It was best that when they told the police they knew nothing, they spoke with the conviction of truth.

Still, when he gave Sophia and Katya a parting hug, he could not help if it was a bit more intense than a casual good-bye warranted. When Yuri walked him to the door, his emotions were stretched thin.

"Good-bye, Yuri." His voice was rough and caught on his friend's name.

"Good-bye, Alex. Have a good time in Leningrad."

Alex merely nodded, afraid to speak lest his rising emotions escape.

Then Yuri flung his arms around Alex in a firm Russian bear hug. His arms were trembling. Only when Yuri kissed him on both cheeks and stood back, revealing moisture on his own cheeks, did Alex realize he had fooled no one. Cameron had always told him how transparent he was.

"I love you as my own son, Alex, and always will," Yuri said with undisguised emotion in his voice. "No amount of distance will ever dull that feeling I know you return."

"Yuri . . ." Alex tried unsuccessfully to dash away the moisture in his eyes.

"You need say no more. Take care, and God be with you!"

15

Leningrad, Soviet Union

THE RED ARROW from Moscow arrived in Leningrad at eleven-thirty in the morning. Alex was accompanied by four of his colleagues, also representing Moscow at the convention, and their two "assistants,"—who all knew were merely MVD guards. They were met at the train station by an official from the convention, an attractive middle-aged woman who carried a clipboard and was the picture of efficiency. She seemed to have every moment of their week-long stay well in hand, causing Alex some concern about how he was to fulfill his personal agenda.

They all packed into an automobile and were driven to the Moskva Hotel. As they traversed Nevsky Prospekt, the main thoroughfare in the city, Alex noted much war damage, but on one side of the avenue a large complex of buildings was being rebuilt. Somehow it didn't look as dismal as it had when he had come here during the height of the German siege. For one thing, at this hour of the morning the street was bustling with activity, with pedestrians and vehicles hurrying about purposefully. When he had come here last, the city was dying by inches, and even the living had plodded around more dead than alive.

It pleased him that the city had rebounded to such an extent, for this was his birthplace and the birthplace of his parents, both revolutionaries who had been forced into exile in 1912 when he had been two years old. Suddenly Alex remembered the key he had given to Cameron during the war when she had left Russia the first time, unsure if she would return. It once had opened the door to his mother's home, a stately mansion in what had been called during tsarist times the South Side of Petersburg. Her family had been of minor nobility, but what really had allowed them to live in the posh neighborhood was her father's affluent shipping business. Since the Revolution, those mansions had for the most part been turned into apartments.

He didn't think he'd have time to visit the place on this trip. And now that he thought of it, he doubted if he and Cameron would ever visit it together. Freedom might come to Russia in his lifetime, but it seemed a remote possibility. In any case, until that time it would be impossible for him to return without fear of arrest. He realized it was in God's hands. Regardless, the key had been symbolic, serving as a tangible reminder of the promise that one day they would be together.

And that would happen—soon! He had only a couple of hurdles left to jump.

On the first day of the convention, Alex quickly established the habit of taking long constitutionals after the last meeting of the day. He roamed for several miles all over the city in the two hours of free time they usually had before dinner. Since the hotel was perched practically on top of a metro station, he often would take a train to some point, then walk in that region. He was always followed, and the MVD agent made no pretense of hiding his presence. During these outings, Alex would contrive to lose his shadow for a few minutes, reappearing after five or ten minutes. It always appeared to be accidental. Alex hoped the ruse would somewhat anesthetize the agent into not becoming overly concerned at losing his charge occasionally—until it was too late, at least.

Only once during one of these slips did Alex take care of business, and that was early in the week. There was only one means of contacting the Naval officer Alex was to meet. The man had made the acquaintance of an American businessman in Leningrad some months earlier. This American had been the one to inform American intelligence of the officer's desire to sell information. The officer had given the American the location of a drop box, a safe place in which to leave communications, which he would check every three days in case the Americans wanted to deal with him. Alex was to leave a message at this place telling the officer the specifics about the meeting.

Alex had been leery of this method and had told Marquet so. "What if the box is compromised and my note falls into MVD hands? We could both be walking into a trap."

"It won't happen," Marquet had replied with that annoying flippancy of his. "You'll both be careful."

"It's not your neck on the chopping block," Alex retorted. "Isn't there some kind of code we can use?"

"None that we can communicate to our contact. But we will consider that for the future."

"What about his American friend?"

"Long gone back to the States. But the Navy guy assured his friend this drop box is safe from his end. So you only have to worry about yourself. And you learned from the best." Marquet grinned with smug assurance. Then he added with a rare touch of sincerity, "Hey, I know you are going to do the best you can. But if you sense the mission is going to go sour, you have my permission to abort—with your honor intact. Got it? No one wants your head to roll."

In the year of their association, Marquet had never failed to surprise Alex.

Alex had made sure the drop box was in the general area of one of his established routes for his daily walk, though not exactly on the route. He had to disappear for only about ten minutes in order to find the spot, leave his message, and then connect up again with the MVD agent. The place was in an alley between two run-down apartment buildings near the end of the trash-strewn alley. Here there was a wooden flower box that contained several dead plants, with the rest of the container overgrown with weeds. It was the only such box in the alley. Alex was to drop his message in the small crack between the box and the wall. As he did so, he wondered if this was where the officer lived. It seemed rather shabby for a Russian officer. The man must have a plausible reason that allowed him to come here every three days. Perhaps an elderly relative lived here whom he cared for.

When Alex caught up with his shadow again, he was certain his little side trip had not been observed. Now all Alex had to do was wait five days—he had given the officer three days to find the message in case he had recently checked the box, then two days beyond that to give the man time to arrange matters so he could make the rendezvous. That would be the day before the close of the conference. Alex had coordinated the meeting with the departure of the train for Helsinki. He was going to have to perform two huge gambits in the space of a couple of hours. But his only other choice was to plan his escape for the following day, but then he would have to lose his MVD man twice in less than twenty-four hours. He felt his chances were better with the former plan.

In order for all to be timed right, he had to schedule his daily walk for later than usual. This he managed by scheduling some meetings with other physicians right up to the dinner hour so that it was not suspicious when he was forced to take his exercise later.

Alex wished it wasn't the middle of Leningrad's White Nights, for the cover of darkness would have been a boon. But it had been threatening rain all day, so the low clouds helped somewhat to shroud the evening and give Alex a sense of cover. He walked for an hour, appearing to be combining a last-minute shopping trip with his constitutional. He went into every souvenir shop he found still open at that hour in the evening. He'd already made it known he had several close friends for whom he had promised to bring back trinkets from Leningrad.

Finally, he made his break—a simple ploy really, just going into a shop and exiting by the back door. By the time his agent would realize he'd been inside far too long, Alex would be three blocks away, jumping aboard a subway train and on his way to a cinema on the other side of town, purposely not far from Finland Station.

He arrived at the theater a half hour before the meeting. He was confident he'd lost his tail, but he wanted to be certain the Naval man didn't bring any unwanted interlopers with him. He saw no one suspicious loitering outside the theater, and about ten minutes before the film was to begin, he saw a man enter the theater. He fit the description he'd been given. The man was alone.

Alex paid for his ticket and entered the theater. The officer was in the seat Alex had instructed him to find. Alex waited a moment as another patron tried to take the only vacant seat next to the man. He hadn't anticipated something like this occurring. What if the officer took that fellow to be his contact?

Quickly Alex strode forward, praying this didn't become a scene.

"Excuse me. That's my seat," Alex said.

The man gave Alex a sour look.

"You're late," the officer said to Alex.

The other man, seeing that Alex was indeed with the man already seated, rose and relinquished his seat. Alex slipped into the seat, barely restraining a relieved sigh. His heart was pounding inside his chest.

"I have been looking forward to seeing this film," Alex said to the officer, his casual tone belying his edgy nerves.

"Yes, it should be a good one," said the man. His tone was also casual, matter-of-fact. He was about forty years old, well-dressed in civilian clothes. Alex thought he sat with a military reserve.

"But the seats don't seem as comfortable as they were before the war," Alex said.

"My Aunt Nadezhda says that twenty-five years ago this theater served only the elite and was very luxurious."

"There is no elite in Russia today."

"No, only good Socialists."

The exchange was letter perfect, exactly as Alex had instructed in his message to the officer.

The officer chuckled. "Who thinks up these lines?"

A bit defensively, Alex replied, "It isn't as easy as it would appear." In fact, Alex had been the one to compose the recognition exchange, and he had given it great thought. The words had to be specific enough so there would be no mistake in the contact but also apropos enough to the situation that if anyone chanced to hear, it would not seem suspicious. Alex had included the last about the Russian elite somewhat tongue-in-cheek but now could see how ridiculous it sounded.

"I was a little surprised to find a note after over two months," said the man. "I had begun to think no one cared."

"It takes time to arrange these things."

"You are Russian, are you not? You have no accent except for a Muscovite twang."

Alex wondered if the man was as anxious inside as he. His tone revealed nothing, but perhaps that was his military discipline.

Alex felt uncomfortable with the question. It shouldn't matter what this man knew about him, yet it still made him uneasy. "Do you have something for me?" He wanted to get this over with and be on his way as soon as possible. The train for Helsinki departed in an hour.

"Wait for the lights to dim."

After a few minutes the theater went dark a moment before the screen burst into light. A picture of Red Square filled the screen overlaid with the words, "Eight Hundred Years of Glory." All the buildings were draped with vivid red buntings, while at the entrance of the square was a full-length portrait of Stalin at least thirty feet high. The newsreel told of the eight-hundredth birthday of Moscow, celebrated recently in the kind of pomp and splendor only Russians could imagine. Alex had managed to avoid the snarl of parades and the drone of oratory during the observance. He'd had a few more patients than usual as a result

of traffic mishaps and other altercations due to overzealous cele-
brating.

After several excruciating moments of this exaltation of the
glorious Party, which ironically had hardly existed eight hundred
years ago, Alex felt a nudge from his companion. Glancing
toward him, he saw an envelope in the man's hand. Alex reached
for it.

"You have something for me?" asked the officer.

Instinctively Alex glanced furtively around before taking
from his pocket the envelope Marquet had given him. It contained one thousand American dollars. A small fortune for most
Russians.

They exchanged envelopes. Alex glanced in his and saw several film negatives, as he had expected. The officer put his envelope in his pocket without even looking.

"You are very trusting," Alex commented.

The man shrugged. "Where would we be without trust, eh?"

"Your envelope also includes a code that will be used in
future communications," said Alex.

"The future? Ah yes. . . ."

"When can they expect to hear from you again?"

"I can't say . . . I don't know."

Alex thought it odd the man wasn't anxious to make arrangements for future exchanges. This had been, after all, quite lucra-
tive for him.

Alex started to rise, but the officer put a restraining hand on
his arm.

"I will go first," he said.

Alex didn't see that it should matter one way or the other, so
he resumed his seat. The man rose and made his way to the aisle.

Unable to explain it at first, a sudden sense of unease weighed
down upon Alex. Everything had gone smoothly, but was that
the problem—that it had been too easy? Was something truly
wrong or was his imagination just overactive? But he could not
discount his feelings that simply.

What was it, though? He couldn't quite put his finger on it—

Then it hit him. Too late.

He groaned.

It hadn't been military discipline that had steadied the officer. No one engaging in such a dangerous activity could be that cool—no one except a man who knew he was perfectly safe.

"How stupid could I be?" Alex muttered to himself.

He had walked right into a trap. At least he must assume so, as he must assume that the moment he walked out of the theater, he'd be met by a squad of MVD agents. He wondered if the officer had been found out and turned by the police, or if he had been working for them all along, using the American business-man merely to ferret out intelligence leaks. Not that it mattered.

The only thing that mattered now was how to get out of the theater alive. One thing seemed clear—the police were not going to storm the theater and make a public arrest. Why, Alex didn't know, but if they hadn't already, then they were likely going to content themselves with waiting him out. Alex understood now why the officer wanted to leave first, so that he could give a description of Alex to the police. They would have no problem now identifying him.

Alex's only chance was to wait until the end of the movie and try to get away in the exodus of the crowd. Yet if he waited, he would miss his train, and he didn't know when the next train would leave.

The main feature came on the screen. Eisenstein's *Alexander Nevsky*. At least he only had to sit through one film because the first of the double feature had played before the newsreel. But sitting there for even ten minutes would have been excruciating knowing what waited outside. Two hours was pure torture. He almost wished the police would swoop down on him and drag him bodily from the theater. However, as long as he sat there unmolested, there remained hope.

Perhaps he was wrong about the whole thing. Perhaps he should discount his fears and leave. But even after a year of this cloak-and-dagger business, he had never acquired an instinct for the work, thus he had to believe this current sense of danger had come from elsewhere. Perhaps from God. If so, he wished God would have warned him long before this.

The movie droned on. Amazingly, he must have dozed near the end, for he suddenly woke with a start. The closing credits were rolling on the screen. People were leaving. He rubbed his face and shook away any lingering sluggishness.

He rose and tried to lose himself in the exiting crowd. He turned to a woman next to him and struck up a conversation, hoping if he appeared to be with someone, they would miss him.

"Do you know of the restaurant Tbilisi?" he asked.

"Oh yes, very good Georgian food," she replied.

They came to the exit doors. He leaned closer to her, glad she didn't respond to the familiarity of his action with a scream.

"Do you know if it is open now?" he asked, a pleasant smile on his face. "I was to meet friends there, but the movie was longer than I expected."

They stepped outside onto the sidewalk. It had started to rain during the movie. A few umbrellas went up. Alex regretted that neither he nor his erstwhile companion had one. It would have given nice cover.

"I'm not sure," the woman said. "I haven't been there in a while." She turned to her companion. "Paval, do you know how late the restaurant Tbilisi is open?"

"What? Feeling Stalinist, are you?" the fellow quipped.

"No. This gentleman—"

"There!" came a discordant shout from another direction.

Alex did not wait to hear more. He supposed his pursuers had waited too long now to care much about making a messy public arrest. He dashed through the crowd which, in alarm, scattered away from him. Anyone running on a Soviet street was to be avoided.

Without the theater crowd around him, Alex was starkly exposed, but it was too late now for subterfuge. He had no choice but to make an all-out run for it. He headed toward Finland Station. He didn't know to what purpose. There would not be a train waiting just to accommodate him, but he couldn't help it. In his mind, the way to freedom, the way to Cameron lay in that direction.

He sprinted around a corner, down the street that ran alongside the theater. Too late he realized his mistake, for the police had men waiting at the side exit. They hurtled toward him, and he tried to dodge them, but his foot struck a muddy puddle and skidded out from under him. With a painful thump, he went down. A moment later two huge MVD agents were on top of him.

As he struggled against certain capture, he thought, or imagined, he heard a train whistle in the distance.

16

Los Angeles, California

CAMERON WAS GLAD Jackie had talked her into spending Saturday at the beach. She had never been one to enjoy lolling about in the sunshine—or lolling about anywhere, for that matter. But on this most recent stint home she had discovered a subtle change in herself.

"This is great," Cameron commented as she adjusted her wide-brimmed straw hat. Unlike Jackie, with her golden California tan, Cameron had been much further north for the last year. She was also a bit self-conscious about being in a swimsuit. She hadn't worn one since before the war, and the only decent ones she could find in the stores now were far more revealing than she was used to.

"Now, don't make too much shade on your face," Jackie said. "You could use some sun."

"Yes, but I don't want to burn."

"Here, put some of this on—Mom swears by it as a protection." She handed Cameron a small bottle.

Cameron took it and unscrewed the lid, taking a whiff. "Hmm, smells like . . . is that vanilla?"

"I don't know what's in it. I use it on Emi, and she hasn't burned."

"Well, if I do burn, at least I'll smell like a sugar cookie."

Jackie laughed, then turned her attention to Emi, who was engrossed in digging in the sand a few feet from the blanket. She was four and a half now and, since losing some of her baby fat, was growing into a pretty little girl. Her hair was more dark brown than black, as were her large tilted eyes. She was an enchanting blend of two races.

"I'm glad you came with me, Cameron," Jackie said. "I hate to come alone. Emi loves it here—I do, too, for that matter. Now that it is finally summer, we try to get to the beach every chance we can. I only wish I hadn't volunteered to teach summer school so we could come during the week when it isn't as crowded."

"You must have plenty of friends who would love to join you," replied Cameron. Jackie's words had struck Cameron as odd because, of the three sisters, Jackie had always been the one with a bevy of friends. Was she still being shunned because of her marriage and Emi? Cameron didn't feel comfortable broaching that subject head on.

"I do and I am thankful for them, but . . ." as Jackie paused, she lifted her gaze to the horizon where the blue sea met the even bluer sky.

"If you don't want to talk about it, I understand."

Jackie smiled faintly. "It's not that. Actually, you are about the only person lately who hasn't been hounding me about finding a husband."

"You're kidding!"

"Everyone—Mom, even Mother Okuda, all my friends. That's why I tend not to go to their beach parties and such. I wouldn't mind if I was the only one who wasn't a couple, but what I can't bear is that they always make sure there's a single guy present to set me up with. And the guys, Cameron, you wouldn't believe . . . !" She paused and rolled her eyes with disdain. "Were all the good ones killed in the war?"

"You mean you haven't met one single decent man?"

"There are those who think I am being too picky."

"Maybe you're simply not ready."

With a confused shrug, Jackie said, "It's been over two years.

In one sense I am ready, at least I would like once again to have a special person, as I had with Sam."

"Perhaps the problem is that you are trying to find a duplicate of Sam," suggested Cameron. "It might be you are missing someone perfect because he isn't exactly like Sam."

"I married Sam because he was perfect for me, so it stands to reason my perfect mate would be like him. Doesn't it?"

Thoughtfully Cameron poured some lotion into her hand from the bottle Jackie had given her and began smoothing it onto her arms. "I am not one to be giving advice to the lovelorn. But don't you think there is more than one perfect man out there for you? More than one like Sam? Gentle, intelligent, funny . . . he may not be Japanese or the same size and shape. He may love vegetables."

Jackie tittered with embarrassment. "The last man I was set up with was a vegetarian. I understand now what you mean. I couldn't seem to see beyond that. The perfect man must hate vegetables, like Sam. I have been narrowing down the odds, haven't I?"

"Well, don't settle for just anyone. You're a smart girl. You'll do the right thing."

"My friend Peggy, the only one besides you who supports my reticence with dating, said much the same thing. I have to find a happy medium—"

"No no!" cut in Cameron with mock censure. "Nothing medium, please. Fall in love, sis, truly in love." Then she laughed. "Listen to me, the romantic."

"You have changed, Cameron. In more ways than one. No, not changed, but grown."

"I even surprise myself at times." This wasn't the only change Cameron had noted within herself since coming home for her mother's surgery. "I've noticed it more this trip home than I have before. You know, I'm actually glad to be home," she admitted. "That really is a shock."

"What can it all mean?"

"A good question." Cameron started smearing lotion on her

legs. "But the answer is simple, I think. I'm growing weary of all the moving around. I think I'm ready to stay in one place for a while. Lately I believe I have been traveling just to take my mind off the separation from Alex. It's not working, though."

"I'm so sorry, Cameron—" Jackie had to stop as Emi jogged up to their blanket.

"Mommy, can I have that cup?"

"Are you thirsty, honey?"

"I need it for my house I'm building."

Smiling, Jackie handed her daughter one of the paper cups they had used for their picnic lunch. Then she continued as Emi bounded back to her pile of sand. "At least you will be ready when Alex and you are finally together. You were always so ambivalent about settling down."

"I appreciate you, Jackie, for looking at the bright side of things." She tried to smile for her sister's benefit. "I am ready to settle down, but I won't, not until Alex is here with me—or, I suppose, until I am there with him. I can't commit to anything because I know I will drop everything at a moment's notice if the chance to get into Russia materializes."

"There still is a chance?"

"Yes, I am sure it will happen. Gary is looking into some possibilities through the State Department."

"I hope it happens," Jackie said, "but I will be a little envious now since Mom's big revelation. It's hard knowing we have a brother there we have never met. I'd really like to know him."

"I've felt that way for a long time."

"I wonder what he's like. Do you think he is anything like us? I thought perhaps I saw some small resemblance in the picture."

"In his eyes."

"Certainly not in his hair," chuckled Jackie. "I'd kill for his curls."

"He must have got them from his father—"

But with the word *father* the conversation stopped abruptly. Cameron knew they were both thinking of their father and how this secret might crush him. Jackie had never said how she truly felt about the deception. She was such an honest, open person that it must rankle at her. Cameron sensed that she was the only one of the sisters who firmly believed that keeping the secret from Keagan was the right thing to do. Maybe her faith in God wasn't as strong as Jackie's or Blair's. Maybe she didn't know her father as well as they did. Perhaps she and Keagan were too much alike for her to be objective about him.

Thankfully, they were distracted from further pursuing that conversation when Emi returned requesting other items for her house—Aunt Cameron's beach sandals, a pencil, her mother's sun hat, and . . .

Sensing the child was growing bored with playing in the sand and looking for an excuse herself not to resume the discussion about Semyon, Cameron jumped up.

"Emi, would you like to play in the water?" she suggested.

"Oh yes!" Emi replied enthusiastically.

Cameron took her niece's hand. "Do you want to join us, Jackie?"

"I think I'll just watch this time."

Cameron and Emi strolled down to the water. Cameron found she liked the feel of the child's hand in hers. She liked her niece's innocent questions and enjoyed trying to think up answers that would satisfy a child. Could it be that she was coming to like children in general? Was that another aspect of this strange metamorphosis she was experiencing?

Cameron returned to her apartment late in the afternoon with that sluggish feeling a day of sun and sand and swimming often induces. She decided to continue the indulgence by running herself a hot bath. While she was waiting for the tub to fill, the telephone rang.

"Hello," she spoke into the receiver.

"Hi, Cameron, this is Jerry." One of the cub reporters at the *Journal*.

"Hi, Jerry. What's up?"

"Someone has been trying to reach you. He's called here, your apartment, even your parents' home. Called here a couple of times. He wanted me to keep calling till I reached you."

"Okay. Who was it?"

"A Robert Wood from West Germany."

"West Germany?"

"Yeah. He left a number for you to call him back. He said as soon as possible. Don't worry about the time."

"West Germany?" she repeated, a bit stunned. Why there? More importantly, why was Robert calling at all? It had to be something bad.

"You want the number?"

"Yes . . ." She fumbled around for a pencil and jotted down the number.

When she hung up the phone, she quickly calculated the time in West Berlin. Midnight. He'd said to call no matter the time. What could be so urgent? Had Robert been deported for some reason? Could he have been caught, along with Sophia, for exchanging the letters? There had been no communication from Russia in months. Cameron had assumed that it was simply getting more difficult, as was everything else in Russia.

Suddenly the sound of running water penetrated her senses. With a gasp she ran into the bathroom. Quickly, she turned off the faucet. She'd caught it just in time. The water was nearly to the top of the tub. Sliding up the sleeve of her robe, she reached in and pulled the plug. She doubted she'd have a chance for a relaxing bath now. She left enough water in for a quick dip to wash off the sand.

Returning to the living room, she paused by the phone. She was reluctant to call anyone at midnight, even if she had been instructed to do so. But she got the overseas operator and gave her the number, then hung up the phone. It would be a few minutes before the call could be put through. While she waited, she slipped into the tub, cleaning off the grit of sand and perspiration. Then she dressed in sensible work clothes, a gray suit with a blue cotton blouse and her most comfortable shoes. She usually spent Saturday night prowling around a couple of police precincts, for this was often a big night for the crime beat.

Since returning home from Europe, she had gone back to her old job on the city desk. Her father had been unusually flexible with her lately. Maybe he felt she was doing him a favor in coming home, in giving up the excitement of her job as a foreign correspondent. If only he knew how her attitude was changing, even to the extent that the thought of taking over the paper as publisher one day wasn't as outrageous as it once had been. But she hadn't said anything to her father because she was afraid he'd expect too much of her too soon. He wouldn't understand that much as she wanted to, she could not take any steady position because of the situation with Alex. Her father had not really accepted that Alex was a part of her life, much less her husband.

She supposed that had been one motivation for getting her own apartment. It made it more difficult for her mother and father to ask too many questions. She was near enough should her mother need her, yet far enough away to give her the independence she needed.

Cameron went to the kitchen for a cup of coffee. Who knew how long the wait would be. She reheated what was left from the morning and filled a clean cup. Her living situation had not changed much since before the war. This place was nearly a replica of the place she'd had back then. Sparsely furnished, little or nothing in the icebox, and only the fixings for coffee in the cupboards. She still ate all her meals out and had not a clue about cooking or keeping house.

And she thought she was ready to settle down? Well, emotionally at least. When the time came—please, God, let it be soon!—she would learn to do the rest. She'd heard Blair had become quite a proficient housewife. If her sister could do it, so could she.

The ringing telephone made her jerk, sloshing coffee over her hand. She put down the cup and ran to the living room. She grabbed the receiver on the third ring.

An operator informed her the call had been connected.

Cameron waited a moment before hearing a groggy voice.

"Uh . . . yeah . . . uh . . . hello . . ."

"Robert, is that you? This is Cameron."

"Cameron!" Instant alertness came into his voice. She could almost picture him lurching to a sitting position on his bed.

"I woke you," she said apologetically.

"No—ah yes . . . it's okay. I am so glad to hear from you."

"What's wrong, Robert? What's so urgent?" She silently bemoaned her penchant for getting to the point. The least she could do was exchange benign pleasantries. But she couldn't quell her natural curiosity, not to mention the pressure of the cost of an overseas call.

"I've got bad news, Cameron," he said. "I didn't think it could wait for the mail. Besides, I wanted to tell you in person, well, at least person-to-person." He paused.

Even over thousands of miles, with static intervening every now and then, she could tell he was having a hard time with this. Someone must be dead. That's all she could think.

Finally he continued. "Alex has been arrested."

Her first thought was *He's not dead!* Relief washed over her, then was instantly obliterated as the reality of Robert's words struck her. Alex had been arrested!

"Cameron, are you there?"

"Yes . . ." More than a moment must have passed before she realized she was now sitting in the chair by the phone.

"Are you okay?"

"Yes . . ." she answered mechanically. Another moment passed before she forced the dullness from her senses. This call could be cut off at any time, and there were things she had to know. "Robert, do you know how it happened?"

"Things are bad here, Cameron. Any Russian with even the smallest ties to foreigners is under suspicion. Russian employees disappear from the embassy nearly every week. But . . . that may not be the entire reason for Alex's trouble."

"What do you mean?"

"I can't talk about it on the telephone, even here, where it is probably fairly safe."

"What are you doing in West Berlin, Robert?"

"I couldn't call you from Moscow. And there was business here, so I used that as an excuse."

Cameron tried to read between the lines, a habit she had not lost since her years as a correspondent in the Soviet Union. There were things Robert couldn't say, she understood that, but there was something else in his tone. A sense of responsibility? Was it just friendship or something else? He'd gone to a lot of trouble to make this call.

He went on, "I tried to learn from Soviet authorities about Alex's disposition, but they became irate that I would attempt to interfere into the affairs of a Soviet citizen. I wish I could tell you more."

Cameron thought of Oleg Gorbenko, Sophia's husband. He'd been arrested in 1942, and except for once when Sophia's father had been able to see him in prison when he'd been ill, no one had seen or heard from him. He had seemed to disappear from the face of the earth. All the blood rushed from Cameron's head.

"Dear God . . ." she murmured, unable to utter more of a prayer than that.

"What will you do, Cameron?" came Robert's voice over the line.

Do? Yes . . . do something. That had always been her way. To act. But what could she do? In two years it had been impossible for her to breech the Soviet embargo against her. For two years she had pounded her head against that wall. For two years she'd been forced to face failure after failure.

What would she do?

"I'm going to Russia," she heard herself saying in spite of her more rational thoughts.

"How?"

"I'll find a way. God will find a way."

"If I could help, I would," Robert said.

"I know."

"One thing I can do is pray, and I will do that."

"Thank you, Robert. And thank you for calling. It means a lot that you told me personally."

"I'll be looking for you at the embassy."

"I'll be there, and soon."

"Heaven help the Red Menace now!" he declared. She appreciated the amusement in his tone. At least he wasn't consumed with despair.

After the phone call Cameron could not sit still. However, she didn't go to a police precinct as planned. Instead, after making a couple of phone calls, she went to Jackie's apartment.

"What are you going to do now?" Jackie asked after Cameron had told her about Robert's phone call. Like Robert, she knew Cameron wasn't planning to take this sitting still.

"I've booked a seat on the redeye to Washington D.C.," she replied. "I'm going to light a fire under someone. Maybe Gary or someone at the State Department. Maybe at the Soviet embassy. I only know I can't light fires or rattle cages from here."

"I wish I could help you," offered Jackie. "I would go with you to Russia if I could. Not just to find Semyon, but to be there to support you. I know I can't do a whole lot, but at least you'd have a friend to lean on."

Cameron reached her arms around her sister. Sudden tears filled her eyes. "I don't know why I'm crying. It's not like someone has . . . died."

"That's right, sis. And you'll get him out—I know you will!"

"No reason to cry at all!" But she sobbed anyway.

"Dear God, please be with my sister now. Fill her with hope and with some ingenuity, too, so she can figure out what to do. And, especially, Lord, be with Alex. Help him to keep his eyes on you in this difficult time. Help him to feel your love and to feel Cameron's love and to know that his rescue is close. Thank you, Father. Amen."

Cameron kissed her sister's cheek. "Thank you, Jackie." She wiped a hand over her eyes. "I'm going to miss not having you with me through this."

"It's still a few weeks till the end of summer school," Jackie said dismally. "I've got to see it through. I can't leave the school in the lurch. If I did, they would never rehire me."

"I understand. Please don't worry. Just keep praying for me . . . for us."

"I will. And if you are still in Russia when school is out—no no, you won't be. You and Alex will be home long before that."

Cameron nodded, appreciating her sister's positive attitude, though this time she thought it was a bit unrealistic. Still . . . who could say? Maybe . . .

Cameron had to firmly put her life, as well as Alex's life, into God's hands. Yes, she would do whatever she could. But in the end, God *was* in control.

Probably the most difficult task that day was saying good-bye to her parents. Her father wasn't happy about her flitting off on a wild goose chase. He subtly hinted that her time would be better spent getting an annulment from her ill-fated marriage, and just when she thought she might at last be able to expect some sympathy from him, too.

Then her mother sent Keagan from the room to bring her some coffee. When he was gone, she said, "Cameron, I don't want you to worry about the other matter in Russia if—when—you get there."

"If the opportunity arises, Mom—"

"I know your heart is in the right place, and I know it would weigh on you. But I don't want it to. I release you from any obligation to me. You concentrate on your Alex."

"Thank you, Mom." She bent over and kissed her mother. "Like I said, if the opportunity arises I won't forget. Everything in Russia takes time. I don't expect to rush in like gangbusters and get Alex out of prison in a day."

"Well, that is something coming from you, dear." Cecilia smiled warmly. "It shouldn't, but sometimes your maturity surprises me."

"Maybe I am finally learning some patience."

She knew she was going to need that and so much more if she was going to accomplish anything.

17

Moscow, Soviet Union

THEY SAT IN the kitchen of their small apartment. The room was cramped, and the table they sat at was a bit worn, but at least he'd made sure his Vera had a modern gas stove and refrigerator. Anatoly Bogorodsk was a colonel in the MVD, so he could afford that much. It wasn't easy to ask her to give it all up.

"I wish it hadn't come to this," he said to his wife.

She smiled tenderly. "You are doing what is right. You must help Aleksei. I understand."

"This terrible thing would not have happened to him if I hadn't abandoned him. I only thought I could protect you and our boy," he lamented. "Yet, I now think we would have had to do this one day soon regardless of our friend. No one, especially one in a position such as mine, is safe in this country. A new purge is coming very soon, and I doubt I would escape it."

"Only if you grovel at the feet of your superiors," she said with a touch of irony in her tone.

"Even bootlickers have been purged."

"But you are no bootlicker, my Anatoly." She paused and sighed. "I would not want you so, even for me. Still, I wish we could go together."

"They would never let us do that. Not even I have that much favor," he said, reaching across the table and gripping her hand in his. He gazed at her round rosy face—much like the cheerful faces on the matryoshka dolls the tourists liked to buy. She had the pleasant, sweet personality to go with that face. He often wondered how he, a despicable secret police agent, could have deserved a woman like her. He went on, "They have given permission for you and Stephan to go to Finland to visit your sick aunt. That's more than I hoped for. I am not under as much suspicion as I feared—yet."

"But how will you get out, Anatoly?"

"I still have many resources at my disposal, my love. I will be able to get out. After I have helped Aleksei."

"Do you know how you will help him? Can you help him escape?"

"I haven't figured it out yet. That may be possible. But one thing I know, I am going to get someone here who might be able to do more than even I. Someone he cares about, perhaps even loves. Her presence might at least give him hope."

"The American woman?" Vera said with a little twinkle in her blue eyes. "Such a romantic story."

"She brought him nothing but trouble," Anatoly grated. "I am probably crazy to think her presence can help."

"But it will, and you know it." She gave her husband's hand a gentle squeeze. "If you were in trouble, Anatoly, I would want to be as close to you as possible. And it will give him hope. But if she is as feisty as you imply, who knows what she could do?"

"Well, whatever the result, it is done. I have expedited her visa application. I can only hope it is not too late. Who knows what they will do to Aleksei. Even I cannot get in to see him."

The dank gray stone walls of Lubyanka Prison rose six stories. From its roof one could glimpse the spires of the Kremlin and the cupola domes of St. Basil's Cathedral. Not many Russians, however, would claim to know the location of the prison or even of its existence. But the profusion of burly men in the dark blue uniforms of the MVD in this vicinity was no coincidence. The upper floors housed the headquarters of the secret police. The lower floors, especially the cellars, housed their victims. A new wing was in the process of being added because Stalin's great paranoia had caused much overcrowding.

Like most cellars and most prisons, this one boasted the usual dark, damp, dismal interior. The cells were windowless, lacking in most cases even the most basic furnishings. The cold penetrated so deeply that Alex had been shivering for five straight days since his arrival. It didn't help that he had been stripped down to his underwear and had only the cold stone floor on which to sit. He was glad now that at least he could sit. For the last three days he had been forced to stand in an interrogation room under guard. When his legs tried to buckle, he was strapped to a post. Seventy-two hours on his feet, no sleep, no food, nothing to drink, no means to relieve himself except where he stood, and then he had to endure the horrible filth and stench. Afterward, he had not been allowed the luxury of a bath but had been dumped back into his cell.

Only the hours and hours of interrogation had been worse.

"Where did you get these falsified documents?"

"Name your contact."

"Name your accomplices."

"We know you weren't working alone. Give us names."

Surely it must have been torture for the interrogators themselves to ask the same questions over and over and over. They changed interrogators once in a while but not the questions.

"Give us names."

"Who gave you the documents?"

"Names. Give us names."

"Tell us who you are working with."

"Names."

He stood naked, hungry, his mouth so dry it was far beyond thirst. He knew their goal was to rob him of any sense of humanity. He who was less than human was less likely to cling to the highest hallmarks of humanity—honor and loyalty among them. Reduced to the level of an animal, a man would betray friends and even family with hardly a thought. At least that was the supposition of the police. Alex had proven them wrong—so far. But maybe it would only be a matter of time. He didn't know. What was the limit of his endurance? He didn't know that, either.

At least since returning him to his cell they had given him a bucket of water, but nothing to drink it with. He had to dip his dirty hands into the bucket and scoop the liquid up to his parched lips. He guzzled it down as best he could, trying not to think about the bacteria that must be floating in it from the grimy pail. He drank as much as he could, for he had no idea when they would take the water away.

He stopped thinking about food. He was a doctor, so he knew what a human could endure. Jesus had fasted for forty days. It was possible.

He slept for a while, amazed at how good the hard floor felt after standing for so long. He slept and he dreamt. Not dreams of freedom and happiness. Not of Cameron. But nightmarish images that were, if possible, even worse than the actual nightmare of his imprisonment. Faces of friends and enemies alike, even Cameron's face, turned ghoulish. They chased him and tormented him.

Voices screamed at him.

Names . . . names . . . names . . . !

Until he babbled every name he ever knew.

He awoke with a start, drenched in perspiration. He was so cold, how could he be sweating? And all the water he'd drunk was now lost through his pores. He turned toward the bucket to quench this renewed thirst, but it was gone. He'd slept so soundly he hadn't even heard the cell door open when the guard must have retrieved the bucket.

A sudden panic gripped him.

Names! Had he spoken them only in his sleep? What irony if he had suffered all that earlier torture in silence only to spew out his guts in his sleep. He crawled to the door, then clawed his way to his feet so he could look out the small barred opening at the top. His legs and arms were so weak and painful that every movement was agony. Finally he reached the opening and saw that the single light bulb burning at the end of the corridor outside showed all was deserted. No one could have heard even if he had mumbled the names out loud.

He slumped back to the ground.

He had to be careful. Maybe it was a blessing when they forced him to stand up without sleep.

But without sleep, his resistance would surely wear away no matter how strong his will was to keep silent.

"God, protect my dreams so I can sleep."

Instantly he knew what he must do. For the five days of his imprisonment, his faith had been always on the fringes of his mind. God must have understood that he had been so numbed by the agony of his torture that he hadn't given his Lord the focus he should have. But that simple prayer made him realize his faith was his salvation. Jesus had fasted for forty days, not out of the strength of his own fortitude, but because the spirit of the Lord was upon him.

Of course, since his arrest Alex had asked God to help him. But he realized now that he had to do more, he had to immerse himself in God, drown himself in Christ's love, fill himself with the bread of life.

He laughed suddenly at his analogies. He *was* thirsty and hungry. But the Scriptures were true nonetheless.

"'The weapons of our warfare are not carnal, but mighty through God to the pulling down of strong holds,'" he heard himself murmur.

There was something else about armor. What was it? A week ago his mind knew every bone and muscle and organ in the body. He could draw from memory the name of nearly every drug for every disease. He knew the name of every surgical instrument, every vein and artery in the body.

Now his mind felt like a hunk of Swiss cheese. He squeezed his head between his hands, as if to force out thoughts hidden deep in his brain's cortex.

"'Put on the whole armour of God, that ye may be able to

stand against the wiles of the devil. . . .'"

He spent the next hour trying to remember what each piece of armor represented. He'd learned it all once long ago.

Loins protected with truth.

The breastplate of righteousness.

Feet shod with the Gospel.

The shield of faith.

The helmet of salvation.

The sword of the Word of God.

He smiled. Not bad. What else was locked inside his head? He'd spent a lot of time in Sunday school in the States. He'd won prizes reciting Scripture verses. He'd always had a good memory.

Another part of that same passage came to him. "'We wrestle not against flesh and blood, but against principalities, against powers, against the rulers of the darkness of this world, against—'"

The sound of footsteps in the corridor stopped him. His stomach twisted. He wasn't the only prisoner in this section, but when the footsteps came, he could not help the fear it brought.

He made himself repeat, "'We wrestle not against flesh and blood—'"

The footsteps stopped. Metal ground against metal as a key turned in the lock of his door. A moment later the door flung open. Two guards came in, grabbed his arms, and yanked him to his feet.

"They want you again, Dr. Traitor," said one with a sneer.

Half dragging him because they were walking faster than he could in his weakened state, they took him to the terrible room in another part of the cellar where his torment would begin all over again.

18

Washington D.C.

BLAIR STIRRED a pot of spaghetti sauce while Cameron, perched on a high stool in the kitchen, watched her sister cook. She still couldn't get over Blair's domestic proficiency.

"This recipe came from the chef at the Italian embassy," Blair commented, adding a pinch of salt to the pot.

"I'm impressed," Cameron said.

"Time was I would have learned a skill solely to impress," Blair commented thoughtfully. "But I am not trying to do that now. I truly enjoy all this." Pausing, she smiled wryly. "Well, to be honest, it does feel a tad good to impress others."

Cameron had been enjoying her time in her sister's lovely home. Blair was a flawless hostess. But there were times when Cameron sensed that her sister was trying a bit too hard, if not to impress, then for some other reason Cameron could not fathom. However, Cameron knew the restlessness she herself was feeling, especially lately, had nothing to do with her sister. She had been almost two weeks in Washington and wasn't anywhere close to getting a visa to Russia. She was ready to come unglued. Alex had been in a Soviet prison now for two weeks. Only God knew what he must be suffering while Cameron enjoyed her sister's gourmet food and the comforts of a finely appointed home.

To get her mind off these thoughts, Cameron said, "Don't

worry about it, Blair. You deserve to be proud of what you have accomplished and have a right to show it off a little. As much as I have said I'm ready to settle down, I still can do little more in the kitchen than boil water for coffee."

"You'll learn."

"Would it be a terrible thing if I didn't *want* to learn?"

Shock flickered on Blair's face for a brief instant before she quickly smoothed it away, replacing it with a more pensive expression. "It once had no appeal to me, but now I truly love it."

"What if I never do? Couldn't Alex and I have a normal life regardless?"

"But who would do the cooking?"

Cameron laughed. "Maybe Alex likes to cook. I doubt it, though. He works twenty-five hours a day."

"So do you." Was there a touch of criticism in Blair's tone?

A bit defensively Cameron responded, "Well, what's wrong with that? Our lives might not be normal by general standards, but why couldn't we make our own *normal*?"

"What if you have children?"

Cameron groaned. "I don't know," she said dismally.

Blair put down her spoon and laid a comforting hand on Cameron's shoulder. "It will work out, Cameron. I'm sure of it."

"My relationship with Alex has always been on the edge of some drama or another. We know each other's heart and soul, of that I am certain, but I don't know what his favorite color is."

"And you worry that a relationship built on such drama might not be able to survive a normal environment?"

"Yes, that fear is there, of course."

"I worried about that with Gary and me, too. But we have never been happier than we are now, with our delightfully boring, normal lives." Blair's eyes became unfocused and inward for a moment, and Cameron knew she wasn't telling all.

"I would just like to get to the point of finding out," said Cameron.

"Anyone home?" Gary's voice came from the front room.

"We're in the kitchen," Blair called.

In a moment the swinging kitchen door opened, and Gary appeared.

"Mmm . . . what is that delicious smell?" he asked, taking a big whiff of the fragrant air.

"Spaghetti sauce," answered Blair.

"I'm gonna have to get new uniforms made if you keep feeding me like this." Gary laughed.

Cameron thought he was as trim as ever. And as handsome. As he bent down to kiss his wife, Cameron mused that they were probably the most beautiful couple she had ever seen. Both had recovered completely from their ordeal in the Philippines during the war. If anything, they looked better now, filled with the depth of their love for each other and their faith in God. They appeared to have everything, yet Cameron recalled that brief look of unease she had seen in Blair's face earlier and on a few other occasions. Blair's life wasn't as perfect as it appeared. Something was missing. Not faith, not love, but something.

Still with his arm about Blair, Gary turned to Cameron. "Please excuse us, Cameron. But a man has to kiss his wife hello."

"You are definitely excused." She smiled. The last thing she wanted was for them to feel awkward because of her presence or because of her situation with Alex.

"I better put on water for the spaghetti," Blair said, slipping from Gary's embrace with a final peck on his cheek.

"I've got some news," Gary said. He slipped off his uniform jacket and laid it over the back of a kitchen chair. "I don't know if you'll think it's good or bad. Maybe just better than no news at all."

"Well, what is it, Gary?" Blair asked over the sound of running water.

"You know the friend I have been communicating with in Moscow?" he said, loosening his necktie. "He just wrote me with an idea. Seems he is getting tired of the Moscow scene. I think he got the idea I had an interest in Russia beyond my sister-in-law's needs. Anyway, he suggested I switch places with him for the remainder of his tour in Moscow, a little more than a year."

Out of the corner of her eye, Cameron noted that Blair, who was about to place the pot of water on the stove, stopped in midair. All color drained from her face.

Quickly interpreting the meaning of her sister's reaction, Cameron spoke hurriedly. "Gary, I don't want or expect you to disrupt your lives for me."

"But if you can't get into the country," Gary reasoned, "at least there would be someone there with your interests at heart."

Into the moment of silence after Gary's statement came the clank of the pot hitting the burner of the stove. Both Cameron and Gary looked in Blair's direction. For a woman who was a pretty good actress, there was a wealth of undisguised emotion on her face now. Gary hurried to her side and put an arm around her.

"Blair, honey!" He spoke with intensity. "We would go together, you know. Both of us."

"You . . . won't go by yourself?"

"No, never. I wouldn't leave you."

Some of the color returned to Blair's face. Cameron had assumed that Blair's reaction had been because she didn't like the idea of giving up her home and present life, and Cameron wouldn't have blamed her. Apparently that wasn't all of it.

"Listen, you two," Cameron said firmly. "I will not let you disrupt your lives like this." She forced resolve into her tone because, in truth, if she couldn't get into Russia, the next best thing would be to have a man like Gary, who cared for her interests, interceding for her and Alex. But she could not ask it of them.

Then Blair surprised Cameron again. "Wait a minute. Gary, you are saying there is a chance that you and I"—she put some emphasis on *you and I*—"can go to Russia for a year, during which time we can possibly act on Cameron's behalf? Not to mention the possibility of seeing my half brother?"

Cameron wasn't surprised that Gary appeared to know about

Semyon. Of course Blair would have told her husband. Cameron had no problem with that.

"I spoke with General McDowell about it," Gary said, "and he thinks it is a marvelous opportunity for me. Foreign experience can be good for me if I plan to advance in the State Department. So what do you think?"

"I think we should do it," Blair said with more confidence than Cameron could believe.

"Now both of you wait a minute," Cameron said. "Especially you, Blair. A few minutes ago you were telling me how much you loved your life, and now you are willing to traipse off to the other side of the world, just like that. I won't have you do this for me!"

Blair chuckled. "I can see that it looks kind of inconsistent, sis." She gave Gary an intimate look and said to him, "It is more for you, too, isn't it, sweetheart?"

"I love you like a sister, Cameron," Gary said with sincerity, "but I have to admit it is more. I love our life here, as well. I do, I honestly do. And I hated that life we had in the Philippines. But being away from it is hard sometimes, like having withdrawal from a drug—only in this case the drug was adventure. I get restless sometimes."

"So do I," put in Blair.

"Restless not only for adventure but for the kind of . . . I don't know, I guess for an urgent meaning, as our lives had there."

"A sense of purpose," said Blair. Gary nodded, and Blair went on, "We have spoken to . . . ah . . . professionals—well, to a psychiatrist. Don't tell Dad. He'll think we are insane or something. But we wanted to understand the emotions we were feeling. Anyway, he felt it would take time to truly settle down. It is a common thing they are seeing in many returning veterans. They hated much about the war, but it still was the experience of a lifetime."

"I understand," Cameron said. "I guess I feel that way myself sometimes."

"I think going to Russia would be good for us," Blair added. "Personally, I need something important to do right now. Perhaps a distraction from . . ." Pausing, she glanced at Gary, then said, "Cameron, I didn't say anything to you when we were home because I didn't want to detract from Mom's needs. But just before I was to leave for California, Gary and I received the news that we would not be able to have children. That's why I postponed my flight. Not because of malaria, but because I was too upset."

"Blair, I am so sorry," responded Cameron.

"Well, at least we know for sure now and don't have to live with false hope." Blair's tone was a little too upbeat. Though she was trying, she obviously hadn't fully accepted the truth. "So you see why going to Russia would be a good thing for many reasons?"

"I guess I do." Cameron jumped up, reached her sister and brother-in-law in two strides, and threw her arms around them both. "Thank you so much! I don't care if you are going to get something out of this for yourself. I will be forever in your debt."

Cameron was with Blair in her bedroom helping her pack. Only five days had passed since Gary's announcement, and Blair was already hard at work making preparations for their upcoming trip. Their paper work was being expedited, and as members of the embassy staff, there should be no problems. They planned to leave in nine days.

"Do you think I should take any summer clothes?" Blair asked, holding up a charming yellow sundress.

"August can get warm, sometimes in the eighties," Cameron replied. "But I don't know about something sleeveless like that." Cameron eyed the dress, knowing even in the tropics she'd feel uncomfortable in that style. Their tastes were vastly different. "All I ever wore were skirts and blouses," she added sheepishly.

"And sensible shoes?"

"Of course." Cameron chuckled.

Blair giggled. "I don't even own a pair of sensible shoes!" Then, with a grin, she added, "Guess I will have to go shopping."

Three suitcases were open on the bed and filling fast. None of them belonged to Gary. Blair had already done some research and had gotten a list of things she should be sure to take. There were several packing crates downstairs for household items and nonperishable foods that they would not be able to get in Russia.

"Goodness," said Blair, "I never thought I'd ever be going to Russia again. If I had known, I would have taken Russian lessons."

"I'll teach you some. You've got a head for languages, so you should learn fast. I've had to work hard not to forget what I learned in Russia. I had a couple of Russian refugees tutor me while I was in Germany, but since I have been home, I feel it's slipping away. It will be good for me."

"Okay. Tell me something now."

"Well, the most important word is *spasiba,* which means thank you."

"*Spasiba,*" Blair repeated.

"*Pazhalusta,*" Cameron responded. "That's the standard response to thank you and means please, or the equivalent of you're welcome."

The telephone rang, but before Blair could reach the extension phone on the bedside table, it stopped ringing. A moment later Gary called from downstairs.

"Cameron, it's for you."

Cameron exchanged a puzzled look with Blair, and they both thought the same thing.

"Mom," Blair said with concern.

"But they would have asked for you, since it's your house."

Blair went to the bedroom door and called down to Gary, "She'll get the extension."

Cameron lifted the receiver. "Hello?" She listened a moment, then mouthed to her sister, "It's not Mom." She listened some more, nodding and murmuring, "Uh-huh." Finally, she said thank you and put down the receiver.

"Well?" prompted Blair when Cameron stood silently a moment too long.

"It was the State Department. My visa came through," she explained a bit numbly. Finally the news hit her, and she grinned. "My visa came through! I'm going to Russia!"

Blair squealed with delight and hugged her sister. "I knew it! I knew everything would work out! Maybe you can leave with us."

Cameron gaped at Blair. "You're leaving in nine days, right?"

"I know that isn't much time, but—"

"I'm leaving tomorrow or on the next flight I can get. I'd go crazy if I had to wait more than a week now."

"But you've got to pack!"

"I have everything I need in that suitcase in your spare room." She started for the door as if she would grab the suitcase right then and leave. She paused. "May I use your phone to call the airline?" Blair had barely nodded before Cameron picked up the receiver and dialed the operator. In a few moments she had the airline and made her arrangements. When she hung up, she said to her sister, "I'm on a flight to Berlin tomorrow afternoon."

Blair laughed. "And I thought *I* had made a snap decision! Can I do anything to help you?"

"I'm ready to go, sis. I've been ready for two years."

"They told us we would fly to Berlin and then take the Berlin-Moscow express the rest of the way. Will it be the same for you?"

"Yes. It is far too difficult to fly into Russia since the war. But I've heard that train to Moscow is awful. It could take as long as five days. Be sure to bring enough food for that long, and water, too. You don't know what kind of services they will provide."

"This will be an adventure, won't it?"

"I do think you and Gary will have your fill of adventure when it is all over," Cameron assured. "But you know, now that I am going, you and Gary don't have to go."

Blair pushed aside a suitcase and sat on the edge of the bed. "He's already made the commitment. His West Point buddy is really anxious to come home. But I would go anyway, to be there to give you support—that is, if you'd like that. . . ."

"I would, Blair!"

"That's it, then. There will be no more feeling beholden or any such thing. I truly believe this is where God wants us all to be now. And isn't He working it out perfectly? I guess the only thing not quite perfect is that Jackie won't be there with us."

"Well, who knows about that? This whole process has taken so long, her school session is about to end in a few days. She'd still have to get her visa, though."

Blair nodded. "Anything can happen. Russia is supposed to be so closed, yet we three got visas."

"It would be wonderful if Jackie could be there, too."

———

Jackie found her mother sitting in the sunshine on the patio facing the rose garden. The roses were in full bloom, the fragrance almost intoxicating. Thanks to the Southern California sunshine, color was returning to Cecilia's face. She was much stronger now, though not completely recovered from her surgery.

"Mom, did you hear about Blair and Cameron?" Jackie asked, taking a seat in one of the wrought-iron chairs beside her mother.

"Yes, Blair called me this morning," said Cecilia. "I can't believe they called you, as well. Gary must be making better money than we thought."

"They were just so excited."

"Yes, I can see that." Cecilia smiled thoughtfully, then glanced at her watch. "Cameron should be leaving Washington about now. She'll be in Russia in less than a week probably."

"It is wonderful. After all this time, her visa came just like that. Pretty amazing!"

"How do you feel about it, Jacqueline? Do you feel a bit left out?"

"I know it is selfish, but I do." Jackie shrugged. "At least Cameron will have Blair with her."

Cecilia patted her daughter's hand sympathetically. "I feel left out, too, if it is any comfort. I do believe if it wasn't for my physical condition, I'd be on an airplane this minute." Pausing, she leaned closer to her daughter and added in low confidential tones, "I asked the doctor about travel. He nearly had a conniption!"

This was quite astounding, considering that Cecilia had always hated Russia. But Jackie had her own surprising news.

"Mom, I have to tell you that the day after Cameron left for Washington, I put in an application for a visa to Russia." She gave a tentative smile.

"But what about Emi?"

"Before I applied for the visa, I asked Sam's parents if they would mind taking care of her if my visa came through. I know it is kind of selfish, leaving Emi and you when you are still—"

"As your father would say, hogwash, Jacqueline!" Cecilia gave her head a censorious shake. "Don't be so hard on yourself. Emi will not suffer if you go away for a while. She will be totally spoiled by her grandparents and loving every minute of it. I think a trip like this would be good for you. Maybe you need to shake your life up a little."

"You're hoping I will meet a man over there like Cameron did."

Cecilia's gaze became shadowed momentarily, then she said, "I know Alex must be a wonderful man, but please, if you go, don't fall in love with a Russian."

"I don't plan on falling in love with anyone. I just want to be there for Cameron. And maybe meet . . . well, you know." She simply could not speak her half brother's name in her father's house.

"I must admit, I have my own reasons for hoping you get there," said Cecilia. "When Cameron left, I released her from any obligations toward me. But if you and Blair are there . . ."

"I know, Mom. We will do whatever we can in that area."

A week later, Jackie brought her mother the news that her visa to Russia had been approved.

Cecilia smiled slyly. "For a country that is supposedly closed, they are dishing out a lot of visas lately. It sounds . . . almost miraculous."

"It does, doesn't it? And those Russians haven't a clue that three of those visas are for three sisters who are about to invade them like the Mongol hordes!"

PART III

"*Russia's past was wonderful, her present magnificent, and as to her future—it is beyond the grasp of the most daring imagination. This is the point of view from which Russian history must be written.*"

COUNT ALEKSANDER BENKENDORFF
Russian Secret Police Chief, 1830s

19

BLAIR COULD not believe they would soon cross the border into Russia. As Cameron had hinted, the Berlin-Moscow express was an adventure in itself. For one thing, the term *express* was some kind of euphemism, because the train made many stops, and they would change trains in Brest-Litovsk for the final stretch of the journey from the Soviet border into Moscow.

Everywhere along the track there was horrible evidence of the war. Trenches, foxholes, bomb craters, and worst of all, many crosses where the dead had been buried. The wreckage of Berlin had been shocking. Warsaw was just as bad but more eerie, because when the train stopped at the platform, there was no station! It had been completely destroyed.

At every stop peasants would swarm around the train selling produce from the farms. Blair and Gary had no local money, so they could buy nothing. Luckily Blair had followed Cameron's suggestion and brought sufficient food and water, for there was no dining car on the train—not even running water. And there was no one on the train they could communicate with except for the porter, who spoke a little English. Blair nearly wore out her main word of Russian, "Spasiba!" But that, with a smile, went a long way to create good relations with passengers and staff alike.

Crossing the Polish border had been sticky.

"You must have Polish visa to cross Poland," the conductor told them with the help of the porter's translation.

"Intourist didn't tell us that when they sold us these tickets," Gary argued.

The conductor had a discussion with his assistant in Russian for several minutes and then took all of Gary's and Blair's papers and left. Gary, who was usually unflappable, looked worried. These people were obviously not the most competent lot, and they now possessed all of their precious identity documents.

Hours later everything was returned, properly stamped for the Poland crossing. But no explanations were given.

At the Bug River, which formed part of the border between Poland and Russia, the train stopped. No one was allowed off—all the doors were locked. The day was hot and muggy, but they were not allowed to even crack a window. Armed soldiers searched every inch of the train, even the undercarriage. Blair's skin prickled. This was too much like being in prison, and she didn't like it at all. Past experiences flooded over her, and for the first time since hearing of Alex's predicament, she felt true empathy for him. She had tried to blot out her time in Jap prisons, with the terrifying interrogations and the cruel privations, but with little success. From what little she had heard of Soviet prisons, she realized Alex must be experiencing something similar. Her heart went out to her brother-in-law, and she uttered a fervent prayer for him.

The new train they boarded in Brest-Litovsk was better appointed than the previous one. There was water and a dining car and fairly comfortable seating. Gary said he'd heard the train was German made. But once in Russia the devastation of war continued to be visible. Cities like Minsk and Smolensk had been reduced to such rubble, they looked more like villages, pathetic ones at that. And now beggars hounded the passengers at every stop.

"Give bread! Give bread!" was a new Russian phrase Blair quickly learned.

Blair found out from a passenger who could speak a bit of

English that these were not true beggars but actually peasants who were suffering from the terrible famine. Blair gave them all the remaining food she had packed for the trip, for she and Gary no longer needed it.

As they neared Moscow, such dismal signs of poverty diminished. Then suddenly they arrived at the Moscow station. Moscow, one of the great cities of the world, did not rise up from the ground like the concrete and skyscrapers of New York City. Rather, it was unpretentious, like a huge overgrown village.

Blair remembered very little of this place from her childhood. She had been here for four years between the ages of five and eight and had been totally encapsulated in the world of foreigners. Unlike Cameron, who had constantly traipsed off with their father, Blair had been tied to her mother, who had ventured little outside of the world of her home.

Blair glanced at Gary. He was as wide-eyed as she. They were no strangers to exotic places or adventure, but this, Blair innately sensed, was going to be like nothing they had ever experienced before.

They were met at the station by Donald Malone, the aide Gary would be relieving. He was smiling and ebullient as he greeted them. "Hey, you made it!" He laughed. "Not that I had any doubt."

"It was quite a trip," said Gary after he introduced Blair to his old classmate.

"Yeah. We don't have adventures like that in the States anymore. Come on, let's load up your gear and get you to your new home." He seemed in a hurry.

A porter helped them load their hand luggage into an embassy car. All their other belongings would be brought to the embassy later. Blair noted they had a chauffeur.

"Very few foreigners drive in this country," Malone explained. "Not only is it next to impossible to get a license, but navigating here can be pretty hair-raising."

As they drove into the center of Moscow, Blair had more of a definite feel of being in a huge city. She could see what Malone meant about driving—even *riding* was hair-raising! There were few vehicles on the road but swarms of pedestrians. Those on foot had no regard for crosswalks, traffic signals, or even the traffic itself, crossing the street anywhere and walking down the middle of the street. Horn blasts filled the air.

Then the true grandeur of Moscow came into view, that which sets it apart from all other cities—the Kremlin. A walled city within a city. Its reddish brick towers hinting at medieval fortifications were in one sense forbidding, yet oddly also inviting, perhaps because of their rich beauty. The ancient spires and domes were indeed otherworldly. The sun glinting off the golden domes of what Blair believed to be St. Basil's Cathedral took her breath away.

"It's a miracle so little of it was damaged in the war," Gary murmured in awe.

"The Muscovites are quite proud of having stopped Hitler at their gates," Malone said.

"Greatest proud achievement of our history!" intoned the driver.

Blair was surprised he could speak English, but he said no more on the drive.

As they neared the embassy, Malone spoke again, "The assistant military attachés have houses of their own—well, they are more like dormitories. Spiridonovka House for the Navy, near the Arbat district, and Khlebny House for the Army and Air Force. But since Blair is the only wife here, we thought you might feel more comfortable with one of the apartments in the embassy, which are usually reserved for the senior embassy staff and the military attachés. They tell me the available apartment is small, but at least there will be other women close at hand."

Blair remembered how miserable and alone her mother had been in Russia and was grateful for the accommodation they were making. "Thank you so much," Blair said. "I don't expect special privileges, though."

"Don't give it a thought," Malone said sincerely. "I, for one, want you to be happy here. You don't know how grateful I am for the chance to leave."

"It's not that bad, is it?" commented Gary with a hint of trepidation in his tone.

Malone chuckled nervously. "Oh no! It's really a great experience. I wouldn't trade it for anything." His tone lacked its earlier sincerity, but Blair tried to ignore that. He did add, as if it would help, "There are other reasons why I'm anxious to get away. You see, there's a girl back home I've been courting—that is, trying to court as best as I can from over here. I'm hoping I'll now have a chance to marry her."

"How romantic," said Blair. "We do wish you the best."

To herself, however, Blair wondered at the wisdom of giving up a year of their lives in order to help Cameron. But she firmly reminded herself that her sister hadn't been the only reason for this decision. They had wanted distraction and purpose. Well, this should provide all that, even if their main purpose was merely to survive.

The American embassy, called Mokhavaya House, was located near the Kremlin facing a broad plaza called Manezhnaya Place, where in tsarist times the tsar's horses were trained. The seven-story building itself had once been an art school, and the interior had many spacious rooms and vaulted ceilings. Blair thought she could be quite comfortable here for a year and was sure of it when she saw their fifth-floor apartment. It had a bedroom with a stone balcony facing the Kremlin, a kitchen, small but serviceable, and two larger rooms, one that most likely had been used by its former occupants as a living room, because there was already a sofa and easy chair there, along with a few other pieces of furniture. The other somewhat smaller room Blair thought would make a perfect dining room, since it was adjacent to the kitchen. Captain Malone informed them there were some spare furnishings in the basement that they should be able to procure. The apartment had the basics.

When they were alone, Gary gestured for Blair to sit beside him on the sofa, upholstered in a tasteful floral fabric.

"What do you think of all this, sweetheart?" he asked, placing his arm around her and drawing her close.

"Better than a jungle hut," she teased.

He laughed. "Yes, we have certainly had worse. But it isn't just the physical conditions I wonder about. We will doubtless be followed every moment by the police. And while inside, we will have to mind our every word."

"Do you really think the place is bugged?" she asked, astonished.

"We have to assume so. While you were looking at the kitchen, Don told me that all assistant military attachés are followed. The Soviets think that they, rather than the senior staff, are most likely to be spies."

"Goodness! We have fallen into a Hollywood movie, haven't we?" Maybe this would be more fun than she'd thought.

Encircling her with both arms, he leaned close and kissed her with passion. "I love you so much, Blair!"

She snuggled as close as she could to him, always feeling safe and secure in his arms. "I have to admit I was a little afraid when I saw that Don Malone seemed so anxious to get away from here. I thought there must be more to his hasty departure than his desire to get back home to his girl. But, Gary, I do feel right about being here."

"I do, too. I think we'll do okay." She liked the confidence in his tone. He then added, "Do you want to go find Cameron?"

Blair was anxious to do just that. They had told Cameron not to meet them at the train station, since the embassy was taking care of transportation. She thought, too, they would want to get settled first. But now that they were ready to find Cameron, they found it wasn't easily done. First Gary had to report in to his superior, General Stoddard, the Army attaché. This took longer than expected because the general was a talker. Luckily, his wife, Janet, was away on a shopping excursion, or they would have had to stay for dinner. As it was, they were invited to have dinner with the general and his wife the following evening.

Then there was the difficulty of getting a car and a driver.

General Stoddard made a call to the motor pool, but nothing was immediately available, so they didn't get away until about six in the evening. They found Cameron at the Metropole Hotel, where she met them in the lobby and took them up to her room.

"It's not the same room I had before," she said. "I think this one is nicer. They apparently save the better suites for tourists, which is how I entered the country this time."

The suite had a sitting room, a bedroom, and a private bath, all furnished rather shabbily, but not too much so. Blair knew Cameron would not mind it. They sat on the sofa while Cameron took a chair. Blair told about the embassy, forgetting that Cameron must have been there often. Then for a time, they swapped travel stories. Cameron had had an even more adventurous journey than Blair and Gary. In Berlin her father had tracked her down and asked her to fill in for an ailing *Journal* correspondent and cover an important diplomatic meeting. Though furious that he would take advantage of her like that when he knew how anxious she was to get to Russia, Cameron couldn't very well say no, since he was paying for the entire trip. That little favor had tied her up for two days. Then at the Polish border she had run into the same difficulty that Gary and Blair did—having failed to obtain a Polish passport. And when she turned over her papers, they had been promptly lost. She had spent three days in Warsaw straightening out the mess.

"Have you learned anything about Alex?" Gary asked.

"I haven't even been here a week," sighed Cameron, "and as much as I want to, I can't just plow through Soviet bureaucracy. I've got to be subtle or get kicked out of the country again. I have only learned—and that from Robert Wood—that Alex is probably in Lubyanka Prison."

"That's in Moscow, isn't it?" Gary asked.

"Yes, but don't try to find it. Most Russians will tell you they don't know it exists. I know its location, though precious good it does me. I've imagined a dozen escape scenarios, all completely impossible."

"Do you really think it will come to an escape?" asked Blair.

With a heavy sigh and a frustrated shake of her head, Cameron replied, "I don't know."

"There are some diplomatic approaches we can try first," Gary said. "Perhaps a trade. I'm sure we have some Soviet agents they would like to have back."

"Our government may not be too anxious to do that."

"Why's that?"

Cameron took a breath. "There are some things about Alex's history I haven't told anyone about. . . ." She looked down at her hands nervously twisting in her lap. She was uncharacteristically reticent. "I guess you should know. . . . You have a right. Goodness, you have already sacrificed a lot—"

"Cameron, I told you there will be none of that!" Blair admonished gently.

"Still, you ought to know. Alex's family emigrated to America when he was two years old. Alex received his education in the States and practiced medicine there for a couple of years. But he became addicted to medication, and . . . well, a patient he was operating on died. He lost his medical license. In shame and bitterness he returned to Russia. He had never relinquished his Russian citizenship. Not only that, at some point, out of rebellion or something, he joined the Communist Party." She paused and glanced back and forth between Blair and Gary. Blair tried to mask the shock she felt.

Cameron continued, "In Russia he was able to practice medicine again. He has been completely free of any addiction. But why would our government extend themselves for a man with that history?"

There followed a long silence. Of course no one could answer that question. Finally Blair reached over and grasped Cameron's hand.

"We'll find a way, Cameron. We will!"

Cameron smiled tentatively, and Blair saw moisture rise in her eyes. "I know we will, Cameron. We must."

"God will find a way," added Gary.

Both women nodded, realizing that was the only way.

Obviously wishing to move on from this topic, which, despite their attempts to inject hope into it, was still depressing, Cameron said, "I haven't told you the best news. Jackie is coming to Russia."

"What!" Gary and Blair exclaimed in unison.

Smiling, Cameron went on, "You were traveling, so we couldn't tell you. Apparently Jackie is more savvy of things of the world than we give her credit for. She applied for a visa a month ago, hoping that all this would work out. Well, she got it and will soon be on her way."

"That is wonderful news!" said Blair. "That sly girl. She never said a thing."

"She didn't want to say anything until she was sure. Dad will give her the money for the trip, and her mother-in-law and sisters-in-law will watch Emi."

"Dad is paying her way, too," Blair said thoughtfully. "Now, that is incredible. Maybe we have underestimated him."

"Perhaps so. He still told me to get my marriage annulled."

"But he gave you the money even though he didn't approve."

"I guess you're right."

Blair wondered at Cameron's reluctance to give their father credit for his positive actions. She had hoped to be able to confess to Cameron about her slip in telling him about Semyon. Now she wasn't sure if she could, or should.

But Cameron had steered the conversation back to more pleasant ground. "I can't believe we are all going to be here together. Something good will come of it. I know it!"

20

Jackie had little remembrance of her years in Russia. Like her sister Blair, she had been tied to her mother, not that she would have been old enough anyway to remember much. She had been two when they arrived and not quite six when she left. She had one abiding memory of that time—her mother's melancholy. One image remained, that of her mother seated by a frosted window, snow falling outside. Her mother was weeping, but all Jackie thought at the time was that she was crying because, for some reason the young Jackie could not understand, Mom could not go outside and play. Jackie had wanted to play in the snow but didn't get to do so very often.

Now, of course, the reason for Cecilia's sadness was clear. Probably during her whole time in Russia she had been unable to shake the grief of knowing she had a son somewhere, lost to her forever.

Jackie sat by the huge tall window in Blair's living room at the embassy thinking on these things. She was waiting for Gary and Blair to finish dressing so they could attend an embassy party. She was staying at the Metropole with Cameron, who was supposed to meet them at the party later.

Soon Blair and Gary emerged from the bedroom, both looking stunning. Gary was as handsome as ever in his full dress uniform, while Blair, in a powder-blue day-length gown with a stylish full skirt belted with a wide sash, looked as though she had stepped from a fashion magazine. Jackie was wearing her best evening dress, the burgundy crepe with sheer sleeves and velvet trim that she had bought last year. She had always felt overdressed wearing it to the kinds of places she frequented at home, but next to Blair she felt almost dowdy. She had to firmly remind herself that her dress was lovely and she looked good in it. She was just nervous to be attending an embassy function. At home she had had some occasion to mingle with California's elite because of her father's position, but she had never felt comfortable with it.

"Do you think we should wait for Cameron?" Blair asked, picking up from a side table her silk clutch bag that matched her dress.

"She said she might be late, so we should go ahead."

"Do you know where she went?"

Jackie shrugged. "She was a bit mysterious about it."

"I hope she isn't going to get herself into trouble."

"She is pretty frustrated. She's been here almost two weeks with nothing to show for it. Her patience is wearing thin." Jackie had only been here two days, but she could tell Cameron was ready to blow like a live volcano. Patience was a trait none of the Hayes women could honestly claim, but Cameron least of all.

"We'd best be on our way," said Gary. "We don't want to be late for our first formal function. Cameron will find us, I'm sure."

The embassy ballroom was brightly lit with chandeliers. The sound of classical music, played by a live orchestra, mingled with the murmuring voices of about a hundred guests. The women were clad as brightly as the lights overhead—a rainbow of colors glittering with jewels—while the men were handsomely decked in black tie or dress uniform. Many countries were represented, and several different languages could be heard rising from the many knots of guests as they conversed. A large area of the floor was designated for dancing, but no one had ventured there yet. Perhaps, Jackie thought, they would as the evening progressed.

Blair and Gary stayed at her side, and feeling a bit lost among all the strange faces, Jackie was thankful for that. She was no shrinking violet, but neither was she a belle of the ball. And since her marriage to Sam, she had become even less so. There had never been anything like this in a Japanese internment camp, and now as a widow she shied away from social events.

"Let me introduce you to some of the people we have met," Blair suggested.

Taking Jackie's arm in hers, Blair led her over to a group of men in uniform and several women standing with them. Everyone offered friendly greetings as Gary made the introductions. The men were assistant Army and Air Force attachés, Gary's equals at the embassy, about three or four assistants representing each service.

A few minutes later guests began to migrate toward the dance floor. Gary asked Blair to join him, and the others in the group also began to pair off. There was one man left, and he asked Jackie to dance with him, though she had the feeling he did so only because he was odd man out. She sensed he was really interested in the redheaded woman who had paired off with someone else. So as not to appear rude, she accepted his invitation, but as they danced he seemed to always be looking in the redhead's direction. She nearly sighed out loud with relief when there was a momentary pause in the music and she could make her escape.

"I think I'll go to the powder room," she said.

"Thank you for the dance," he said stiffly.

She hurried away so quickly she wasn't watching where she was going and crashed into a passerby.

"Oh, I am terribly sorry!" she exclaimed.

To her horror, the man had been holding a glass of punch, which splashed all over his tuxedo at her collision. He was brushing the spill from his jacket with a small cocktail napkin. "That's okay," he said, his full attention on the task at hand.

"Let me get you another napkin," she offered lamely.

He then glanced up, blinked, then smiled warmly. "No, honestly, it was only a small spill."

Jackie found herself looking at a man of slender frame, about two inches taller than her. He had medium brown hair, dark brown eyes behind wire-rimmed glasses, a fine-featured face and good looking in its own way, though he looked like a college student dressed for the prom rather than an employee of a foreign embassy, as she assumed he must be.

"You are too generous," she said.

He blinked again. Did he have something in his eyes?

"You look very familiar," he said. "Have we met?"

"I don't think so."

"No . . . I'm sure I'd remember meeting you."

She felt a bit embarrassed at the awed tone of his voice.

"Wait a minute! She said her sister was coming. . . . I'm going to take a bit of a stab in the dark here—well, let's say an educated guess. Are you related to Cameron Hayes?"

"I'm her sister. I've been told we bear a strong resemblance, but I never really believed it."

"You do indeed. But you're—" He stopped, smiled awkwardly, then seemed to deflect himself from what he had been about to say. "I'm Robert Wood, second assistant to the ambassador."

"My name is Jackie Okuda, youngest sister to the renowned foreign correspondent."

They both chuckled at her lame attempt at wit. "You have a different last name. You are married then?"

"A widow," she said, amazed at how smoothly, how conversationally, she spoke the word that still seared her heart. "My husband was killed in the war."

"I'm very sorry."

She never knew how to respond to that sentiment, which always followed the revelation of her husband's death. But she was spared this time when another man approached them.

"There you are, Mr. Wood! I see you have cornered the most beautiful woman here." The man grinned and bowed gallantly toward her.

Jackie blushed at the fellow's attention, which seemed less

glib than it appeared. But that wasn't the only reason pink rose in her cheeks. This man was so handsome she nearly gasped out loud when she saw him. Six feet tall, broad shouldered, stunning in his Navy dress whites. His features seemed carved in granite, not that they were by any means stony, but his appearance was like a work of art. And unlike Michelangelo's David, he was tan and very much alive, topped with a shock of thick sandy hair.

"Captain Rigdon," said Robert, "may I present Mrs. Jackie Hayes—I mean—"

"Just call me Jackie," she put in quickly. She had never been ashamed of her husband's name, though it was often the first stumbling block in her disastrous foray into the world of dating. For the first time in that world she thought she might like a small chance at success before revealing her entire history.

"Charmed, as I know I will be," he said with a grin. "Mr. Wood, I was asked to give you a message," Rigdon added. He glanced offhandedly at Robert, almost in a superior way; however, by Rigdon's use of *Mr.,* Jackie guessed that Wood held the superior position.

"And what would that be?" Wood prompted Rigdon, whose eyes had strayed toward Jackie, apparently causing him to lose his train of thought.

"Oh, the ambassador wants to see you in the east reception room," Rigdon answered.

"I guess I must go then," said Wood.

"I'll keep the lady company in your absence, sir," Rigdon offered.

"If you don't mind, Jackie. It was nice meeting you. I hope—"

"It was nice meeting you, too, Mr. Wood." Vaguely Jackie realized that even as she spoke, her eyes were still all but ogling the stunning Captain Rigdon. Suddenly aware of her rudeness, she turned to amend her faux pas, but Wood's back was already to her as he threaded his way through the crowd. She made a mental note to apologize if she saw him later, and then she returned her attention to the captain.

"Would you care to dance?" he asked.

"Oh yes!" she breathed.

Her heart was fluttering, and when he slipped his arm around her on the dance floor, she tingled all over. What was happening to her? She was not the kind of woman to be stultified by a handsome man. Nor was she the kind of woman to be turned by a man's physical appearance. But she *was* a woman, and she couldn't deny it was thrilling just looking at this man. She couldn't help all the fluttering and tingling.

He remained with her exclusively for the rest of the evening. They danced, talked, drank punch, and ate canapés together. She nearly forgot there was anyone else in the room. His name was Captain Troy Rigdon. Troy . . . what a wonderful name, like a Greek god. When she mentioned her real name was Jacqueline, he asked if he could call her that.

"It fits you better," he said. "It's like a song, a beautiful song."

Blushing, she said, "My mother thought so, too." She blushed even more when she realized it was a stupid thing to say.

He laughed, seeming to think anything she said was charming. The one thing she didn't say, and only because it never came up, was that she was a widow, that her husband had been Japanese, and she had a half-Japanese daughter.

Robert didn't blame Jackie for her behavior. When a man like Rigdon came into a room, women could not be held responsible for their actions.

It was too bad, though, that their conversation had been cut short. It had gotten off to such a good start. He would have liked the opportunity to get to know her better, but now that Rigdon had made his move, Robert's chances were slim. Not that he was on the prowl for women. His interest was no doubt more because she was Cameron's sister. Robert had always had a certain fondness for Cameron. Nothing romantic but enough of a friendship that she was the only person outside his family who knew the secret of his heritage. If Jackie was anything like her sister, she would be worth knowing. He hoped she was like Cameron and not a giddy bobby-soxer smitten by a pretty man.

As he approached the east reception room, he turned his thoughts to what the ambassador might want. Only that morning Ambassador Smith had chided Robert about working too hard, telling him he must forget work this evening and enjoy himself. Yes, Robert worked hard and kept long hours, mostly because he had few other distractions in life. Perhaps if he had a family . . . but he couldn't get on that tangent now. Perhaps soon, when he worked out the mysteries of his life.

He came to the door he was looking for, knocked lightly, then opened it. Inside, seated on a red velvet settee, was not the ambassador but rather the person he had been thinking of only moments before. Cameron Hayes.

"Hello, Cameron," he said, glancing around the room thinking Smith might still be there, but he quickly realized it hadn't been his boss who had called him at all.

"Hi, Robert." She offered him a slanted sheepish smile, confirming his deduction. "Sorry to trick you like that."

He grinned, remembering how she had always spiced up his life in Russia before and rather pleased to think she might do so again. Of course, he had already seen her since her arrival in Moscow, but he'd still been able to do little to help her.

"Don't give it a thought. I'm sure it must be important." He strode to the settee and sat beside her. "So what's up?"

"Another chapter in the drama of my life," she sighed. "I need a big favor from you, Robert."

"Always at your service!"

"You better hear it first." She lifted a rather forlorn gaze toward him. He thought it an incongruent look for the feisty woman he'd known. Yet war, and life itself, had seasoned her. And he knew the arrest of the man she loved was a deep distress for her.

"First we best go someplace secure to talk," Robert said.

The reception room had a servants' entrance that connected to a series of corridors leading to the kitchens. Grabbing her coat, Cameron followed Robert to the kitchen and through a back door into an alley where deliveries were made and where the garbage was stowed. It smelled faintly of refuse, but there was a slight breeze that helped dispel some of the odor.

After they were securely in the open air, Robert said, "Cameron, you know I'll do anything I can for you. I might even do something illegal—well, at least what is illegal by Soviet standards, which doesn't define legality in the true sense." He grinned. "You do know I am a lawyer?"

She chuckled, but the lost look remained in her eyes, visible even in the dim light that came from a single bulb over the door. He was prompted to add with deep compassion, "I'm sorry to be glib, Cameron. I know this is a terribly difficult time for you. I haven't done as much for you as I should. I admit to a certain helplessness, but . . ." Pausing for a moment, he made a hasty decision. "Cameron, I want you to meet someone. I should have had you do so when you first arrived, yet I was held in check by the specter of national security. I don't think you should be in the dark any longer. Besides, this man may have resources that could help, even though he was part of the cause of Alex's problems."

"Who is it? How did he cause Alex's problems?" she asked, her brow creased in confusion.

"I think you should hear it from him. I'll arrange something for tomorrow. I'll call you at your hotel in the morning. But I must be honest, I had some part in all this, as well."

"Now I really am confused, Robert. What is this all about?"

"Please wait until tomorrow. You need to talk to this other person. Now what can I do for you?"

"You mean what *else* can you do." She studied him for such a long moment that he began to feel uncomfortable. She shook her head a bit bewildered, shrugged uneasily, then went on, "There's a man at the party tonight I want to see. Boris Tiulenev. I was shocked when I walked in and saw him across the room. I made sure he didn't see me, and then I waylaid that Navy man and asked him to give you my message. I have been trying for the last two weeks to get in to see Tiulenev. He's an old acquaintance of my father's and was very kind and helpful when I was here during the war. I feel he is the only contact in the government that I can trust. He is an important Party official now, and I think he could help me with Alex. But he has refused all my attempts to see him."

"If he won't see you," Robert reasoned, "maybe he can no longer be trusted."

"I think he won't see me because he is afraid of being compromised. My gut tells me he still can be trusted. If I could just get him in a place where he wouldn't have to worry about being seen by the police. Perhaps if you invited him back here—"

"You mean lured?"

Her lips quirked into a smile. "Yes . . . that, too."

"How would I recognize him?" he asked, to which she responded by giving a description of a plump sixtyish man with distinctively long white eyebrows. He could hardly be missed.

"It's risky," said Robert, not convinced this was the right thing to do, "not only for you, should he turn on you, but also for him. Just coming to a private room with me could be dangerous for him. Getting him out here where you can talk freely . . . that'll be a trick."

"Make it appear a chance thing," she suggested. "Spill a drink on him, then bring him back here to clean up."

Robert arched a skeptical brow, then burst out laughing. "I knew you were going to make my life interesting again."

"It's the least I can do for you, my friend!" She flashed a grin.

The only other time Jackie noticed Robert Wood that evening was a short time later when she saw him involved in a bit of a scene with a guest—a burly gray-haired man with incredibly long white eyebrows. Robert bumped into the man, spilling red punch all over the poor fellow's suit and white shirt. Jackie wondered if perhaps Wood had been the clumsy one in her mishap with him.

Captain Rigdon, with whom Jackie was still dancing, snickered. "I don't know how that man got to be third in command of the embassy," he said with more than a touch of disdain.

"I must admit that's how I met Mr. Wood," Jackie commented, trying to be more amused than snide.

"He spilled punch over you?"

"Well, I wasn't looking and bumped into him, and there was punch involved, but it got on him, not me."

As they talked, Wood was trying to blot up the punch with his handkerchief. Then he tried to gesture for the man to come with him, probably to find a rest room where he could more properly clean the stain. It seemed the man tried to protest, though they were speaking in Russian, Jackie thought. Finally, with some reluctance the man let Wood lead him away.

"They say he's some kind of genius," Troy was saying, obviously referring to Wood. "First in his class at Harvard or something. I don't know . . ." He shook his head and chuckled. "But it does make me thirsty. Would you care for some punch?"

Troy slipped his arm around Jackie and led her to the refreshment table. She gave no more thought to the clumsy embassy official for the rest of the night.

21

As CAMERON WAITED, she thought of all her failures since coming to Russia, the worst of which was her inability to see her friends the Fedorcenkos, especially Sophia. She knew if she could somehow connect with them, they would be able to help. She had tried once to go to Yuri Fedorcenko's hospital but had been unable to shake her MVD shadow. Either they had become better at their jobs with the change of their name, or she had grown rusty. Every attempt to shake them had failed.

Yet she had to remind herself that Yuri and Sophia must know about Alex's arrest and were already doing whatever they could, if anything. She felt now that old Uncle Boris was her only hope.

Restless, she paced to the end of the alley. Despite the fact that it was early August, it was a bit chilly and the narrow alley acted like a wind tunnel for the cool night air. She shivered and pulled her coat closer around her. Blair would be appalled that she hadn't bothered to dress for the formal embassy function. Under her coat, she was still wearing the skirt and blouse and cardigan sweater she'd put on that morning. After making her last unsuccessful attempt to see Tiulenev in the afternoon, there hadn't been time to change. Perhaps she would have made time if she had cared, but she was in no mood for a party.

It wasn't the chill in the alley that bothered Cameron. She was cold with fear over Alex. It never left her, even haunted her dreams. She knew he was suffering. And now there was Robert's talk about someone else being to blame; even taking some blame upon himself. What did it mean? Why had he not said something before this? Why had Alex really been arrested? Had it been more than a run-of-the-mill mishap with the government that happened all too often to innocents in the Soviet Union? If so, then it must be that much worse for Alex.

Another door toward the end of the alley opened, spilling light onto the dark pavement. Cameron started, then saw that Robert Wood was holding the door for Boris Tiulenev. He must have found another exit in order to avoid the Russian workers in the kitchen, who could easily be informers for the police. Tiulenev did not look pleased with the situation. Robert had to nudge the man into the alley in order to shut the door.

"Comrade Tiulenev," Cameron said, stepping into the light of the single outdoor bulb so she could be seen.

Tiulenev looked up, and sudden awareness dawned on his creased and furrowed countenance.

"Now I see," the man said in broken though adequate English. He cast a sharp glance at Robert, who shrugged with a touch of apology.

They strode toward Cameron.

"I will leave you two alone—" Robert began.

Tiulenev cut in, "No, you will not! If you return to the party without me, it will only raise suspicions. I do take it correctly that this ruse was to protect me, yes?"

"Yes, Colonel Tiulenev," answered Cameron quickly.

"I no longer hold rank in the Red Army. As you know, I am now the commissar of defense and munitions production. You may call me Mr. Tiulenev, as I know the term *comrade* is an uncomfortable one for you Western capitalists."

When Cameron had last seen this man, he had told her to call him Uncle Boris. Had he changed that much? Could he still be trusted? Did she have any other choice? That past friendship was the only tool she had in order to get through to the man.

"Am I to take it, *Mr.* Tiulenev," she said evenly, forcefully calming her inward tremors, "that past friendships no longer exist?"

"It is dangerous in this country to have friends, Miss Hayes, when those so-called friends continually take advantage."

She knew she was guilty as charged. "Forgive me for doing so," she responded with deep sincerity, "especially since I seek to take further advantage of that friendship. I don't know where else to turn. A dear friend of mine has been arrested by your government."

"An American?"

"No, a Russian citizen—"

"Have you not learned!" he said sharply. "Even my letter to your father imploring him to talk some sense into you didn't help?"

"My father? What do you mean?"

"I told him you were taking dangerous risks by involving yourself in the affairs of Russians. I suggested that he talk to you. He obviously did not, and now I must be the one to . . . how is it you Americans say? 'Knock some sense into you.' Yes?"

Quickly Cameron tried to assimilate this surprising information. He had written to her father? Why hadn't Keagan said anything? It would have been perfect fodder for him to browbeat her.

"All I want to know is where this prisoner is and how he is faring," she said, pushing all else from her mind.

"I cannot help you." He shook his head sharply. "No! I *will* not help you. For your protection as well as mine. That, Miss Hayes will be my last act of *friendship* toward you. That, and my not reporting this incident. In the future do not expect further leniency. I will report you. You will be deported again." He turned and strode to the second door, opened it, and stepped inside, not once looking back.

Cameron watched his exit in shock. She simply could not believe her last avenue of hope had ended with such finality. Robert immediately came to her side and put an arm around her.

"I am so sorry, Cameron."

"I was so sure he would help," she said dismally.

"You're trembling. Come on, let's go inside and warm you up."

She let him lead her back to the reception room. In a daze she sank down on a settee. Robert sat beside her, holding her hand.

"What am I going to do now?" she said, fighting back tears.

"Cameron, you're not going to let one little setback get to you, are you?"

She didn't want a pep talk. She wanted to wallow in her misery for a while. Everyone expected her to be the plucky one, the fighter. She didn't know if she had much verve left in her. Was it possible she'd used up all her miracles just getting to Moscow?

"Listen," Robert went on, "I know you've got faith in God. You have to trust that He is going to see this through. I can't believe God got you this far only to drop you into midair."

She knew he was right. She simply did not feel it. "Thank you, Robert. But I feel so . . . not hopeless, I suppose, just weak."

"I don't claim to be a paragon of Christian wisdom," he answered gently, "but I believe it is all right to be weak. Isn't that when God can truly be powerful within us? The Scripture says that when we are weak, then we are made strong, does it not?"

Her lips twitched into a small smile as she remembered back to when she had first given her heart to God. "Yes . . ." she murmured. "That was one of the first things I learned about faith in God, one of the first promises I truly claimed."

"There you go!" He pressed her hands between his. "God will help you. He will hold you up. And He will use other Christians to hold you. I will do what I can. And didn't you once tell me your sisters were Christians? You have them, too. It is no small miracle that they are here with you now."

She nodded, trying to grasp the gift he was offering. She brushed her hands across her face, pushing back the tears that had started to rise in her eyes.

They sat in silence for a few minutes before she said, "Robert,

I mustn't keep you from the party. I know you are expected to be present."

"Why don't you come with me? It will help you get your mind off these things."

"No, I'm not dressed. Maybe I'll catch my sisters when it's over." As Robert rose and headed for the door, Cameron had a change of mind. "Wait! I will go, after all. No sense sitting here and wallowing in self-pity any longer than I have to."

But she couldn't enter into the gaiety of the party, and though Robert would have stayed by her side, she insisted that he mingle with the guests. She had monopolized him far too long. Standing alone, she looked around for her sisters. Blair and Gary were in the center of a small group of diplomats. She recognized the Swiss chargé d'affaires and his wife and Ambassador Smith's wife among the group. In another part of the room Jackie was talking and laughing and sipping punch with a handsome Naval officer, the same one who had delivered Cameron's message earlier. She didn't want to disturb them while they seemed to be having such a good time. She stood idly, thinking twice about her decision to join the party.

A young servant approached her with a tray of drinks.

"Refreshments, madam?" he said with a thick Russian accent.

"No, thank you." But the minute she spoke the words she noted an extremely odd look on his face. An intensity that was quickly followed by an almost imperceptible twitch of his eye toward the tray. She had no idea what it meant, but she knew better than to ignore mysterious gestures, if indeed that's what this was. She took a glass of punch from the tray. The waiter's hand flickered toward his pocket so quickly she almost missed the movement. Then he took a cocktail napkin from the tray and handed it to her. She took it, and he turned and strode away.

The napkin crunched in an odd way. She wasn't surprised to find a small slip of paper hidden beneath the napkin. Surreptitiously, she slipped the paper, wrapped in the napkin, into her pocket. She would look at it as soon as she was alone. What could it be? Had Tiulenev changed his mind? She was dying to get away, but just as she turned to leave, Blair spotted her and drew her into the group.

———

It was midnight before the party wound down and the three sisters found themselves climbing the stairs to Blair's apartment. As so often seemed the case, the elevator wasn't working.

Bounding into the apartment, they were gasping for air. Gary, who was hardly affected at all by the physical exertion, laughed at them. "Hey, you don't want our Russian servants to think American women are puny fragile sorts!"

"I don't care!" gasped Blair. "If they don't fix that elevator soon, I'm going to stage a revolution of my own."

"It kind of invigorated me," quipped Jackie. "I'm ready for another round of dancing."

"It wasn't the climb," said Blair. "I think it was that dashing sailor you want to get back to."

Jackie turned beet red.

"Oh, Jackie," said Blair, "why are you embarrassed? You snagged the most handsome man there—well, the second most handsome man," she added with a wink at her husband.

The women plopped down, Jackie and Cameron on the sofa and Blair on the big upholstered chair. They kicked off their shoes and tucked up their legs, truly relaxing for the first time that evening.

"Does anyone want a drink?" offered Gary. When everyone chorused an enthusiastic yes, he asked, "Cold or hot?" All agreed on tea.

"Thank you, Gary," Blair said sweetly as he disappeared into the kitchen. "Isn't he a gem?" Then she turned back to Jackie. "So . . . tell us everything. Who is that lovely man? Are you going to see him again?"

Jackie mused that her sister had changed in so many ways that it was difficult to remember she was still the same in other ways. She was deeper, more thoughtful than in the past, but she still had her shallow side. Not that there was really anything wrong with that. Why not unwind and act like girls at a slumber party for a change? They couldn't always be steeped in troubles and angst. Maybe even Cameron would be grateful for a few lighter moments. She was looking pale, even bedraggled. They would talk about it soon enough, but for now she might like to think of another's woes.

So Jackie made the sacrifice despite the blush that kept heating her cheeks. "I made an absolute fool of myself tonight," she confessed. "I behaved like a kid. No, when I was a kid, I didn't act like that. I don't know what came over me!"

Cameron chuckled, and Jackie thought she'd made the right choice in diverting the conversation to her love life. "I know what came over you," Cameron asserted, "the cutest sailor I have ever seen. But I don't think he thought you were in any way a fool. He seemed equally taken with you, my dear sister."

"Yes, he was," agreed Blair. "I saw other women drooling over him, but they couldn't get within a mile of you two. Who is he?"

"His name is Captain Troy Rigdon," Jackie said. "He's an assistant Naval attaché, I guess Gary's counterpart in the Navy. He's twenty-eight years old, an Annapolis alumni, and he's from Pennsylvania. His father is a congressman. And he is a Christian. I don't know . . . what else is there?"

"What's your verdict of the fellow?" asked Cameron.

"Well, I don't feel like running in the other direction. I guess that says something."

"Indeed it does," Blair said with enthusiasm. "You could do a lot worse."

Jackie cringed inwardly. It seemed to her that Blair had put a bit too much emphasis on the words *a lot*. She seemed to come just short of implying that Jackie *had* done a lot worse when she had married Sam. But she shook away the thought. The important thing was that Blair *hadn't* said she'd done worse. Jackie wasn't going to stir old tensions, not now when she and Blair had been getting along so well.

Gary entered with a tray of tea things. "Who's that you're

talking about? Troy Rigdon?" He set the tray on the coffee table.

"I'll take it from here," Blair said as she rose and began pouring tea.

"Do you know him?" asked Cameron.

Gary turned a straight-backed wood chair around and sat straddling it. "I've met him. Seems a nice fellow. Very personable."

"So you approve of his dating your sister-in-law?" Blair asked coyly, handing him the first cup of tea.

"Wait a minute!" protested Jackie. "Who said anything about dating?"

"You're not seeing him again?"

Heat flushed Jackie's cheeks again. "Well ... ah ..." She couldn't help a quick glance at Cameron. Suddenly she lost her confidence about this whole silly topic of conversation. After all, they weren't here on some lark. Meeting men, *dating* men, for heaven's sake! It seemed too incongruent with the seriousness of their main intent.

Cameron instantly perceived her dilemma. "Jackie, you are in Russia! This is the adventure of a lifetime. Yes, there are some serious things facing us here, but no one wants or expects you to drag around like you're at a wake. I want you to see as much of the country as you can, and if you have a handsome sailor on your arm as you do so, all the better. You may as well enjoy yourself while you are here. I know you'll be there when I need you. I know where your heart is." She took in both Jackie and Blair, with a glance toward Gary, as well. "My quest is going to take time. You all have my permission—if you think you need it—to go about your lives, to have a good time if it comes along. Please!"

Jackie twisted around to hug her sister. She had to sniff back tears.

"Now, Jackie," Cameron asked wryly, "are you going to see this Captain Troy again?"

Jackie nodded. "Since it's all right with you. He wanted to take me sightseeing tomorrow. But please don't make so much of it." She couldn't resist a pointed look toward Blair. "It's not a big deal, honestly. I'm sure he is just wanting to be polite."

"Uh-huh . . ." Blair responded skeptically. "Polite."

"You be careful of smooth-talking sailors, sis," Gary added, the sage judgment of an Army man.

"But if he doesn't work out," Cameron said, "I could try to fix you up with my friend Robert Wood. He's a very decent guy."

"I met him," said Jackie. "He did seem nice." She may as well have yawned as she spoke the words.

"Oh, I've met Robert Wood," put in Blair. "Nice is the right word for him. But notice that Jackie's eyes didn't sparkle when she spoke of him like they do when she talks about Troy. Robert Wood doesn't hold a candle to the stunning captain."

"If looks are all that interest you," said Cameron with the barest edge to her voice.

"That is so rude of us, Cameron," apologized Jackie, "especially since he is your friend. To be honest, I was kind of rude to him when I met him. I'm going to apologize to him the first chance I get."

"What did you do?" asked Blair.

"I ignored him after I met Troy."

"Jackie," Cameron said patiently, "Robert isn't going to sulk around with hurt feelings because you slighted him. He is far too much of a man for that."

Jackie gave a self-deprecating laugh. "One handsome man pays me some attention, and I get a head bigger than one of those onion domes out there. That's what I mean about the fool I have been acting like."

"Don't worry about it," soothed Cameron. "You deserve some attention. And don't worry about Robert. He's a big boy."

"I certainly won't demean him by apologizing for something that he probably didn't even realize happened."

"You are going to see Troy tomorrow, aren't you?" asked Blair.

"Sure. Why not?"

But inside, Jackie was indeed trying to find some reasons why not, and she couldn't. She couldn't find one thing wrong with Captain Troy Rigdon.

22

ROBERT WOOD ushered Cameron into his office. Looking around, she saw he was alone.

"You did want me to meet someone, didn't you?" she asked.

"He's been detained," Robert said. "Have a seat." His tone was rather formal.

Cameron didn't know him as well as she would like, but she knew him well enough to realize this was the way he got when tense. Normally he was warm and personable.

"Robert, what's going on?" she probed. "I'd rather hear it from you than from some stranger."

She sat in the chair adjacent to his desk. There was a leather sofa in the room, which, with a couple of leather chairs and a coffee table, formed a small sitting area, all very nicely appointed. This was a new office and far nicer than the one she remembered from before. Robert had indeed become important at the embassy. He resumed his seat behind his desk. This was not going to be a friendly meeting. Cameron couldn't understand it.

She pressed on like a persistent puppy who could not let go once she got her teeth around a bone. "Have I pushed our friendship too far? I know I have. I am sorry—"

"Goodness! Cameron, no!" Shaking his head dismally, he

added, "I'm the one who should be sorry. I'm hiding behind this desk, I suppose, behind the austerity of my office. Trying to, at least. It's not working."

Robert glanced at his watch, then rose. "It's time," he said. "Do you care for a stroll in the park?"

She understood, of course, that they couldn't talk freely in his office. She got up, and they left the office and the embassy and walked down the street to a park adjacent to the Kremlin. Cameron thought it was called Alexander Park.

She couldn't enjoy the sunny summer morning nor the tree-lined grassy paths. She was still disturbed by Robert's behavior. Unable to wait any longer for answers, she asked, "Robert, why do you feel so responsible for what happened to Alex?"

With a determined sigh, he answered, "It was I who got him hooked up with U.S. intelligence."

"U.S. intelligence!" she repeated, stunned.

"That's who you will soon meet. The head of the Moscow station. I am cowardly enough to have hoped his presence would deflect my own culpability. He's not the most likable fellow, so I thought maybe you would hate him instead of me."

Cameron was silent as she assimilated this astounding information. Alex was involved with American intelligence? How could that be? He was not a political man. He'd joined the Communist Party out of rebellion toward the capitalist nation that had revoked his medical license and his life. He would never become involved in spying, especially against Russia. He loved Russia.

"I can't believe this, Robert," she murmured.

"I met your Alex. I can see how this is hard to fathom. After a single meeting I could tell he was a decent, honorable man." He shook his head dismally. For the first time since knowing him, Robert looked old, at least as old as his thirty-five years. The creases around his eyes and lips stood out, and his eyes seemed darker than usual. "I could have ended it before it began. I told myself he ought to have the right to choose for himself, but I knew the temptation would be too great for him to choose any other way."

"What temptation?"

Before Robert could answer, a man approached them. Robert introduced Larry Marquet to Cameron. Cameron hoped he never had to do undercover work, because his appearance glared "intelligence agent." He was about five feet eleven, built solid and muscular. Otherwise, his looks were nondescript, so perhaps he could pass as a spy.

Marquet studied Cameron for a long moment. If she were anyone else, she might have squirmed under the sharp, almost lurid, appraisal. Her stomach knotted, but he couldn't see that. She made sure all he could see was her steady gaze returning his. He had hardly spoken a word beyond a perfunctory greeting, but she already knew she wasn't going to like him. When he nodded as if in approval of her, she had the strongest urge to kick him in the shins.

"It all adds up now," Marquet said slyly, a small grin on his face.

"Funny, nothing adds up to me," Cameron replied without humor.

"Well, I know now why our Alex took the risks he did." Marquet arched a brow. "Who could ever blame him?"

"Tell me about those risks, Mr. Marquet," she said sharply. "Tell me how he got involved with you."

"There are certain matters of national security—" Marquet began.

"Tell her!" Robert demanded.

"Okay, okay!" Marquet gave a disgusted grunt. "But none— I emphasize *none*—of this finds its way into any newspapers. You understand, Miss Hayes?"

"I understand," she conceded, though her tone was in no way conciliatory. She sensed to her very core this man was the enemy.

"It's very simple," Marquet said. "Your Dr. Rostov came to our attention when some sensitive material was discovered in a diplomatic pouch. Material from him that was being sent to you, as a matter of fact."

Cameron glanced at Robert for corroboration. It didn't sound like something Alex would do.

"It's true," Robert verified. "Alex admitted to it. He was passing information to U.S. intelligence from a Soviet friend of his who happened to be a nuclear physicist. He had hoped you would get it to the proper authorities. However, it never reached you."

Yes, she could see how Alex would be caught up in doing a favor for a friend.

"We thought," Marquet continued, "he held a position that would enable him to act as an agent-in-place for us. So we recruited him to perform a few sensitive tasks. I won't go into the details if you don't mind."

"Why? Why would he do that?" Cameron asked, still befuddled by it all.

"I thought that was obvious. To get out of the country. To get back to his . . . lady love."

"Marquet!" growled Robert. Cameron was a bit surprised by the protectiveness of his tone.

"Oh yes, by the way, I am sorry about what happened to him," Marquet added as an afterthought.

Cameron nearly lost control of her foot then. But this man deserved more than a kick in the shin.

"I want to be clear," Cameron said tightly. "You offered him the means for escape in exchange for doing certain tasks for you?"

"That's about it."

"How long did this go on?"

"Look, Miss Hayes, Alex knew the risks—"

"How long?" She spit each word like a nail.

"That's not important—"

"We first made contact with him in September of '46," Robert replied.

She let out a sharp breath. "That's almost a year!"

"So?" Marquet practically challenged.

"What promises did you make him?"

"That is between him and me."

"It's between you and me now, Marquet," Cameron intoned evenly, as even as the edge of a blade. "What promises?"

"I have already told you far more than I have to—"

Cameron glanced at Robert. "Do you know, Robert?"

"I'm afraid I don't," he replied. "I was not involved beyond that first meeting. I'm sorry."

Cameron eyed Marquet, trying to skewer him with a single glare. She supposed knowing these things really didn't matter, but she still had to know. Learning the truth seemed to be the only thing she could do for now.

"I've been trained in resisting interrogation, Miss Hayes," Marquet said. "Do you think one angry look is going to make me spill my guts? It is very unfortunate that your boyfriend was arrested. But as I said before, he knew the risks every step of the way. He thought they were worth it in order to get to America, to be with you, to practice medicine. It didn't work out for him." He shrugged. "It's a real shame, for him and for us. We lost a great deal with his arrest. Do you realize many are predicting war with the Soviet Union within two years? In that short time we will never be able to find another agent-in-place as valuable as Rostov."

Cameron saw that Alex was no more than a commodity to this man. Appealing to him on any emotional level wasn't going to do any good.

"Tell me what you have done to aid him since his arrest," she said coldly, forcing all feeling from her voice and her expression.

"Aid him?" He chuckled dryly. "You jest, of course. There is absolutely nothing we can do."

"Think again, Marquet," she replied. "You promised to get him out of the country. That's what you are going to do."

"Not while he is in a Soviet gulag, lady! We can't touch him there. He's a Soviet citizen."

"Don't worry about that. You just get documents prepared

211

for him and work out a route of escape after he gets out of prison."

"Are you giving me orders?" he sneered.

"No," Robert put in quickly, "I'm giving you the orders."

"I don't think even you can, Wood."

"The game is wide open," said Robert. "At this moment in Washington the entire intelligence service is being reorganized. For all practical purposes, there is no official intelligence service right now. You work for the embassy, Marquet. The ambassador is your boss. Shall we go to him about this?"

"All right! Don't get your underwear in a bundle!" Marquet shot back with a roll of his eyes. "But don't either of you forget, I'm not the bad guy here. I'm a patriot working for the good of my country. Have you thought that if I could have gotten him out of the country, I would have done it before? It is not easily done, even with the material Alex himself passed to us."

"We'll give you the benefit of the doubt," Robert said. "Just work on getting the proper documents."

"You have some time," added Cameron, "while we organize an escape plan."

"And exactly how do you think you will do that?" asked Marquet.

"Aren't you glad it's not your problem?" Cameron hedged. She didn't want to admit she hadn't a clue.

"I best get to work then." Marquet started to turn, then paused. "It was enchanting to meet you, Miss Hayes," he added with a sneer before striding away.

When she was alone once more with Robert, or as alone as one could be in a Moscow park, she said, "Your plan worked, Robert. I don't hate you at all. But Marquet . . ."

"It wouldn't be a good idea to alienate the man. We need him. He *says* it is impossible for us to get to someone in a Russian prison, but I expect he knows more regarding this than he let on. He may come in handy for us yet."

"Us, Robert? How involved can you get? We don't want it turned into an international incident."

"No, the president of the United States would frown on that."
He smiled. "I can't act in any way on behalf of the embassy, I am
sorry to say, but I will do anything I can as a friend. We'll have
to wade through the fine details when they come along. The line
is very fine, I'm sure, but not impossible to cross."

"Thank you so much."

"What's next?"

"I'm going to take a metro ride," she replied. "I'll let you
know if it leads anywhere."

———

The note Cameron had received at the embassy party contained an address and a day and time. It had been written in
familiar handwriting—Sophia's fine script. Cameron's heart had
raced hopefully when she saw that, and now even the tense meeting with Marquet could not dampen her excitement. Even if
Sophia knew nothing about Alex, just to see her dear friend
would be wonderful.

"This is exciting," Blair exclaimed as she jockeyed for standing room on the train. "Are you sure we're on the right train?"

"Unless that fellow at the newspaper stand purposely led us
astray," Cameron replied, grasping an overhead rail as the train
lurched into motion.

"Or didn't understand you."

"Well, that's possible, too." Even with her improved Russian,
there had been a few gaps in communication. "I'm glad you came
along. At least we'll be lost together."

"I'm glad I insisted." Blair grinned.

Cameron had stopped by Blair's apartment after the meeting
in the park. She thought Blair should know about the conversation with Marquet. He'd said not to print anything about it but
made no mention of not telling her sisters! Also, she wanted to
tell her about going to see Sophia, for there had been no opportunity to do so the night before. Blair and Jackie had seriously
rearranged their lives to be here with her, so she wanted to
include them as much as possible. Jackie was off with Captain

Rigdon at the moment, but Cameron reasoned correctly that Blair might be growing restless and bored.

Blair's suggestion that she accompany Cameron, that a random shopping trip would look less suspicious with them together, might have come from that boredom. But it made sense, as well.

Once they reached the Arbat, finding the address was still going to be a task. There were no maps in Russia, or at least none that Cameron had been able to get her hands on. During the war she had thought the purpose was to befuddle the Germans. Now she realized the Soviet government wanted to befuddle everyone!

Nor could Cameron ask directions. She was still being followed, so her outing had to appear random. She had to assume the address was a place of business because Sophia would know the dangers of going to a residence. When she asked Robert before leaving him a couple of hours ago, he could only guess it might be in the Arbat district. The street name looked like one on which he thought several bookshops were located. Thus, she and Blair took the metro to the district and began their meander in and out of shops. They made a number of purchases and were able to innocently inquire of the location of bookshops. This at last led them to the location on the note. They had about twenty minutes to spare.

"Do you speak English?" Cameron asked the proprietor, a small bell overhead having announced their entry. It was a small bookshop, very cluttered, with several tall shelves of books and the musty fragrance that went with them.

He shook his head. "No English."

Cameron thought she would need to kill time before Sophia's arrival so she attempted a conversation in Russian. "Do you have a first edition of *Anna Karenina*?"

"I wish I did. It would be very expensive. You are American, yes?"

Cameron nodded.

The shopkeeper went on. "You might find something of interest toward the back." He pointed casually.

"Spasiba," Cameron said.

She gestured for Blair to follow her back to where the man had pointed.

"You are managing pretty well with the language," Blair said. "Did I tell you that Gary and I have acquired a Russian teacher?"

Cameron hardly heard her sister, for when she turned a corner of bookshelves, she saw her friend. It took everything in her not to squeal with delight and fling her arms around Sophia. But she dared not attract attention. She merely grinned and her friend grinned back. Then she looked around, saw there were no windows in this area of the store and no one but Blair around, so she did what she wanted to do. She threw her arms around Sophia in a warm embrace.

"Oh, Sophia! I am so happy to see you, I'm gonna cry," she exclaimed.

"I know how you dislike crying," Sophia replied, her own voice shaky.

"T-too late!"

They held on to each other for a long moment before Cameron remembered her sister.

She stood back and dashed a hand across her damp eyes. "Sophia, this is my sister Blair."

"I am so happy to meet you," responded Sophia with deep sincerity. "You are the sister who was in the Philippines, yes?"

"Yes, that's me," answered Blair. "And I am pleased to meet you, Sophia. Cameron has spoken so highly of you."

"I have few dearer friends. She said you are a movie star. I have never met a real movie star."

"I don't think you have yet," Blair answered with a modest chuckle. "I only aspired to that once—not anymore."

"We have all changed, I think," said Sophia. "The war left nothing the same."

"Some of the changes were good. The best for me was that it led me to God. Cameron tells me you helped her find her path to God."

"I am honored she thinks of me in this way. Knowing Cameron brought me closer to God, too."

Cameron laughed. "I was that much of a trial!"

"Oh, I did not mean—" Sophia responded, flustered.

"I'm sorry, Sophia," Cameron put in quickly. "I forgot you are not exposed to American humor much."

"Yes." Sophia laughed with her friend to show her feelings were not hurt. "I used to be much more on my toes. How I wish we could have time to spend together like we used to! The shopkeeper is a friend, so until we hear the bell over the door ring, we can be fairly free, but it still isn't like when we used to talk for hours in your room. We cannot sit together over a cup of tea anymore."

Cameron sighed as she came face to face with reality. Boris Tiulenev had recently remarked that it was dangerous to have friends in Russia. What a pitiful reality that was!

"We don't have much time," Cameron said regretfully. "You know about Alex, don't you?"

"Yes. I am so sorry, Cameron. I know that doesn't help. I wish I could do more."

"I know it is as hard on you as it is on me." Cameron turned to Blair and explained, "The Fedorcenkos are like family to Alex. Sophia is like a little sister, and her father, Yuri, is very much like a father to Alex."

"This loss touches us all deeply," Sophia said.

"Loss?" Cameron repeated, feeling a hollowness inside. "You don't mean it in that way, do you, Sophia?"

"No . . . no . . . of course not. I try so hard not to lose hope."

Cameron knew they were not only talking about Alex.

"You have never heard from Oleg, then?"

Sophia dismally shook her head. "Nothing. There are many Russians who were German POWs now in gulags. When they were liberated in Germany right after the war, they were brought back here, only to be incarcerated once again. Stalin says there are no prisoners of war, only traitors. What hope does that offer for my Oleg?" She sniffed back tears, and Blair handed her a handkerchief. Dabbing at her eyes, Sophia added, "But it might be better for Alex. He is a political prisoner. As long as they think he has information—" She broke off and started again. "My father has learned that he is in Lubyanka. They still have not moved him. This could be good."

"It will make him easier to get to." Cameron was glad the conversation had been diverted. She would never cease to feel self-recrimination over Oleg's arrest. "Sophia, I have wanted to share something with you for the longest time. I don't know if Alex ever told you, but he and I were married in Germany just before the war ended."

"Married!" she cried, her eyes lighting up, the pall of her own husband's arrest lifting temporarily. "I am so pleased to hear this. You know, when Alex was away and we were fairly certain his unit would be in Germany, I prayed that somehow you would meet. I thought for sure you would be where the war was hottest."

"Your prayers were answered. He is my husband—" Suddenly her voice broke as joy and fear collided within her.

Sophia now embraced her friend. "We *must not* give up hope!"

"I won't if you won't." Cameron sniffed, and with a wan smile Sophia handed her Blair's hankie.

"My father has felt so helpless over Alex," Sophia said. "When he heard you were in the country, he thought he might at least help you in another way. He went to your half brother's father to try to convince him to see you."

"And?"

"No success yet. The man refused, but my father thought there was a little waver in his tone. Papa thinks the idea that Semyon has a right to decide for himself is beginning to take root."

"So Semyon still knows nothing of any of this?" asked Blair.

"No. His father is very protective of him."

"I don't suppose you will tell us the man's name?" asked Cameron.

"I cannot. My father gave his word to the man."

"I understand. Just thought I'd try."

"My father will keep trying."

"I don't want him to get into trouble over this."

"He won't."

Cameron wondered at the confidence in Sophia's voice. In Russia one could get into trouble for sneezing. Yet Yuri Fedorcenko had in his life dodged not only Soviet "bullets" but tsarist ones, as well. If Cameron didn't know any better, she might think the man led a charmed life. Only God knew why Dr. Fedorcenko remained safe in a world where everyone was in danger.

23

Stanislav Tveritinov looked at his wife with rare tenderness. It wasn't that he did not often feel tenderness toward her, but he had learned long ago to keep his emotions under a tight rein.

That rein was loosening with each day, each moment. Tveritinov could feel his neat, tidy world slipping away from his control.

"I'm sorry, Mathilde," he said. "I thought I could contain this. But now I must tell you."

"What? You look like the world is ending. Is the situation in the Ukraine worse? Will they finally reinstate you to where you belong?"

These last two years after the war had been hard for Russia but particularly so for Ukraine, which had sustained some of the worst fighting of the war and had suffered years of Nazi occupation. Millions of Ukrainians dead; hundreds of towns and cities destroyed. Forty percent of the Ukrainian economy lost. On top of all that, one of the worst droughts in Russian history had plagued the region, setting off a terrible famine. Khrushchev, as head of the Communist Party in Ukraine, had in his bombastic way promised sweeping relief of these problems to his subjects and to his leader, Stalin. When he had failed to deliver, he was lucky to survive with his head intact. Instead, Stalin stripped him of his Party leadership, and Khrushchev was forced into exile. He was now at his dacha outside Moscow recovering from a serious illness, an illness Tveritinov feared had been brought on by his political reversals.

Tveritinov, one of Khrushchev's closest advisors, had followed his boss into obscurity, thankful that he, too, had not only survived with his life but also with relative freedom. He and his wife had moved back to Moscow to be nearer to their son, Semyon. Rumors were now afoot that Khrushchev was trying to worm his way back into Stalin's good graces. The last time Stanislav had spoken to Khrushchev, only a few weeks ago, he had hinted that they would soon return to power in the Ukraine.

"I wish politics were my only problem," Stanislav said to his wife after a long thoughtful pause.

"I know you have chafed, sitting here in Moscow with so little to do," she said.

"That may soon end," he sighed, "but that is not what troubles me."

"What is it, then?" Her brow knit with concern. She was a beautiful woman, though her hair was now completely gray, and fine lines around her mouth and eyes marked the turmoil of her life. She'd been the child of aristocracy before the Revolution, and the refinement of her birth showed clearly in her bearing and the gentility of her speech. He had always wondered how such a woman could have loved a coarse miner such as he. True, when they met he had already risen to the position of a superintendent in the Ural mining district. But he was from humbler beginnings than she. The men in his family had always been miners. He was the only one to have risen literally out of the black depths.

He told her then everything about Zharenov, who had arranged the adoption of their son, and about the encounter with Dr. Yuri Fedorcenko several years ago. With great reluctance he also told her about the most recent visit from Fedorcenko, when the man had told Tveritinov that members of Semyon's birth family were in Russia once more and hoping to meet the young man.

Mathilde stared at him in silent shock. Many years ago she had lost her own birth child to scarlet fever. His death had nearly broken her, because of her love for the child, of course, but also because she had known at his birth that she would not be able to bear more children. She had fallen into a deep depression, relieved only by the adoption of Semyon. She had let this child fill the void left in her heart by the death of the other. She had nearly cracked again when Semyon had announced that he was being assigned to the Front during the war. Stanislav and Semyon had tried to protect her by lying, saying that he would be in the rear echelon of the fighting. Tveritinov had never told her about the minor wound Semyon had received.

"Please say something, Mathilde," he implored when the silence stretched on for several minutes.

"Why did you keep this from me?" she finally responded, her tone harsh.

"It seemed pointless to worry you unduly. I am telling you now."

"Because now there is a point?" she said sharply. "Because now there is reason to worry?"

He shook his head. His next words were hard to admit. "Because I need your help. I don't know what to do."

She reached out and grasped his hand, all ire fading from her expression. She understood.

"Do you fear losing him?" she asked.

"Don't you?"

"I have feared losing him since the day he came into our home," she replied sadly. "But my fears were that he would die, not that his heart would be stolen away by his blood family."

"Could that happen?" he asked plaintively. For as much as his wife had suffered with the loss of their first child, he too had suffered, though he had never dared reveal the true extent of his pain. But he had arranged the adoption of Semyon for his wife's sake, for her sanity. He had not believed that he would become attached to a child who was not his own. But he had.

He remembered the moment it had happened. The boy—he

had at that time always thought of Semyon as "the boy," little more than his charity case—had been with them about six months. During that time the child suffered from constant nightmares. Doctors were consulted, and it was then they realized that he not only did not want to talk about his past, but he had blocked it totally from his young mind. One day Stanislav came upon the boy sitting under a tree in the yard crying. Awkwardly Stanislav approached and asked what was the matter.

"I don't know, sir." Semyon shrugged.

"Young men should not cry unless it is a very severe matter." That's what Stanislav had learned. It was the only way he knew.

"I just feel all alone," admitted the boy.

"Are you afraid of being alone?"

The eight-year-old child merely nodded.

Stanislav continued. "Well, men do not fear being alone."

In a shaky voice Semyon muttered, "I-I'm n-not a man." He sniffed loudly and wiped a grubby hand across his tear-streaked face, leaving smudges of dirt in the place of tears.

Stanislav took out his handkerchief and tried to wipe away the dirt. "Your mother will be upset if you come in all messy."

"M-my mother?"

They had told him to call her Mother. Was he slow-witted as well as orphaned?

"Of course," Stanislav said, knowing no other response.

"She is not really my mother," the child said.

"Yes, she is, and you must never say otherwise to her, or you will break her heart. I can see she already loves you like a mother would."

Semyon nodded. "She has told me she loves me. That's not why I feel alone."

"Why then?"

"Something is missing."

"What?"

"I don't know. I dream of looking everywhere for it, but I can't ever find it. Mother comes in and comforts me when I wake crying from these dreams, and I like that. But that isn't what I'm looking for. I don't think I ever had a mother's love to miss it."

"Everyone has a mother," Stanislav replied reasonably enough.

"And a father?"

"Is that what you are missing?" Stanislav's heart began to quake. In six months he had never suggested that the boy call him Father. Somehow they had fallen into the use of *sir*. Stanislav knew little of the boy's history except he had been raised by his father, who had been arrested as a subversive. The trauma of being separated from this man had made him shut the memories from his mind. Semyon didn't realize that in his dreams he was probably searching for his father. But Stanislav knew, or he did now. The boy needed a father. Only when Stanislav embraced this notion and extended himself to the child did he realize how much he himself needed a son. The empty places in both of their hearts were filled by the other. When Semyon had first called Stanislav Father, the man had nearly wept. Semyon's nightmares had stopped for a while, too, and though they were to return periodically, it was never again as bad as in those first months.

The three had, over the years, melded into a close family. Stanislav could not believe their bonds could be destroyed so easily. But his wife's brow was now knit together in painful consideration of his question.

"Mathilde, don't tell me you have the slightest doubt of our son's loyalty toward us?"

"A mother's love, Stanislav," she answered, "they say there is nothing stronger."

"You are his mother!"

She rose from her chair. They had been seated in the parlor of their finely appointed Moscow apartment. She walked to the window, which looked out on a small park. It was green now with a bed of bright flowers in bloom. Mathilde loved to garden. In their dacha in the country she had a large flower garden that she tended herself, eschewing her husband's frequent suggestions for her to hire someone to help. They would be at the dacha now for the summer months, but Khrushchev had requested that he remain close to Moscow to be ready in case the call came for them to return to Kiev. He decided he would take Mathilde to the country on the weekend. The further away from Moscow now, the better. He'd figure out a way for his superiors to reach him.

After several moments of silence she said, "Find out who these people are, Stanislav, and have them deported. They must never meet him."

"What harm can they do? They cannot steal his love from us, can they? The mother deserted him. The father all but deserted him by placing his political fervor above the welfare of his son. Semyon could never embrace them because of that alone. Blood cannot win over all we have given him."

Dismally she shook her head. "He still has the nightmares."

"No, that stopped long ago."

"He hides it from you, from me, as well, except once shortly before he went away to war. I came upon him crying out in his sleep like he used to do when he was young. He is still haunted by his birth family—"

Outside the door of the parlor a floorboard creaked. Mathilde stopped suddenly and cast a fearful look at her husband.

The door opened and Semyon entered. "Mother? Father? What are you talking about?"

"And who taught you to eavesdrop behind closed doors, young man?" Stanislav countered irritably, hoping to cast a smokescreen over everything else.

"You didn't hear me knock on the front door," he answered. "So I came in. I have a key anyway. I heard voices. You never have this door closed."

"What did you hear?" Mathilde asked in a tremulous voice.

"Something about my birth family."

"That's all?" pressed Stanislav.

"What are you hiding from me?"

"Nothing. It is none of your business—" Stanislav began until he realized how ludicrous the words were.

Semyon picked up the trailing sentence. "It is my business,

though I have never asked about these things."

"You had good reason not to ask. Those things that happened before you came here were so terrible you shut them from your mind." And we let you do so, Stanislav thought. But was it now fated to be revealed? Was it no accident that after all these years Semyon should chance upon such a conversation between his parents? But when he looked upon his wife and saw her agonized expression, he knew this was not the time for revelations. "Look at your mother," he hedged. "Would you break her heart?"

Semyon ran a hand through his tight caramel-colored curls. His hair had grown out since the war. Stanislav hated to make the comparison, but his son looked a bit like the outcast Trotsky at times, at least when he let his hair go wild. But this wasn't the time to nag him, as he often did about his grooming.

"Listen, son," Stanislav said as gently as he could considering his pounding heart and throbbing head, "what you overheard was just idle speculation. We sometimes wonder if your choosing not to marry is because of the uncertainties about your past. We question if we could do more to better direct you in this area."

"Mother has a new girl for me to meet every week," Semyon said with a dry chuckle. "You are doing quite enough."

"My friend Galina has a daughter you haven't met," offered Mathilde. "She's very pretty."

"I have no objections to meeting her," Semyon said agreeably. "Especially if she's pretty. I'd like to find a wife, too, you know." He smiled amiably.

Stanislav was surprised at how easily the conversation was deflected. But then again, was it so surprising? None of them truly wanted to dig up the past, least of all Semyon.

———

Semyon cried out and woke, drenched in perspiration. The dreams were back. He'd had a few years' reprieve, at least since the war. He'd hoped that maybe he had finally chased away the demons that had haunted him since childhood.

It did not surprise him that this nightmare had come on the

heels of the encounter with his parents the previous evening. They had all tried to brush it cleanly under the carpet, Semyon most of all. He did not wish to know about the family of his birth, he never had, because he'd always realized the dreams were somehow related to them. And the dreams were terrifying.

He glanced at the clock by his bed. Five-thirty in the morning. No sense trying to go back to sleep.

Kicking off his covers, he rose and went to the bathroom. In the dim light of the bulb that hung over the sink he studied himself in the mirror. He needed a haircut. Proof that whatever was troubling his parents was serious if it had kept his father from harping at him over that need.

"You have an important position in the Party," his father told him all too often. "You should not go to work looking like a wild Cossack, or worse, Trotsky's twin. Cut your hair and shave that beard closer!"

Semyon rubbed a hand over the dark stubble on his chin. A day's growth on him looked like two days' on most men. But under it, his skin was sensitive to the scraping of the blade. He might try to rebel in these areas, but he always eventually did what his father asked. He was thirty-one years old, yet he still wanted little more than to please his father.

Why else had he not pressed him yesterday regarding the conversation about his birth family? Why had he hidden the fact that the dreams had never stopped haunting him? Why had he never once since coming to this home inquired about his past? In memory, this was the only family that had ever loved and nurtured him. If they withdrew that, he'd have nothing.

Once when he had still been a boy, about ten years old, he had remembered something of his past. An image had formed in his mind of a man who looked a lot like him. It had been a gentle face, smiling, eyes full of love. He'd known even as a child that it had been a real memory of something from his past. But it was so incongruent from the terror of his dreams that he did not understand it. And he did not want to understand it. So he pushed it from his mind, almost as completely as he had unconsciously pushed other memories away. Almost. For a long time he could call up that face at will if he chose to, not that he often did. Only the passing of years made that image grow dim, the details fuzzy.

But that's how it should be. He had no need of the past.

Except he knew, even if his parents had only guessed, that was why he had never started a family of his own. Each time he met a woman who might interest him, he found a reason to end the relationship just as it was on the verge of growing deeper. The uncertainties of his past seemed to make him fear the uncertainties of the future.

"Ah, Semyon, you are a fool!" he muttered as he turned on the faucet and splashed water onto his face.

Toweling off, he went to the front room where the kitchen and sitting area formed one room. It was a small room, a small apartment, but in Russia having his own apartment in a fairly decent area of Moscow signified he was quite well off. He filled a porcelain kettle with water and put it on the burner of the stove. He had most of the modern conveniences. No samovar, though. He didn't see the point for just one person. While the water came to a boil, he took a loaf of bread—good white bread, an expensive luxury—and cut off a couple of slices.

He had a good life. Why spoil that? As chief photographic editor of *Party Life,* the Communist Party journal, he had achieved one of his highest dreams. He helped shape Party propaganda. And though there were few photographs in Soviet newspapers, those they published came mostly from the free-lance work he did for the TASS news agency. Through these he liked to think he helped to shape the view the Soviet Union presented to the world. He was proud of his achievements, even if at times he might question the leadership of Stalin—only within himself, however, never in the public forum of his work. He believed Stalin had failed the Party and the country by refusing to mete out greater liberty as a reward for the sacrifices of the war. And though he wasn't stupid enough to voice these criticisms now, he hoped his rising favor in the Party would one day give him the power to right some of the wrongs he had witnessed and to enable the Communist Party to realize its full glory.

His father often talked of his days as a miner in the Urals, and he had spoken of the care that had to be taken not to dig too deeply into the earth for fear of releasing poisonous gases. Birds were often taken down into the mine to detect these gases, and if a bird dropped dead, the men knew to evacuate. Semyon perceived his own past like the depths of the mines. The dangers of digging too deeply were far too risky. If his parents knew something about his birth family, let the secret stay with them. He didn't need a past. He'd lived with the nightmares this long. Why couldn't he do so forever?

24

THE VEHICLE BOUNCED along the rutted muddy road. Jackie now began to understand why people often said Russia was better in winter. At least the snow and ice would fill in the potholes.

"I wish I could have ordered you up a tank for the ride," commented Troy with a wry chuckle.

"It's n-not t-too bad!" Jackie said, then laughed as her teeth jarred at a harsh jolt. "I'm just glad for an excursion so far out of town. I heard tourists weren't allowed to go more than sixty miles away from Moscow."

"Our destination is a bit less than that. I hope you'll think it is worth the effort."

"Tchaikovsky's house? Should be fascinating," Jackie responded with enthusiasm. She had been a little surprised when he had come that morning to pick her up and suggested a drive to the town of Klin, where Tchaikovsky had resided for a short time before his death.

The driver turned and spoke to Troy in Russian. They conversed back and forth a few moments.

"Andreyev says the road leading to the house is in pretty bad shape, and it would be best if we parked in town and walked the rest of the way, perhaps a ten-minute walk," Troy explained.

"That's fine with me," said Jackie. "I wore comfortable shoes.

By the way, I didn't know you spoke such good Russian."

"Our Naval attaché is very firm that his assistants have some knowledge of the language. Your brother-in-law would never have made the Naval requirements."

Jackie wasn't surprised to note the pride of service in Troy's tone. She thought it would be funny if she ended up with a military rival to Gary. As if she and Blair needed more tension between them.

Troy went on. "Most likely he received some special favor because of your sister's plight." Jackie had given him only brief details of her sister's reason for coming to Russia.

"Where did you learn the language?" she asked.

"My maternal grandmother is from Russia. I learned the rudiments from her, then when my background was discovered at the Academy, my superiors suggested that I build on my knowledge. Even then, before the war brought the Soviet Union and America to the forefront of world politics, it was deemed advantageous to have such a background. My father encouraged me, thinking of a career in the State Department for me. I was more interested in commanding battleships, but you do things for your parents, you know."

"Yes, I know. So do you like what you are doing better than commanding a ship?"

"I never got to command a ship." His tone was tinged with both regret and resignation. "But I like what I am doing. After hearing my grandmother's stories of the old country, I'm happy to finally see it for myself."

As he spoke, they came into the environs of a small town—what was left of it, at least. Rubble was everywhere, and many ruined buildings dotted the streets.

"The Germans occupied Klin for twenty-seven days," Troy said.

"It looks like they only recently left."

"I guess other places have priority for the money necessary for repairs."

Andreyev pulled to a stop in front of what looked like a tavern. It was one of the few whole buildings on the street. The passengers got out of the car, Jackie just missing a huge puddle by an inch. Troy hurried around to her side and gave her a hand. She realized she should have waited, for he was anxious to be the attentive host. Troy arranged a meeting time with the driver, because Andreyev was more interested in the tavern than in classical music. Troy also carried a small hamper with a picnic lunch.

Their destination was on the edge of town, and the road leading there was indeed very rough. One huge puddle nearly bisecting the road would have done serious damage to the car had they decided to drive. Jackie didn't mind the walk. Troy held her hand, ostensibly to aid her, as they almost literally danced around puddles and potholes. She liked the warmth of his strong hand around hers. She liked laughing with him each time they barely made it over large obstacles. It had been a long time since she had so enjoyed herself with a man. She wondered what was different about him.

Then she realized it with such a shock her foot didn't clear one puddle, landing instead with a splash. Troy flung an arm around her so that she didn't completely lose her balance.

"Thank you," she said breathlessly and forgot for a moment the previous revelation.

His closeness momentarily put everything else from her mind. His strong arm, gripping her close, lingered longer than necessary. She tingled all over, and when their eyes met, she knew he felt the same electric charge. His luminous blue eyes held her gaze for an extended moment. His sudden smile completely took away her breath. This was a magic she had not experienced in a long time.

But her previous thoughts came back with a sickening reality. She attempted a laugh to deflect the thud of the cruel truth. But her laughter rang hollow. Of course she was getting along with Troy. Of course it was magical and thrilling. Why shouldn't it be when they hadn't talked about anything serious since meeting? There had only been brief, superficial references to the war. She told herself there simply had not been an opening to let her talk of her loss or to mention she'd been married. What had they been talking about all this time since the party yesterday evening and during the hour-and-a-half drive to Klin? Troy seemed comfortable talking about his interests, mostly his recent experiences and what he knew about Russia. He needed little encouragement to talk about ships and other nautical topics. Nothing profound. She had never known she could talk about trivial things for so long!

What really jarred her was that there *had* been openings for more serious conversation. She had merely deflected them. She had made sure this man knew nothing of the things that were most important to her.

Couldn't it wait a bit longer? Couldn't she just *enjoy* the company of a man for another hour before it all had to crash and burn?

"Something wrong?" he asked a moment later. "I've never seen a smile turn to a frown so quickly."

There it was, the perfect opening. "No, nothing. Just . . . nothing, really."

I will tell him, but later. I want one day, that's all.

"We should be there in a minute. It's just beyond those trees."

In a few moments, as promised, the house came into view. It had the look of a Victorian manor house, though perhaps a bit simpler of line, with clapboard siding and two stories. By the standards of the Russian gentility of the 1890s when Tchaikovsky occupied the place, it was rather modest, but it was far grander than any of the peasant farmhouses they had passed along the road.

On entering the house after paying their admission fee, they saw it had been maintained with loving care. Though much of the furniture had been taken by the Germans and some of the wood paneling torn off to use as firewood, most of the interior still contained many original pieces, including Tchaikovsky's piano. They were greeted at the door by one of the composer's nephews, Davidov. Jackie noted from a photograph of the composer that his nephew bore a distinctive resemblance to the famous Russian. Mr. Davidov was a stately older man with a neatly trimmed gray beard and carried a natural elegance about him that spoke of a bygone age.

"Captain Rigdon, I am so glad you were able to come," he said in thickly accented English.

"I'm glad I called today instead of waiting until tomorrow," said Troy. Turning to Jackie, he explained, "I called him this morning to arrange a visit. But he plans to go away for a few days, so this was the only day we could come."

"I, too, am happy it worked out," said Jackie. "Mr. Davidov, Tchaikovsky was truly your uncle, then?"

"Yes, he was, and it has been my honor to assume the family business, as it were, of keeping his memory alive in Russia. It is our labor of love, yes?"

"Was this the family estate?" Jackie asked.

"No, it wasn't. My uncle rented this house a little more than a year before his death. But he wrote his sixth symphony here, so it seems fitting that here is maintained a tribute to him, perhaps Russia's most celebrated citizen."

Davidov invited them to hang their coats in a coatroom, and then he took them on a tour of the house. The ground floor had once been occupied by Tchaikovsky's servant and was closed to the public. The composer lived on the second floor. His grand piano dominated the reception area, which was bare of other furnishings except for a few chairs.

"We are in the process of collecting period pieces to bring the house back to as near its original condition as possible," explained Davidov.

There was a shelf in the reception room that Jackie found particularly interesting. It held an odd assortment of trinkets, mostly cheap souvenirs that Tchaikovsky was fond of collecting. One was a Statue of Liberty inkwell, which he brought back from his tour of America.

"I can just imagine him stopping at a vendor on Fifth Avenue and buying this," Jackie said. "It makes him seem more real, not merely a historical presence."

"That's an interesting perspective," replied Troy. Was there a hint of condescension in his tone?

"I guess it's silly, but it does make him more interesting to me. I suppose that's because I'm not much of a musical aficionado."

"Come, you will like this, then," said Davidov.

There was a curtained alcove right off the reception room, and upon entering, Jackie discovered a bedroom. It was an odd location for a bedroom, lacking privacy. Jackie wondered if the composer received many visitors. But the room was cozy, even warm. Davidov pointed out the satin coverlet on the bed and proudly related that it had been made by the composer's niece. On the carpet next to the bed was a pair of slippers, set in place as if ready at any moment to receive the feet of their owner. They were small enough to fit Jackie, so she was surprised to learn they had really belonged to Tchaikovsky. She didn't care what Troy said, she thought they gave a wonderful personal touch.

Davidov gestured to a table by the window. "This is where he finished the sixth symphony."

This appeared to interest Troy far more than had the Statue of Liberty inkwell. He ran a hand upon the wood surface, then stood gazing out the window for a long moment.

Next they were shown Tchaikovsky's study and the stately wood-paneled library, where Davidov was still in the process of cataloging many of the composer's manuscripts. When they returned to the reception area once again, Davidov had another surprise for Jackie.

"So, Captain Troy, you will please to honor us by playing something on my uncle's piano?" asked their guide.

Jackie gaped at her companion and was even more shocked when he smiled and nodded in response.

"That is so kind of you, Davidov," Troy said. Then he sat at the piano and began to play the famous composer's sixth symphony.

Jackie didn't know enough about music to judge his effort, but to her ear it was pretty good. She began to view her Naval officer in a new light. Not only was he a handsome, thrilling man, but now she saw there was a sensitive, creative side to him. A Renaissance man! She rather liked that.

She applauded him when he finished, and he blushed slightly.

"Stop, please!" he said with an awkward laugh. To Davidov, he said, "You don't know what it does for me to sit here and actually play where he played. I just hope if he's listening, he's not cringing too badly."

"I understand, my boy," Davidov said earnestly. "I know what it means to you."

Outside, the sound of an approaching vehicle could be heard as it crunched over the gravel. Glancing out a window, Jackie saw a school bus.

"I must tend to the children," Davidov said. "Please feel free to wander about. I noticed you brought a lunch. You may eat in the garden if you like. The children will be inside for at least an hour, so you will not be disturbed."

They took his suggestion and, retrieving their coats and the lunch basket, headed out, meeting a line of about thirty children on their way in. Jackie was torn between having a quiet, possibly romantic lunch with her date and joining the tour once again with the children, who were about the age of her own class at home. She would have loved to interact with a group of foreign children, but when she hinted of her interest, Troy showed no enthusiasm at all, and she thought it would be rude to desert him.

What was she thinking? She certainly did not want to abandon this wonderful man. She did decide, though, that she would try to visit some Soviet schools while she was in Moscow.

It had warmed up enough outside so that they could shed their coats. The clouds of the morning had finally parted, and now there was more blue in the sky than gray. The ground, however, was still damp from a rainstorm during the night, so they would not be able to spread a blanket on the grass for a traditional picnic. They contented themselves with a fairly dry wooden bench set among the shrubbery.

As Jackie nibbled on a sandwich, she commented, "You play

the piano wonderfully. I'm discovering you are a man of many talents."

"Hardly what I'd call talented," he said, oddly without modesty, but rather as if stating a fact. "I left music behind in order to live the adventure of the high seas."

"You've obviously had more than just a few lessons as a kid. I had some lessons as a child, and I can only play Chopsticks."

"Music has always been important in my family. My mother is a music teacher. She tried to groom me for greatness, but it was with my . . . brother that she was successful."

"Is he a professional musician?"

"He was very accomplished. He would have gone far. Tchaikovsky was his favorite composer. That's why I'm familiar with this place. When I come here, it makes me feel closer to him."

"He's passed away, then?"

Troy nodded, then added in a husky tone, "Killed in the war."

"I'm so sorry, Troy. I do understand your loss. My husband was killed in France." There, she'd said it—that much at least.

He reached out and grasped her hand, deep sympathy filling his vivid blue eyes. "I'm sorry for you, as well. Do you think the pain will ever go away? Sometimes I think I am finally able to deal with the grief, but then I think of him and it all comes back like the day I heard the news."

"Yes, it's the same for me. But doesn't visiting a place like this make it worse for you?"

"It makes me sad, but at the same time it gives me comfort. I know it would have given him great joy to visit here, and that gives me joy, also. That's why Davidov doesn't mind my playing the great man's piano. In a way I feel as if I am desecrating a holy place, yet at the same time I think of how thrilling it would be for Ron to sit on that stool and touch the keys where the world's greatest music was created. Somehow God uses it to lift me a little from my grief. Do you have something like this to help you?"

Immediately Jackie thought of Emi and how her daughter always brought her close to Sam, and how, instead of emphasizing her grief, Emi lifted her from it.

"I have a daughter," she said, her heart now pounding so against her chest that she was sure he could hear. "She's . . ." She barely breathed that word which was to begin her great confession.

Troy must not have heard, for he spoke over her word. "Wow! You are very lucky!" he said almost reverently, tenderly. "I wish Ron had had time to have children. It would be nice to have a nephew or niece around to remind me of him. But those dirty Japs ended his life before it had a chance to really begin. He was only eighteen when they killed him." His lip quivered into a sneer when he spoke the word *they*. The gentleness of his earlier tone hardened. "I know it's wrong to hate, but God forgive me, I can't help it. Maybe He will—forgive me, that is—because isn't it really evil I hate? The Japs' evil designs on the world brought so much ruin."

She wanted to tell him that Christ even forgave his own murderers, but she couldn't find her voice.

"I know that shouldn't matter," he went on, and she could clearly perceive his deep inner turmoil over these things. "The Lord says to love our enemies. Don't you feel the same way about the Germans?"

Oddly, Jackie had never once felt hatred toward the enemy who had killed her husband. Not because she was more saintly than the man seated next to her, but because she'd always felt the German soldiers had been doing their duty just as Sam had been. The true evil had been Hitler, but even him she didn't hate. However, Jackie understood Troy's emotions. She had faced the same reaction many times from others in the States, from her friends, from men she had tried to date. From her own sister. Yes, she understood very well.

She also understood that this would be the perfect opportunity to tell Troy about Sam and Emi.

"Oh, Jacqueline, I'm sorry," he said suddenly. "I've spoiled our day."

"No matter how much we try to avoid it," she said, "it always comes back to the war. It has scarred us all so deeply."

"Let's not talk about the war, then," he implored. "Let's forget about it, for now, at least."

"Can we?" she responded, her lip trembled with emotion because she knew she was not asking a question but making a request.

How could she continue to enjoy this man when he had actually said he hated the Japanese? If he ever met Emi, he would feel toward her as Blair did, though Jackie had always believed that Blair did not truly hate. She had been wounded deeply by the Japanese when she was captured in the Philippines, and it was going to take time to heal those wounds. In the same way the wounds of a nation would take time to heal. It must be the same for Troy. She could see he was a decent man despite his scars. Just as she wanted to be given a chance, shouldn't she also give him a chance?

So when he jumped up and took her hand, she rose to her feet and joined him.

"I want to show you something," he said, and he led her down a narrow path behind the bench. He paused before a patch of lilies of the valley.

"Why, they're beautiful."

"These were Tchaikovsky's favorite flower," Troy said. "These are believed to be the very ones he planted. I don't know, though. A lot has happened in almost sixty years."

"It is still nice to imagine they are the very flowers he gazed upon," she offered.

Troy grasped her hand. "I wish I could pick you some, but Davidov would probably not appreciate it."

He drew her close and slipped his arm around her waist. She didn't want to kiss him. She didn't want this relationship to progress to that point. She wanted to back away as he lowered his lips to hers. But just as she did not have the will to tell him about Sam, she could not resist the power of his closeness. He had but one glaring flaw that she could see, and she was willing to believe he had good reason for it. If she condemned every man for such a defect, she'd be alone for the rest of her life.

She didn't back away. For the moment she wanted to forget all the past and simply be held and kissed by a very desirable man.

His lips against hers were soft and warm, and as the kiss deepened and his arms wrapped completely around her, there was more than mere physical passion in their embrace. His intensity was caring and tender, and she returned it willingly.

25

Before Troy left Jackie at her hotel, he invited her to attend church with him on Sunday, two days from then. Jackie had wondered what she would do about church in a place like Russia. She had looked into a couple of the beautiful Eastern Orthodox cathedrals in Moscow and had found that, though quite beautiful with their rich icons and ornate altars, they were a bit cloying with heavy incense, not to mention that the services were conducted in Russian.

Troy said the best church for foreigners was the Church of St. Louis, an old French Roman Catholic church. It was made available to foreigners when the United States first opened diplomatic relations with the Soviets. An American priest and a French priest presented the services in English, French, and Russian. At present, the church was open to Russian citizens, but there were rumors afloat that the Soviets soon planned to close it to all but foreigners.

Sunday morning appeared bright and sunny; in fact the temperature had soared to nearly seventy-five degrees. Everyone decided to meet at the Metropole, since it was on the way to the church. Blair and Gary had decided to join Jackie and Troy, as did Cameron, who had invited her friend Robert Wood. Jackie was glad for the other companions. They kept her from melting completely to Troy's charms.

After their kiss in Klin, Jackie had been walking in the clouds. It had been the first time a man had kissed her since Sam. Later when she thought of it, she felt a little as if she were betraying Sam, yet mostly she thought he would be glad she was happy and moving on with her life.

Was she happy? Was that tingling feeling she experienced when she remembered Troy's touch a sign of happiness? Could she be happy with Troy? He was so good-looking and decent, as well. And she knew her father would be thrilled with a son-in-law like Troy. It had always stung Jackie to see her father so taken with Gary, when Sam had been every bit the man Gary was. Would it be wrong for her to look for a man who would win her father's approval?

But was the real reason she felt she was betraying Sam because of Troy's feelings about the Japanese? Once again she tried to convince herself that if she ruled out every man who was the least bitter toward the Japanese, she'd have no one to choose from. Most eligible men her age had fought the Japanese and were sure to feel some animosity toward them. It didn't necessarily mean they would hate Emi. Even her father loved Emi, and he had never made any bones about his feelings toward the Japanese in general.

At least she could give Troy a chance, though that would mean she had to tell him about Sam and Emi. She felt confident she had not misjudged the man to such an extent and determined she'd tell him after church.

The service was long, spoken in three languages, and she didn't get much out of it, partly because she was unfamiliar with the Catholic liturgy but mostly because she couldn't concentrate. Troy's nearness and the prospect of what she planned afterward kept her thoughts in a whirl.

What struck her most about the service was that the church was jammed with Russians. The few pews in the building had been saved for the foreign worshipers, but all standing room was filled with Russians. Jackie had heard so much about atheistic Communism that she expected little interest in religion among the people. Cameron had said the churches were packed during the war, and now, two years later, it appeared still to be the case. It warmed her heart to see religion was not as dead in the Soviet Union as the government wanted one to think. She had never before seen worshipers kneel on the floor and touch their foreheads to the ground in contrition, as several Russians did during the service. Some even made their way to the altar on their knees, which appeared to be sincere rather than a customary form of worship.

Jackie had hoped Cameron would be able to get them into one of the underground churches that Cameron had attended when she had been in Russia before. Unfortunately, Cameron said it was now too dangerous for that.

At the end of the service they exited through the throngs of Russians. It had been a never-to-be-forgotten experience, but Jackie didn't feel completely refreshed spiritually. She hoped if they were to be in Russia much longer, she could find a church more of the kind to which she was accustomed.

Blair invited everyone to her apartment for luncheon. Robert regretfully declined because he had a previous engagement with the ambassador. Everyone else accepted, though Jackie was determined do what she had to do before lunch. She could not put it off another hour and thus mentioned to Troy that she would like to take a little walk with him.

To her sister she said, "Blair, do you mind if Troy and I get there in about a half hour? I . . . uh . . . want to talk with him a bit first."

Blair grinned knowingly. "I'll never have everything ready that fast anyway, even with our Russian cook helping. Why don't we say we'll eat in an hour?"

Everyone else departed in the embassy car while Jackie and Troy headed off on foot. It wasn't that far to the embassy.

She couldn't have chosen a finer day for a stroll, and when Troy took her hand, she almost decided to let it be just that. His hand was large and warm as it enveloped hers, and his touch reminded her of that kiss and made her think how much she wanted him to kiss her again. In the romantic haze of her vision she pictured how their conversation would go.

"So, you see, Troy, my husband was Japanese. And, of course, so is our daughter. Look at her picture. Isn't she sweet?"

"She is as beautiful as her mother!"

"I'm sorry I didn't tell you sooner."

"I understand."

"And you don't mind—about Sam and Emi, that is?"

His eyes shimmering with tender caring, he would reply, "Of course not! I love you. How could I not love your child! I know she has nothing to do with those who were our enemy."

Back to reality, Jackie, she told herself. But she couldn't help gazing up at Troy with renewed hope.

"I've thought a lot about you since Klin," he said. "I was worried . . . after, you know . . . that you would think me too forward. But I truly could not help myself." He gazed down on her now as if he might kiss her again, right there on the sidewalk!

"I liked it, too, Troy," she replied, her heart racing for several different reasons, least of all because of her plan to tell her secret to him. She was close to scrapping that idea altogether.

"I'd like to be alone with you again right now," he said. His hand tightened around hers. "I'd kiss you right here, but these Russians are odd birds. They might arrest us if we did."

"Well . . ." She came just short of lifting her lips closer to his. But she had *some* good sense left. "Maybe it's for the best," she murmured with little conviction. "Things are going rather quickly."

"I feel the press of time," he answered. "You won't be here forever. Do you think two people could fall in love this quickly?"

The word *love* yanked her back to reality with the force of an atomic blast. He couldn't love her. She didn't love him. But . . . maybe she could.

Not until he knows about Sam. She didn't know if those words came from her own thoughts or from outside herself. But she knew they were true.

"Troy, I must tell you something." Each word was an effort of will.

"I knew it!" he exclaimed. "I've spoiled it by rushing things, haven't I?"

"No, it's not that. I haven't told you everything about myself. It probably won't matter, but whatever is to happen between us has to be built on honesty. Right?" He nodded, and she felt a small pang of disappointment. Had she really hoped he would tell her to forget honesty? Reaching into her pocketbook, she took out the small photos she carried with her, one of Sam in his Army uniform and the other a recent one of Emi. "I guess a picture is worth a thousand words," she said almost glibly. "Those are of my husband and daughter."

He took the photos. The one of Sam was on top. Jackie had never seen such a complete transformation of a person's expression. In an instant it changed from one full of warm affection to that of a stone wall.

"You're joking, right?" he said after a brief but agonizing silence.

"Do I look like I'm joking?" she replied in a steady tone, though her insides felt like a rock falling into a pit.

"Your husband was a Jap?"

She just nodded, biting back the sudden surge of emotion that threatened her. His question had been spoken with the same disdain she'd heard so often before.

"You were married to a Jap?" he repeated, still shocked and appalled. Then almost reflexively he flipped the other photo to the top. Whatever color had remained in his face after the horrible revelation of Sam now drained away completely. As he looked at Jackie's sweet daughter, it seemed as if he might be sick.

"I'm sorry," she heard herself say. She meant she was sorry for not telling him sooner, but she knew it might appear as if she'd meant she was sorry for committing the ghastly sin of loving a man of a different race. To her eternal shame she did not immediately repair the disparity.

Not until he said, "You should be. Defiling yourself with the enemy—"

That brought her to her senses. "Wait a minute! That's not what I meant at all. I am not in the least sorry I married Sam. I loved him dearly, and we have the most precious child a person could want." At first it was hard to utter a word without bursting into tears, but as anger gained a foothold, tears were forgotten.

"And to think I had started to care for you," he muttered.

"And I had started to care for you," she shot back, "before I realized just what sort of person you are!"

"Me? You slept with the enemy!"

"You can't truly believe all Japanese were the enemy!" Perhaps she could reason with him, though why she should try, she didn't know. "Sam was an American citizen. He died for his country. He earned two Purple Hearts and a Distinguished Service Cross. How dare you call him the enemy!"

"A Jap's a Jap," he intoned.

"I am sorry for what happened to your brother." She tried to calm her emotions. She knew he was still in much pain over the death of his brother. "But Sam had nothing to do with that."

By now they were near the embassy. They stopped a short distance away from the gate. Neither wanted to have this discussion in full view of the embassy staff. She asked herself if it was worth having any discussion at all. She wasn't going to change that deeply entrenched disdain she'd seen in his expression.

But she was compelled to make one more attempt. She had been through this very scene so many times, and she hated to admit defeat again.

"I don't hate all Germans for killing Sam," she said. "I don't even hate the one who shot him. It's pointless. He was doing his duty, like Sam was. Like your brother was. And so were the Japanese—"

"No, they're different."

"Because they are a different race?"

He shook his head, a sneer on his lips. "Because they are sneaky little rascals. Because . . . they killed *my* brother! I'll never be able to look at one without wanting to wring his neck. And you . . . ! That you were with one—" he shuddered—"that's disgusting!" He touched his lips as if he wanted to wipe away the filth of her touch.

That gesture nearly did Jackie in completely. She could say no more without releasing a flood of emotion.

26

TROY WAS GENTLEMAN enough to leave Jackie at the embassy door. But he left in a hurry after that. Jackie was grateful he didn't linger, because she was fighting desperately to hold her emotions in reign. She refused to cry in front of him.

Numbly she shambled her way to the elevator and pressed the button. What had she done wrong? Why was God denying her the life she dreamed of? It was bad enough that she'd been denied the lifetime she had intended with Sam, but now was she doomed to be alone forever?

The thought barely formed before the dam of pent-up anguish burst. Tears spilled over the rims of her eyes, and a sob choked her. The elevator arrived just then.

"Floor, please?" asked the elevator operator.

He might as well have asked her the meaning of life. As she stepped inside, she gaped at him tearfully, not knowing what to answer.

Another voice called behind her. For a fleeting moment she thought it might be Troy, suddenly realizing how wrong he had been.

"Hold, please!"

She turned, but it wasn't Troy. It was Robert Wood. Another sob broke through her lips.

Robert hurried into the elevator. "Six, please," he said to the operator. Then he noticed Jackie. "Ah, Jackie, hello."

Her response was something close to "Whaa!"

Dismay flooded his expression. "Is something wrong? Of course something is wrong. What am I saying? Have you received bad news? Not Alex—"

She shook her head and managed a wobbly "N-no."

The elevator came to a stop on the sixth floor. Robert said, "Aren't you going to your sister's for lunch?" Fresh sobs clogged Jackie's speech as she nodded. Robert said to the operator, "The fifth floor, please."

With a small scowl the operator pulled the lever to close the doors and pressed the button for five.

"Y-you d-don't have to come with me," Jackie managed when she saw Robert wasn't getting off at the floor he had requested. She remembered he had a luncheon engagement with the ambassador.

"I can see you to your sister's apartment. Blair will know what to do."

But that suggestion only ignited more distress as Jackie realized the last person she wanted to see just then was Blair. Jackie would have to explain her tears, and Blair would never understand. Or worse, she would support Troy.

"I c-can't see her," sobbed Jackie.

"But I'm sure both your sisters will be there. Surely you want to talk to them. They'll know what to do . . . Cameron will know," he said with a helpless, almost desperate, quality to his tone.

"I c-can't," she blubbered as the elevator bounced to a stop on the fifth floor. "Blair won't understand."

"Can I take you to your hotel, then?"

Jackie thought being alone would be the worst thing of all, but maybe she'd better get used to it, since it looked as if she'd be alone for the rest of her life. She was about to choke back another sob and take up the man's offer when he added, "Perhaps being alone isn't a good idea. You could come to my place.

I could leave you there and get Cameron to come there for you."

She nodded gratefully, her lip trembling too much to speak.

With a wan smile Robert told the elevator operator, "Six, please."

The man's scowl was heavy now as he gave the lever a hard pull. He muttered something in Russian, which Jackie thought was just as well she couldn't understand.

"Let me take your coat," Robert offered as he ushered her inside his apartment. She slipped out of the garment, and he hung it on an antique hall tree. "Would you like some tea?" he offered. "In Russia they think tea fixes everything. Tea and vodka, but I have no vodka." He chuckled nervously. "Not that I believe vodka would fix anything . . . even if I had some, which I don't, of course."

Suddenly Jackie became intensely aware of the awkward position into which she had placed this man. She wanted to somehow ease his discomfort. After all, she was usually the fixer, not the one needing to be fixed. That only made her realize anew how botched up her life seemed at the moment. Fresh tears rose in her eyes.

"Tea w-would be fine," she said.

He led her into the front parlor. "Make yourself comfortable. I'll be back in a jiffy."

"Don't you have an appointment this afternoon?"

"I'll ring up the ambassador. He'll understand."

"Will you tell him about me?"

"Certainly not!" He started to turn, then added, "I can also call down for Cameron." Was that hopefulness in his tone? Hopeful for a reprieve from the distasteful task of comforting an emotional woman?

She hated to impose on him this way, but she had to be honest. "I don't want to burden her with my problems. She has so much to worry her now."

"I understand," he said. "Let me get that tea. Then you can talk to me if you like, or I can leave you alone, and you can sit here quietly until you feel better. Whatever suits you."

"Thank you so much."

When he disappeared into the kitchen, she took a moment to assess her surroundings. The apartment was furnished simply but tastefully, with a lot of oak antique pieces. He had really made a home of what must be a temporary situation. For a single man he had done quite well with the decorating. The look of the place and the general layout was very much like Blair's apartment. Because this was on a higher floor and had a slightly different orientation, there was a magnificent view of Red Square from a parlor window. The grandeur of the Kremlin and the delicate beauty of St. Basil's, with the sun glinting off its golden domes, somehow calmed Jackie. These glorious symbols of this country that had suffered so deeply made her own problems seem small and insignificant.

Yet still she suffered. Small by comparison to the far greater woes in this world, yet very real to her. She had never been more confused. The worst of it was that small inkling of bitterness that had struck her in the elevator. Bitterness toward Sam! For dying, certainly, but even for being Japanese, which was now causing her such strife.

I'm sorry, Sam, for even the fraction of a moment I might have felt that way. This is not your fault, nor is it our fault!

"Here we go!" came Robert's voice.

She turned, and he was setting a loaded tray on the oval coffee table.

"You have a wonderful view," she said as she seated herself on the Victorian-style sofa, upholstered in a floral brocade fabric of rich fall colors.

"One of the perks of being at this post so long," he replied. "You see, as I was promoted and others moved back home, I got to move into better digs." He sat next to her on the sofa.

"How long have you been here?"

"I first came in the spring of '41. What timing, eh? But then most everyone believed in Stalin and Hitler's nonaggression pact. How drastically the world has changed since then. We have a bomb now that could wipe out half the world and two powers that are standing toe to toe, eye to eye, with the will to use it if they had to."

"But Russia doesn't have the bomb."

"Not yet, but it won't be long—" Stopping abruptly, he shook his head dismally. "Please forgive me! That's hardly conversation to cheer you up."

"It's a distraction, at least." She offered him a smile. "But please, don't feel that you have to cheer me up, or even stay. If you have plans—"

"That's taken care of, but if you'd like me to leave . . ."

"No," she answered quickly. "I . . . I really don't want to be alone. I'd rather talk about the bomb, or anything else."

"You must be in a bad way, then." He chuckled drolly.

She smiled. "I'm feeling a bit better."

"I can see. I think the tea is ready." He poured out two cups. "Do you take anything in yours?"

"No, just plain, please."

He handed her a cup, then stirred sugar and milk into his. "Are you hungry?" he asked. "You haven't had lunch. I let the cook go for the day, but I could try to fix something."

"I'm fine." She gazed into her tea for a moment, realizing she needed to talk. Would he mind listening? "Robert, don't ever try to hide who you are."

"What?" he said, nearly choking on the sip of tea he'd taken.

"It doesn't pay," she added.

"Has Cameron told you about me?"

She wasn't certain what he meant but said, "Only that you are very nice. And I see she was right."

"She said nothing else?"

"No. Why do you ask?"

"It's just what you said about hiding who you are."

"Oh, that. I guess that's what I have learned today about myself. I hope I've learned, anyway." She studied him a moment and saw something akin to understanding in his eyes, even though he could not have any idea of what she was speaking. She was encouraged to continue. "You'll think me a horrible person if I tell you—maybe I deserve to be thought of as terrible. I'm not really ashamed of it. It's just that no one understands, especially men like Troy. And the war has made it much worse." She gave a dry chuckle and added, "I'm babbling, aren't I? Do you want to know my problem, my awful secret?"

"If you want to talk about it, I can be a good listener," he said earnestly. "There's plenty of tea."

Instead of answering directly, she picked up her pocketbook, which she had laid on an end table. This method hadn't worked well with Troy, but she still thought it was the most effective way to approach the matter. Opening her purse, she took out the two photographs, the ones she had shown Troy, and handed them to Robert.

"My secret," she sighed. "My husband and daughter. But I don't really want them to be a secret. I am proud of them."

The photo of Emi was on top, and she couldn't resist giving Robert an incisive gaze as he took it in, gauging his reaction.

"She's beautiful!" he said with sincere feeling. "You have every right to be proud, I am sure." Then he shuffled the next photo to the top. He studied it a long moment. She could not read his expression. Perhaps he hadn't realized Emi was her birth daughter, not until he saw who her husband had been. She braced herself for the usual recoil.

"Was he in the 442nd Combat Unit?" Robert asked.

The question took her aback. It contained none of the disdain she had come to expect.

"Yes," she answered. "He was killed in France."

"They were all heroes. I read about their exploits in the papers."

"They were all Japanese," she said inanely, but she was stunned by Robert's response.

"Yes," he replied, and his tone seemed to say, "So what of it?"

"I don't usually get that kind of response," she explained.

"No, I don't suppose you do," he replied thoughtfully. He handed back the photos. "Is that why you were crying, then? Did someone make disparaging remarks? Did Captain Rigdon—"

"He made no remarks," she answered, unable to hide the residue of bitterness she still felt toward him, "except to say that he hates Japs, and he nearly vomited when he saw the photo of my husband. Can't blame him, though, can I?"

"I am so sorry, Jackie." He set down his cup and grasped her hands. "That was boorish of him."

"It wasn't really his fault. I guess I blindsided him. I should have told him right at the beginning, but—" Emotions—grief, sadness, despair, anger—she thought she had under control began to rise once again. She slipped one of her hands from his and swiped it across her eyes. "Every time I tell a man about my husband, he runs in the opposite direction. I get everything from pity to revulsion, as if I am some kind of fallen woman." She sniffed and fumbled in her purse for a hankie. She needed both hands to blow her nose but felt regret at having to remove them from the warm comfort of his hands. She looked at Robert again and realized Blair had been wrong when she said he didn't hold a candle to the likes of Troy Rigdon. No, he wasn't as handsome or as brawny, but he had a depth in his dark eyes that she had never seen in Troy's. Caring was there, and understanding, too. "You don't feel that way, though, do you?"

"Heavens no!"

"Why not?"

"There are many reasons, but this isn't the time to go into them all. However, at the bottom of it is the simple fact that I know the importance of judging people by who they are, not by what they are or what color or religion they are. I expect your Sam was a fine man, and you loved him very much."

Tearfully, she smiled. "He was and I did. I still do. The issue of our different races was only important to others. For us . . . well, I can't say the issue of race didn't exist, but it was just one more facet of each other that made us love all that much more. Sam used to say it was a package deal." She dabbed her eyes again. How her heart ached for him still. How she missed him! "Our daughter's name is Emi," she said quietly.

"It's a beautiful name."

"She's named for a dear friend of Sam's, a Japanese friend. His friend Emi was in love with a white man around the time that Sam and I first fell in love. Emi got into trouble, and I guess she wasn't able to handle the adversity that would come with a mixed marriage. And she couldn't face telling her parents about her condition. So she committed suicide."

"How tragic," he murmured.

"It might seem rather morbid that we named our daughter after her, but we wanted to pay her tribute and be reminded always of how much God had blessed us in being together. I don't know what to think now. I always believed our marriage was right, yet I must admit there are moments, especially when I must face the reaction of others, that I have a tiny seed of doubt. Did God kill Sam because it wasn't right to mix the races? I hate myself for even momentarily entertaining such a thought. But there it is, like a worm boring into my soul."

He was silent for a moment, and she wondered if she had opened up too much to this stranger. But he was so easy to talk to. She could tell he was really listening, that the sincerity of his responses and the depth of his gaze were real.

Finally he said, "I wonder if God sees race. He created them, though I am not entirely certain why. But all men were created in His image, weren't they?" He shrugged. "I really don't know the answer to that question, but I can say with confidence that God did not kill your Sam. A German soldier killed him, or if you will, Hitler killed him. God gives life. He doesn't take it."

"I know in my heart you are right," she replied. "But I have had people actually tell me that God took Sam because it wasn't right for us to be together."

"You mustn't listen to them. Listen to your heart."

"Troy said you are a genius. Now I believe him," she said with a smile.

Red crept up his neck, and he gave a self-deprecating chuckle.

"I didn't mean to embarrass you," she apologized.

"I guess I am a genius according to my IQ, but that is not an assessment of wisdom. Believe me, I constantly wrestle over life's questions. I suppose it is just easier to solve other people's problems." He laughed. "Not that I have solved anything for you. You still have to face bigots and hateful people."

"Or those who have been truly hurt by the Japanese and have legitimate bitterness toward them, like Troy and my sister Blair."

"I recall now that your sister was in the Philippines during the war. I never heard what happened there."

"She was caught in the Philippines until nearly the end of the war. She lived as a fugitive for a couple of years, a really hard existence. Then she was captured and tortured. Because of the torture, she lost the baby she was carrying. I guess she has every right to hate the Japanese. But she includes Emi in that, as well. I think every time she looks at Emi, she sees the faces of the men who tortured her. I know she struggles with it because, as a Christian, she knows her bitterness is wrong. It still hurts—her as much as me."

"I wonder if those in our generation will ever be able to escape the cruel effects of the war." For a moment the small furrow between his brows deepened, and he seemed to be thinking of something far more personal than the general terms of his words. "I've always been a bit ashamed I didn't get to fight. When I tried to enlist, I was told my knowledge of the Russian language made me indispensable at the embassy at that crucial time. So in many ways I was protected from some of the real horrors of war. But even I often feel the backlash from that time. I expect it is especially difficult for those of you who were in the middle of it all."

"I was hardly in the middle of it, either," she said. "Even living for a time in a Japanese internment camp in the States, I was fairly protected, until Sam's death, that is."

"You were in one of those camps?" he asked, incredulous.

"Yes. I wanted to be with my husband and daughter. There were a few other whites, mostly women like me married to Japanese men. We were a rarity, though."

He asked about her experience there, and she asked him about his work at the embassy, and after an hour or so Jackie realized that her painful emotions had quieted substantially.

"Robert, thank you for spending this time with me," she said. "I feel so much better."

"I am glad I happened along."

"I haven't talked so freely with anyone in a long time." Since Sam, she thought, but she did not voice that insight.

"I suppose sometimes it's easier to open up to a stranger."

"I hope you are no longer a stranger," she said earnestly. "I don't think of you as one now."

Smiling, he briefly took her hands once more. "I would be pleased to count you as a friend."

"Me too." She gave his hands a heartfelt squeeze before rising. "But I don't want to take further advantage of that friendship. I really should be going. Blair will wonder what has become of me. And now I think I can face her."

Robert walked her to the door. As he helped her with her coat, he seemed to be preoccupied. He was still distracted as he opened the door.

"I'll see you soon, then," she said.

"Yes . . ." Letting the word trail away, he added, "Good-bye."

"Yes, good-bye." She lingered a moment more.

"I can walk you to the elevator," he said.

That seemed unnecessary, yet she didn't protest. He still had that distracted look when the car arrived with the same operator.

"Floor, please?" the man asked.

"Five," Jackie answered as she stepped inside.

"You are certain, yes?"

"Yes, I am. Five."

He started to pull the lever to close the door.

"Wait!" Robert said suddenly.

The operator growled and uttered something in Russian to which Robert responded with raised eyebrows and a slightly shocked look.

"I am sorry," the man muttered.

Ignoring him, Robert turned his attention back to Jackie. "I have tickets to the theater tomorrow night. I'm attending with some friends from the Swiss embassy. Would you care to have one of the tickets? Um, I really mean . . . would you like to join me?"

"I'd like that," Jackie said, barely restraining a smile at his discomfiture and his attempt to avoid making this appear like a date. Were it a true date she might not be so inclined to accept his invitation, but she took it to be just a gathering of friends. That she could handle.

"I'll pick you up at your hotel at seven." He nodded toward the elevator operator.

The fellow wasted no time in closing the doors should these strange indecisive foreigners change their minds once more.

27

WHEN JACKIE LEFT Robert's apartment she had just enough courage to face Blair. That is, until she reached her sister's door. She began to quake inside. Maybe Cameron would still be there to help diffuse any situation that might arise. Or perhaps Jackie could simply say nothing about Troy. But her sisters were sure to question her, and she didn't want to lie to them.

Perhaps it would be best to get everything out in the open. She could deal with Troy's rejection—he was only one of a string after all, and moreover, he was just a casual acquaintance despite the fact that he had mentioned that frightening word *love*.

Blair was different, of course. She and Jackie would always be sisters. She did not want the rest of their lives spent in tension and emotional distance.

She raised her hand and knocked on Blair's door.

Gary answered, and much to Jackie's relief Cameron was still there. They were seated in the parlor. Cameron was in the upholstered chair, and Blair was on the sofa, where apparently Gary had also been sitting. He politely offered his place to Jackie, which she politely took. Merely the fact that she was reluctant to even sit beside Blair made Jackie more certain than ever that they must face this problem.

While Gary was pulling up a straight-backed chair and straddling it, Blair promptly started the dreaded grilling.

"Okay, I won't be mad about you missing lunch, but only if you tell us every detail." Her tone was amused and light. Obviously she expected a tale of a romantic interlude.

Out of the corner of her eye Jackie caught Cameron rolling her eyes.

"Give the girl a break, Blair," Cameron said. "Maybe she doesn't want to talk. Maybe she's starved and wants to eat first."

"It's that notorious Hayes patience," Gary put in drolly.

"I'm not hungry," Jackie said. But her stomach rumbled just then and everyone laughed. Everyone except Jackie. She felt a little better than when she'd been on the elevator with Robert, but she was still too overwrought to make jokes.

"Jackie, sweetie," Cameron said sympathetically, "are you okay? Do you want to talk?"

"Well . . ." Jackie looked up at Cameron but pointedly kept her gaze from Blair. "It didn't go so well with Troy. I . . . uh . . . I told him about Sam and Emi." She heard a sound beside her. Was that a muffled groan from Blair? She knew it was, and that small sound ignited an anger in her she had no idea existed. She jerked a gaze full of fury toward her sister. "What was that for, Blair?" she snapped. "Did I do wrong to speak of the two most important people in my life? The two people I have loved more than life itself? Was it a mistake to speak of a man who—" suddenly anger dissolved into tearful emotion, but she forced herself to finish—"was more noble and dear and honorable than any man I have ever known!" She jerked her gaze toward Gary. "You are a professional soldier, Gary. You fought in that stinking war. You know, don't you, what Sam suffered, what he sacrificed, what it took for him to do what he did? You know he had no ordinary courage—" Choking on a sob, she stopped.

"I didn't say anything—" Blair began petulantly.

But Gary's voice went over hers. "Yes, Jackie, I know. I'm ashamed of many things I did in the war, because the life of a guerilla isn't always honorable. But the more I learn of Sam's tour of duty in Europe, the more I am convinced he always acted honorably and courageously. I am proud to name him brother-in-law. I wish I could have known him."

"Th-thank you, Gary," Jackie said.

Blair sat stiffly at the other end of the sofa, eyes averted from her sister. But Cameron came and sat between the sisters and put an arm around Jackie, seeming to know that she needed comforting.

Jackie smiled her thanks. "I thought I was finished crying."

There was a long silence, and even with Cameron between them, Jackie could feel the tension emanating from Blair. Jackie thought it would help if she just said she was sorry, but she simply couldn't get the words out. There was nothing for her to be sorry about. For years everyone had been dancing cautiously around Blair, usually at Jackie's expense.

"Jackie, have patience with Blair. She's been through so much. Give her time. She doesn't really hate Emi. She'll come around. Remember what she has been through. . . ."

Well, Jackie was tired of it. She didn't expect sympathy for herself, and certainly no one was dishing it out as they did with Blair. Maybe Blair would only get over the pain she carried if everyone stopped feeling so sorry for her.

Finally Blair spoke, her words aimed at Gary. "I thought we were in this together, Gary."

"In what?" he asked, appearing baffled.

"What we went through. What we suffered. I thought we shared that. I thought you understood." Her voice was shaky with emotion.

"Yes, we did share it," he replied gently, "and I do understand. But am I betraying you because I am getting over it? Or because I never hated my enemy as much as you did?"

"Maybe you can get over it, but how can I when I live with what they did to me constantly? Two miscarriages, Gary!" She shot a look at Jackie as she spoke. "I have lost three children because of them."

"You don't think I live with it as much as you?" His tone was edged with pain and ire. "Maybe not in the physical way you have, but I've lost three children, as well! I, too, must live with the fact that I will probably never have children of my own. And worse, I have to live with you as you become more and more a bitter shell of a woman because of it—" He stopped suddenly, aghast at his own words.

"I see," Blair said in a strangled tone. She jumped up.

Cameron grasped her hand. "Blair, stay. Let's talk this out."

"Why should I let you all gang up on me?" With that she turned and fled the apartment.

Jackie felt sick. If only she'd been able to say she was sorry. This was all her fault. Jesus had said to forgive seventy times seven, but Jackie had given up before even beginning to reach that number.

"I'll go after her," Jackie said.

"No," Gary said, rising. "I will." He started toward the door, then paused. "Pray for me, will you? I've hurt her badly."

"We'll pray, Gary," Cameron said. "Just keep in mind that Blair is stronger than she appears, and pampering her might not be the best thing for her."

With a nod, he opened the door and left.

To Jackie, Cameron added when they were alone, "And if I know you, you are probably crucifying yourself over this." When Jackie gave only a shrug in reply, Cameron continued. "Well, don't. I know we've been over this ground before, but you have to keep telling yourself that you have done nothing wrong."

"Except that I haven't been constant in forgiving Blair."

"I can't disagree with that," said Cameron wryly, "but for heaven's sake, Jackie, you are not going for sainthood. Even God doesn't expect you to be perfect. Maybe in this case it is a mistake to keep on forgiving Blair. Maybe it is time we take a harder line with her. Sometimes I think she takes our forgiveness and our pity as license to continue to hang on to her bitterness."

"I was thinking the same thing," Jackie admitted, "but aren't you a little afraid she might crack if we don't?"

"She is in God's hands," Cameron said with deep feeling. "He will protect her, even from those who love her if He has to. I think also that He will give us wisdom in knowing how to deal with her."

"Maybe He already has," Jackie said with a smile and squeezed Cameron's hand.

Then together they prayed for Blair and Gary and for whatever was transpiring between them now.

Blair was pounding on the elevator button as Gary strode around the corner.

"Curse Russian inefficiency!" she grumbled.

"Bless it," he said, coming up next to her.

"I don't want to talk to you right now, Gary."

"I don't deserve for you to talk to me or to let me off the hook or anything." The elevator arrived, and the doors slid open. Blair stepped inside with Gary close upon her heels. "Lobby," he said to the operator. To his wife he went on, "I don't deserve it, sweetheart, but I beg you to grant me what I don't deserve."

She said nothing as the car moved down. She wanted to hang on to her anger, because his words had been terribly cruel. She didn't think he had ever said anything so hurtful. Did he really think she was being consumed by bitterness? Was she truly making his life miserable? He'd always given her nothing but love and support. Had that been little more than an act? Had their marriage become a mere shell?

The elevator jerked to a stop, and the doors slid open. For a brief moment when Gary had first approached her at the elevator, she'd thought she might let him off the hook. She needed him too much to stay angry at him for long. Yet now all the questions that had harangued her during the ride down in the elevator left her too confused to be able to look at him, much less confront him.

She hurried out of the elevator, but he was at her side in a moment. He fell into step with her as she exited the embassy. That little thing nearly brought her to tears. They fit so well together. Even now their steps were in sync. Was it possible he had grown tired of her? Oh, not in the sense of boredom, but simply that he could no longer take her weaknesses. She had tried so hard to get over the trauma she had experienced. Obviously not hard enough.

Outside the sun was shining, the air almost sultry. She'd heard Russia could get quite warm at times in the summer. This must be one of those days. It was a day for picnics and swimming, not for confronting painful issues. They walked for some time in silence. She hated the crackle of tension between them. They argued so seldom.

"Blair, I'm a fool," Gary said finally.

"I hate it when you apologize just to placate me!"

"Is that what you think?"

"I don't know what to think." She tossed her head in frustration. "I guess I just know you are right, so your apology has to be a tad insincere, because you must know you are right, as well."

Several people hurried past. She suddenly felt exposed as some passersby glanced in their direction. Though this should be the perfect situation to have such a conversation because no one could understand them, it wasn't, for they stood out both in their foreignness and in their intensity.

Gary, apparently sensing the same thing, said, "Let's go back to the embassy. Maybe I can get a car and we can drive out to the country."

"You know you can't drive here, Gary. Besides, Cameron and Jackie will wonder what became of us." How strange for her to be the practical one for a change.

Gary knew as well as she that they had to request a car and driver days in advance. The senior staff had priority, while Gary was the lowest man on the totem pole at the moment.

"Did we make a mistake coming here?" she asked suddenly.

"I thought it would be a good diversion for us," he replied, "as well as a chance to help Cameron. I thought we needed something, you know."

"*We?*" she said pointedly. "Was this a desperate ploy to save our marriage?"

"What?" he gasped. "Does our marriage need saving?" Stopping, he swung around to face her. "You can't believe that!"

"What am I to think when you say you are having a hard time putting up with me?"

"I told you that was a foolish thing for me to say." Now people were looking at them curiously. He moved back to her side, and they started walking again so as not to draw attention to themselves. "The truth is, what I said was more what I fear could happen, not what really is. And when I see you around your sister and her child, the fear hits me between the eyes. You are not a bitter shell, Blair, but if you don't find a way to deal with your feelings about the Japanese . . ." He shook his head to finish the thought. He didn't have to say more.

"How have *you* dealt with it?" she asked plaintively. They had talked of these things before but had usually just brushed the surface of the matter. Neither wanted to dwell on their wartime experiences. They wanted to forget them.

But this time Gary patiently answered her. "I guess my training as a soldier helped me. You can't let fighting your enemy get personal. You follow orders; you do your duty. It wasn't easy, not when I had to watch my friends die, but the training got me through. There were many aspects of war that West Point didn't prepare me for, but at least it taught me discipline. You didn't have that, Blair. You were thrown into that horrible ordeal with little but your wits to guide you. You had your faith, but what happened over there was almost too much to handle for one so new in their faith. You came out of it pretty good after all."

"I don't need a pep talk." She wasn't angry anymore except with herself for being so dense. "I just want to understand what is going on with me and then do something about it."

"You can't let go of your bitterness?" He knew even before she gave him an arched brow that the question was dumb. "I know you would if you could. But other than simply letting go, I don't know what else you can do."

"And I have done that, or tried to let it go many times," Blair said defensively. "I'm sorry, I know you mean well. Meg Doyle told me the same thing. How did she get over it? She lost her husband, and for years she didn't know if her daughters were alive. It wasn't until the war's end that they were finally reunited. Yet she doesn't carry hatred with her. She didn't have military discipline, either. I'm just not as good a Christian as she is. That's all I can think."

"I can't believe God keeps score like that," Gary said. "There is something standing in your way, Blair, but it's not that. Something is holding you back, and though I have no idea what it is, I am truly confident you will find a way through this."

"Are you, Gary?" She smiled for the first time since all this began. She could tell he meant what he said, and that gave her hope.

She slipped her arm around him. She didn't care any longer if they stood out in the crowd. Let all of Russia know how much she loved this man!

As if he had read her thoughts, he said, "And know this, as well, Blair: We *are* in this together. You don't have to find your way alone. I am committed to you for the rest of my life. And that is not only because of our marriage vows, but also because you are part of me and I of you. Believe this, I love you more now than I did at either of our weddings!" He offered her a lop-sided grin.

"Now I wish we were back at the embassy," she responded, "because I really want to kiss you."

He had placed his arm around her and now tightened his hold. "I know."

They walked a bit farther before turning and heading back to the embassy.

After a few moments' silence, Blair said, "Maybe if I have a baby, I will get over it."

"Maybe . . ."

She detected hesitation in his tone. Though the doctor had all but told them that would be impossible, she still clung to a small hope. "No, that's too simple. If we lived closer to Jackie, I could volunteer to baby-sit and force myself to get close to Emi. Even my dad has conquered his prejudices. I talked to him about that the last time I was home." But as she spoke she wished she hadn't recalled that day. It had started out so well, she and her father really communicating with their hearts. Then she had spoiled it all by telling him her mother's secret. She still hated herself for doing that.

"What did he say?" Gary's voice broke into her grim reverie.

"Just that it would take time. But you and I both know how I hate for things to take time."

He chuckled. "Your family's curse."

"Maybe if nothing else I'll learn patience through all this."

When they finally reached their apartment, Blair was relieved to find Cameron and Jackie gone. There was a note, written in Cameron's hand, saying they thought Blair and Gary would like some time alone and they would all get together tomorrow.

28

Jackie didn't know if she would keep the appointment with Robert to attend the theater—she refused to call it a date. After the scene with Blair, she and Cameron left their sister's apartment and returned to their hotel. Jackie was uncertain how things now stood between them all and could not conceive of having a good time until they cleared the air.

Blair surprised Jackie by showing up at the hotel the next morning.

"Am I still welcome here?" she asked contritely.

"Of course you are," Jackie responded without hesitation. She feared even a slight pause might set things off again, though Blair seemed quite sincere.

Jackie opened the door wide for her sister to enter. Blair came in and sat in the chair at the small table, and Jackie took the other one. Cameron was in the bathroom combing her hair, but she poked her head out to say hi and left the door open so they could continue to visit while she finished dressing.

"Are you both sick of me asking for time to get over this problem of mine?" Blair asked. "You don't have to answer," she quickly added. "Jackie, I am going to work through this, but in the meantime I want you to have no doubts that this is about me, not you."

Jackie shrugged, afraid to agree too heartily to her sister's admission. Silence followed, not entirely awkward. Obviously the situation wasn't resolved, but there was no sense butting their heads if there was no ready solution. The Hayes women had learned this trick from their father. Ignore a problem and maybe it would go away. Jackie wasn't certain if that was a negative or a positive approach. However, in this case she thought it might be the only solution for the time being, and since Cameron didn't press the issue, it seemed apparent her sisters were in silent agreement.

They spent the rest of the morning together walking around the city, shopping and, with Cameron's help, learning the metro system.

They went to a department store called Mostorg, Jackie guessed. It might have once been a fine store, perhaps the Macy's of Moscow, but the selection on the shelves was slim now. And what was there was of shoddy workmanship. Jackie bought a set of wooden dolls that nested inside each other for Emi.

Blair took it in her mind to buy a fur hat, since she intended on being in Russia for the winter. They had fun at the milliner's counter trying on hats, and they drew a bit of a crowd as curious customers stopped to see the foreigners. No one came too close or tried to converse with them, but Jackie sensed they wanted to.

Blair tried on a hat Jackie would have called a Cossack hat, one that was usually associated with Russians in photos. The brown fur contrasted nicely with Blair's fair coloring. In U.S. dollars it would probably cost about thirty dollars. The sales clerk kept trying to steer Blair toward the shelf of more expensive hats, obviously holding the common opinion that Americans were made of money. Russians disdained capitalism until it was time to take the tourist's dollar. The clerk would never believe that Blair was stretching her budget as it was with the thirty dollars.

"What do you think?" Blair asked her sisters as she pirouetted around, the fur hat perched regally on her head.

Cameron and Jackie offered critical appraisal, then pronounced their approval. Cameron told the clerk in Russian that this was the one her sister wanted to buy. Immediately several of the onlookers surged forward and wanted to see the same hat.

"I guess they appreciate foreign fashion sense as well as our money!" Blair said.

But it was certainly difficult to hand over that money. Cameron had informed them of the Russian system of "commerce," but Jackie hadn't believed it could be so inefficient until she actually saw it. First the clerk gave Blair a ticket, and then she had to wait in a long line at a booth in another part of the store, where she presented the ticket to another clerk, paid for the hat, and was given yet another ticket. With that she had to trek back to the millinery department and wait in another line in order to present her purchase ticket and finally receive the hat. Jackie wondered at the long lines, since there was so little to buy; however, that didn't seem to deter the Muscovites, for the store was quite crowded. There must be money somewhere in this war-depressed country.

When they returned home after the shopping excursion, Jackie felt much better. She had enjoyed Blair's company today. Actually she had always been closer to Blair than to Cameron, though Blair's past lifestyle had often separated them. They had more in common, with them both being interested in home and family life. Perhaps that would change once Cameron set up housekeeping with Alex, but as it stood now, Jackie knew that it was she and Blair who were the most likely to be friends. That is, if they could somehow surmount that obstacle between them. But this short time together gave Jackie hope for success.

As evening approached, Cameron encouraged her to go with Robert to the theater, and Jackie reluctantly agreed, even though she felt she shouldn't be enjoying herself with Alex's plight hanging over them.

Robert came to the hotel at seven. He was dressed in evening clothes—a black tuxedo with black tie—and carried a trench coat draped over his arm, for it was threatening rain. Jackie was glad she had learned from Cameron that one usually dressed in evening clothes for the theater. She had brought only the one dressy outfit she had worn to the embassy reception. Perhaps it was vanity, but she hated to wear the same evening dress twice so close together. So she borrowed something from Blair, who always had the proper clothes and never too few of anything. Jackie chose a black day-length gown of lace over crepe. Very elegant but also simple, which suited Jackie. There was a black velvet elbow-length cape that went with it, but always practical, she also carried a raincoat, though she hoped she didn't have to wear it because it didn't exactly complement her outfit.

"You look stunning," Robert said, offering his arm to her. There was an element of sincerity in his tone that almost embarrassed Jackie, though it pleased her, as well.

As they walked out to the waiting embassy car, it dawned on her that this would be the first date—if indeed it was that—she'd had since Sam died in which her marriage and her daughter didn't loom over it like a specter. And for the first time since their conversation in Robert's apartment, she fully realized the incredible significance of the fact that none of her disclosures had bothered him in the least. She directed a rather awed glance in his direction. At that same moment he turned toward her, and his brow arched.

"Is something wrong?" he asked.

She felt so free and unfettered that she wanted to laugh, but she managed a more sedate response.

"Oh no, nothing at all," she said. "I'm just . . . that is, it's just . . ." She didn't know how to respond.

She was spared for the moment when they reached the vehicle and the driver held open the door for her. Once she and Robert were settled in the backseat, she said impulsively, "Robert, this is the first time I've been out with a man since my marriage that I haven't dreaded the moment when I must tell him about Sam and Emi." A laugh slipped from her lips before she could stop it. "You can't believe how wonderful it feels."

He smiled. "I'm pleased to hear that, Jackie," he replied as the car pulled into motion. Then his brow knit in thoughtful reflection. "But it is too bad it had to be that way for you. Those men didn't know what they were missing."

"I had begun to think the war had taken all the good men."

It seemed to take him a moment to realize she was implying that he was one of the good ones to whom she was referring. He smiled again, this time awkwardly. For some reason it pleased her that he wasn't entirely comfortable in his own skin. She'd never much liked slick, smooth-talking men, which made her wonder how she could have been attracted to Troy. Apparently she had been momentarily blinded by the dazzle of his looks. Yet Robert was definitely no slouch. Behind those wire-rimmed eyeglasses and the boyish but unassuming features, there was a handsome man. Eyes so dark they glistened like onyx—not exactly black, more a burnt umber. They were topped by thick brows that could be nearly as expressive as the eyes themselves. His brown hair was wavy and conservatively cut, but there was one unruly strand that had a penchant for falling out of place—just like Sam's had done, she mused. He was neither tall nor muscular, though he seemed trim and fit. And he certainly cut a fine figure in his tuxedo.

Oh, Jackie, what are you doing? Sizing up a hot prospect? She didn't want to think of him in that way. Still, she must admit something about herself: She *was* a single woman looking for a husband, so it was difficult not to have a critical eye on single men. She wanted to remarry and have more children, and she didn't intend to settle for just any man.

She already knew Robert Wood wasn't just any man.

That aside, she still had to question what was happening here in Russia. To have been here less than a week and to have met two single men, both of whom seemed interested in her? Was it possible God had brought her here not only to help Cameron but also to meet the man of her dreams? Was a change of scenery all she had needed?

After less than a ten-minute drive, the car pulled to a stop. She looked out the window and saw they had stopped in front of a row of buildings that looked to be turn-of-the-century vintage.

"We're here already?" she asked.

"It wasn't far. We probably could have walked, but I thought we might not wish to do so in our evening clothes, especially with rain threatening."

He opened his door as the driver came around. But it was Robert who lent a hand to Jackie as she stepped from the car. Other cars were also arriving, and others also dressed in their finest were emerging from them. The theater, however, wasn't directly facing the street. They had to turn into a courtyard of sorts where other buildings were located.

"This is the Moscow Art Theater," Robert said.

She thought the building was rather unassuming, on the outside at least. Two simple double doors were framed in bluish tiles that were chipped and in some disrepair. Jackie had already discovered much of Moscow was thus, and it could not all be attributed to war damage. The one distinctive feature of the theater was a fascinating bas-relief of a huge wave over the doors. She was about to ask Robert about it when a woman called out to them.

There were a couple dozen people milling around in front of the theater waiting for the doors to open. This particular woman was about thirty-five years old, petite and attractive. She was accompanied by a man of about the same age who towered over her small frame.

She greeted Robert in French, and he responded in the same, then added in English, "This is my American friend I told you about, Mrs. Jackie Okuda."

"So pleased to meet you," the woman said in good but accented English.

Robert continued the introductions. "This is Madame Alcina Guignard and her husband, Jules, the Swiss chargé d'affaires."

"*Enchanté!*" said Monsieur Guignard, taking Jackie's hand and kissing it lightly. "It is so good to see a new face. We at times feel so isolated here."

"Thank you," Jackie responded.

"I'm sure Robert feels the same way," Alcina Guignard said with a coy wink. "Robert, I was beginning to think you were afraid of women. But I see now you were just waiting for the most beautiful of them to arrive."

Jackie blushed. She wasn't used to being called beautiful. Blair had always claimed that distinction, and now Jackie realized she was glad of it. It took a moment for her to realize Robert was also uncomfortable with the woman's glib words.

"Really," Alcina went on, seemingly unaware of their discomfort, "I couldn't believe him to be afraid of anything. Not since he almost single-handedly held down the fort at the American embassy during the Battle of Moscow. Did he tell you about that? The city nearly fell to the Germans, but he held his post. So heroic."

"It certainly wasn't as glamorous as you make it sound," Robert demurred. "The Russians stopped the Germans well before they were in sight. I never laid eyes on a real German soldier during the entire war."

"It must have been quite exciting, though," said Jackie. "Cameron saw some of it, too, and even she had moments of fear."

"Yes. I remember her missing the last train out of Moscow," said Robert, seemingly relieved to have the focus of the conversation deflected from him.

They chatted for a few more minutes. Alcina was vivacious, bubbly. Just listening to her wore Jackie out. Her husband, however, was more stoic and did not seem to mind that his wife monopolized the conversation.

Finally the doors opened and the group of patrons filed inside. Beyond the foyer the main auditorium was rather plain, which Robert said was intentional so that audiences were forced to focus entirely on the performance.

Though Jackie's seat was between Alcina and Robert, she was spared the woman's constant chatter when Alcina saw an acquaintance down the aisle and went to visit with her.

"You never did say what we are going to see," Jackie commented to Robert.

"I am so sorry. It's Chekhov's *Cherry Orchard*."

"I've never seen Chekhov performed." Then Jackie added, "To be honest, I've never even read him."

"My Russian teacher made me read everything by him, in Russian of course!" He added in a somewhat apologetic tone, "I hope you'll enjoy it even though it is in Russian. I am told by those who don't speak the language that it still has great merit."

"How many languages do you speak, Robert?"

With a self-effacing shrug, he answered, "A few."

"How many?" she prompted.

"Five, besides English. You do mean fluently, don't you?" He offered a sheepish smile. "I was trying to teach myself Japanese during the war, but I haven't kept it up. And I am now working on Hebrew—"

At that moment the lights dimmed and a hush fell upon the audience. Alcina returned to her seat, and even she was quiet as the orchestra played an introduction.

Robert quietly explained the high points of the play to Jackie as it progressed, but she found it was so captivating in other ways that the dialogue was almost incidental. Jackie learned later that many of the performers in the production had been decorated by the Soviet government for their expertise. But in Russia there were not really "stars" as there were in America. No one performance was allowed to overshadow any other. Many minor characters were performed by accomplished actors, and they shone in their captivating performances.

The sets were also wonderful, every detail given great care. In one scene when the house in the story was vacated and the furniture moved out, there were places on the walls showing where the paint had faded over the years.

Jackie had been to plays at home and had enjoyed many of them, including some outstanding performances by American actors. But in this Russian production there was a level of passion in the actors that seemed to go far beyond anything she had seen before. Perhaps it had to do with something Cameron had said about Russia and Russians—they lived in the extremes. There was no middle ground for them. If they were going to present a play, then it would be glorious indeed.

Afterward, she and Robert were invited to a small soirée at the Swiss embassy. Only twenty or thirty guests were in attendance, most of whom had also attended the play. Jackie was thankful for her sparse French, for that seemed to be the predominant language spoken among the guests. She was even more thankful when, after an hour, Robert asked if she was ready to leave.

Only when the embassy car came around for them did she realize that leaving the party was one thing, having the evening end was quite another. She was enjoying Robert's company. She would have liked more time with him and was happy when they were finally alone. When he walked her into the Metropole, they tarried in the lobby, finding chairs in an out-of-the-way corner. She discovered what she had already guessed—he was a very interesting man, though reluctant to talk about himself. When he did speak of himself, his manner was unassuming. Not that he was stoic like Alcina's husband. He talked freely about many other subjects such as Russia, the world political situation, and what he missed about the States.

"I miss watching the Red Sox play baseball, hamburgers, and all the usual things. But what I miss most is freedom. I know that sounds trite, but you can't imagine what it is like to be under observation nearly every waking moment. I have no doubt they know what I had for breakfast this morning. Having to always be careful what you say and do wears away at you."

"But you have been here so long," she said. "Can't you go home?"

"I went home for a year after the war," he replied. "But . . . I wasn't ready to deal with certain family situations there, so I requested another two-year tour of duty."

"What will you do when that ends?"

"Watch baseball and eat hamburgers, I suppose."

She eyed him skeptically. "No one is going to let a talented fellow like you do that for long. And I bet you'll quickly get bored with that."

"Probably true."

Robert encouraged Jackie to talk about herself, and without even realizing how deftly he had deflected any personal discussion about himself, she was soon sharing about herself on a personal level. She told him more about Sam and Emi. She told him about her family, particularly about her father and how demanding and hard he had been on her and her sisters.

"He has changed more recently, though," she added quickly, regretting placing him in a negative light. "I think when Mother stood up to him over my marrying Sam, it shook his world a little. Not many people have ever stood up to my father, much less my meek mother. I think Emi has also softened him. I hope so, anyway. I guess he will never change entirely until he gives his life to Christ."

"Perhaps God is slowly bringing him around," he suggested.

"That may be the only way to reach my father. He is definitely a hard nut to crack. Are your parents Christians, Robert?"

His brow furrowed slightly. "They attend church regularly. I'm not in a position to judge beyond that, am I?"

"I guess that was a judgmental question, wasn't it? I can definitely say my in-laws aren't Christians." She smiled wryly. "They're Buddhist. But when people attend church and all, who are we to say where they stand in God's eyes?"

"It's an easy habit to fall into. And perhaps there is validity in judging others by their actions, but judging anyone at all makes me uncomfortable. I have my own reasons why I am sensitive to that issue." He paused, seemingly on the verge of saying more. There was a distant look in his eyes momentarily, and then he focused fully on Jackie. "I guess you are not the only one wrestling with secrets."

"I understand. I truly do," she said. "I don't expect you to reveal your secrets to me. We hardly know each other."

"You've shared some pretty personal things with me."

She ran a hand through her hair, not knowing what to say when she didn't understand herself why she had felt so free with him. Nevertheless, she wasn't going to get her feelings hurt if he didn't feel the same with her.

He rushed ahead. "It's not that I don't want to tell you. . . ." Pausing, he lifted his eyes to meet hers. His gaze was frank and open. It sent an odd thrill through her, and before she even realized what she was doing, she took his hand in hers.

"I understand, Robert," she murmured.

His gaze dropped to their clasped hands. Then he swallowed hard and jumped up. "I better be going," he said. "An early day tomorrow, you know."

She nodded, momentarily dazed by whatever had just transpired between them. It took a heartbeat or two for her to remember to rise, as well.

Finally she found her voice. "Thank you for a lovely evening."

"You're welcome." His tone was a bit curt, but more, she thought, from a sudden discomfiture than anything else. He turned, paused, and turned back to her. "I'll call you," he said.

He hurried out the door as she focused a bemused gaze on his back. She stood there long after he had disappeared outside. Only as she turned to head for the elevator did emotion shake away the fog. It wasn't the emotion she expected, that of a dreamy sensation after experiencing a grand time with a man. What she felt was not euphoria but rather an inexplicable fear.

What was the meaning of that? She had not had such a pleasing evening with a man for years. Fear just didn't make sense.

Cameron was still awake in their room, reading in bed.

"It's almost midnight, missy," she said with mock umbrage as Jackie entered. "It's past your curfew."

Jackie offered an amused chuckle, but she didn't feel it inside where that strange knot still hung on.

"Everything okay?" Cameron closed her book and rolled onto an elbow, giving her sister her full attention.

"Oh yes," Jackie said. "I had a wonderful time. Your Robert Wood is an incredible person, I think."

"But . . . ?"

Jackie kicked off her shoes and plopped down on her bed, a cot that the hotel had provided when she first arrived.

With a confused sigh, she said, "Everything was going perfectly. But as I left him, I got this horrible knot in my stomach. It was like . . . fear. I don't know what it means."

"That's odd," Cameron said, disappointing Jackie, who had hoped for some astounding gem of wisdom from her big sister.

"Absolutely nothing transpired to make me afraid," Jackie exclaimed, more frustrated than ever. "It was perfect."

"Could it have been too perfect?"

Jackie was ready to shrug the comment off as her sister's usual pessimistic outlook. Then she gasped.

"What is it?" Cameron asked with real concern in her voice.

"This is crazy, truly crazy," Jackie said with a dismal shake of her head. "I've felt ready to get married again for some time. And now I meet someone who . . . well, someone I like."

"Someone who could be perfect?"

"Oh, Cameron!"

Cameron smiled knowingly. "It makes complete sense." Her smile broadened. "You've just spent an evening with your future husband."

"But I'm not in love with him," Jackie argued.

"Not yet." Was there a hint of smug assurance in Cameron's tone?

Jackie groaned. "I think you're right. And it scares me to death!"

"But in a good way," Cameron said drolly.

Jackie nodded. This was so strange. She didn't understand it at all. And it was definitely nothing like she had experienced with Sam. Maybe that was a good thing.

Could what Cameron suggested really be true? She knew of only one way to find out. After she climbed into bed and Cameron switched off the lights, Jackie turned her heart toward prayer. Only the Lord knew the answer to her questions.

29

ALEX HAD JUST begun to recover from the previous interrogation sessions when the guards came for him. They had left him alone for several days since the last round of brutal questioning. He'd relished the relief, but fear of new interrogation continually hung over him, which was probably their intent. Give him time to stew in fear so that the reprisal would weaken his resolve rather than strengthen it.

Braced between the guards because the inactivity and dampness of the cell had served to stiffen his muscles, he was led upstairs. Cringing with dread, he wondered if he could take another round of interrogation. He'd been toying with the idea of giving them false information in hopes of satisfying them and ending the torture. But that was a route fraught with disaster. For one thing, the false information had to be plausible enough to fool them, and he simply did not know enough to put on much of a show. Besides, once they got information out of him, they might just decide to shoot him.

He felt his only option was to continue to stonewall them. If he could. Yet what would be the harm in talking? He knew very little. A few names. But he kept thinking that one name might possibly unravel something far larger than he could imagine.

Much to his surprise, he wasn't brought to the usual interrogation room. Instead, he was led to a new cell. This was far more comfortable than the dank crypt he'd occupied in the cellar. There was a cot with a fairly decent mattress and a plain table and chair. Best of all there was a window! Screened and barred, it still let in light. Though it was higher than his eye level, he could see a patch of blue sky. That small glimpse was like a gift of diamonds. He could almost smell the clean summer air outside.

In this new "home" he was given two decent meals a day with clean water to drink. He'd also been given a shower and new clothing—clay-colored prison garb, but it was better than nothing. They were letting him feel like a human being again. Why?

Because Lubyanka held political prisoners, care was taken so there could be no communication between them. Through the window in the cell door, Alex could see colored lights going off and on in the corridors. These he learned were meant to announce traffic in the hallway so he would not by chance meet another prisoner. His captors had thought of everything. It had occurred to Alex to try to get a message to the outside via a prisoner who might be leaving, either released—though few were ever released—or being transferred. Though he didn't know who he would send a message to. His friends must know of his arrest, yet they were helpless to do anything for him. Did Cameron know what had become of him? During their separations in wartime, they had feared losing each other, and in an often chaotic country like Russia, that was more than possible. Such a thing had happened with Cameron's mother and half brother. It was not an idle fear.

Were those fears now to be realized? Would he rot here or in some gulag in Siberia, never to be found again? It could happen.

These new quarters, however, renewed his hope. Nevertheless, he continued with his routine of mind-sharpening exercises. First, he mentally went though all the Scriptures he could remember. Then he started in on anatomy and physiology, naming all the bones in the body, the muscles, and the organs and their purposes. Each day he did two mental surgeries, sometimes more if sheer exhaustion didn't overtake him. As his body weakened, he was more determined than ever to guard the acuity of his mind.

He was two days in the new cell and had begun to feel restored when an interrogator came to his cell.

"Do you like your new place, Comrade Rostovscikov?" asked the man who had questioned him in the past. His tone was pleasant, almost hiding the cruel character that Alex had so painfully experienced previously.

"Yes, thank you," Alex answered.

"Would you like to remain here?"

This, he knew, was a loaded question, but he wished to keep up the civility as long as possible. After two days of relief he feared more than ever a return to the miseries he'd experienced before. He now saw that this was exactly what they were hoping for.

Still, he answered honestly, "Yes."

"Good. And we would like this for you, as well. But these cells are only for those who cooperate. You understand, yes?"

Alex nodded.

"So you wish to cooperate?"

Alex shook his head.

"Come now." The interrogator shook his head in dismay. "We probably already know everything you have to tell us. We merely want confirmation. What would it hurt for you to talk?"

"I don't know anything. I am sorry," Alex said, bracing himself for a blow, or worse, waiting for a more terrible punishment. Sleep deprivation. Starvation. Or one of their favorites, letting him drop off to sleep only to waken him a moment later so he could never grasp the much craved rest.

But the interrogator merely nodded. "As I thought," he said evenly, then rose and exited.

A few moments later another man, this one dressed in a white lab coat, entered.

"Good morning, Dr. Rostovscikov. I am Dr. Soroka." In one hand he held a black bag—Alex had one just like it that he used when he made house calls. Soroka set it down on the table. In his other hand he was holding a metal clipboard holding some papers. He flipped through a couple of pages, as if he were a real doctor. Perhaps he was real. What was he doing here? Certainly they had not taken a sudden interest in his health.

Alex said nothing, but his mind was racing with possibilities. How could he use this? Maybe if he feigned illness they would take him to a less secure prison hospital from which there might be hope of escape. His mind was truly dull for not thinking of this sooner.

But Soroka's next words shocked him to such an extent all else fled his mind.

"I see here you were once addicted to amphetamines and depressants. What were the specific drugs?"

Alex's mouth had gone so dry he could not form words. A cold fear engulfed him.

"No matter, just curious," the doctor went on without waiting for his tardy response. "It is more common than you would think, is it not? Physicians falling prey to the temptation of drugs. What drew you? Some injury for which you were taking pain medication? Or simply the incredibly long hours we are forced to work? We can get dangerous drugs so easily." He gave a shake of his head.

Alex felt perspiration bead on his own head. He'd had weeks to do nothing but think, but he had never once considered this. He'd almost forgotten this weakness of his, this glaring red flag in his history.

The doctor eyed him carefully. "Yes . . . Dr. Rostovscikov. I think you begin to understand. They—meaning your captors—believe you know a great deal. But you have a strong resistance. What else can they do?"

Finally Alex found words. "Please . . . don't do this!" he begged.

"I don't want to. I am a physician like you, and I feel great sympathy toward your plight. Tell these people what they want to know and save yourself this agony."

"I . . . can't" was all Alex could respond.

He told himself this might not be so bad. He'd withstood so many physical tortures, how much harder could this new method be? But like so many ex-addicts, he had sorely forgotten the effects of the bondage of addiction.

Soroka reached for his bag.

"No! Please . . . no!" Alex cried, backing away until his legs bumped against the cot.

"Guards!" called the doctor.

Two burly men entered. They grabbed Alex, forcing him down on the bed. Alex fought wildly. Suddenly he didn't care if they killed him in the struggle. That would be preferable to what the doctor intended. Feeling the tip of the needle touch his arm, Alex gave a mighty jerk. He heard a snap of metal. The doctor cursed.

"Can't you imbeciles do better than that?" Soroka snapped.

Alex continued to struggle. The guards cursed and yelled at him. But even in the best physical condition Alex was no fighter. Weakened by weeks of starvation and abuse, he was no more than a mere annoyance to the muscular men who held him. Eventually they subdued him.

Groaning in agony over their victory, he felt the needle pierce his skin, and then came the warmth of the drug as it entered his vein. What were they giving him? There were many legal substances that would do the job, but the most effective for fast and complete addiction would be heroin. He suspected the MVD would have no trouble obtaining it.

The effect was quick. First a warmth spread throughout his body, followed by a similar warmth enveloping his mind. It . . . felt good. And he instantly hated himself for thinking it. But after weeks of suffering, the mental euphoria, the sense of peace and well-being, however artificial, was comforting. He tried to convince himself that it was a false peace. Only the peace of Christ was abiding.

Still . . . God help him . . . it felt good.

Soon he was left alone. He lay back on the cot, relaxed. He

even began to forget his fears. He went through his mind-sharpening exercises. They went well. This wasn't going to be so bad.

Exactly four hours later the doctor returned with the two guards. Alex struggled again as he was given another injection. He fought as wildly as before.

After that the injections came every four hours. Sometime after the fifth injection Alex stopped fighting. When he tried to do his mind-sharpening exercises, he realized he just didn't care and let them go. For the next twenty-four hours he became a clock watcher instead. Yes, he now noticed there was a clock on the wall of the cell. Had they placed it there intentionally? He didn't care.

Near the end of each four-hour period, he began to look toward the door and listen for footsteps in the corridor outside. When the key scraped within the lock of his cell, relief washed over him. Then a day came when the clock struck the four-hour mark and there was no key in the lock. Four and a half hours passed. He began pacing the small cell. Where was that doctor? Were they toying with him? A vague niggling in the back of his mind told him they were doing just that. But he didn't care.

Five hours. Six.

He began feeling the initial effects of withdrawal. Jitters, sweats, cramps. He paced and cursed.

Finally, the key scraped in the lock. This time it wasn't Soroka who entered but the interrogator.

"Good afternoon, Comrade Rostovscikov," he said.

"Where's the doctor?" Alex grated irritably.

"You are anxious to see the doctor, hmm?" Was that a small triumphant smirk on the man's face? Alex was very close to physically attacking the ogre. "Of course you are. He will be here in a moment. But first I thought you and I could have a little talk."

"I'll talk after."

"Oh, but that's not how it works. You talk, *then* the doctor comes. I know you must be gauging the possibility of surviving withdrawal. Thinking that perhaps you could handle it as you have other tortures. And I am quite certain you are strong-minded enough to be successful. However, you must realize we won't allow you to withdraw, not completely, only enough to feel the agony before we start all over again. We won't let you die, either. You see, we are in complete control."

Alex scraped his hands through his hair, pulling hard at the roots, but he could not inflict enough pain there to dull the ache in his gut. They weren't even going to allow him the option of death. But there was still some small spark in him, perhaps a misplaced arrogance. Maybe it was mere defiance, a desire to push his tormentors to their limit. So he put them to the test. When he refused to talk, the interrogator exited the cell. Alex spent the next hours in withdrawal agony. And just when he knew he would either die or find victory over the addiction, the doctor returned with the guards who held him down. The cycle began all over again.

Finally the interrogator returned one day as Alex was again awaiting his fix.

"How much longer?" the interrogator asked with a sneer. "Admit that we have won, and your suffering ends."

Alex crumbled inside. His eyes were still on the clock. He could not face another withdrawal.

"I'll give you one name," Alex rasped. He knew now that holding back was useless. Yet there was still a small hope of stalling them, and though he was loath to admit it, the hope of keeping the injections from ceasing.

"That's good. Yes, a good start. You give a little, we give a little. I can be reasonable. So give me a name."

"Larry Marquet."

"A Frenchman?"

"An American. U.S. intelligence."

"Doctor!" called the interrogator, turning toward the cell door. Focusing back on Alex he said, "You see, comrade, I won't even verify it first."

The doctor entered the cell and did his deed. When Alex was alone, basking in the warm euphoria of the drug, he tried to think of more names he could give.

PART IV

"*The only kind of love worth having
is the kind that goes on loving,
laughing, fighting . . .*"

Spencer Tracy
A Guy Named Joe, 1944

30

CAMERON FELT AS if she were running on a treadmill. Running . . . running . . . and getting nowhere.

As the days passed, frustration and boredom collided within her. She just wasn't made for the endless rounds of embassy gatherings, theater, and shopping. Jackie and Blair were having a grand time, at least as much as was possible under the circumstances. Blair was perfectly suited for the social though insulated lifestyle those in the foreign colony had adopted in this place where freedom was so limited. Though here a short time, she had become quite popular, not only among the Americans but also with members of other foreign legations. She and Gary were invited to many functions that assistant military Army attachés were usually excluded from.

Jackie's social rounds were more limited—limited to the company of Robert Wood. Whenever Cameron saw them together, they both looked starry-eyed. Jackie would never be so forward as to tell Robert of her premonition of their possible future, but Cameron saw the definite beginnings of something special.

She did not begrudge them their happiness nor Blair her parties.

Maybe if she enjoyed such things, she'd do them herself just to kill the boredom. In fact, she was going to some of the parties.

She was that desperate. One never knew what useful connections one might make at such events, though nothing had transpired yet.

What she really wanted was to get off the treadmill. She wanted something to happen.

That's what eventually induced her to go the Narkomindel, or Commissariat of Foreign Affairs, where the pressroom of the foreign correspondents was located. Until then, she had purposely avoided mingling with the correspondents. She was in Russia on a tourist visa, and she hoped the Soviets had forgotten her connections to the press and her past mistakes. If so, she didn't want to do anything to remind them. She tried to forget what long memories Russians had.

Still, journalism was too much in her blood to keep her away altogether. Besides, some of her old newspaper friends were still in Russia, and she wasn't sure they understood why she was avoiding them. Perhaps a small conciliatory gesture on her part would help her save face a bit.

An old press pass she still carried got her into the Narkomindel. None of the Russians seemed alarmed at her presence, so she boldly proceeded upstairs.

The pressroom hadn't changed except for some new faces. It was still cramped quarters, sending the message that the press wasn't exactly welcome in the Soviet Union. The lovely sound of clacking typewriters filled the air.

"Hey, look who's decided to mingle with the masses," said Henry Cassidy, who had been in Russia during the war.

"It's not like that, really, Hank," Cameron said apologetically.

"It seems like you've been snubbing us, Cameron," said Ed Reed, another wartime correspondent she had worked with. "Even at parties you've barely given us the time of day."

"Ah, give her a break," said Jed Donovan, the *New York Tribune* reporter. "I'm sure she has her reasons." His brow furrowed a bit, and she thought he knew more than he was saying.

These men were reporters, so she had hoped they might have ferreted out the real reason for her being in Russia. But perhaps it was just as well they hadn't. The fewer who knew, the better.

"So what brings you out of the woodwork now?" asked Donovan.

"Newspaper ink runs in my veins, Jed. It's hard to stay away."

"Was it the Ruskies—?" began a correspondent she didn't know. But he stopped, having forgotten they couldn't talk too freely indoors.

Donovan scraped back his chair and rose. "Cameron, I'm about to get something to eat. Want to join me?"

Sensing this was more than an invitation for lunch, especially since it was only ten-thirty in the morning, she accepted without hesitation.

Leaving the building, they walked a couple of blocks to a corner where there was a street vendor selling pirogi. Donovan bought them each one. They chatted as they walked and ate.

"What's up, Jed?" Cameron asked, figuring they were far enough away from unwelcome ears.

"I've heard rumors about why you're here," he said.

"What rumors?"

"You're looking for a certain doctor."

"I'm not looking. I more or less know where he is. What I don't know is how to get him out."

Donovan offered a sympathetic nod. "That's a tough break. You haven't had any luck?"

"None, and I am about to go crazy. Looking back, I see now that during the war we were freer than fleas on a hound despite our frequent complaints."

"You only know the half of it. . . ." He paused, then amended, "No, I think you probably know everything. You can't blink around here now without taking a risk. Have you noticed the fleet of correspondents is cut nearly in half from the wartime numbers? Every chance they get, the Soviets edge someone out. All the radio newsmen are gone. Stalin now forbids all broadcasts from the country. But it's not just foreigners who are at risk. Did you hear about that old so-and-so Lozovsky?"

"They make him vice-premier?" She knew that during the

war Solomon Lozovsky had been Deputy Commissar for Foreign Affairs and responsible for the foreign correspondents. He had delivered war communiqués and had been an expert at skirting questions and issues.

"He's disappeared."

"You're kidding! We used to think he wrote the Party line." That news stunned Cameron more than almost anything. If a man like Lozovsky could go down, no one was safe. "What did he do?"

"Made someone unhappy is all we know. No one will say outright, but I think he's been executed."

Cameron exhaled a ragged breath. Her knees felt weak. She took a bite of the pirogi to help her focus.

"I admire you and the others who have stuck around this long," she said finally.

"I've had my reasons." Pausing, he turned his attention to his lunch. He chewed the pastry slowly, thoughtfully, as if savoring the morsel, but Cameron knew that couldn't be his intent, for the crust of the pie was rather tough and the filling was dry and almost meatless. "I was hoping for a chance to talk to you," he said when he had swallowed. "Like I said before, I have my reasons for staying on. You see, I met a girl—a Russian."

"Oh, Donovan, you haven't." She regretted her words as soon as they left her lips. How she had hated it when people had responded that way to her relationship with Alex. As if doom were ready to fall. But considering her present plight, maybe that was the only possible response there was.

"Yeah, pretty dumb," he said.

"It is," she said, "but I wouldn't trade what Alex and I have for anything."

"You mean that, don't you? Even considering present circumstances?"

"Yes," she said unequivocally. "But, Jed, how did you manage to meet a Russian girl with all the current restrictions?"

"We met just after the war, when the blush of victory was still on the land. We fell in love and have been stealing moments together ever since."

They came to a low brick planter that encircled a scraggly tree. Donovan suggested they sit for a few minutes. "I can't get too far away from the pressroom. I've got a deadline to meet."

She couldn't resist an envious glance. "I do miss all that," she said wistfully.

"Don't. The news they give us now is even more paltry than it was during the war. If it wasn't for Elena, I'd shake off the dust of this town and head home."

And I wouldn't be here at all if it weren't for Alex, she thought. But she was in no way resentful of that. As much as journalism was in her blood, so was Russia. However, she knew that as soon as Alex was freed, she would have to leave and never return.

"Do you know what you are going to do about it?" she asked.

"I've considered marrying her and relinquishing my U.S. citizenship," he replied. They both knew that was the only way the Soviets would even consider a marriage between a Russian citizen and a foreigner.

"I thought of that many times myself," she said, "but Alex always talked me out of it. He believed I was too accustomed to freedom and would soon come to resent him for it. I think he was right—about freedom being too deeply inbred in me to accept life in a police state."

"That's the same as saying repression is inbred in Russians, which may be true, as well. They've had hundreds of years of it to make a pretty lasting impression. When I was in the States, I saw some Russian defectors who told me it took them a long time to stop looking over their shoulders. Even after years, they flew into a panic for the most minor run-in with the police. A simple parking ticket almost gave them heart failure."

With a philosophical sigh Cameron said, "Still, it is probably easier to shake that than to shake freedom. Chances are, if we did become Russian citizens, we'd end up in prison faster than ice melts in summer."

"Escape, then, is our only answer." He sighed.

"That's your intent?"

"We'll wait it out for a while. I'm hoping for a thaw in the political climate. That will be the time to go." He snorted humorously. "*Thaw*. An apt choice of words, isn't it? You know they have started calling the relations between the Soviet Union and the West a Cold War."

"I've heard that. Cold or hot, though, I haven't the luxury of many choices. Alex can't wait for that." Even as she spoke, she whispered a silent prayer that he was waiting, that he was still— No! If he were dead, she'd know it. He was alive, and in his heart he knew she was coming for him, and that hope would keep him going.

"If I could help in any way, you know I would," he said earnestly. "But to tell the truth, that's why I wanted to talk to you. I had hoped to ask you for help. I know while you were here you were able to curry connections others weren't." He chuckled with the memory. "You took a few more risks than the rest of us. And there are your father's connections."

"I'm sorry, Jed. Those seem to have dried up. The one Soviet who was friendly to me back then, and whom I was counting on, won't touch me with a ten-foot pole." She thought for a moment, then added, "There is a family I can trust. I'll tell them about you. But they have been unable to help with Alex, and he is like family to them, so I wouldn't pin my hopes on them."

"We can only hope for a change in power."

"And pray it is a good change."

"Stalin can't live forever," he said. "There have been rumors of ill health."

"Who will succeed him? Beria? Trade one monster for another."

He rose. "I better get back to that deadline. Thanks for talking with me."

"My prayers are with you, Jed."

They walked together back to the Narkomindel. Cameron

thought she'd hang around for a while and visit with some of her other friends for a time.

As they reached the building, a man came up behind them and laid a hand on Cameron's shoulder. She started at the sudden contact.

"Please to excuse me," he said in broken but fairly understandable English. "I did not mean to frighten you, but I hoped to speak to you, Miss Hayes, before you went inside."

This man was familiar to Cameron, though she hadn't seen him in four years. It would be difficult to forget a man who looked like a football linebacker and had once arrested Cameron.

"What do you want?" Cameron asked.

"Only for to talk." His English was much improved.

Donovan must have guessed—it wouldn't take a genius—that the stranger was MVD despite the fact that he was not in uniform. "Look here," Donovan protested. "There are plenty of places to talk inside."

"Please to come with me, Miss Hayes?" Incredibly, the man was asking rather than demanding.

"Cameron, don't go with him," said Donovan. "You remember what happened last time this happened to you."

She remembered all too well. Within hours after going away with the then NKVD agents, she was on a plane back to the States.

"I assure you," said the agent, "I only wish to talk—outside."

His emphasis on the word *outside* gave Cameron pause. There was usually only one reason people talked out of doors in Russia. But why would a member of the police worry about bugs *he'd* probably installed?

"I think it will be okay, Jed," she said with more confidence than she felt.

Donovan eyed the agent skeptically.

The man reassured him once more, "Only talk. Nothing else."

"You better have her back here within an hour, or I'll make

sure the full weight of the United States embassy falls on you," warned Donovan.

The agent must have known what an empty threat that was, but he said, "One hour should be enough time."

Cameron didn't know how to take that. A bruiser like this fellow could do a lot of damage in an hour. But she went with him anyway. She had prayed for something to happen. Maybe this was it. Of course, God would have a pretty unusual sense of humor if the thing that happened was her arrest and deportation.

"I'll see you in an hour," Donovan said pointedly.

As she and the agent walked away, she was sure her correspondent friend remained on the steps of the building watching until she turned a corner and was out of sight.

"It is a good thing to have friends," said the agent.

"What do you want?" she demanded.

"Do you remember me?"

"Yes, you got me deported once."

"I thought I was doing you a favor."

"That's what you people call it?"

He gave his big muscle-bound shoulder a shrug.

"My name is Colonel Anatoly Bogorodsk," he said. "I am, as you must know, with the MVD."

"You must be very proud," she replied snidely.

"That is a subject for another conversation," he answered vaguely.

Cameron did not trust this man. He looked like a thug, and his high rank in the most evil police force in the world only proved he must have curried great favor with the thug of all thugs, Josef Stalin. Yet, despite all that, Cameron sensed, as she had years ago when he'd had her alone in an interrogation room in police headquarters, an element of sympathy in this man. She didn't know what to make of it, but she determined to keep up her guard. Sympathy would be an excellent tactic to use in order to wheedle information from her.

"You do not trust me, yes?" he said.

"Should I?"

"What I said before about having friends, it is true."

"Do you have friends, Colonel?" She half expected some of these friends at any moment to jump from the bushes and slap handcuffs on her.

"Yes, I do. I know this must surprise you. There are not many, to be sure, so I value the ones I do have." He paused, perhaps for effect.

They passed an old church. It was boarded up now, and there were some beggars hovering in front. They held out grimy hands, asking for alms. The sight never failed to shock Cameron. Russian beggars were unbelievably ragged and filthy. But what disturbed her most was the legless man among them who still wore his Red Army uniform, though it was so tattered and faded it was barely recognizable as such.

Bogorodsk surprised Cameron by dropping a coin into the soldier's upturned cap.

"There but for grace," murmured the MVD agent.

"In my country," Cameron said, "that is a very religious statement."

"Yes, and how can an atheistic Communist speak of God's grace?" He shook his head. "It has been said that if there were no God it would be necessary to invent Him. I doubt you will find many true atheists in this country, even among such scum as myself. I have seen enough evil to make me often wonder about the existence of God. But . . . I have seen good, as well. And that brings me back to friendship. Would it surprise you to know that you and I have a mutual friend?"

"Yes."

"But surely you, too, have seen enough of the world to know surprising things do happen?"

"I suppose I have. Who is this mutual friend?" Many names passed through her head, but none of them was the one he indicated.

Bogorodsk replied, "Even now, out in the open air, where presumably we are safe from eavesdropping devices, I will not mention him by name. But he is one to whom you are very close, and one whom you feared you have lost."

She gasped and nearly spoke his name. Her heart skipped a beat as she swung her head around and gaped at her companion.

Pure instinct made her ask. "How can I believe you are his friend?" But she did remember Alex speaking of a friendly NKVD agent during the war. She'd wondered four years ago if this was that man.

"I can offer you no irrefutable proof, but I will tell you a story and you can judge from that." He glanced her way as if looking for her sanction to continue.

She nodded.

"My story begins about eight years ago," he began, "with a man who found himself a part of Russia's feared and hated secret police."

"That would be you?" Cameron prompted.

For some reason he didn't want to relate the story in the first person. Perhaps there was really no safe place in Russia, especially for one of Stalin's cops who somehow had befriended an outsider.

"This man," he continued, "had only two good things in his life. If there is a God, then it is a mystery why He would bestow on such a man the precious gift of a dear wife and a son." As he spoke, his English failed him at times, and he reverted to Russian, but Cameron's improved Russian helped her to follow easily. "These two made the man feel half human when he returned home after a day of his evil work."

"Why didn't this man give up the work if he thought it was so evil?" Cameron could not keep from asking.

"Only one reared in freedom could ask such a thing," Bogorodsk said. "There is but one way to leave a boss like Stalin, especially for a member of his police who knows far too much to be allowed to run loose in the country. You are either loyal to the Party or—you are dead. This man did not wish to be dead, yes? And besides, he half believed what he did was for the good of the Party and thus was justifiable." He paused, as though waiting for a protest from her. But she was too interested in the rest of the story to begin a political debate, so she nodded for him to continue.

He did so. "This man's son was ten years old at the time, a healthy, happy boy. But in a flash all that changed. One day while chasing a ball into the street, he was struck down by a truck. When the boy's father reached the hospital, the boy was truly at death's door. His doctor said only surgery could save him, though even that held only a slim hope. Of course his parents gave their permission. The father was leery, however, of the doctor, for he knew the man had recently arrived in Russia from America under cloudy circumstances. But other doctors he conferred with said flatly there was no hope. The boy would die with or without surgery, and they were not at all certain surgery would not just hasten the end. So the father grasped at the only straw of hope that was offered him.

"The surgery lasted ten hours. During that time the father expected at any minute for the doctor to appear to announce the boy's death. He knew his wife could have no more children. This child was everything to the father. Perhaps he was even the father's only hope of redemption for his sins. When the doctor finally appeared, he looked as near death as the patient had. One can only imagine the kind of exhaustion produced by standing for ten hours engrossed in such highly intensive work. The father learned later that many times during the procedure, the doctor's colleagues urged him to give up. The child even experienced what they call cardiac arrest. But the doctor would not give up."

Even if she hadn't already guessed, Cameron would have no doubt now who that doctor was. She'd seen Alex at work. She knew the kind of dogged tenacity he gave to his labor.

"The father's son was returned to him, Miss Hayes. He is now a remarkable young man dedicated to becoming a doctor himself. And this father had no doubt who was responsible for that gift. The doctor tried to protest the man's deep indebtedness. For years afterward, he tried to insist nothing was owed him. But the father knew differently. He knew he owed everything—everything!—to this doctor. He owed his very life to him."

Cameron could not respond immediately. They walked in silence for some time. But the scenes on the street were a blur to her—the gusts of wind blowing scattered trash, the kiosk selling brightly colored flowers from the Crimea, the vendor loudly hawking sausages. All Cameron could see was Alex, bent over the pale, helpless body of a child. Alex, barely able to stand but unwilling to sacrifice even one soul to death. He must have had enough faith even then to know death wasn't the end, yet he still prized life, especially for a mere boy who still had so much ahead of him. She could see the passion for medicine glow in his wonderful blue eyes, his eagerness to solve the puzzle of piecing back together a crushed body. All that was Alex. And that more than anything lent the ring of truth to Bogorodsk's story.

Bogorodsk had yet another surprise for Cameron. "Do you know that the doctor had no idea who the father was? He was not performing under fear of the man's position. Later, when the father told him, the doctor laughed. 'I'm glad you didn't tell me before the surgery, or I might have trembled too much to do any good,' he said."

Tears sprang to Cameron's eyes. She could hear Alex's voice, wry and sincere at the same time. Her heart suddenly ached to hear that voice again for real.

Plaintively, she asked, "Where is he, Colonel?"

"Then you believe my story?"

"Yes, I do."

"I know where he is, Miss Hayes."

"If you are his friend, why haven't you helped him? Surely a man of your position—"

"No man is safe in this country," he said bitterly, "and though I would give my own life freely for him, I would not sacrifice my family. I've had to wait until I could ensure their safety."

She nodded. "I'm sorry. I understand. They are safe now?"

"As safe as I can make them. They are no longer in Russia."

"So now what?"

"It is time to act."

"What do you propose?"

He hesitated. "My association with the doctor is known. Some have questioned whether I am too friendly with him. Some still look upon him as a foreigner despite the fact that he is not only a citizen but also a hero in the war. I have not been allowed near him, but I have not pressed the issue because of my family. Now I will try to get in to see him and attempt to assure him not to give up hope."

"Do you know if he is okay?"

"He is alive and has been interrogated. I don't think he has revealed any information, or they would have moved him out of the city by now. That is, if he had any information to give them. They think he does. Do you know if he has any?"

She visibly tensed and drew away from the MVD agent.

He snorted dryly. "It was a stupid question. Do not answer it. I don't want to know, believe me. You can trust me, Miss Hayes, but I realize it is not an easy thing to do."

"I have to trust you, don't I?" she said. "I had only one other hope of helping him, but that hasn't panned out."

"What was that?" he asked. "Perhaps I can make use of it."

She decided to throw caution to the wind and trust this man. But she backed this up with a silent prayer and felt a deep assurance that his story had been no fabrication. He indeed believed he owed Alex his life and was determined to not fail him at this most critical stage.

"Believe me it is a small hope," she confided. "Before I came to Russia during the war, I learned that I have a half brother here. It's a very long story, which I won't go into. I still don't know his name, but I have learned that he is alive. As a child he lost his real father, and his mother—my mother—was forced to return to America. At the age of six or seven he was adopted by a Russian family. A Russian friend of mine has located him but has given his word to the man's adopted father not to reveal his identity. One thing I know is that my half brother's adopted father is a very important man in the Party. Oh, my brother's first name is Semyon. In the back of my mind I had hoped to find this man and get him to help with our mutual friend. If he is truly important, he might have the resources to do so."

Bogorodsk give Cameron a sly smile. "I had always believed your man had found himself a remarkable woman, even if she is a foreigner. Now I am certain. You were busier than I thought while you were here as a correspondent."

"I guess the secret police are not omnipotent."

"No, they are not. And that may be—how do you say?—our ace in the hole."

"You never said where they have him."

"In Lubyanka."

She gulped dismally. "I feared as much."

"That works in our favor, actually. My office is there, and I come and go freely. How much harder can it be for me to go downstairs instead of up, yes?"

"Will it be difficult for you to contact me in the future?"

"I will manage. No one is entirely safe in this country, and while it is possible I am being watched, it is nothing I cannot deal with. Now, we have talked long enough."

"I truly can't thank you enough, Colonel," she said.

"Thank me when our friend is free."

31

CAMERON WAS TORN about whether to go to the embassy to see Blair or to find Jackie at the hotel. She had to tell them what had just happened. First, however, she returned to the pressroom to assure Donovan that she was okay before he started an international incident. She could only hint to him that her encounter with Bogorodsk had been a positive one.

When she left, she headed for the hotel. She remembered Blair mentioning she'd been invited to a luncheon at the British embassy, so she probably would not be at the apartment now anyway.

At the Metropole, Cameron found Jackie in the dining room lunching with Robert.

"Good, I've got both of you together," she said, slipping into the vacant chair at their table. "I've had an incredible day!"

Jackie grinned. "I haven't seen you this gay since . . . I can't remember when."

Cameron knew exactly when it had been, though Jackie hadn't been there to see it. The day she married Alex.

Just as she was about to blurt out her good news, she remembered where she was and why she couldn't.

"Oh!" she moaned. "I can't tell you here."

"Want to take a walk outside?" Robert offered.

"But you're eating." She realized then that she was hungry. That pirogi had not been very substantial, and now she had an appetite for the first time in a long while. "I think I want something, too," she said. "Then we can go for that walk."

"Unless you burst first," quipped Jackie.

"Let's just not dawdle over the food," Cameron suggested wryly.

Cameron had forgotten about the slow Russian service. By the time the meal was over, she was about to burst with impatience. But she was glad for the food because the place she wanted to take Robert and Jackie was a bit of a trek from where they were.

Once outside in the free air, she steered them toward her destination as she told them about her encounter with Bogorodsk.

"I'd call that a breakthrough," Robert said.

"I'd call it a miracle," amended Jackie.

Cameron noted the pleased look Robert directed toward Jackie. The look of a man who was proud he was with a woman whose first instinct was a godly one.

"It's both," Cameron said. "But who would ever have thought we'd have an MVD agent on our side? I feel anything is possible now!"

"It's going to be torture for you to wait to hear from him," said Jackie.

"You know me too well."

"Do you think he will also find out something about Semyon?"

"Who is Semyon?" Robert asked.

Cameron and Jackie exchanged glances.

Jackie said to Cameron, "I didn't know if I should tell anyone."

"I don't see why not." Cameron shrugged. "Semyon is our long-lost half brother who lives in Russia and whom we are trying to find—well, he's been found, but we don't know exactly who he is."

"I'll tell you all about it later, Robert," promised Jackie.

"Bogorodsk might try to find him," said Cameron, "but I don't see why he would have to in order to help Alex. He's a colonel in the MVD, for heaven's sake! He ought to be able to move mountains."

"You mentioned something about his relationship with Alex bringing him under some suspicion," commented Robert. He seemed a bit reluctant to interject reality into Cameron's rare optimistic mood.

"True," she said glibly, "but he didn't place any emphasis on that. It's probably just that natural Russian suspicion they all have."

They chatted and walked until they were a fair distance from the hotel. A light rain began to fall, surprising Cameron. She hadn't noticed the sky clouding up. Robert bought a couple of newspapers when they passed a newsstand near the metro station. These, held over their heads, gave them some protection. In a few minutes they reached their destination. Robert was the first to realize where Cameron had led them.

"Lubyanka" was all he said.

"He's in there," Cameron said.

"Oh my!" breathed Jackie.

They hovered under the eaves of a building across the street from the prison to keep dry.

"I've always had a feeling he was here," Cameron said, "but until now I was afraid to come near it."

"We should still be afraid," Robert said.

The infamous building stood before them like a forbidden wall, a barrier between Cameron and her heart's desire. Several MVD agents were coming and going from what was not only a prison, but also the headquarters of the secret police. In the center of the square that fronted the building, rain splattered against the statue of the man who was nearly as infamous as the prison. Feliks Dzerzhinsky, for whom the square was also named, had been the first head of the secret police, then called the Cheka, after the Revolution. There had been at the time no man more hated, not to mention feared. Still, he warranted a statue.

Cameron thought it was probably less to honor him than to continue to evoke fear in the Russian people.

I won't be afraid, Cameron stubbornly told herself, even though inside she quaked at the obstacle that lay before her. She remembered a Scripture verse she had recently read in her Bible. "There is no fear in love; but perfect love casteth out fear." Somehow Christ's love and her love for Alex would transcend her fears. A promise she would hold close.

"What's going on over there?" Jackie asked, nodding her head in the direction she meant, knowing it wasn't wise to point.

"They're building an addition to the prison," Robert said. "Stalin has been a busy fellow since the war. The old building didn't have enough room for his victims."

"It makes me sick," said Jackie.

"No matter." Cameron forced resolve into her tone. "I'm going to get in there. I'm going to get Alex out."

"Perhaps your new friend will get in for you," Robert suggested.

"One way or another," Cameron conceded.

"You know," Jackie offered, seeming to be getting into the spirit of the matter, "that construction over there might not be as bad a sign as it looks."

"What do you mean?" asked Robert, a bit of alarm showing in his expression. No doubt he had begun to guess what she was implying.

"Well, there's always confusion at construction sites, isn't there?" Jackie said. "Routines are interfered with, strangers are around as part of the construction crew . . ."

"Oh, my wonderful devious sister!" Cameron exclaimed. "You may have something there."

"I want you both to note," said Robert in his most reasonable tone, "that there are no female construction workers over there."

"We're not close enough to tell," argued Jackie. "And this is Russia, where women do men's work."

Robert's expression was so full of distress, Cameron feared it might draw observation from nearby police.

Jackie chuckled teasingly. "I'm just joking, Robert." She glanced at Cameron. "Right?"

Cameron nodded. "Yes, of course." She even forced out a chuckle of her own. But she knew she would do whatever it took to free Alex.

———

Jackie and Robert parted from Cameron in the hotel lobby. Jackie thought her sister looked exhausted and was glad she had decided to go up to their room for a nap. Maybe she would finally be able to sleep now that her hope had been boosted.

Jackie and Robert stood in the hotel lobby, both uncertain about what to do next. Jackie wasn't ready for him to leave, and she was too keyed up to return to her room and possibly disturb her sister.

"Robert, would you like me to tell you about Semyon?"

"I'd like that," he said. "Are you up for another stroll outside?"

Smiling, she replied, "I nearly forgot! It must be terrible when you have to share secrets in the winter. The rain is bad enough."

He laughed. "We try to have no secrets in winter."

"Everyone walks the straight and narrow, is that it?"

"Don't we wish."

Laughing, they exited the hotel once more, this time armed with their raincoats and an umbrella borrowed from the desk clerk.

"Actually, I like walking in the rain," Jackie said. "My Emi loves to splash in the puddles. Summer rain, of course, when it's warm enough so wet feet aren't a problem."

"This is more like the start of autumn. It comes early in Russia."

"I regret I won't be here to see it, or winter."

"You won't?"

Was that disappointment in his tone? "I must return home soon. I miss my daughter terribly. And there's my teaching job.

School begins after Labor Day." She, too, felt more regret than she expected.

"Of course," he said. "It's selfish of me to hope you could stay forever."

"You really mean that?"

"I've . . . enjoyed your company enormously."

She thought he might have wanted to say something else, perhaps something more personal. Maybe it was best he hadn't. Despite any silly premonition she may have had, two weeks was far too fast for any relationship to develop. Yet she realized that when she left Russia, she'd be in California and he would be here, thousands of miles away. How could anything grow at all then?

If it is meant to be, she thought, you'll work things out, Lord, won't you?

To distract herself from these thoughts she said, "Why don't I tell you the story of my half brother."

For the next several minutes she did just that, telling him of her mother's sad sojourn in Russia, her neglect by her husband, and her fateful meeting of a Russian bookseller.

"I couldn't have been more shocked," she said finally. "In my mind my mother has always been close to a saint. For a short while after I heard, I felt betrayed, until I reminded myself of her deep heartache in all this. I knew if God forgave her, so must I."

"It must have been difficult, regardless," he said.

"I feel bad for my father," Jackie added. "I know he made mistakes, but he's been betrayed, as well. My mother hasn't told him yet, so he hasn't even had the chance to forgive her. Cameron's afraid he wouldn't. I have to admit I've never heard him apologize for anything, much less offer forgiveness. What do you think, Robert? Do you think we should tell him?"

He seemed surprised she was asking his opinion on such a delicate matter. But she hoped he might have some good insights.

"Not knowing either your father or mother, it is hard to know what would be best. But if I were forced to decide the issue, I would have to choose on the side of truth."

"Yes, I'm sure it must come to that."

Robert seemed to be distracted, as if he'd pulled suddenly inward. Had she told one too many secrets? Had she finally given him cause to doubt a woman from such a mixed-up background?

She didn't know what to say, and they walked in silence, the only sound the splashing of rain against their umbrella. She sensed his sudden pensive mood and was dying to know what he was thinking. She forced down her curiosity.

Soon the rain stopped, and a bit of blue sky peeked around the edges of the gray clouds, hinting that summer had some good days left yet.

Jackie had heard of awkward silences and had experienced her share, but this one was excruciating. He still held the umbrella over their heads, causing her to feel insulated with him on the busy street.

Finally he lowered the umbrella. "The rain's stopped," he said, as if just emerging from a dream.

She only nodded.

"Thank you," he said.

"For what?"

"I needed a few moments to think something over." He gave the umbrella a shake, then closed it. "We've been talking about secrets and truth, and I have offered you neither. You have opened yourself to me, while I have remained safely in my shell, so to speak. Now I want to share one of my secrets with you."

"You don't have to, Robert. I don't expect reciprocation."

"I know, but I'd like to tell you anyway. I've waited a long time to tell someone, and I'd like you to be that person." He paused, his brow creased. "Well, in the interest of honestly, you are not the first person I've told. Cameron was the first, but it was years ago. I feel like this is the first time because now I know you will be the first of many to hear my story." An embarrassed laugh slipped from his lips. "Sounds terribly ominous, doesn't it?"

"A little," she squeaked, feeling some trepidation.

"I'm Jewish!" he blurted.

She took a small misstep and he caught her arm, righting her. She gave him a puzzled look, waiting for more, for some terrible secret.

"That's your secret?" she asked, dismayed that he thought it would bother her. "I can't believe you would be so petty as to keep something like that from me. Are you ashamed of it?"

He blinked at her sharp words.

Well, what had he expected? After she had shared her own experiences with racial prejudice, how could he think she was so bigoted?

"Jackie, please wait," he implored. "You don't understand." He flung a hand across his hair, sending that rebellious strand down into his eyes. He gave it a frustrated brush with his fingers. "Only the second time I've told someone, and I've botched it royally." Self-recrimination laced his words.

"Well," she said, relenting a little, "it sounds to me like you think I would hold that against you, and worse, that you are ashamed of it."

"Neither is true," he said. "The truth is, my family has been hiding our Jewish heritage for many years."

She stared, astonished at what she was hearing. She had heard of such things. She recalled Sam's telling her that many times when he'd been younger he had desperately wished he could be white, for unlike some immigrant nationalities, like the Irish or Germans or Italians, there was no way he could blend in and disappear into white society. Is that what Robert's family had done?

"My name is Robert Grunwald," he said, pausing as if savoring the feel of those words on his lips. "I haven't had the opportunity of speaking that name often. Only to myself. I'm the great-grandson of a German immigrant, a well-educated man, a lawyer. After he got to the promised land of America, he discovered those promises were offered less readily to one with a Jewish-sounding name. So he changed his surname to Wood, found employment, and soon the family rose through the ranks of society. They moved from New York to Boston, where they could start with a clean slate. The Wood family began one of the most successful law firms in the state. My grandfather became a well-respected federal judge. My father is in state government and is considering a run for Congress. He is a pillar of his Presbyterian church, president of his country club—one that excludes Jews."

"My parents' club also forbids Jews," she stated contritely. "Dad was really worried my marriage to Sam would get him blackballed."

"I didn't ask for any of this," he said.

She realized he was not only seeking but also needing her understanding. She freely offered it. "I understand now, Robert. Forgive my initial reaction."

"You had every right. This whole thing is reprehensible. Not only my family's lie, but that they had to lie in the first place."

"When did you find out?"

"Just before I entered college. I discovered some family papers in the attic and confronted my father. He said he was going to tell me. I wonder, though. Maybe it would have been better if I'd never found out." He stopped walking and turned to face her. "Or do I wish I'd grown up Jewish, eating kosher, observing Sabbath, and learning Hebrew at the feet of my rabbi? I just don't know."

"If that had been the case," Jackie said, "what would have become of your Christian faith?"

"There lies another can of worms," he sighed. "My faith is real. I'm sure of it. Still, sometimes I wonder if I became a Christian under false circumstances. What would have happened if I had been raised Jewish rather than Presbyterian? Was I destined to find Christ as my Savior all along, or did it happen because I was raised in Christianity?"

"Only what is in your heart now matters," Jackie said confidently.

"I wish I had your confidence. I've been shaken to the core, and there are moments when my heart is torn in two."

They began moving again. She wasn't certain what to say, but she did know they couldn't keep walking forever, and she had a feeling this conversation wasn't going to end soon.

"Is there someplace safe in this city where we can sit and talk?" she asked.

He looked around, as if noticing their surroundings for the first time. "I think there's a pub not far from here."

It was farther than he'd thought. When he opened the door for her, a quick glance inside told her this was not the ordinary type of establishment frequented by foreigners. It reminded her more of a corner bar in America, where truck drivers or factory workers might stop for a beer after work.

Hesitating at the door, she said, "Is it okay?"

"I don't think anyone bothered to follow us today," he assured. "And there definitely won't be any bugs in here—at least the electronic kind. I'd look out for the other kind, though." He chuckled. "But the tea should be safe to drink."

It wasn't very busy at this time of day. They had no trouble finding a table. Jackie felt a greasy residue on its surface as she brushed it with her hand, so she slid into a chair, trying not to touch the table. Stale cigarette smoke blended with even staler body odors, all topped off with the fragrance of rancid cabbage.

Noting her wrinkled nose, he said, "Sorry I couldn't come up with someplace better. At least we can talk freely here."

"Well, I've wanted to meet the real Russians. I bet I'll find them here."

"Soon as the workday ends, this place will be bustling. I've come here a few times just to hear everyday Russian spoken."

When a waiter came, Robert ordered. "There's tea," he explained to Jackie, "but no food served at this hour."

"I'm not hungry."

"Nor am I."

"Robert, you said that you hoped I would be the first of many you would tell about being Jewish. How does your family feel about that?"

He let out a dry snort. "I'm sure my father feels that telling our secret would be worse than dropping another A-bomb. I went home for a year after the war to try to talk him into breaking the silence about who we are. After what happened to the Jews in Europe, I feel that hiding our true heritage is nearly the same as admitting that Hitler was right, that Jews are subhuman and must be exterminated. When I was in Germany a couple months ago on business, I visited one of Hitler's death camps. Dachau. Of course it is cleaned out now, but I saw one of those gas chambers. I stood inside it and tried to imagine what it must have been like. What they felt when they first realized the unthinkable was happening. I have little doubt many must have continued to believe the delousing lie right until the first person fell over. Even now with the evidence of the truth, it is hard to conceive of such a thing, the systematic murder of millions of people! In that moment as I stood there, I knew I wanted to claim my heritage."

The waiter brought tea and cups, but they hardly noticed it. Jackie's eyes were focused on Robert. She felt ashamed for ever thinking ill of him. As he imagined the suffering of Hitler's victims, she tried to imagine his personal pain and confusion.

He went on, "Two years have passed since the war, since I first heard of this holocaust upon the Jews. Two months have passed since I was in Dachau, and still I've said nothing."

"You've told me."

"I can still back out. I can hold you to secrecy, and that will be that." Absently, he picked up the teapot and filled their cups. "My father has begged me to keep silent. There's more at stake than his career, than the key to the club tennis courts. He's never told my mother. Can you believe that?"

"Yes, I can," she said softly.

"Of course you can—I almost forgot." He fingered the handle of his cup but did not drink. "Do I destroy his life? I can rebuild. My brother and sister can start over. They are younger than I. They have time. But my father is sixty years old. If his life crashes around him, I don't know if he could survive, or if his marriage could. People have asked me why I'm thirty-five years old and have never married. I could never do to a woman what my father did to my mother."

"You have been placed in a horrible position."

"It's all up to me," he said miserably. "I hold all their destinies in my palm." He held up his open hand, then squeezed it together into a fist.

Gently Jackie wrapped her own hand around that fist. "Remember, Robert, God is holding your hand."

He smiled and nodded. "I did forget there for a minute. It doesn't feel such a heavy burden when I remember that." He brought her hand to his lips and gently brushed it with a kiss. That brief touch was filled with such intensity, she could not imagine even a passionate kiss on the lips affecting her more deeply.

"He will help you to know the right thing to do," she said.

"He hasn't yet. Maybe I'm too impatient. Yet if there is one reason for clinging to my Christian faith, it is that. I need Christ in my life. I want His direction."

"Maybe God has already let you know the answer, in what you told me about the truth. 'Ye shall know the truth, and the truth shall make you free.'"

He lowered their still clasped hands but didn't take his away. Instead, he placed his other hand on hers, gazing deeply into her eyes all the while. She thought that look of wonder in his shining dark eyes was odd.

"So simple," he said. "My mother often told me I was too smart for my own good. Thank you for letting me share this with you. I have had so few here in Russia with whom I could open up. Talking it out this way has truly helped."

"I'm glad, Robert."

"I'm going to speak with the ambassador as soon as possible."

"You won't tell your father first?"

"If I wait until I can do that, I may lose my resolve. I'm sure he knows it's coming. I'll send him a cable in the morning, though. The repercussions from what I do here won't reach

America for a while. It will give him time to prepare."

"I'm so proud of you, Robert! It takes an incredible amount of courage to do what you plan."

"I haven't done it yet," he said with a self-deprecating chuckle. "But I will."

They talked for another hour. Soon the pub began to fill with its after-work crowd, and the noise level rose to such that they could barely hear each other. Reluctantly, they admitted it was time to go. Jackie considered suggesting some evening entertainment, a movie or another play perhaps, so they could keep this incredible day going. But they had to be practical, she supposed. She was free, but he still had the duties of his job, and he had a dinner he must attend as the ambassador's representative.

They returned to the hotel. She thought he was sweet to walk her to the elevator. As they were crossing the lobby, she noted a uniformed man rise from one of the seats and approach them.

It was Troy Rigdon.

32

ROBERT STAYED a few moments to exchange polite greetings with Rigdon before making a hasty retreat.

It didn't take a genius—and since he was one, he should know!—to size up the situation with Rigdon as a battle in the making. Well, that was probably too strong a term—a competition might fit better.

No matter what it was called, Robert felt as if he had suddenly lost a great deal of ground. Yes, he and Jackie had been spending some marvelous days together lately. In a short time, they had connected on a profound level.

But he'd pretty much had the field to himself. If Rigdon was back in the picture . . .

Beside a man like the brawny Naval captain, Robert felt like a candle flickering beside a giant searchlight. He'd tried to convince himself that Jackie's initial attraction to Rigdon had been purely a reaction to the man's surface attributes. But who was he kidding? Jackie was not that shallow. And though he didn't know Rigdon well, he did know the fellow was not all spit-and-polish. Maybe he was a bit self-absorbed, but he was a decent sort. He had earned the Silver Star in battle and a battlefield promotion for his heroism. More than that, Robert had seen him often at church services, so he must be a Christian, which would be important to Jackie.

It had started to rain again, and soon water was dripping off the end of Robert's nose and blurring the lenses of his glasses. Too bad he wasn't in the habit of wearing a hat. He'd be soaked before he reached the embassy. Right now he was too miserable to care.

He'd come to care deeply for Jackie. For the first time in years he had lowered his defenses to let a woman get close. And finally he was in a position to commit openly and honestly to a woman. More than that, he felt instinctively he might have found the woman he wanted to have a future with.

But if Rigdon also fancied her and she had to choose . . . He groaned and shook his head in answer to his own silent question, sending a spray of water onto a passerby.

Fancy? Now who used a word like that nowadays? Another strike against him. He'd always been such an awkward egghead. What could possibly make him think a beautiful modern girl like Jackie would be romantically attracted to him? Yes, they'd had some wonderful moments, but none that couldn't be attributed to anything more than friendship.

Rigdon was the kind of man for Jackie. A man who'd laugh at a word like *fancy*. A man who'd say, "I dig you, Jackie. You're the cat's meow." A man who had probably kissed her on their first date. It had taken all of Robert's nerve just to brush his lips against her hand.

There was one other asset Rigdon had going for him. Robert's confession to Jackie about his being Jewish had been an astounding encounter for him. And he'd felt deep sympathy from Jackie. She would never reject him for that. But she had told him how her father had nearly disowned her for her relationship with her Japanese husband. Could she defy her father again? Would she? Robert knew enough about Keagan Hayes to sense he would have nearly as many prejudices against a Jew as he would against a Japanese. Anti-Semitism in America was incredibly widespread. When Cameron had been dealing with the issue of the massacre of Jews that her friend Oleg Gorbenko had witnessed, she had never even hinted that her father would champion the man's cause in his newspaper.

Thinking of encountering prejudice because of his being a Jew was almost as shocking as if it were actually happening to him. He realized if he opened up to the world, as it were, there would doubtless be some of that. Life would be far different for Robert Grunwald than it had been for Robert Wood.

And that sparked his anger.

He was as good as any man! He defied anyone to denigrate him for being Jewish, or anything else, for that matter.

He had as much to offer a beautiful, desirable woman as did the likes of Captain Rigdon. He wasn't entirely unpleasant to look upon, not to mention intelligent. He had a bright future ahead of him regardless of what transpired after the revelation of his heritage. Despite the presence of anti-Semitism, America was far more advanced in that area than it had been fifty years ago. He might not be a he-man or suave with the ladies, but he was decent and honorable. He believed Jackie valued those traits above all.

As the rain washed over him, it seemed to flush away his insecurities. He was suddenly of a mind to march right back to the hotel and give Rigdon a run for his money.

But as he neared the embassy, he realized there was something he had to do first. He could not—he would not!—put it off any longer.

Full of fiery resolve he made his way to Ambassador Smith's office, pausing only for a few moments at his apartment to dry off a bit. He was ushered immediately into the ambassador's office. Only then did Robert's determination start to slip. In the back of his mind he'd thought Smith would not be at the embassy this late in the day, or certainly he would be busy and unable to spare time just then. The suddenness of his reception left Robert feeling as if caught in a whirlwind.

He would not let that deter him. He had a mission.

"Robert, I want to thank you again for attending that dinner for the Italian foreign minister. It's highly important we show our support by our presence. Those Italians have been rather touchy about these things since the war, and we don't want them to think we're snubbing them."

"I don't mind at all," said Robert. "It's my job to run interference for you in your absence."

"Well, the minister's visit was rather a surprise, and my wife's sister's visit has been planned for weeks. I promised I'd be at the welcome dinner for her."

"You just have a good time."

"You don't know my sister-in-law." The ambassador chuckled. "Have a seat, Robert. Did something specific bring you up here?"

Smith had risen from his seat behind his desk to receive Robert. Now he gestured to the sitting area, where three leather upholstered chairs sat around a coffee table.

"I did have something I wanted to talk to you about, sir," Robert began. He wanted to take this slowly, not blurt it out as he had to Jackie.

"Go on."

Robert made a concerted effort not to squirm in his chair. He told himself over and over that he was proud of who he was.

"I have a bit of a confession to make, sir." He paused. No blurting. "But in all honestly I hate to call it a confession as if it were something wrong. Maybe it is somewhere between confessing and bragging. A number of years ago my great-grandfather immigrated to America from Germany. Even then Jews faced great anti-Semitism in Europe."

"Jews, you say?"

"Yes, sir, he was Jewish. He'd hoped to find more acceptance in the New World, but it wasn't to be. He was an educated man, but the only work he could find was as a janitor, and that only because he changed his name from Grunwald to Wood. He moved his family from New York to Boston in order to start over with the new name. They were very successful."

"Yes," mused the ambassador. "I well know the Wood Law Firm. And I knew and respected your grandfather." He crossed his legs and directed an incisive gaze at Robert. "When did you find all this out, Robert?"

"I've known for about fifteen years, since just before I started law school. My father told me then—" Despite his desire for truth, Robert didn't want to cast his father in a bad light.

"You've known all this time?"

Robert nodded, and a long silence followed. The ambassador's face was blank. Robert could not even venture a guess as to what was going on behind that stoic exterior. Robert shifted in his chair, uncrossed his leg, then recrossed the other. He began to worry as the silence dragged on.

"Why are you telling me this now?" Smith finally asked.

"I have never liked living with this lie," Robert answered frankly. "I've done so for my family's sake—well, I can't say I haven't prospered because of it. But what has happened to the Jews in the war has made me acutely aware of who I am and of how hiding it only appears to validate what Hitler did."

"That's very commendable."

It seemed that statement would be followed by a *but,* so Robert waited for more.

"You know, Robert, I am not anti-Semitic. I have many Jewish friends."

It wasn't exactly a *but;* nevertheless, Robert still felt it coming. "I know that, sir." I'm counting on that, he thought.

"I understand that you have been under pressures outside yourself to do what you have done."

"I have."

"But your actions are highly irregular for a member of the State Department."

There it was. Robert waited dismally for the rest.

"You have taken a position in government demanding the highest truth and honor. Yet you have abused that honor with a serious lie."

Robert wanted to cry out, "My father made me do it!" But he was man enough to take full responsibility for his actions. He remembered what Jackie had told him about his courage. He clung to that. His life may crumble, but he would know he had faced it courageously.

"I know, Ambassador," he said.

"I would be well within my rights to fire you on the spot. Not for being a Jew, you understand, but for lying."

Robert swallowed. How he hated being thought of as a liar and deceiver. He'd tried to live his whole life with honor. Would one lie now mark him forever?

"I'm not going to do that," said the ambassador.

Robert blinked at this surprising statement but remained silent.

Smith continued, "For one thing, it would reflect badly on me and on this office, for no matter what was said, it would appear as if your dismissal was due to your being Jewish. Moreover, as I said, I do understand the pressures you were under regarding your family, but some action must be taken."

"Yes, sir. I am prepared to answer for what I have done."

"You have been in Russia for two tours," Smith said. "An extra long tour during the war. A year in the States, and now you are well into another two-year tour. How many ambassadors have you seen come and go?"

"A few."

"You are quite invaluable to this embassy; nevertheless, even ambassadors serve for only two years. All things together, I think your time here should be coming to a natural conclusion. I believe the best course of action would be for you to tender your resignation."

Robert had expected something like that, but he had not expected his reaction. It surprised him that he did not feel as if the rug had been pulled out from under him. It took the ambassador to enlighten him, but he should have known all along he was going to have to resign. There would be strong repercussions within his family over his revelation, and he needed to be there to support them, or to take their blows. And now there were other reasons for him to return to America. If he did have a chance with Jackie, he certainly could not hope to win her if ten thousand miles separated them.

"I'll have my resignation on your desk in the morning."

"You understand how difficult this is for me?"

"I know, Ambassador. But I agree it is the best thing."

"I'm sure you will still have a bright future ahead of you."

"We shall see."

They rose and the ambassador walked Robert to the door.

He paused. "You know, I can't let you go until your replacement arrives."

"I understand," said Robert. "And I will continue to serve you loyally."

Robert walked down the hall with a much lighter step. He'd faced the worst obstacle and survived. Well, the worst obstacle would be his father, but with God's help he'd survive that, too. And his family would survive, also. He was sure of it.

Robert stopped by his office before he went home to change for the reception. He was still an employee of the embassy, and he had grossly neglected his work today. There was correspondence he needed to send off in the morning.

As he worked at his desk, the telephone rang. He picked it up.

"Hello," he said. He listened a moment with an expression of growing alarm. Finally he responded, "Meet me in the ambassador's office in ten minutes."

Disconnecting the call, he dialed a number. "Ambassador Smith, this is Robert. Can you wait a few minutes in your office? Something urgent has come up."

————

"So, Troy, what brings you here?" Jackie asked politely, though she couldn't help the touch of frost in her voice.

"I wanted to talk to you."

"Okay."

"Can we go someplace?"

Jackie considered for a moment, then led him to the sitting

area in the lobby. She couldn't imagine that Troy had anything to say to her that the Soviet eavesdroppers couldn't hear, as well.

When they were settled in adjacent chairs, he said, "I've been thinking a lot about what happened the last time I saw you. I feel pretty bad about it."

Was he here to apologize? Did he want to continue seeing her? Somehow, it didn't really matter to her. Yes, he was handsome, but that's not what she was looking for. She thought she had already found what she was looking for, and he wasn't handsome like Troy, nor as smooth talking. In fact, he wasn't anything like Troy Rigdon at all. He was leagues better in every way.

Still, she had to be polite to Troy, give him a chance to make amends. "I feel bad about it, too, Troy."

"It wasn't all your fault," he said.

All my fault? What does that mean? It was clear he thought some of it was her fault. "Just what part wasn't my fault?"

He didn't notice the sarcastic inflection in her tone. "I didn't give you much of a chance. Everyone makes mistakes, and I shouldn't have been so quick to judge you for yours."

Mistakes? She felt heat infuse her skin, and it wasn't the heat of shame or embarrassment. This heat was about to ignite a terrible fury within her. "I think you've said enough," she managed between gritted teeth.

"Please give me a chance. I know I don't deserve it."

His tone was truly sincere. He really did not have the faintest notion of his error. It made her feel a little sorry for him. She relented. "Please continue."

"I'd like to try to work this out. Maybe I can overlook what you told me."

He wanted to overlook it, while Robert had embraced it.

"I'm sorry, Troy, but that's not good enough."

Her response took him aback.

"Huh? I don't think you understand. I think I can forget about . . . well, about what you did, about that marriage of yours. That would be the Christian thing to do, and I want to do the right thing."

"And would you also like to forget about my daughter, who looks very much like her father?" Jackie felt the heat rise again.

"I don't know. Couldn't we cross that bridge when we get to it? I mean, she's not here now."

"She's here, Captain Rigdon. She's in my heart, as is her father. They are not some afterthought we can deal with as needed."

"I didn't exactly mean that."

"Before you go on any further, Captain, I must tell you that I am not interested in seeing you again." She realized she had let him go this far in order to punish him, to watch him squirm, but now that she realized her intent, she knew it was wrong and couldn't let it continue. "Troy," she said more softly, "when I first met you, I thought you might be someone I'd like, but I know now you are not my type. Even if you were to fall madly in love with my daughter and venerate my husband, I know I would not be interested in you. I don't think we have anything in common."

"Are you sure you can be so choosy, Jackie?" he said, an edge to his tone now. "I mean, I am willing to try to overlook what you did. Not many men would do that."

"Only the special ones," she said, and a gentle smile bent her lips as she thought of that particular man with errant hair, poor vision, and skin that didn't fit exactly right.

Troy might always wonder about the meaning of that mysterious smile. Or maybe he knew. No matter, she had no regrets as she watched him walk away.

She went up to her room. Cameron was awake and seated at her portable Underwood typing. Jackie told her sister about her afternoon, about what Robert had shared, and about Troy's visit. Jackie was touched when Cameron shared how she had found out about Robert being Jewish. Jackie had yet another reason to admire Robert for his compassionate heart.

There was a knock at the door, and Jackie was surprised to find the object of their conversation standing before her when she opened the door.

"Robert! Hi. Come in."

When he looked briefly at her, she saw a lot of things in his shining eyes but couldn't identify any of them. Was there a hint of concern and questioning? Might he be worried about Troy's visit?

"I can't stay long," he said. "I have to be at that reception in a few minutes." He came in, and Jackie closed the door.

"Robert," Cameron said, "you look positively grim."

He took a slip of paper from his pocket and gave it to Cameron. Her face went pale as she read it. Then she gave it to Jackie.

It looked to be hurriedly handwritten. *Can't talk and no time to walk. Larry Marquet has been arrested. We are trying to get more information. All we know is they suspect him of espionage.*

"Robert," Cameron said in a tone as pale as her skin, "does this mean what I fear?"

"It might not, Cameron, but it would be a good idea to get your new friend to expedite things."

Cameron's head dropped into her hands, and her shoulders trembled. Jackie hurried to her side and put an arm around her. She lifted an imploring gaze toward Robert, who looked miserable in his helplessness.

"I have to be at that reception tonight," he said apologetically. "There's got to be an American of some standing in the embassy present, not that I'll qualify for long."

"What do you mean?" Jackie asked with concern.

"We'll talk soon, okay?" When Jackie nodded, he added, "Cameron, please don't lose hope. God has brought you this far. You have to trust Him to finish what He has started." He laid a hand on her shoulder and squeezed it gently.

She lifted reddened eyes and offered a tentative smile. "Thank you, Robert."

Jackie walked Robert to the door.

"I wish I didn't have to leave," he said.

"It's okay. There's little we can do right now."

"Jackie, I—"

"Robert, I—"

Their voices collided. They smiled.

"Go ahead," he said.

"I had an interesting talk with Troy," she said.

"D-did you?" His voice cracked over the words.

"You know, he's kind of a jerk."

"He is?"

"That's my opinion. He thought he'd be magnanimous and overlook my mistakes." She rolled her eyes. "Anyway, just thought you'd be interested in why he came."

"I am. . . . I was . . . I . . ." He seemed frustrated. "There's a lot I'd like to talk to you about, but Cameron needs you, and I have that reception to attend."

"Maybe tomorrow," she suggested.

"Yes, definitely."

33

CAMERON TOSSED a hurried glance over her shoulder as she crossed the crowded station platform. Seeing nothing suspicious, she shouldered her way toward the approaching train.

She had taken Robert's advice, and though it had taken two days, she had contacted Colonel Bogorodsk. Now she was on her way to meet him. She just hoped choosing the busiest time of day at the metro had freed her from MVD scrutiny.

The train rumbled to a stop, its brakes screeching loudly. Like everything else in Russia, the trains were in poor repair, though millions in Moscow relied on them for transportation.

It felt as if every one of those millions had converged on this particular station. It was five in the afternoon, the end of the workday for many, and they all were anxious to get home. She caught an elbow in the ribs and felt her hat knocked askew. Once in the stream of bodies flowing into the train, she couldn't have turned back if she wanted to. The seats were quickly taken. Standing, Cameron grasped the overhead bar, but she needn't have bothered, for the press of other passengers would keep her from falling when the train lurched into motion.

As soon as the train began moving, many of those seated snapped open their newspapers. The Soviet press might not be a free one, but Muscovites gobbled it up regardless. Cameron noted the headline on a paper held by a nearby passenger.

"AMERICAN SPY CAUGHT RED-HANDED!"

Cameron snorted, drawing a look from the man pressed up next to her. The Soviet Ministry of Information always took days to release news, but of course they would jump on this.

She would have liked to read the article and knew her Russian was good enough to allow her to, but she also knew it no doubt sported a tirade about insidious American designs upon the blameless Soviet people.

Cameron waited for three stops, debarked the train, walked to another part of the station, and got on another line. By the time she had changed lines twice more, she was certain she was not followed.

She bought a *Pravda* as she exited the final station. The article about Larry Marquet was as she had guessed, a twisted version of the truth. It said Marquet had confessed to espionage and the American embassy had not in any way attempted to dispute it. All outright lies. According to Robert, Marquet had never confessed, and the embassy was standing staunchly by him. The fact that Marquet actually was engaged in espionage didn't matter. It was entirely possible that the ambassador was not fully apprised of his actions. Even if he was, the embassy would never admit to it.

The article went on to assure that "this threat to the peace-loving Soviet nation" would be deported posthaste. This, at least, was true. Marquet's exit visa was being expedited, and he would no doubt leave in a few days. His diplomatic immunity had kept him from remaining in Soviet hands for long, only about six hours, but it apparently could not keep the Soviet government from forcing him to leave the country. Robert had intimated, though he could not come right out and say it, that some deal had been struck with the Foreign Ministry. Cameron hoped she would have a chance to see Marquet before he departed. She still held on to a scrap of hope that somehow he would come through with the documents for Alex.

Cameron's mood had lifted since that moment in her hotel

room when she had read Robert's note. She knew now why God had directed Blair and Jackie to come to Russia with her. Both of her sisters had helped to strengthen her and get her through what was probably her lowest point since hearing of Alex's arrest. And once she had recovered her emotional stability, she had acted quickly.

She was to meet the MVD colonel in Pushkin Square. Once there, she found a bench that had another bench backing it and waited. The park was nearly deserted this time of day. Those who had come earlier to enjoy one of the last sunny days of summer had gone home. Soon a woman came along and sat on the adjacent bench.

Why she would choose that place when there were other empty places to sit in the park, Cameron did not know. But Bogorodsk would not approach if anyone was near, that was certain. Cameron's stomach twisted and knotted as she prayed this would not scare off the man.

Ten anxious minutes passed before the woman rose and strolled away. A few moments later, out of the corner of her eye, Cameron saw the big agent stride toward her. She kept her eyes averted, however. As he sat, his back toward her on the other bench, she opened her copy of *Pravda* and pretended to read. He did the same. With their heads buried in the newspapers, no one could tell they were talking.

"You were not followed?" he asked.

"I'm sure of it."

"It was very dangerous of you to contact me."

She had taken great precautions in doing so. She had contacted Sophia, who in turn had called upon a friend, who enlisted yet another friend, who delivered the message to the colonel.

"The messenger could not be traced back to me," she assured.

"Nevertheless, I said I would contact you."

"Why has it taken so long?"

"I must be careful."

She wondered then if her confidence in him was misplaced. No matter, he was still her only resource.

"I fear time is running out for him," she said.

"Why?"

"Have you heard about the captured spy? Alex . . . knew him."

Bogorodsk must have caught her slight hesitation. "So he *was* involved in espionage. Was Aleksei, as well?"

"Would it matter?"

There was a long silence. Cameron resisted the urge to turn and assess the agent's expression. Now she would find out just how deep his debt to Alex went.

"If so, I am sure he had his reasons. I am sure they were noble," he said at last.

Cameron let out her held breath. "You understand, don't you, that the news of Marquet indicates that Alex may be breaking."

"Yes, I understand time is growing short. I have been cut off from everything regarding Aleksei's case. They know of my close relationship to him. Besides that, the departure of my family might cast me in a suspicious light. I've had to move slowly so as not to bring attention to myself." He paused. She heard him take a shuddering breath. "I will press harder to see him."

"Please, Colonel," Cameron said desperately, "if you can't help him, I don't know where else to turn."

"I will not fail him." His tone was resigned, like that of a man about to step off a precipice.

———

Anatoly was close to the edge. One misstep and he would plummet over. But he was still a colonel in the MVD. He still had resources. Those resources had been aiding him in digging into the mystery of Cameron's half brother. He felt he was getting near some answers. He wasn't certain how that could help, but years as a police agent had taught him the value of even the smallest nugget of information.

His main problem, however, was getting in to see Aleksei. If he could do that, then he'd be fairly certain the door would be open for him to do even more. That newspaper article about the

American spy might be the perfect opening now that he knew it involved Aleksei.

Armed with the copy of *Pravda,* he went to the office of Colonel Podolsk, the man who was in charge of Aleksei's case.

"So, Sergei," Anatoly said without preamble when he had been let into the man's office, "you have had Rostovscikov in custody for weeks now, and this is all you have ferreted out of him?" He waggled *Pravda* in the man's face. "'American spy caught red-handed!'" he quoted in a mocking tone.

"How do you know this story relates to Rostovscikov?"

Though the men were of the same rank, Anatoly had been promoted a few months earlier so held slight superiority over Podolsk. He intended to use that to his full advantage.

"Do you think I have my head in the sand?" Anatoly strode boldly in and sat in a chair. "Sit down, Sergei. It is time we talked."

With a shrug Podolsk took the seat behind his desk. "This is my case, Anatoly. And you know the reason for that."

"Yes, I well know," sneered Anatoly. "You consider me too friendly to the doctor. So I accepted that. I have a lot of my own work to do. I don't need your cases also."

"Then why are you here?"

"You and I have been friends for how long? Fifteen years at least. We took our training together and rose up the ladder almost side by side." He placed the slightest emphasis on the word *almost.* Podolsk knew he had more often than not ridden on Anatoly's coattails. There even had been a couple of promotions that had come just because Anatoly had spoken for him. He might not want to admit it, but he owed much of his career to the big tough agent. What he might not realize yet was the fact that it was now time to pay his debt.

"Yes, Anatoly, this is true." Podolsk spoke cautiously. There were friendships and there were friendships in the MVD. One could never be too free with anyone.

"Well, in the name of that friendship, I want to help you."

"*You* want to help me?"

"Have you ever considered that my friendship with Rostov-scikov might be the ideal way to extract information from him?" Anatoly slapped the newspaper against the desk. "Had I not been so busy with other matters, I would have offered my services earlier. This article prompted me to act."

"We consider this an enormous breakthrough," Podolsk said defensively.

"Bah!" Anatoly stabbed a finger at the article. "This is nothing. Surely you can see that. So you deport an American spy. We know all the Americans at the embassy are engaged in espionage. You can't deport them all."

"It is a start."

"That is the kind of thinking that has held you back, Sergei. Foreign spies are one thing, but the far worse danger is the spies and traitors among our own people. Those are the ones we must ferret out. We must break the networks polluting our own people."

"What has that to do with Rostovscikov?"

Anatoly shook his head and directed a look at his comrade as he might look upon a slow-witted child. "Marquet was obviously controlling Rostovscikov, who despite his past, is a Russian citizen in good standing, or shall I say *was*? Do you think he was the only Russian Marquet controlled? Do you think Rostovscikov acted alone? I know the man. He knows nothing of these matters, thus he must have been working with others."

"Why do you think we continue to question the man? We are certain he knows more than he is telling."

"You have learned only one name—a most insignificant name." This was a guess on Anatoly's part, but the fact that they were still questioning Aleksei gave it strong credence.

"We have learned one or two others," said Podolsk. His shoulders sagged slightly as he added, "Well, none as significant as the American. A fellow in the business of printing false papers, but we'd already suspected him. A couple of others who had already been arrested, though Rostovscikov might not have been aware of that."

"Sounds to me like he is playing you along."

Podolsk visibly bristled, and Anatoly feared he'd gone too far. This was a tricky game he was playing. Podolsk was a mite slower than some, but he was no fool.

Anatoly quickly added, "How severe has his interrogation been? How much longer can he last?"

Podolsk steepled his fingers and tapped them thoughtfully against his chin. Anatoly could almost see the gears of his mind working.

Finally he said, "I admit he is about at the end of his rope."

Anatoly groaned inwardly, though he let none of his distress at this news show on his face.

Podolsk continued. "What do you propose, Anatoly? Because to be frank, though I believe he knows more, I am close to giving up, executing him, and having done with it."

"You know the saying that you can attract more flies with honey than with vinegar? It is time you plied him with honey. Introduce a friend to him who is ready to offer him succor. He trusts me. He will talk to me, or he will talk to no one."

"Perhaps . . ."

"Sergei, I have heard rumors that you will soon be taken off the case. Do you wish to be assigned to some post in Siberia?"

"I have heard the same rumors." Podolsk sighed.

Anatoly had fabricated the comment about rumors, though anyone with an ounce of intelligence had to know their superiors would not put up with Podolsk's incompetence much longer.

"Then it is time you changed your tactics."

"I'll make arrangements immediately."

Within the hour Anatoly was admitted into an interrogation room where Aleksei was waiting.

Anatoly gasped at the sight of his friend. Aleksei was slouched in a chair at a small table, halfway draped over the table. His shoulders were bony from weight loss, and when he lifted his head to see who had entered the room, Anatoly felt sick at what greeted him. The once bright and vigorous doctor now looked worse than any of his patients ever had. His skin was gray, dark circles ringed sunken eyes. The eyes themselves were vague, almost to the point of being glassy.

"My God, Aleksei! What have they done to you?" Because of the plan he had discussed with Podolsk, he could be open with his concern. Podolsk would think it an act.

Aleksei squinted and drew a hand over his hair, lank and plastered to his head with dried sweat.

"Am I dreaming? That you, Anatoly?" he slurred.

Anatoly pulled out the other chair by the table and sat down heavily. He'd been apprised of the methods that had been used in order to extract information from Aleksei, but the results were still shocking.

"I'm here to help you, my friend," Anatoly said.

"You got somethin' for me?"

"No—"

"Then how can you help?" snapped Alex, some vigor reaching his voice.

"I've ordered a good meal for you."

"I don't want food."

"You must eat. You must get your strength back."

"Why?" The question was more challenge than entreaty.

"Let me help you, Aleksei." He placed emphasis on the word *help* and put added expression into his eyes, hoping Alex would catch deeper meaning to the statement. There were, of course, listening devices in the room, and he could say nothing outright. But he had devised a way to surmount this problem. He took a handkerchief from his pocket to blow his nose. When he pocketed the handkerchief, he still had something else in his hand. It was a paper which he laid on the table, shielding it from view of the small window on the door in case anyone was watching. Anatoly only hoped Aleksei was lucid enough to read it.

The paper had two words: *Cameron* and *Escape*.

Aleksei burst out laughing, such a dry, brittle imitation of the action, lacking all mirth, that Anatoly wondered if his friend had lost his sanity.

When he ceased his laughter, Aleksei said, "You always were

a dreamer, Anatoly." He lifted a hand to wipe spittle from his lips. "I remember reading Dostoyevsky, and in his character's prison, there was a sign that said, 'Abandon hope, all ye who enter here.' So true, my old friend . . . so true. . . ."

"You mustn't, Aleksei," said Anatoly, deftly pocketing the paper.

Aleksei shrugged. All the while as they had conversed, he had been glancing up at the clock on the wall. Now he slurred roughly, "It is almost time for me to get an injection of hope."

"Let me tell you about my family," Anatoly said. "My boy received the highest marks possible on his university entrance exams. He is well on his way to fulfilling his dream of becoming a doctor like you."

"I stopped being a doctor long ago," Aleksei muttered.

"Bah! Impossible. For you it is not a job but a life. When you are released from here, it will all come back to you."

"Will I ever be released?"

Anatoly patted his chest, his hand over the place where he had put the note. "I am sure of it."

"I think the only release is death." Aleksei lifted eyes full of moisture. "They won't even let me die."

"Don't talk like that. You have reason to live."

Aleksei wiped a grimy hand across his wet eyes. "She would have been better off never to have met me."

"Who is she?" Anatoly hoped it would help to get him to talk about Cameron. Revealing even her name shouldn't be harmful at this point.

"No one."

"Is she someone you care about?"

Aleksei's eyes narrowed. "You are not my friend at all!" he spat. "You are just like the rest. All you want is information."

"No, no, Aleksei," Anatoly protested. "I only thought it would be good for you to talk of happier times."

"Is that just another way of torture?"

"I assure you, it isn't. I will go now and have them bring your . . . ah, medication. And also some food."

"I said no food."

"You must get back your strength!" And to himself Anatoly wondered how they could effect an escape if the escapee was too weak or too drugged to help. But the great dilemma was, how could he help him escape in the midst of withdrawal? If the withdrawal itself did not kill him. They certainly could not wait until the drugs were completely out of his system.

Aleksei's eyes went to the clock. "Hurry!" he begged. And something about the sudden brief clarity in his tone made Anatoly believe his friend also meant more than it would appear.

Anatoly left the prison and met Podolsk in the observation room where the police listened to the interrogations.

"That was a failure!" Podolsk said smugly.

"What do you mean?" Anatoly replied. "You knew this would take time. I must build his confidence. I almost lost him at the end by pushing too hard."

"That woman he spoke of, do you think she is an accomplice?"

"No doubt about it." There was a carrot to dangle before Podolsk's eyes. "A couple more sessions, and I will learn her name."

"You seem certain."

"I am certain. This is child's play. But it would go easier if he wasn't so incoherent. Can you cut back on the drugs?"

"No. It is the only hold I have over him, and if you should fail, I don't want to lose it."

"No matter. Bring him some food and have him back in the interrogation room this same time tomorrow. No, now that I think of it, make it an hour earlier."

The rush hour would be slowing by now, and when the streets were busiest would be the best cover for an escape when it happened. *When* was the question. He did not have all the pieces of the puzzle yet, but he would find them or die trying.

When he returned to his office, he called in his assistant.

"How are you coming along with that assignment I gave you, Pavel?"

"It is a tedious process going through so many records. If I had some help . . ."

"I can't allow that. This is a highly sensitive matter."

Captain Pavel Orlov was perhaps the only man Anatoly even dared to trust in the MVD. He'd worked for Anatoly for years, their families socialized together, and their sons were best friends. More than that, a year ago, when Pavel had come under suspicion of treason for a misspoken political remark, Anatoly had made the situation go away.

If he could not trust, Pavel . . . Well, he had to trust someone. He could not do something as stupendous as breaking a prized prisoner from the depths of Lubyanka all alone.

"I'll do my best, then, sir."

"I know you will, Pavel. As I have told you before, when we are alone, we can speak familiarly with one another."

"Perhaps when we are out of the office," said Pavel. "But not here."

Sighing, Anatoly muttered, "I suppose so."

"Colonel, General Markov sent some of his men over today to question me."

"About what?"

"About your family's departure."

Anatoly's stomach sank, though he had known this was coming. "Let them question," he blustered as if he wasn't quaking inside. "My poor wife hasn't had a vacation since the war. You well know she threatened to leave me if she didn't get one."

"Perhaps you should have gone with her." A slight inflection in his tone implied a double meaning.

How good they all were becoming at speaking in double meanings, and hearing them, as well!

"Too much work." When Pavel hesitated, Anatoly asked, "What else, Pavel?"

"They also questioned me about your relation to the prisoner Rostovscikov."

"They already know what that is," Anatoly said dismissively. "I was assigned to ease him into his repatriation to Russia, to watch him and assure his loyalty." With that final word, Anatoly suddenly realized another aspect of Aleksei's arrest and how it might reflect upon him.

Pavel nodded understanding. "And now he has been arrested for espionage."

"I am positive he wasn't engaged in such activities until recently. He wanted to return to America to . . . visit a sick relative." Pausing, Anatoly felt as if quicksand were closing over him. He just hoped he could keep track of all the subterfuge.

"I told them as much, Anatoly."

"I'm glad you did, because it's the truth."

"I know what the doctor did for your son. I know you must feel some obligation toward him."

"Did you tell them that?"

"Of course not!" Pavel bit his lip, obviously debating his next words. "Anatoly, I beg you not to do anything foolish!"

"I don't know what you are talking about."

"I am talking about all the secret tasks you have set for me to do. I am talking about you meeting with the woman who was a correspondent here during the war and who had, uh, dealings with Rostovscikov—"

"You followed me!"

"Only once—because I am worried about you. You have been behaving strangely since the doctor's arrest. I doubt anyone else sees most of it. I only do because of our close association. But how long before it draws attention? Don't waste your life because of some false sense of obligation."

"Don't tell me what to do, Pavel."

"Do you plan to help him escape?"

"It is time you returned to your work, Captain Orlov."

"Yes . . . sir." Pavel turned to leave but then paused and turned back, looking as if he might say something else. He changed his mind and exited.

Anatoly had been surprised to see the worry and distress on

his assistant's face, perhaps some fear, also. Anatoly probably had one foot over the edge of the precipice. He feared he would fall and take his friends with him. But he could not turn back from the edge.

34

THE GUARDS PRODDED Alex back to his cell, where a few minutes later a nurse arrived with the injection he had desperately wanted.

No! He groaned inwardly, not wanted. *They* want it, not I. But he could not deny that he lapped up the sense of relief and euphoria it gave him.

He lay back on his cot and let the drug infuse his body, hating himself for it but not caring at the same time.

Only when a tray of food was brought did he rise a little from his stupor. He did not want food. His gut was such a twisted ball that even the thought of food make him sick. Yet that tray represented something.

What was it?

His numb brain had almost forgotten the events of a half hour ago. But the tray helped clear the fog a little.

Anatoly.

His friend had come to him.

Was he really a friend? Could it be just another ploy to extract a confession from him? Was Anatoly using him? Why should he trust him? He was one of *them*.

Then Alex remembered a slip of paper with a name. But he couldn't remember the name.

But you have to! It was important, came a small voice deep inside him, a tiny remnant of the man who was not ravaged by poison.

I . . . can't remember.

Remember! You fool! That name was a message of hope.

She is better off if I don't.

She is here for you!

No . . . no! I am lost to her.

Say the name, you fool!

I . . . can't.

Then with great effort his voice rasped the word out loud like a dry, brittle hand clawing for life, "C-Cameron!"

Again, softly like a prayer, "Cameron."

"Oh . . . God . . . she's here."

———

Larry Marquet was hurriedly packing the things from his desk in the office he shared with other Army attachés.

When Cameron strode toward him, he stopped, holding a fistful of pencils in midair.

"When do you leave?" she asked.

"Couple hours."

"You never contacted me."

"I had a few things on my mind. You were on my list, though."

"Not at the top if it."

"You vaunt yourself too highly, Miss Hayes," he sneered, tossing the pencils into his briefcase. "I have other irons in the fire and more than one puppet dancing on a string, which will all collapse with me gone. Even more so since it is obvious your precious doctor has spilled his guts. I had lots of other lives to save."

Cameron didn't want to think of this arrogant piece of work as some humanitarian. Yet, though it grated at her to admit it, he was right.

"I guess a spy's work is never done." That was as much relenting as she could muster.

"Righto, missy." He seemed quite willing to accept her meager stab at understanding. "Do you realize how hard it was to get any inroad at all in this country? Your boyfriend was my foot in the door. But now it could take years to get back to square one. First they're going to have to train someone else to fill my shoes. That ain't gonna be easy."

"I know. Good men are hard to find." And the best of them, she thought, was locked up and withering away with each breath she took.

Marquet shuffled through a disheveled stack of papers on his desk. He threw some into the briefcase and then held out a folder.

"Here," he said.

She stared. She hadn't expected this. "You've got them."

"Maybe I ain't such a bad guy after all, huh?"

"Maybe not." She grasped the folder as if grabbing a lifeline.

"They came through just before my arrest. I was gonna give them to Wood before I left."

"Thank you," she breathed. She knew when to bury the hatchet.

"Lotta good they'll do you. Your boyfriend won't be worth spit to them now that he's spilled the beans."

"Unless they think there is more where that came from."

Marquet snapped shut his briefcase and took the coat and hat lying over the back of a chair.

"I gotta go," he said, "and this is no place for this conversation."

He strode to the door, and Cameron fell into step with him.

"Look, Miss Hayes," Marquet said as they stepped into the open air, "I don't know what you have up your sleeve, but whatever it is, you have to know it's doomed from the start. You have no idea what you're doing."

"I wish I could have had your expertise, Marquet, but that won't stop me."

"Hey, no skin off my nose if you want to hang on to illusions. As for me, I'd rather rely on facts. And the fact is, sweetheart, if you go through with some harebrained escape plan, you'll just end up eating gruel next to Rostov. You don't have diplomatic immunity. The Ruskies will eat you alive."

"I'll take my chances."

"So be it." He shrugged. "I got a plane to catch. I doubt I'll ever see you again, but I'll enjoy telling folks the story of a dame with more moxie than is probably good for her."

"Oh, I'll see you again, Marquet. I'll look under every rock until I find you so I can let you know how wrong you were."

He smiled. "I do hope so."

———

Sunday after church, Robert found a place where they could all meet that could not possibly be bugged by the Soviets—the embassy basement. Even the Soviets weren't that paranoid. But for added security, he brought along a record player and dropped on a record. The strains of Benny Goodman and Tommy Dorsey filled the damp air.

Perched upon crates and boxes, the group made an intriguing concave of conspirators. Jackie, Blair, Cameron, Gary, and Robert. None looked well suited to this business of subterfuge, with the possible exception of Gary—tall, broad-shouldered, and commanding in his uniform. He was certainly the only one with any experience in this sort of enterprise. Then Cameron remembered that Blair had dabbled in a bit of espionage in the Philippines. She didn't count her own foray into this realm, since Oleg's escape attempt had been such a miserable failure.

"I guess I'll start," Cameron said. "I met once more with Hawk." They had decided to give all the players code names. That had been Blair's idea, probably a good one, even if she had gleaned it from the movies. Hawk was the name given Colonel Bogorodsk. "He has gotten into see Al—I mean Eagle. He—" she swallowed, determined to curb her emotions—"he isn't well. They've been drugging him. He's weak and malnourished. We are not going to be able to whisk him immediately out of the country. He's going to need time for recovery." Anatoly had actually said *withdrawal,* but Cameron could not bring herself to say the word. She could barely accept the fact that those animals had gotten him addicted to drugs again.

Robert, apparently noting that her voice was deteriorating, jumped in. "What Cameron is saying is that we need to find a place for Eagle to stay or to hide out for a short time in order to gain some strength so his physical condition doesn't attract attention when he leaves the country. And we need a way to get him to that place right after the escape. Hawk will handle springing Eagle from his present nest, but it will doubtless be on us to do the rest."

"Could we hide him in the embassy?" Jackie asked.

"That's got to be the last resort," Robert replied. "You cannot imagine how unorthodox, illegal, and undiplomatic what we are doing is. That's why, Gary and Blair, you are to stay in the background as much as possible. Gary, you are a member of the embassy staff, and if you are implicated in something like this, it will not only mean the end of your career but possibly a diplomatic breech of incredible proportions in U.S.-Soviet relations."

"What about your career?" asked Blair.

"I'm not worried about that," he said vaguely. Jackie had mentioned to Cameron that Robert was seriously considering telling the ambassador about his family's secret. Perhaps he figured after that he wouldn't have a career to worry about. She wanted to protest but reminded herself of his earlier words of commitment to her and Alex and knew she could say little to change his mind.

"Well, that Marquet fellow didn't cause a war with what he did," argued Blair. Cameron knew she didn't want to be left out.

"He didn't have as much to lose," Robert said.

"I can't believe I have come all this way and won't have a chance to help," said Blair with a pout.

Cameron scooted over to her sister and put an arm around her. "Blair, you have already helped, and Jackie, you too. The love and support you both have given me is beyond what I ever expected. And I have desperately needed it. Please know you have done your part."

Blair offered her a grateful smile. "Thank you. And I am sorry for my childish tirade."

"Will there be anything I can do?" Jackie asked, somewhat reluctantly. "I'll understand if not, but remember, I don't have anything to lose, either."

Cameron thought about what Marquet had said. Neither she nor her sisters had diplomatic immunity. They could easily disappear, and the Soviets could play dumb while they were locked away somewhere in Siberia. They all had a great deal to lose. That's why Cameron had already decided she would place none but herself in harm's way. If this plan went awry, she didn't care much what the Soviets did to her.

Cameron and Robert exchanged a quick glance. He of all people clearly understood the risks.

"I'm sure there will be plenty for everyone to do," he said dismissively.

Cameron continued the previous vein of the conversation. "I'll contact my friend . . ." She paused, unable to remember the code name for Sophia. Then it came to her. "Dove. I'll contact Dove. She might be able to provide a hideout."

"Dove is probably too close to Eagle," said Robert. "The MVD will search and question all his known friends."

"Still, she might have other ideas. And the fact that her father is . . . well, his profession will help. I fear Eagle will need lots of the kind of attention he can provide."

"We'll have to figure out a way to get him from the . . . uh . . . nest to the hiding place," Gary said. "A couple of different routes should be lined out. You may need some transportation if he can't walk."

They discussed these matters for a while, trying to touch on all possibilities and possible snags. Finally the discussion stumbled to an end, leaving them all feeling more helpless and incompetent than when they first began. Many ideas had been offered, but most had ended up in the figurative trash. Robert said ruling out one another's ideas was a good thing because they didn't want to go down a path only to have it blow up in their faces later when it was too late to fix. But they were discouraged because so many of their ideas had turned out bad. As they dispersed, no one said it, but they all realized it would take a miracle to get Alex out.

Leaving the group, Jackie and Robert went outside. The fine summer day was a good one for walking and talking. Robert had been so occupied with the Marquet matter that Jackie had hardly seen him since it began.

"I feel so wrung out," Jackie said as they walked through the embassy gates.

Despite the sunshine, the afternoon air was brisk with a chill breeze. It blew leaves from the trees, and they tumbled to the ground, brown and brittle.

"Would I sound callous if I said I feel invigorated?" Robert hurried on to explain. "It's the first time in a long while that I've felt I am doing something useful. The rewards of embassy work here in Russia aren't exactly forthcoming. I guess that's why it's considered a hardship post."

"I thought you loved your work."

"Perhaps I am just trying to convince myself that I won't miss it as much as I thought."

"What do you mean?"

He sighed. "I told the ambassador about my being Jewish. The only thing that bothered him about it was that I had lied for so long."

"But you had your reasons!" It amazed her how quick she was to defend him, to take his burden on her shoulders.

"It is still a lie, an abuse of a position that requires trust, not to mention high security clearance. It could have placed the embassy here in jeopardy, opening me up for blackmail—" He snorted. "Well, that might be a bit of an overdramatization. Still, the ambassador was within his rights to censure me. He thought I should tender my resignation."

"That's unfair! That's—"

He smiled. "I think the time is right for it. And, if for no other reason, I should be home now to deal with the repercussions of what I have done."

"I suppose you are right. What will you do?"

"You mean in the future? I have no idea. I could practice law. The world is open to me—or maybe not. I really don't know how the world will accept Robert Grunwald."

"You'll make out fine, Robert. I'm sure of it."

They walked past one of the Kremlin gates, an interesting medieval-looking structure. Just beyond this was the entrance to a park Robert called the Alexander Gardens. They were greeted by a bed of bright mums, another reminder that summer was starting to fade. But there were many Muscovites enjoying the lovely crisp day, reclining on benches or on grassy areas. Jackie and Robert passed a tall, plain obelisk. Pausing, Robert read some of the names engraved on it, the names of old revolutionaries, most of whom Jackie had not heard.

They came to an unoccupied bench and sat for a time in a comfortable silence. Jackie became absorbed in watching the passersby. She thought the Russian people were fascinating. Any one of them could be an intriguing character in a story. Many bore a scar or deformity, perhaps a consequence of the war. An old man with a blind eye, a boy with a limp, a woman who could not be older than Jackie because she was carrying a baby in her arms, yet she gazed down at her child with ancient eyes. These no doubt bore testimony to the hard life they lived. There was something else unusual about them, though she could not quite name it. She regretted once again never having had the chance to get to know these people. It made her realize her time in Russia would soon end, and she discovered she had mixed feelings about that.

"I'm going to miss this place," Robert said, as if reading her own thoughts. "Despite the Soviet obsession with keeping foreigners apart from the real people, they have still managed to get under my skin."

"When will you go?" she asked.

"Not until they find my replacement." He hesitated, then

plunged ahead. "Maybe you and I should say our good-byes now. I have a feeling things regarding Alex will soon start to move very fast."

"But it will take time for us to get exit visas." She was growing anxious to get home, but she didn't want this time to end, either.

"Yes. Funny thing about the Soviets," he mused. "They do everything they can to keep people out of the country, then when they've got you, they seem reluctant to let you go. Jackie, I'm reluctant to let you go, too."

She wrinkled her brow. Was this it, then? Just a summer fling? Time now to go back to the real world? She was too unsure of herself to question him. She'd had too many rejections lately to feel confident in taking that kind of risk, even though she felt different about Robert.

"All good things must come to an end," she heard herself say in a glib tone she used like armor.

He sucked in a ragged breath. "I had a great time with you."

"So did I." Was that all it was then? Had she misread it all so badly?

Silence enveloped them, this time not so comfortable. A bent old woman hobbled by, a cane gripped in an arthritic hand. A little boy with a smudged face and ragged clothes towed a rusty wagon carrying a younger child as bedraggled as the boy.

Then she realized what the elusive thing was about these people. There were few young men among them. It was Sunday afternoon, a fair day, and hundreds of people were enjoying the park. She had seen one or two young men with missing limbs or other scars of war, but hardly in a proportionate number to the rest. It wasn't like that in America. Though thousands of American young men had lost their lives or were maimed in some way, she'd never noticed the gap as acutely as she did now. She wanted to ask Robert if he knew how many Russians were killed in the war, but she was sensing a heavy cloud over them, so she kept silent. She wondered if he was feeling it, too, but she was afraid to even venture a glance in his direction.

At length he said, "Funny that at the end there should be such a loss of words between us. I never could talk to anyone as I have with you."

"The end?" she said. "It sounds so grim."

"It is to me. Maybe you don't—"

"I do!"

"You do what?"

She took a breath, though she didn't know what she dare say. But he hurried on. "Wait! Don't say anything. Let me say something. I don't want to be a coward anymore."

"I don't think you ever were a coward, Robert."

"Thank you, but still . . ." He hesitated. "Jackie, I don't want this to be the end—for us, I mean. I may be no Troy Rigdon—"

"I already told you I thought he was a jerk."

"I didn't know if you were just trying to make me feel good—"

"Why would I want to do that?" She knew that didn't come out quite right, but before she could amend it, he was speaking.

"I guess because you cared about me."

"I do care about you!"

"You do?"

She rolled her eyes. "Being a genius really isn't much help in life, is it?"

"Not at all," he said with a self-effacing chuckle. "Especially not in this area." He turned to face her, lifting dark eyes to her.

She thought at that moment she could almost see to his soul through them, they were suddenly so clear and open.

"I'm well versed in many subjects. I know several languages, but I still can't find the words to express what I feel to a woman. Little experience, I guess."

"Maybe you want more experience," she suggested in spite of herself. "I mean now that you don't have to worry about your secret."

His brow furrowed as his gaze grew even more intense. "Is that your way of letting me down easy?"

She let out a frustrated breath. She'd had an easier time communicating with her second graders. But she couldn't blame it all on Robert. Her own insecurities were making it hard, as well.

"Robert, we both—"

"Jackie, I do care about you!"

Her statement tumbled over his, but she quickly forgot what she had intended to say. She stared in amazement at him, then it struck her as funny how hard it had been for either of them to get those simple words out. A giggle bubbled from her lips.

She quickly sobered when she realized how it must appear, her laughing at his words of affection. "Oh, I am so sorry!" she exclaimed. "I'm not laughing at you."

"I never thought you were—well, for an instant my ego was jarred, but I know you would never do that. What is so funny?"

"Oh, just this . . ." She didn't know quite what to call it, so she gestured with her hands to indicate this situation between them.

"I've never been so insecure," he admitted. "But you showed up and put me in a regular dither!"

"Thank you very much!" she said with mock affront.

She could see a sudden transformation in him. His confidence had returned.

"I do care for you," he said, "and I don't need a lot of experience with other women to know that I've never met one quite like you. I want us to have a chance to get to know each other better."

"I do, too, Robert. I was afraid to say it because I've been rejected so many times. And I was afraid it would be a betrayal of Sam if I cared about another man as I did him." When she said the words *as I did him,* Robert swallowed and looked slightly awestruck. "Do you know what? I don't feel bad at all. I feel . . . his blessing."

"Wow!" Robert breathed, taking her hands in his.

She felt a tremor in his hands and knew they both were dancing around that scary four-letter word. But if ever she felt love, it was now. She wanted desperately for him to kiss her. But when he continued, it was almost better than a kiss. "Jackie, when or if our feelings develop more deeply, I want you to know I'd never expect to replace Sam. I know he will always occupy a part of your heart, and that doesn't bother me. I believe you have a heart big enough for both of us."

She wanted to weep, shout, and dance all at once, she was so happy. When Robert drew close to her and put his arm around her, she laid her head on his shoulder. It wasn't a shoulder as broad as Troy Rigdon's, but her head fit on it perfectly.

WORKING IN THE darkroom was one element of photography
Semyon was not fond of. He couldn't wait until he had enough
stature in the field that he could have someone else develop his
photographs.

Being so enveloped in darkness was too reminiscent of his
nightmares. His friends and colleagues would laugh if they knew
he had lately taken to sleeping with a light on—that is, when he
slept, which hadn't been much in the last week.

A knock came at the door.

"What is it?" he snapped. He didn't like being disturbed in
the darkroom because there was always the fear some idiot
would come barging in and ruin his work. He didn't like locking
the door, either. Once he had tried that and had ended up hyper-
ventilating because he had felt so trapped.

"Don't worry, Semyon, I see the red light on," said the person
outside. "I'm not stupid."

"All right. What do you want?" Semyon replied, still irked,
but it was probably just the sleepless nights talking.

"Someone to see you."

"I can't come out now without ruining my pictures." He lifted
a photograph from a pan of solution.

"They said it was important."

"Who is it?"

The other fellow spoke after a pause. "MVD, Semyon."

The picture slipped from the tweezers, splashing back into the pan. What did he have to fear from the police? He was a loyal Party member. He did what he was told. He had never published anything that had not been duly approved by the censors.

But were men with secrets ever safe from the police? Even if a man did not know exactly what those secrets were?

"I'll be out in five minutes," he said, forcing a steady voice.

"They won't like waiting."

"Tell them I can't help it." Hurriedly he did what he could to protect the photos still needing time in the developing solution. Then he exited the room. A few lost photos were a small price to pay for appeasing the MVD.

Two agents awaited him in the outer office. They always seemed to come in pairs. They must know one was enough to strike fear in any man.

"Comrade Semyon Tveritinov?" said one. The men looked almost identical, though the one who spoke had brown hair while the other's was blond.

"Yes."

"We wish to question you about the activities of your father."

"What?" But the moment they had said the word *father*, his stomach clenched.

"You may be unaware, but this morning he was arrested for treason."

For a brief moment the room seemed to tip on end. Semyon stumbled back as his knees grew weak. He grasped the edge of a nearby desk.

"That's impossible," he managed to protest, even if his voice was nearly as weak as his knees.

"What do you know of his activities?"

"I only know he is the most loyal man in this country. He has served the Party faithfully all his life." Semyon kept clinging to the desk while he felt detached from his own voice. If he'd had to lie just then, he would have been lost. But he spoke the truth, and it came by pure instinct.

"Do you know the name Vasily Zharenov?"

"I never heard of him."

"You did not know your father had paid this man to find means to blackmail certain loyal Party members, including his boss, Comrade Khrushchev?"

Semyon stared, incredulous, unable to speak.

The agent pressed on, "We have Zharenov's confession to this fact."

"He's lying. My father would never—"

"At this point," the agent cut in, "you are not implicated in your father's activities. So I advise you to take a moment to consider your own loyalties. He is not your blood father, correct?"

Now the room and the two agents all swam before Semyon's eyes. He was suddenly back in one of his nightmares. Only by sheer force of will did he keep from tumbling into dark oblivion.

He had to think straight or all would be lost. All—a thought struck him that finally did send him over the edge. His mother!

His knees gave out. Only the proximity of a chair kept him from crumbling to the floor. He sank into the seat and dropped his head into his hands.

"This can't be happening!" he muttered.

"Are you a loyal Party member, comrade?" demanded the agent.

Since I was a child, he agonized silently. I marched in parades with the Young Pioneers. I proudly carried the Red banner, learned the litany. I have loved the Party. I have served the Party, sacrificed for it. Sometimes I have even sacrificed my own honor for it. Visions of the war flashed through his head. The lies of a boy presented as truth; the bodies of his guards dead as he sought news to glorify the Party. How could they now question his loyalty?

How could they question his father's loyalty?

The anger fostered by this thought strengthened him a little.

"How dare you question my loyalty!" he spat. Or my father's, but he could not say that. Good sense was beginning to penetrate his shocked mind. He couldn't help his father if he was arrested, too.

"The traitor's family is always brought in to question," said the agent.

"He isn't even my blood father, as you pointed out." *Forgive me, Father!*

"Then surely you can offer us more evidence against him."

"I would if I could, but he never confided anything to me. He considered me little more than a ward for whom he had a responsibility to feed and clothe. When I became an adult, even that ceased."

"You were not close, then?"

"Hardly."

"You make regular visits to your parents' home."

"Well, I do feel a certain responsibility to my m—to his wife. She has been decent to me. And I felt it wouldn't hurt my career to do what I could to curry the man's favor."

"That was a mistake," sneered the blond agent.

"An error in judgment," amended Semyon. "But certainly not worthy of arrest."

"We decide what is worthy of arrest, comrade," said the other agent.

Ignoring that ominous statement, Semyon asked, "Surely you have more evidence against my father than this Zharenov's testimony? I have never even heard of the man. He must be an insignificant cog in the wheel."

"That is not your concern."

"It would be my concern if I denounce my father and he is later released and reinstated. I would go down a lot faster than a man of my father's stature in the Party. You must have more weighty evidence against him."

"I can only tell you to speak to his former boss about that."

Semyon should have guessed that from the start and would have had not his mind taken so long to start focusing. The arrest of a man of his father's standing in the Party would have to be backed by more than the word of some low-level Party flunky; therefore, it should not surprise him at all that Khrushchev would use his father as a scapegoat in order to regain his former power. Stanislav Tveritinov would not be the first man the vice-roy of the Ukraine had sacrificed to his ambition.

Swallowing bile, Semyon forced himself to his feet. "If I can be of further service to you, comrades, please do not hesitate to call upon me."

The agents left. Semyon remained planted in that same spot for some time, feeling numb and bewildered. But he fought off the desire to crumble once more into the chair and cave in to his emotions. He must be strong for what he had to do next.

In his beat-up old sedan, it took him two hours to get to his parents' dacha in the countryside. Traffic at that hour of the afternoon was horrendous. The roads leading to the outskirts of the poor village had been neglected since the war and were rutted and muddy from recent rains. The house itself was not palatial by any means, though it was one of the finer ones in the village. He'd known happy days here as a boy, though the visits were few because so much of their time was spent in Kiev in the Ukraine. That memory made him think of how hard his father had worked for the Party and how faithfully he had served Nikita Khrushchev.

It was inconceivable that a man like Stanislav Tveritinov could have been betrayed in this way. It was as if his own mother had plunged a knife into the man's back.

Dahlias were blooming in the planters in front of the house. Their cheerful oranges and yellows and reds detracted from the chipped and peeling green house paint. His mother was so proud of the bright flowers with their large full heads.

There was no telephone service to the house, not that he dared to telephone her anyway. He had no idea what her state of mind would be or what she might blurt out over the phone. They must be careful now. None of them was safe.

He opened the front door. It was never locked.

"Mother!" he called.

A panic seized him when there was no immediate answer. Wives were often arrested with their husbands despite their innocence.

"Mother!" he cried, rushing through the house, looking in every room as he hurried toward the back, where her bedroom was located.

The room was dark. All the drapes were drawn, and it took a moment for his eyes to adjust.

"Mother, are you here?"

There was movement on the bed, and as his vision cleared, he saw her curled up on top of the covers, her face buried in a pillow.

"Semushka." Her voice was strained and muffled by the pillow. He could tell she had been crying.

He rushed to the bed and sat on the edge. "Mama! It will be all right." He laid a hand on her shoulder.

She lifted her head up, then flung her arms around him. "Oh, my baby! I had feared they had you, too! What will we do, Semushka! What will we do . . . ?" She sank against him as tears again racked her body.

He didn't know what to say or how to comfort her. In his heart he knew her husband was lost to her. If they had not already executed him, it was only a matter of time. There was little grace for the crime of treason, whether real or trumped up. He just held her tightly, cooing meaningless words of solace into her ear. How many times had she done the same with him? Mostly when he woke screaming from one of his nightmares.

Now they were both in a nightmare.

"How could this happen to us, Semyon?" she sobbed. "Your father never did anything to deserve—"

"Do you think it matters what one deserves?" he said bitterly. He desperately needed to vent his anger, and here he knew he was safe. His father had always made sure of that. "Do you know that Khrushchev denounced him?"

"But they were friends." Her tone held an innocence that shocked him, but he and his father had always protected her from the harsh world. "I even tried to telephone Nikita to see if he would help," she said.

"And of course he would not speak to you."

"They said he was sleeping."

"Asleep while his friend burns?" He snorted harshly. "Why didn't you call me from the village market?"

"I was so afraid. Your father always kept his distance from any who were in trouble. I thought I should distance you from us."

"That is what I have thought, as well, Mother. Though it kills us, we must keep apart from Father now, even if we must also denounce him."

"Semyon!" she gasped. "You would not?"

"I have already," he admitted miserably. "I can't help him if I am arrested, too. You know that is a possibility."

"We are doomed, Semyon! I know it. They will come for us— for me, especially. They always arrest the wife." She broke down once more in body-racking sobs.

"Not always, Mother," he said gently, speaking a lie even he wanted to believe. "They have not yet, and that is a good sign."

"I cannot live without my Stanushka!"

He'd never before heard his mother refer to his father by a diminutive. Father simply was not a man such terms of endearment fit, though perhaps she reserved those for when they were alone. It nearly broke his heart, realizing they had a love, an intimacy that transcended even the family circle.

She lifted beseeching eyes to him, reddened and wet. He stroked back strands of graying brown hair that clung to the damp places on her face.

"Mama, you must be strong," he said.

"I have never been a strong person. He was my strength."

For the first time in his life, Semyon cursed the Party.

His father had occasionally hinted that Semyon had an idealistic view of the Party. He saw now how true that was, for in the past when he had seen the shortcomings of the Party or some seeming injustice done, he had overlooked it, holding the firm

belief in a higher good. A photograph censored—the Party officials must know what was best for the people to see. A friend
arrested—he must have committed some offense. A wholesale
purge—our Little Father, our exalted leader Stalin, has only the
good of the Party at heart.

At times he had wrestled mightily with these moral questions.
But he had felt he had to believe in the rightness of the Party. If
his loyalty had proved unfounded, what would become of his
world?

Now he would find out. How could he remain faithful after
this? There was no way in heaven or earth to justify the betrayal
of a man like his father.

As Semyon debated these weighty matters in his mind, he
realized his mother was waging her own mental debates.

"I said we should take it to our deaths," she said suddenly, as
if in the midst of an ongoing conversation.

"What are you talking about, Mother?" Her sanity always
had been fragile. Could this now push it over the edge?

She cocked her head and frowned. "He wanted to tell you,
but I was so afraid."

"Tell me what?"

"I can't bear the thought of you losing your father and
mother all over again," she said, her voice shaking, still on the
edge of tears.

He cringed inside as he remembered that bit of conversation
he'd overheard a couple of weeks ago. He'd tried to forget about
it. He certainly had not probed his parents for more information.
He'd never wanted to know about the past. That's why, in his
mind, there was still a wall protecting him from it. Except . . .
when in his mind's eye a little ray of light shone on the face of a
stranger, who he knew was no stranger. Dim and shadowed
though it was, he had sensed the man's face was not to be feared.
Fear still gripped him, yet he knew he could run from it no
longer. What if both his parents were taken from him? What if
this secret died with them? He'd never find succor from his nightmares.

"Tell me, Mama. Tell me about it," he said softly.

"I did not want to lose your love. . . ."

"That is not possible, Mama."

"You mean that, don't you?" She touched his chin tenderly. Always at this time of day she would tease him about his bearded shadow, wrinkling her nose when she kissed the scratchy surface. She said nothing now, though his chin was dark with stubble.

Then an incredible story poured from her thin pale lips.

"He was a subversive, your birth father. That's all we know. He left you with an uncle when he feared arrest." She searched her son's eyes, perhaps hoping for a signal for her to stop. But he only nodded, and she went on. "Those were hard times. Civil war and famine. Many peasants died of starvation. Your uncle could not afford to feed you and his own children, as well, so he found a family to adopt you—he found us. We saved you, Semushka."

"I know, Mama."

"Your f—the man who sired you, died in prison."

"And my—the woman who gave birth to me?"

She shook her head in misery. "Believe me, Semyon, we thought she was dead until shortly before the war's end. Your father learned that she was a foreigner and that her daughter had been in Russia recently looking for you."

"Then this . . . this woman lives?" It was almost better thinking her dead than that she had abandoned him.

"I think she was forced to leave the country for some reason. She had to give you up."

"Where is she from?"

"I don't know. I never want to know. I wish she never existed!"

So did he in a way, but now that the floodgates were open, he could no longer shut out the truth. "Why were you and Father talking about it recently?" he asked.

"She's here, Semyon!"

"My mother?" Too late he realized he'd spoken in reference to another that one word he had been avoiding.

"I've lost you!" She gripped his shirt in her fists even as she buried her head on his shoulder and wept.

"No, no! You haven't," he insisted. "She may be my mother by birth, but you are my Mama. That will never change."

"If only . . ."

He stroked her head, though he knew the only real comfort he could give her was to end this painful discussion now. But he couldn't, if only to free himself from the torments of the past.

"Mama, I must know. I haven't slept in a week because of the nightmares."

"Forgive me, Semyon." She lifted her head away from him. Her eyes grew clear, and her voice was steady. "I could have spared you with the truth. The daughter is in Russia now, looking for you once more."

The daughter . . . his sister?

His mother added resolutely, "I still do not know who she is, but there is a Dr. Fedorcenko who can tell you."

"Thank you, Mama!" he murmured as he wrapped his arms tightly around the woman who had loved him, cared for him. Who had earned the name *Mother*.

36

IT TOOK ALL Semyon's restraint to keep from rushing out right then to find this Dr. Fedorcenko. But this was definitely not the time for such a search. He was surely being watched, and though he might be able to lose the police, it wasn't worth the risk. He'd have to live with the nightmares awhile longer. He only hoped the foreign woman didn't leave the country before he could get to her.

Putting all this from his mind, he returned to Moscow intent upon seeing his father. With that in mind, he convinced the police that he might be able to induce him to make a confession. Generally Stalin's hatchet men were not squeamish about dispensing with tedious formalities such as confessions. But in Tveritinov's case, being such a high Soviet official, they had felt obliged to extend at least the appearance of legality. Semyon had counted on this.

Immediately upon entering his father's cell, he feared all his pretenses might be destroyed.

"What are you doing here?" his father demanded. "Get out, you fool! Get out!"

He understood his father's fears, but he quickly twisted them to his own cause.

"What? Am I not even good enough to visit you in your

prison?" he spat. "Give me that, at least, a moment to gloat over your downfall!"

For a moment Tveritinov stared in bewilderment. But Semyon knew his father was intelligent enough to assess the situation for what it was—a mere performance. It would kill him if his father actually believed Semyon could turn on him thus.

"If it wasn't for me, you'd be nothing!" retorted Tveritinov. "I rescued you from sure death, fed you, clothed you—"

"Yes, and you never ceased to throw that into my face." Semyon could only speak his true heart with his eyes. He prayed they expressed the agony he felt inside, but more, the love he felt for this man.

An almost imperceptible nod from Tveritinov gave him the assurance he craved.

"What do you want? Besides to gloat?" demanded Tveritinov.

"Confess your sins, Father," said Semyon. "They say it will go easier on you if you do."

"As if you cared!"

I do care, my father! But he said, "You still have your wife to think of."

"Bah! What is your real reason for this visit?" sneered Tveritinov.

Semyon almost smiled at how heartily his father had taken up the performance. "You never did give me any credit."

"Why should I? You are only here now in order to save your own skin. If they only knew what a loyal Party minion you are."

"You raised me to love the Party."

"I did a good job, then."

"And your Party loyalties, Father? Where do they lie?"

Tveritinov laughed. "If I confess, it won't be to the likes of you. I told you to get out—and never show your face to me again."

Semyon left. He apologized to the police for his failure. But his arms ached because of his real failure in never having the chance to embrace his father one last time. The harsh words between them might have been an act, but it was torture thinking that they could well be the last words they ever spoke to each other.

Bitterness embedded itself deeper into Semyon's soul.

When he returned to his apartment, a neighbor told him an MVD agent had been inside. That didn't surprise him except the neighbor mentioned that the agent—he was alone, of all things!—had made certain Semyon wasn't home before searching the apartment. The MVD were usually not so delicate in their invasion of a man's home. Out of curiosity Semyon got a description of the agent.

Back at his office he discovered this same agent had been asking questions about him. No surprise there, either.

Semyon kept wondering if there was yet something he could do to help his father. The only thing he could think of was to launch his own investigation. It was risky, but if discovered he could always say he'd hoped to expedite the case against his father.

The place to start was with this man Zharenov.

Years ago Semyon's father had obtained for his son security clearances in order to access higher levels of the Party machinery. This had given Semyon a certain edge in his work, and he'd been able to impress his superiors many times. So it was easy for him to gain access to Party records. He'd done so often before, and when he entered the records office, he discovered the police had not yet cut off this privilege. They probably knew nothing of it.

He asked the clerk for Vasily Zharenov's file.

"Of course, Comrade Tveritinov," said the clerk. He went to the files and withdrew a folder. As he handed it to Semyon, he added, "Funny you should come here now. Only an hour ago, an MVD agent was here requesting your file."

"Did he give his name?"

"I try not to ask the police questions," said the clerk, "but he had to sign it out like anyone." He pointed at the name in the ledger. It was right above Semyon's own name, which he had just scribbled into the book.

Colonel Anatoly Bogorodsk.

The clerk gave a description of the man that fit the man who had searched Semyon's apartment.

After learning the identity and address of Zharenov from his file, Semyon returned to his office and made a couple of phone calls.

"You are sure Colonel Bogorodsk is not handling the matter of Stanislav Tveritinov?"

He listened to the negative response and then hung up, perplexed. It was not inconceivable the police were investigating him about another matter. Frightening, but not impossible.

Trying to put the matter out of his mind, he finished his workday. Regardless of recent events, he still had a job to perform, and he must give the impression that his father's arrest was no more than an inconvenience to be endured.

At five o'clock he left the office and went to the address in Zharenov's file. The man was not home, though Semyon knew the police had released him from custody earlier in the day. Feeling at loose ends, hating the thought of spending an evening alone in his apartment, and knowing it was best if he avoided his mother for a time, he returned to his office. There would be a late shift working, people around, and work to distract him.

Approaching his door, he thought he glimpsed a flicker of a shadow behind the frosted glass of the door. He always locked his office before leaving, but even if a colleague had entered seeking something, why was there no light on? Of course there were burglaries in Russia, but the penalties were so severe, no one dared them unless the rewards were great. He had nothing of value in his office.

Because of his natural Russian reluctance to call the police, he had but two choices of action—to leave whoever it was to his work or to stop him. The fact that there was nothing to steal roused his curiosity. Who would be riffling through his office after hours? Not the police—they could do such things anytime.

Semyon looked around for a weapon, finding only an umbrella in the stand by the elevator. This he grabbed and, holding it like a club, flung open his door.

"Don't move!" he cried. "The police are on the way."

A dim light flicked on—the desk lamp. Its slanted glow threw the usurper's features into odd relief.

"I am the police," said the man.

He was big and brawny and certainly could have been the police, but he was dressed in street clothes—a dark sweater, dark trousers, and a dark wool hat on his head. He looked like a burglar. He also fit the description of the man who had searched his apartment.

"How do I know that?" Semyon asked, still wielding the umbrella, as if it would do any good. Russian made, it would snap in two against the man's muscles.

"Put that thing down and close the door," ordered the stranger.

Semyon obeyed the edge of command in the man's voice. "What are you doing in my office?" he demanded. He wasn't accustomed to making demands of the police, but if this man was one, there was definitely something fishy about him.

"You are Semyon Tveritinov?" the man asked, ignoring Semyon's question.

"If this is about my father, I have told you people all I know."

"Your father?"

"His arrest?" Semyon thought he already knew the answer to that question, but he wasn't certain how else to deal with this man.

"Your father was arrested?"

"Yesterday morning."

An odd look crossed the man's face. Was it worry? Fear? Very peculiar.

"Curse it! I didn't know," said the man.

"Are you Anatoly Bogorodsk?"

"I'll ask the questions!" The way he snapped those words out almost by reflex were so typically MVD.

"I'm entitled to some curiosity. I am not the one who broke into another's office."

"Sit down. We must talk."

Semyon hesitated only a moment before grabbing a chair. Bogorodsk sat in the chair behind the desk, which was fitting, since he seemed the one most in control of the situation.

"Why have you been investigating me if it is not regarding my father?" Semyon asked.

"I said . . ." Colonel Bogorodsk paused, put an elbow on the desk, and rubbed his chin thoughtfully. "I will answer your questions, I assure you. But first, what of your father's arrest?"

"They are accusing him of treason."

"But you remain free?"

"I have denounced him. I am a loyal Party member."

Bogorodsk leaned back in the chair, his bulk making it creak dangerously. "That is what I have discovered, Comrade Tveritinov. Loyal to the point of betraying the man who rescued you from poverty and possibly death; the man who gave a home to a poor orphan boy. You would see the father and mother who cared for you destroyed in order to save yourself?"

Semyon swallowed. How he hated being cast in that light. The visit with his father still tormented him. Maybe it was better to live in honor even if it meant death. His father had taught him the value of honor.

"What choice have I?" he cried.

"No one has any choices these days, do they?" Bogorodsk mused almost as if to himself alone. "Your father's arrest limits my choices almost to none."

"What are you talking about?"

"I want the truth from you, Tveritinov," said Bogorodsk. "I am an officer in the MVD. I can have you arrested. As you well know, I hardly even need a reason for doing so. I could have you buried so deep in Lubyanka, or better, in a Siberian labor camp that you would never see the light of day again." He leaned forward, his huge head looming before Semyon like an angry bear ready to strike. The intensity of his gaze was surely capable of boring two holes into Semyon's heart. "The truth, you hear! Are you loyal to the Party or to your father?"

It was clear now to Semyon that he was going to prison one

way or another. Let it be as his father had always taught him.

"Both," he answered.

"That is not good enough."

"But it's true. I love my father. He is completely innocent of any of these trumped up charges. I would die defending him. I only denounced him in order to protect my mother and in the hope that I might remain free to help him in some way. I have served the Party all my life. I have believed in the Party. What has happened has made me doubt, but it is hard to shake a lifelong loyalty."

"Yes . . ." Bogorodsk breathed regretfully, "it is hard." He cast another incisive gaze at Semyon before continuing. "I had hoped you could help me, but I see now that is doubtful, though perhaps not. Still, I see no reason not to impart to you the information I have. But I swear to you, if this person is compromised in any way, I will crush both you and your father."

"If you thought I could harm anyone, I doubt you'd give me the time of day," said Semyon. He was confused, befuddled, but mostly curious.

"You are right. But it's always good to have an ace in the hole—that's an American reference to their game of poker." A ghost of a smile twitched his lips. "This is an interesting game, poker, by the way. Everyone holds their cards 'close to the vest.' They try to reveal nothing in their facial expressions of the value of their hand. But they bluff freely, and one never knows if his opponent is holding a pair of twos or a royal flush, the best hand you can have. Sometimes a player will bet all he has in order to fool the others into believing his hand is better than it truly is."

"Is that what you are doing, Colonel?" Semyon asked.

"I think I am in the biggest poker game of a man's life. The stakes are high—for both of us." The MVD agent shifted again. The chair groaned. "I have information regarding your birth mother."

Semyon blinked. He had never expected this.

"This surprises you, yes?" Bogorodsk went on. "Coming out of the blue as it does. I was hoping to use this information against you, perhaps to blackmail your father in assisting me in another matter. Well, that hope is gone. Now I am merely doing a good deed." He chuckled, and oddly, the sound was not entirely out of place coming from this big dangerous-looking man. "I realize that is the strangest thing about this whole conversation. So be it. Do you want this information, comrade?"

"Yes."

"Good. If you were to have said no, I would have told you anyway, as a service to a friend. Actually, I have little specific information, but I can arrange a meeting between you and your half sister, who is a foreigner but is in Russia at this time."

"Would it be safe? Considering my precarious position?"

"I can make it safe."

"Then do so," Semyon said, suddenly full of an odd mix of misgiving and anticipation.

The big agent rose and strode to the door. Semyon jumped up and joined him. Before he opened the door, Semyon laid a restraining hand on it.

"You are the strangest MVD agent I have ever met, Colonel," he said. "But you have taken a chance with me, so I will take one with you. Can you help my father?"

"I will do what I can."

Anatoly walked away from the offices of *Party Life* with a heavy step. All that risk, all that posturing, and he had done little good for his friend Aleksei.

Still, he felt he had an ally in this Semyon Tveritinov. Too bad the son did not wield the same power as the father. But an ally was an ally, and on the dangerous path upon which he was now embarking, he needed all he could get.

Anatoly had more than one ace up his sleeve, though when he had heard of the elder Tveritinov's arrest, he'd felt as if he had plunged through an abyss. He had pinned a lot of hope on the blackmail scheme.

Maybe there was hope yet in all this. If he could effect Tveritinov's release, he'd have garnered himself a true royal flush. The man would do anything for him then.

Sometimes he had to wonder if this was a poker game or a circus juggling act.

37

CAMERON WAS AMAZED at how adept Sophia was in getting around the restraints of her homeland. She had gotten a message to Cameron requesting a meeting, this time in a bakery in the Arbat. Because Jackie wanted to meet Sophia, and because in the past it had proved a good cover having more than one person along, Cameron welcomed her sister. Since Blair happened to be there at the hotel when the message had arrived, Cameron saw no reason why she should not come along, too.

They took their time getting there, stopping at some tourist sites along the way so that it seemed quite natural for them to stop at the bakery for a rest and a bite to eat after a morning of touring. Sophia was already there, seated at a table in a corner away from any windows. The four women were crowded around the small table, but that served to nearly block little Sophia from view should anyone take an interest in the group of foreign women. If the police had followed Cameron, they would watch from outside, as usual.

Sophia and Jackie were thrilled to meet each other.

Sophia took a moment to study all three sisters, then grinned. "Cameron has told me you are all so different from one another. Yet now I see, so much alike, too. I feel like the picture is now complete."

"Maybe a bit more Picasso than Rembrandt," Cameron said with a chuckle.

"But that is part of the beauty!" returned Sophia.

"We'd be terribly boring if we were three peas in a pod," Blair said.

"Do you have sisters, Sophia?" asked Jackie.

"Yes. One who is ten years older than I, but we are not very close because she had been gone from home so much, first in school, then in the Army. My next sister, Valentina, is only two years older, but we are not very close, either. Our interests have always been different. You three are lucky to be close."

The three Hayes women exchanged glances. Cameron thought she knew what they were thinking—they had never been close, either, but lately they were making up for lost time.

"We are now," said Jackie, seeming to voice that look between them, "and I think we realize what a gift God has given us in each other."

A waitress brought them a pot of tea and pastries.

"I took the liberty of ordering," said Sophia when they were alone again. "I wasn't certain how much time we would have. I know it is risky for us to meet."

"I was about to attempt contacting you anyway," said Cameron. "But why did you want to see us?"

"I have news I had to tell you." Sophia's eyes glittered, and her usually pale, fragile countenance was absolutely rosy. "I have heard from my Oleg!"

"Oh, Sophia! How wonderful!" exclaimed Cameron. Though she knew the news must be good from Sophia's appearance, she asked anyway. "How is he?"

"I have no details and haven't heard directly from him," Sophia replied. "The authorities contacted me. It seems Stalin, in his great magnanimity, has granted amnesty to many of the repatriated Russian POWs."

"The ones he threw in prison after they were repatriated from the Germans and whom he called traitors?" asked Cameron caustically.

Sophia nodded. "I, too, am bitter, but I won't let that ruin my joy. Oleg was never technically in that group. He had been a POW, but as you know, Cameron, his case was unusual. Nevertheless, he has been grouped with these and will receive the same amnesty."

"So he's coming home?"

"Not quite. These men will be released into a lifetime exile in Siberia." Sophia smiled bravely. "At least it is something. Their families are permitted to join them if they wish. I will finally be with Oleg, even if it is on the other side of the world. My parents are trying to share my joy and be brave, but I know our parting will be hard on them—on all of us. Even in this day of modern transportation, visiting anyone in the remote villages where the prisoners will be placed would be difficult. Yet at least the possibility is there."

"Perhaps possibility for other things, as well?" queried Cameron cryptically.

"We will be closely watched," Sophia said, comprehending Cameron's meaning, "and must make weekly reports to the authorities. We will, as you say, be on a short leash."

Cameron grasped her friend's hands in hers. "You always have a friend you can call upon if . . ." She finished the thought with a shrug. No more needed to be said. The idea of escaping Russia had to be in the back of Sophia's mind, yet there also was the memory of the terrible debacle the last time she and Oleg had tried. Cameron began to feel bad that she had perhaps cast a damper over the joyous news, so she added, "I am so happy for you, Sophia!"

"I must leave in a couple of days."

"I am glad we have had some time together then," said Cameron. "You know I feel that you are my adopted sister!"

"And you are mine!" A grin was on Sophia's lips, but her eyes were full of moisture. "I am sorry I will not be here to continue to help you and Alex."

"You must not worry about that. Since I last saw you, God has provided help I never expected." In a lower tone, despite the fact that they were alone in the bakery except for the clerk, she added, "Sophia, we have an MVD agent on our side now!"

"What? Unbelievable!"

"I best not go into any details, but I feel confident Alex and I will be together soon."

"Thank God!"

"Sophia, there is one last thing you can do for me," said Cameron. "Perhaps your father can help in this. We need a place to hide Alex for a few days after his escape. He will be too weak and sick to travel right away. It can't be your place, though, because the police will surely be watching for him there."

"I'll ask him. You know he will do all he can."

They all chatted awhile longer until the tea and sweets were gone, and then they had to part. Cameron and Sophia hugged for a long time, both in tears. Cameron knew better than to believe partings were forever, even if they might appear to be. The miracle of Sophia and Oleg's soon-to-be reunion after a six-year separation was witness to that. Moreover it bolstered Cameron's assurance for a reunion with her own husband.

The three Hayes women returned to the Metropole after seeing Sophia. As they entered the lobby, two men garbed in MVD uniforms strode up to them.

This was certainly déjà vu to Cameron, but it was no less daunting. As for her sisters, alarm etched each of their faces.

"Please come with us," said one of the agents.

Blair and Jackie cast bewildered helpless eyes toward Cameron.

"May I ask why?" Cameron asked.

"We wish to question you."

"All of us?"

The two agents glanced at each other. "He said all of them, didn't he?" one of them said in Russian, apparently unaware of Cameron's knowledge of the language.

"Only if we didn't have to enter the embassy," replied the other.

"Then we are in luck," said his partner, who then spoke in his broken English to Cameron. "Yes, all."

"What do you wish to question us about?"

"I am told only to bring you in."

"We do have rights."

"You are in no jeopardy, Miss Hayes. This is only for questions, I assure you."

Cameron looked at her sisters. They appeared about to swallow their tongues, and for good reason, because they knew, even if the police didn't, that they were planning to break some serious Russian laws and probably already had.

"It'll be all right," she told them, wondering where her bravado was coming from.

They were led to a black sedan and driven to MVD headquarters. Cameron had been here before, to the upper floors, when she had been questioned during the war—once when they had wanted information about Oleg Gorbenko and another time before they deported her. She felt no fond sense of homecoming, by any means, but her heart did beat faster. She had not been this close to Alex since their wedding in a bombed-out German village.

The women were taken to an interrogation room, where they were invited to take seats around a table and told to wait.

As the door clicked shut, Blair jumped up from her chair, raced to the door, and tried the knob. It was not locked. Obviously feeling foolish, she resumed her seat.

"They've found out!" Jackie exclaimed when they were alone.

"Quiet, Jackie," said Blair and Cameron together.

"I'm sorry . . . I forgot." She rubbed her hands over her face. "Cameron, I thought I could take these risks. I am so sorry, but I am scared to death!"

It was Blair who put a comforting arm around her sister. Cameron was reminded that Blair was the only one of them who had truly suffered interrogation and imprisonment.

"I was scared, too," Blair admitted. "The idea of being locked up—" She shook her head with a shudder to complete the appalling thought. "But they can't do anything to us—not to all three of us together! Imagine what kind of an international uproar that would cause."

"Yes," Cameron said, "we are safe as long as we are together."

Jackie nodded, but her lips still trembled as she tried to smile. "That reminds me of when I first realized we were all Christians, that we were like the three-fold cord mentioned in the Bible. We are now stronger together than we ever were apart."

"It's true," Cameron said. "I've felt that especially here in Russia. I know my strength is in God, but I also know He sent both of you to strengthen me, as well."

They laid their right hands on the table and joined them. "Together!" they said in unison.

In less than ten minutes, the door opened. Cameron felt only mild surprise when Colonel Bogorodsk entered, but she gasped when she saw his companion. She heard similar reactions from her sisters. They all rose to their feet. Perhaps like her, they had an instinct, barely restrained, to run to the colonel's companion and throw their arms around him.

"I see I don't need to make introductions," said Bogorodsk as he closed the door.

The young man at Bogorodsk's side was gazing at the sisters with as much wonder as they looked upon him.

Shaking away some of his daze, he said in Russian, "I have a feeling they know far more about me than I do about them."

Cameron stepped forward, replying in Russian, "My name is Cameron. These are my sisters, Blair and Jackie." She gestured to each. "May we call you Semyon?"

"Why don't you sit?" Bogorodsk said. "I can assure you this room is completely safe. I have personally disabled all eavesdropping devices."

Cameron didn't want to sit. She wanted to embrace this man . . . this stranger . . . her brother. He may have only just learned about her, but she had been thinking of him, imagining him for years. She had come to love the chubby little cherubic child with a mop of curly hair and a glint of mischief in his eyes.

She had never been quite sure how to feel about the grown man in the photo her mother now had, except that he was her big brother, and she had longed for a big brother almost as much as her father had longed for a son.

He was here now standing before her like a vision, still with a head of kinky hair, caramel-colored, fighting to escape the bounds of the leather-visored cap he wore. He was dressed in a brown Argyle V-neck sweater over shirt and tie, and a tweed suit. She knew his clothes were unimportant, yet she wanted to remember all the details of this moment. Who knew if she would see him again or if her mother ever would, and it would fall to Cameron and her sisters to impart the specifics of this meeting to their mother.

Glancing at her sisters, Cameron saw that they were reluctant to sit, as well, as if that act conceded the fact that this momentous meeting would be no more than a formal, sterile encounter. But they realized that Semyon might well have only learned of their existence recently. He was going to need time to absorb this knowledge, and it wouldn't help to have three emotional women fawning at him.

They all sat. Only by reflex of long experience was Cameron able to muster up the many questions she had.

"How long have you known?" she asked.

"Two days."

"We've had much longer." She smiled sympathetically. "I can understand your shock. We found one brother—you are faced with three sisters."

He swallowed hard. "You speak good Russian. I'm surprised. I speak no English." For an instant a hard look marred his visage, dulling completely the hint of the cherubic child. "My father wanted me to learn English, but I refused to learn the language of capitalism."

Cameron recalled Sophia telling her that Semyon's father was an important Party official. There had also been hints that Semyon, too, was loyal to the Communist Party. She admitted that in her idealizing of her brother, she had conveniently left out this detail. Perhaps sensing this, he had felt the need to remind her, though his tone was more like that of a man desperately clinging to a shadow.

"I will translate to the other women," offered Bogorodsk quickly. "I assume they speak no Russian."

Cameron was thankful for the colonel's glossing over of the subject of Semyon's political loyalties. She wanted to entertain her ideal as long as possible.

Bogorodsk then proceeded to translate, first explaining the gist of the previous remarks. Then he continued to do so throughout the exchange.

Because of the palatable tension, mostly emanating from Semyon, Cameron sought to put him at ease with a few innocuous inquiries. Blair and Jackie, also perceiving this need, contributed.

"What do you do for a living?" Cameron asked.

"I am on the staff of *Party Life,* a photographer for the most part."

The three sisters exchanged astounded looks.

"This surprises you?" asked Semyon.

"I also work for a newspaper," Cameron replied. "Our father publishes a newspaper."

His brow arched. "Most interesting. But *Party Life* is a journal. As you know, Russian newspapers have few photographs."

Cameron did know this. She also knew the journal was the official publication of the Communist Party. Only very loyal members would work for it.

"Are you married?" Blair asked.

"No, I am not," he said. "And you? Are all of you married? Do I have little nieces and nephews?"

"Blair and I are married. Jackie is a widow, and she has a daughter."

The question-and-answer session continued for a few minutes and then, seeming to play itself out, trailed away in silence. They all knew they were skirting what was in each of their hearts. But Cameron hesitated, for once curbing her incisive interview style.

Instinctively, she knew he must still be in shock.

But it was Semyon who finally broke the silence. His own instinct must have clued him that they were handling him with kid gloves. "I guess we all have many questions. But we must sooner or later speak of what is truly in our hearts. I will be frank about something first. I have never asked questions of my adopted parents. I did not want to know."

"But you must have memories, Semyon?" said Cameron. "You were six when you were adopted."

"For some reason the memories of my life before I came into my parents' home are blocked. They—" pausing, he seemed to shudder—"they come out a bit in . . . in my dreams. Never clearly."

"Do you want to know now?"

He hesitated a long moment.

Cameron could see in his eyes the struggle he was experiencing. "You are close to your adopted family?" she asked.

He nodded. "Perhaps I feel that voicing interest in these . . . strangers who gave me life would be a betrayal of my adoptive parents."

Cameron winced at the word *strangers*. Yet how could she fault him for feeling that way? He had no clue of how they felt about him. He might feel he'd been abandoned by them. Yet she was desperate for him to know of his birth mother's love and anguish.

Finally he said, "Tell me . . . tell me about them."

She did, and when her Russian failed her, Colonel Bogorodsk aided. In simple terms she imparted the story of the love affair between her mother and Yakov Luban, knowing he was Russian and no doubt could read between the lines. Her loyalty toward her mother made her emphasize how miserable Cecilia was, all but abandoned by her husband in a strange country. Cameron's own emotion was enough to underscore Cecilia's torment over having to leave her newborn son behind.

"She would never have done so," Cameron said, "if she hadn't been certain she was leaving you in good, loving hands.

Your father adored you, Semyon. If only you could read the letters he wrote about you. I wish I had his photos and letters with me now to show you. But you were his world."

He nodded. Perhaps there had always been some small part of him that could not entirely blot out the truth of a father's love. She hoped so, at least.

"He read to me," Semyon said, his tone embracing the words he spoke as if he was just discovering them. "I sat on his lap, and he smelled of mint and tobacco."

"He would never have left you except that he was forced to do so."

"I am told he died in prison only a few years ago."

"Yes."

His face twisted with anguish, but he fought back any other show of emotion. "It seems my fathers are all doomed to leave me. . . ." he murmured, shooting a glance at Bogorodsk. He seemed to want to say more, but his lips trembled, and he appeared determined to rein in his emotion.

"His father has recently been arrested," Bogorodsk said.

That revelation was like a kick in Cameron's stomach, not only because of sorrow for her half brother, but because she had been hoping that Semyon's father could intercede for Alex, preventing a desperate and risky escape attempt.

"I'm so sorry," she said.

"I know you were hoping for help from him regarding your problem," he said.

"I understand."

"I would help if I could," he said defensively, his eyes flicking briefly toward the colonel once more. "But I must protect my mother. If she were to lose both her husband and her son . . ." Taking in a sharp breath, he closed his eyes in a vain attempt to squeeze back tears. "I . . . cannot!"

"I'm not asking, Semyon," Cameron assured, barely able to see him through her own tears.

When he had regained his composure, he said, "My parents are good people."

"I am sure they are."

"My father would have helped if he could."

Cameron reached across the table and grasped his hands, which were folded together on the tabletop. That moment, the first time she had ever touched her brother, sent a tingle through her body. It made him real to her.

"Semyon, please know this meeting was not for the purpose of enlisting your help," Cameron said, trying to infuse into her voice the sincerity in her heart. "I have been looking for you for years. I have longed to find you, as has my mother. It is only coincidence it has happened in tandem to this . . . other matter."

"I wish I could give you more time then," he said. "I don't know if another meeting would be safe."

"I understand." She lifted her hands, unable to broach the one subject they had been seemingly avoiding.

As he moved his chair away from the table to rise, it was Jackie who ventured upon this uncertain ground.

"Semyon," she said as Bogorodsk translated, "before you go, would you . . . like to see your birth mother's picture?"

He appeared to freeze, his face pale as ice. He had obviously been avoiding that subject. The few moments of silence that followed Jackie's risky words were agonizing.

Finally, in a voice taut with emotion, he said yes.

Jackie opened her pocketbook and withdrew a small photo of Cecilia. It was a few years old, taken shortly before the war, but she had changed little. Jackie slid the photograph across the table.

He did not pick it up but looked at it where it lay. Then a sound like a sob escaped his barely disciplined lips. Cameron wondered if he saw the resemblance that she saw. The likeness to her mother was clear.

Jackie said, "You may keep it."

Still he did not touch the photo. But as if voicing an inner debate, he said, "I could not see her even if . . . no, it would be impossible."

"We realize that now," Cameron said.

When the words had been translated, Blair spoke up. "We've seen many impossible things happen lately. If it were possible, Semyon, would you want to?"

His eyes skittered to the photo, then away, as if it were dangerous to look too long.

"Perhaps . . ." he breathed.

When they all rose to leave, he palmed the photo and slipped it quickly into his pocket.

They parted then, with no embraces exchanged. But Cameron took comfort in the fact that he now carried with him tangible evidence of a family who loved him, a mother who had not abandoned him in her heart.

38

THE THREE WOMEN wanted desperately to talk when the agents took them back to the hotel. But neither the hotel nor the embassy was safe. Jackie took them to the park that Robert had shown her.

"In all the time I was in Russia, I've only been here once, and only recently," Cameron said as they passed the bed of flowers at the entrance.

"It's called Alexander Gardens," said Jackie. "It's so close to the hotel, I'm surprised you never frequented it."

Cameron shrugged. "You know me and the great outdoors. Unless there was news to be found there, it held little interest."

"Places like these must be indispensable here," commented Blair. "I've never done so much talking out of doors!"

"Back during the war there didn't seem as much of a need for all these walks outside," said Cameron. "There wasn't near the paranoia then that there is now."

The day was overcast and a bit chilly. Jackie hoped it didn't rain on them, for they had not come prepared except for light jackets. They found a bench protected from the breeze.

Blair began. "So what did you think of our brother?"

"Kind of intense," offered Jackie. "But I guess he had good reason to be with all that has been dealt him lately."

"That comment he made about not wanting to learn the language of capitalism was a bit daunting," said Blair. "I suppose he must really be a Communist, then."

"He works at *Party Life*," said Cameron. "That's the official Party mouthpiece. His father was assistant to Nikita Khrushchev, who is the head of the Ukrainian Party. I would say our brother is very enmeshed in the Communist Party."

"He seemed to be a decent man," said Jackie. "Very sensitive. Not the sort of raving radical we've been conditioned to expect."

"Yes, but imagine having a Communist in the family!" Blair had no doubt forgotten that Alex was, or had been, a member of the Communist Party.

"Dad would have a conniption!" said Jackie.

"Speaking of Dad . . . and Mom," Cameron said, "where do we go from here?"

Blair shifted on the bench, seeming restless all at once.

"Do you have an idea, Blair?" asked Jackie, thinking that was the cause of her sudden edginess.

"No. Should I?" Blair snapped, her brows rising. She added in a softened tone, "No, really, I don't."

"Cameron, would it really be impossible for Semyon and Mom to meet?" Jackie asked.

"I'm sure Semyon will be under close police scrutiny since his father's arrest. No way would they let him leave the country. And even if Mom came here . . ." Pausing, Cameron looked down at her lap, fingering her pocketbook, then dashed a hand across her eyes. "There must be a way! How can we tell Mom we met her son knowing she will never have the chance to meet him for herself. It's just not right!"

"Well, one thing is certain," said Jackie, grasping her sister's hand, her own voice unsteady. "If there was a way for Mom to meet him, there would be no way to keep it from Dad any longer."

"Dad . . ." groaned Cameron. "I almost forgot."

"I thought for sure Mom would tell him after her surgery,"

Jackie said, "but I'm positive she didn't. We'd surely know if she had—"

"Why would you think that?" cut in Blair, her voice edged in accusation. "You've never given him credit. But what if—" she gasped a sharp breath. "I can't do this!" she moaned. She shifted again, looking as if she wanted to flee.

"Do what?" asked Cameron.

Blair looked away. "Please don't hate me, but . . . Dad knows." She hiccoughed a sob. "I told him."

Jackie and Cameron were stunned. A glance at Cameron's face told Jackie that Cameron was more than shocked. She was angry. For once Jackie wished she were sitting in the middle, but that had become Cameron's accustomed place, to act as a buffer between Blair and Jackie. Now it was up to Jackie to intercede before someone did or said something she would regret.

"Blair," Jackie gently entreated, "please look at us. Maybe it's not so bad what you did." With a pointed look at Cameron she added, "Maybe it is for the best."

"It doesn't matter if it is for the best," Cameron said tightly. "We agreed not to say anything to him."

"You were the only one who wanted that," said Jackie, trying to maintain a conciliatory tone. "I went along because I didn't have the courage to go against you."

"It wasn't courageous what I did," Blair said in a trembling voice. Still she didn't turn around. "I betrayed your trust. I betrayed Mom. Dad was right."

Jackie rubbed Cameron's shoulder as she might soothe her four-year-old daughter's hurt feelings. "Cameron, let's give Blair a chance to tell us what happened before we judge."

Though her lips were still taut, Cameron nodded. "Tell us, Blair," she said. "But turn around and look at us when you do so. I know you are not a coward."

Blair drew back her shoulders and turned. Her eyes were moist, her lips quivering as she spoke. "I went to Dad for advice about—" she shot a glance at Jackie, and for a moment looked even more miserable than before—"I wanted his advice about

Emi and . . . and my . . . feelings."

Jackie didn't know which was more astonishing, that Blair had revealed their mother's secret to their father, or that she, of all people, had gone to him for advice. Of only one thing could there be no doubt, and that was where her misery sprang from. Not only had she admitted her betrayal and then lied about it all these months, but in telling about that she also had to broach another volatile subject. Jackie wanted to allay Blair's worries regarding the subject of Emi. She wanted to assure her sister she had no intention of taking up that cause just now, but Blair hurried on before Jackie could speak.

"Dad was so understanding at first, when I was asking for his advice," said Blair. "I guess I was thrown off-guard. I thought we had underestimated him. So it just came out. You know what a ninny I can be! It just slipped out. But you must believe me, he didn't seem all that surprised. It was almost as if he already knew. Yet I'm sure Mom never told him."

"He wasn't surprised?" said Cameron, incredulous. "He didn't blow a gasket?"

"Honestly, Cameron, he didn't," Blair insisted. "Except . . . he did blow up at me. He upbraided me for betraying a trust. He said he was ashamed of me." She sniffed back rising emotion. "He was right." She fumbled in her purse for a handkerchief. Finding one, she blew her nose. When she calmed, she added, "What's more, I am almost positive he never said anything to Mom."

"I think you're right there," said Jackie. "We would have known. Mom would have told us."

"It would be like Dad, wouldn't it," Cameron said, "to brush this under the carpet like he always does."

"Maybe it's the only way he feels he can save face," suggested Blair.

"At Mom's expense," said Cameron bitterly. "She is suffering torment at keeping this secret while all along he has known. It's not fair."

As gently as she could, Jackie said, "Mom should never have kept the secret."

"Don't judge her, Jackie!" Cameron retorted.

"I don't mean to," Jackie said, "but I hate all this subterfuge! It makes my stomach ache when I think of it." Blowing out an exasperated breath, she added in a rush of passion that she only now realized had been pent up for months, perhaps years, "Sometimes this whole family makes me ache. Here we are, the three of us, finally all Christians, yet we are still struggling over the same ground we stumbled over as kids. Will it never end! Why can't God heal us?" She gave her head a shake. "I don't really expect an answer, but it hurts so bad!"

Cameron responded. "Maybe all this that is happening, maybe Semyon himself, will be a catalyst to that healing." She reached out to Blair. "I'll start here, sis. I'm sorry for my harsh words."

Tearfully Blair threw her arms around Cameron. People in the park stared at the scene, then tried to pretend they didn't see the strange foreigners. Well, if it embarrassed them, Jackie didn't care. What did they expect when they didn't give foreigners many opportunities for privacy.

When Blair and Cameron finished their hug, Blair reached across Cameron for Jackie, and Cameron moved to the other side of Blair.

Blair and Jackie stared at each other for a long moment. There was so much between them, and it had been repressed for so long that even in this moment when the walls were surely breeched, it was hard to know how to take the first step. Jackie choked up as she realized her words about healing had meant more than healing for the family in general. Perhaps the deepest hurt she bore was the one between her and Blair. They both suffered very specific wounds, gaping and painful.

Blair nodded. "It must start with us. With me, because I made the wound." Jackie started to protest, but Blair gently hushed her. "Jackie, I caused the problems between us. Maybe I had good reason, but I was never justified and certainly not to keep it up for so long. How stupid and lame of me to hate people who never harmed me—no, it was wrong for me to hate anyone. I've told myself a hundred times that Jesus loved His enemies. I don't know why it never helped. But my eyes are open. For the first time I can truly see how my hatred has wounded you. Years ago when I was hurting and so near to taking my life, you alone stood by me. Though everything I was and everything I did must have repulsed you, you kept loving me, caring for me. And how did I repay you? When your need was great, when your heart was breaking, I turned my back on you." Sniffing back a new rush of tears, she reached out a hand and brushed a strand of Jackie's hair from her eyes. "Oh, Jackie, please forgive me for hurting you so! What a fool I am."

Blair embraced Jackie, and this time Jackie knew something was different from the other times they had tried to assuage each other's feelings. This was not assuaging. This was major surgery, digging in and cutting out all the rottenness between them.

"Of course I forgive you, sis!" Jackie kissed Blair's cheek.

It was difficult to effect a three-way hug, but the sisters, desiring to somehow, in some physical way, cement their newfound union, clasped their right hands together in the way that was becoming symbolic to them. All three sensed that they were now more together than ever before.

Jackie knew the healing had truly begun. And now she could hardly wait for all of them to be home again, for she was certain the strides the three sisters had made this day would be felt in a wonderful way with the rest of the family.

39

ANATOLY RETURNED to his office after the gathering with the Hayes women and their half brother. The meeting itself was of little consequence to him. He'd arranged it as a gesture of goodwill and in part to distract Cameron Hayes from his slowness in effecting what she really desired.

But when she waylaid him in the interrogation room after Semyon had departed, he'd had to be honest with her about the difficulties he was encountering.

"How close are we?" she had asked in that infuriatingly direct manner he recognized from when she was a correspondent during the war.

"You must understand the implications of Tveritinov's arrest, Miss Hayes."

She nodded dismally. "I didn't think it would matter one way or the other to you." For a brief moment hope had flickered in her eyes.

He didn't want to admit even then how much he'd counted on the elder Tveritinov's intercession. It would have meant avoiding a messy and dangerous escape. With a wave of a pen Tveritinov could have signed an order for Aleksei's release. Yet Anatoly could see in the woman's look that she believed Anatoly also held that power. She thought him a Superman, like in the

American comic book he had once read. Impervious to the bullets of his enemies, he would fly into the prison, perhaps right through a wall, and rescue her lover.

Then he had told her, "I have insinuated myself into Aleksei's interrogation regime. But you must understand, I can't just walk out of Lubyanka with him."

"But you are—"

He didn't let her finish. "When I have a plan, I will notify you. Remember, Miss Hayes, *I* will notify *you*!"

She'd nodded contritely. He'd always sensed this was a woman who lived life on her own terms, who stood up for herself and feared nothing. He supposed that's what Aleksei loved about her, for surely these were traits seldom found in Russian women. But the expression she wore was helpless enough to make his heart break. She was looking to Anatoly for her salvation, or for that of her man.

If she only knew...

Anatoly was hoping the rescue of his friend would bring about his own salvation, his own redemption. But even he knew one act of good would not free him from the burden of his many acts of evil as a member of the secret police. Would freeing one man from prison erase the fact that he'd put hundreds *into* prison? Many were innocent of any egregious crimes, though he'd convinced himself they must be traitors and enemies of the Party. Aleksei had often attempted to talk to him about God. He had told Anatoly that Christ died for the sins of mankind. Accepting this Christ meant forgiveness. He'd said something about God removing a man's sins from him as far as the east is from the west.

Anatoly was not a religious man and doubted he could become so at this stage of his life. Yet... how sweet it would be to have his many sins taken so far away they no longer weighed him down.

All he could do now was try to redeem a little of his evil. And even as he thought this, he realized that Aleksei's freedom would mean a kind of freedom for Anatoly. Not so much from his sins, for Anatoly had a very hard time believing there really was a god out there who could wipe a man's slate clean for no more payment than belief. Yet now Anatoly was sure that when this matter of Aleksei was over, he would leave Russia and join his family. He would forever wash his hands—which he thought was also a religious phrase—of the evil work of the secret police.

He felt better with this settled in his mind. In fact he felt so good he thought he might commit some other acts of good before it was over. He still had some power, and though he would do nothing to jeopardize either Aleksei's escape or his own, there must be something he could do.

The matter of Stanislav Tveritinov immediately came to mind. Here was a decent man. Freeing him might count for a great deal of good on Anatoly's record, for Tveritinov not only was in a position to make some positive changes in the country but also was the kind of man who had the will to do so. The good he might produce would spread wide.

Anatoly was about to call in his assistant, Pavel, to enlist him in launching a covert investigation into the matter. But he lifted his finger from the intercom, remembering what Pavel had said about the secret tasks of late inviting suspicion. Moreover, Pavel had been acting very nervous lately. Best not to push him too far. Anatoly decided he would handle the Tveritinov investigation himself.

Checking his watch, he saw he had some time before Aleksei's daily interrogation. Semyon had mentioned a man named Zharenov as a key in the case against his father. That would be a good starting place.

After examining the man's record, Anatoly began his investigation, not with Zharenov himself, but with some of his cohorts. He spent the next three hours driving around, questioning some very low characters, and visiting some of the more seedy Moscow haunts of this man. The next day he did the same thing, and it was in the course of these pursuits that he had an epiphany of a different sort. Perhaps it was a reward for his mission of doing good. One of the men he wanted to question was in the hospital for an appendectomy. In order to get information from the patient, he had to go to the hospital, not one of his favorite places, and listen to the man's grisly description of his illness. The fellow could hardly describe the sudden onset of such agony, though it took a half hour for him to do so anyway.

Walking through the hospital after this encounter, which had done nothing to aid Tveritinov's case, Anatoly naturally thought of his friend. This wasn't Aleksei's hospital, but still it conjured up images of his friend nonetheless. It also conjured up an image of the doctor's present dire physical straits. By the time Anatoly reached his car, a plan had begun to form in his mind.

He made one stop before returning to Lubyanka and his appointment to interrogate his friend. At the hospital where Aleksei had worked Anatoly found the one man in that hospital he knew he could trust implicitly, the one man whose devotion to Aleksei was no doubt as great as Anatoly's own.

Dr. Yuri Fedorcenko had to be called on the loudspeaker, for he was off making afternoon rounds. Anatoly was asked to wait in the doctor's office. He had to sit there for a half hour before the doctor came. Only a doctor, especially one of this man's importance, would have the temerity to make an MVD agent wait so long.

The doctor was somewhat alarmed when Anatoly escorted him outside, but only then could the agent be certain they could talk in privacy.

Though it was very un-Russian, he decided to be frank and succinct. "Dr. Fedorcenko, I plan to effect Aleksei Rostovscikov's escape from prison. I need your help."

The doctor nodded calmly, as if this statement did not shock him to the core. Perhaps it hadn't. Anatoly knew a bit of Fedorcenko's history. He'd no doubt experienced enough in his life so that little surprised him.

"What can I do?" said the doctor.

"You have no fear that this is a trap of some kind?" Anatoly had seen a lot in his life as a police agent, but he was jolted by the man's trusting response. "I am an MVD agent, after all."

"I know that, Colonel Bogorodsk. I also know of your relationship to Aleksei." He smiled. "And I know of your most recent encounters with Cameron Hayes."

Anatoly laughed. "You have a better network of informants than I have, Doctor!"

"If I did, I would be the one breaking our friend out of prison."

"So you will help?"

"I have racked my brain trying to think how I can help Aleksei. But unfortunately mine is not a very devious brain, and I have been empty of ideas."

"My brain is nothing if it is not devious," said Anatoly slyly. "I have a plan. You tell me if it can work."

An hour later Anatoly returned to the prison to interrogate Aleksei. Podolsk pressured him more than ever for results. Anatoly had hoped for a few more days to iron out the details of the escape and to let the Hayes woman know, but Podolsk informed him that his immediate superior, General Dubnov, was ready to abandon the entire project. Anatoly was able to finagle only two more sessions.

He was now forced to put the plan into motion by tomorrow. He thought that would be just enough time to gather in all the loose ends, but he had to move quickly, and that bothered him. He tended to be a methodical man, always telling his subordinates that slow and thorough was better than fast and frivolous. He made two more stops that night. One was back at the hospital. He didn't like seeing Fedorcenko twice in one day, but he had no choice. He'd been careful he had not been followed. Then he went in search of Cameron Hayes. She was attending the theater with her sisters. He waited until intermission, and when she came into the lobby, he escorted her outside.

"It is time, Miss Hayes."

"Time for what?"

"For what you came to Russia to do."

She gaped at him in disbelief. "When?"

"Tomorrow."

Again, her jaw nearly dropped, but questions were ready to her lips. "What are you planning? What do you want me to do? I still have no place to keep him until he is strong. Where—?"

"I will answer all of your questions. . . ."

40

THAT NEXT DAY there was no choice but to wait until Anatoly's regular interrogation session with Aleksei at five in the afternoon to put the escape plan into motion. It proved an agonizing wait for all.

Cameron wasn't completely idle, though, and began her part by checking out of the Metropole, telling the clerk that she was going to stay at the American embassy in order to care for her sister, who had suddenly become ill. She hugged Jackie in their room, not knowing if she'd see her sister again in Russia. The idea that she might never see either of her sisters if things went awry lurked in the back of her mind.

Blair, Jackie, Gary, and Robert huddled together in Blair and Gary's apartment in the embassy. They had never felt so helpless, but the fact was, it was out of their hands at this point. The only part they could play now was to pray. And though they well knew this was the most powerful, most important, part of the plan, it had been hard to convince them to remain in the background. They nearly wore a path in the carpet with their pacing.

Yuri also paced his office until he was called to attend one of his patients. He was more thankful than ever that shortly after the war he had resigned his position as chief of staff, taking the lesser post of chief of cardiology in which he'd be more involved with patient care. He had missed that terribly, and now his closer involvement with patients would play well into Anatoly's clever but slightly insane plan. This wasn't the first insane endeavor Yuri had participated in. He just hoped and prayed it would be the most successful. He had begun his part by slipping a small package to Anatoly during their last meeting. Now he was trying to remain available for the call he hoped he soon would receive.

If all went according to plan.

———

Helpless to act on his plan until five o'clock, Anatoly spent the morning zeroing in on that slippery devil, Vasily Zharenov. The more Anatoly learned of the man, the easier it was going to be to discredit him and his testimony against Tveritinov.

At five in the afternoon Anatoly made his way to the basement interrogation rooms in Lubyanka. Much to his relief, Podolsk was not anywhere around to breathe down his neck. Still, he had to be careful, knowing Podolsk was no doubt listening to all that transpired.

It still shocked Anatoly every time he saw his friend. And doubts filled him about the wisdom of the plan. He wondered if he had accurately reported Aleksei's physical condition to Dr. Fedorcenko. Perhaps in his zeal to promote his plan, he had underestimated his friend's state of health. Would it all be physically too much for him to bear? He'd heard Aleksei mention the droll saying, "Cure the disease, kill the patient."

"If there is a God," Anatoly intoned silently, "please let that not be the outcome now!"

He slipped into the chair across the table from Aleksei, who barely acknowledged his presence, wearing a dazed, glassy expression.

"Why do you keep coming?" Aleksei said dully.

"Because, my friend, I care about you. I want to spare you suffering."

"We don't always get what we want."

"I must be honest with you, Aleksei, my superiors are losing patience with you." Anatoly needed to keep up the act. Podolsk had given him one more day, but he could change his mind on a whim. "You must give us *something*!"

"I'm so tired, Anatoly."

"I know," Anatoly breathed gently. "I swear to you, my friend, this will end if you can give one more name."

"End how? No, I don't really care."

"You will be sent to a labor camp in Siberia. It will be better than this, yes?" It didn't matter what lies Anatoly told as long as it gave the appearance of getting results.

"Will . . . ?" Aleksei swallowed and rubbed his hands over his face.

Anatoly saw that he was barely hanging on. Perhaps he had discerned this was an act, perhaps not. There had been no other way to convey that message except in that brief note and in meaningful looks. Perhaps it truly didn't matter to him either way.

In a miserable tone, filled with self-loathing, Aleksei asked, "Will they continue the injections?"

"I will see to it," Anatoly promised, then he prodded, "One name, Aleksei?" As he spoke, he slid his hand across the table. Lifting it, he revealed two pills. With a twitch of his eyes and a slight nod, he tried to get across the message that Aleksei was to take the pills.

Aleksei just stared at them. Worried this would draw attention to them should someone be watching from the window on the door, Anatoly pounded his fist on the table and jumped up, at the same time effectively blocking his friend from view of the window.

"Curse you, Aleksei!" Anatoly shouted. "Give me a name or you are a dead man! There are plans to execute you in two days if you don't talk."

He continued to stand as an agonizingly long moment passed. Everything hinged on those pills—no, everything counted on the hope that Aleksei was lucid enough to grasp such subtle significances. Finally Aleksei put the pills in his mouth and swallowed. Anatoly nearly sagged with relief. He still wasn't certain if Aleksei understood what was happening. He had the look of a man taking poison and enjoying it. He might have thought—hoped?—the pills were simply another drug. Of course they were a drug, one that Dr. Fedorcenko had assured would make the prisoner appear very sick.

Aleksei said, "Get me another injection, and I will give you a name." And to Anatoly's amazement, Aleksei winked, or at least it appeared so.

Anatoly decided to interpret it as Aleksei's own subtle way of indicating he did indeed understand something was afoot and was going to play along. Anatoly smiled. "I will arrange it." He could not help exhaling a sigh of relief.

Podolsk was striding down the corridor toward the interrogation room as Anatoly exited.

"He's playing games with you now!" the man said contemptuously.

"I tell you, he's close to breaking."

"Bah! You have done nothing I haven't already tried. A name for an injection! It didn't work before—"

"You did not see the look of terror on his face when I mentioned execution."

"I can use terror. You were supposed to use honey," sneered Podolsk.

Anatoly himself felt like he was barely hanging on. But he just needed an hour, perhaps two.

"Give him the injection, then call me in two hours," said Anatoly. "If he doesn't talk, I will personally take him to the execution room. I will do so happily. The man has tried me to my limit."

"I shouldn't do this, but if there is even a small chance of success, I'll take it. This is it, Anatoly. Tomorrow he will be executed."

Anatoly went to his office and waited. When two hours passed with no word from Podolsk, he sat and perspired. So much could go wrong. Podolsk could have gone ahead and executed Aleksei. Yet the man had a huge stake in Aleksei delivering viable information. Anatoly was counting heavily on that fact.

His assistant looked in once. "Colonel, I just wanted to let you know I've sent that packet to Comrade Khrushchev — Are you ill, sir?"

"No, I am fine."

"You don't look fine."

"Maybe a touch of influenza . . ."

"You should go home."

"I am fine! I don't need a mother hen!"

Pavel exited. At least one matter appeared to be moving along smoothly. If that dossier on Zharenov, detailing the man's many shady, even traitorous, dealings, didn't convince Khrushchev to call off the dogs nipping at Tveritinov, nothing would. If Khrushchev wanted to use Tveritinov as a scapegoat in order to get himself back in Stalin's good graces, he was going to have to find a better informant than Zharenov. Supporting a traitor's lies would only put the ex-Ukrainian party chief in a worse light.

Yet the Tveritinov case had only been a small distraction for Anatoly. It would mean nothing if he could not manage to save his own friend. Anatoly stared at the telephone on his desk, willing it to ring. If they didn't call in five minutes he would go down anyway. His eagerness might be suspect, but it was a lesser risk than not being called at all.

Despite his anticipation, the ringing telephone made him nearly jump out of his skin. He grabbed it, listened, then said, "I'll be right there."

In his cell, Aleksei was draped over his toilet vomiting.

"He started about an hour ago," Podolsk said. "Look, it's bloody now."

"Has the doctor been called?" asked Anatoly.

"Yes. He said he didn't know what it was. Perhaps a reaction to the drugs we've been giving him."

"Why now after all this time?"

"Do you have a better idea?"

"Has he talked yet?"

"No. The illness came on him too soon."

As they talked, Aleksei, who had been propped up only by his grip on the toilet, seemed to lose even that and collapsed to the floor. Anatoly rushed to his sprawled-out figure. Bending down, Anatoly felt the pulse in his neck. This was less an act than real concern. His friend certainly looked near death. Dr. Fedorcenko said the pills were a poison, though in a controlled dose they wouldn't kill. Nevertheless, there was a fine line in determining the dosage, and he wasn't certain how the poison would react with the drugs already in Aleksei's system nor how his physical deterioration would affect things. Fedorcenko was only willing to take the risk when Anatoly had assured him Aleksei would definitely be executed in a day or two if action wasn't taken immediately.

"We need to call a real doctor," Anatoly said, rising.

"Or we can just let him die and have done with him," grated Podolsk, though he must know Aleksei's death would not bode well for the MVD agent.

"I'm going to get information out of this wretch," Anatoly snarled with a curse, "or I will see him executed! I won't have him die like a sick rat and rob us of the pleasure of a firing squad." He turned and strode out of the cell.

"What are you going to do?"

"I'm going to call a doctor who will get him better so I can see him properly shot!"

It took fifteen minutes for the doctor to arrive via ambulance. Fedorcenko swept into the prison with an impressive air of confidence. Using a false name, wearing a fake goatee and mustache with the gray dyed out of his hair, the doctor appeared different enough to fool only the casual observer. But it should be enough to protect the doctor if the escape plan was exposed.

Fedorcenko strode into the cell, not even a twitch on his face to indicate dismay at Aleksei's condition.

By this time Aleksei was all but unconscious, writhing on the floor, gripping his stomach, still vomiting a little but not even bothering to use the toilet. It was clear he didn't have the strength to rise even that distance.

After a thorough examination, Fedorcenko rose to face the two MVD colonels. "This man needs immediate surgery."

"What's wrong with him?" asked Podolsk.

"His appendix has burst. He'll die if he isn't operated on within the hour. There's an ambulance waiting outside."

The two colonels looked at each other. Anatoly knew what was going on in Podolsk's head—debating the need to go through all this trouble for a man they planned to kill anyway.

"Take him, Doctor," Anatoly said peremptorily.

Podolsk shrugged. If there was a shred of hope sparing him from his superior's censure, he apparently was still desperate enough to take it.

As they lifted the stretcher, with Aleksei strapped onto it, into the ambulance, Podolsk motioned for a guard to climb in.

Fedorcenko interceded. "I've got a dying man here. I don't want some inept guard in my way."

"But—" Podolsk started to protest.

Anatoly quickly said, "Sergei, the prisoner is hardly going anywhere. We'll follow the ambulance to the hospital in my car."

Cameron had watched this scene at the entrance to the ambulance with a sinking heart. If a guard were to accompany the prisoner, she would be forced to act the part for which she was now dressed, that of a nurse. She didn't know if she'd be able to pull it off with Alex so close at last.

Only when the doors were shut, with only the patient, the doctor, and herself inside, did she dare to look at the stretcher.

"Oh, Alex!" she moaned. She grasped his hand, but he was not aware of her presence.

"He looks worse than he is," Yuri said, but his tone lacked confidence.

She looked at him with skepticism, then turned her attention back to Alex. She brushed back the damp sweaty hair from his brow. Vomit and spittle were smeared across his dear face, now a ghastly shade of gray, and his lips were blue. His eyes were sunken and ringed, as if smudged with soot. She tried to imagine the eyes she remembered, the blue of them so alive, glistening like a pool in summertime. She tried to conjure up the image of the man she had married. Even then in Germany, he'd been a little pale and thin from the privations experienced in the Red Army. But this! Dear God, this man lying before her was a mere wraith. Had Bogorodsk merely brought about another kind of death for Alex?

While she looked on, Yuri gave Alex an injection.

"What's that?" she asked.

The doctor's expression was grim. "I've got to keep giving him the narcotics, Cameron." His tone was defensive. "If he goes into withdrawal in this condition, he will die."

"Oh, Yuri! What have they done to him!" Silent tears slipped from her eyes, trailing down her face.

Yuri laid a hand on her shoulder. "He'll pull through." As he spoke, he started an IV. "I would have to sedate him anyway for the next step in this cockeyed plan."

She felt foolish in the nurse's uniform when she could do nothing a nurse would do to help. Maybe Blair should have done this part. At least she'd had some experience in nursing.

The ambulance pulled up at the door to the hospital. Continuing the act, they rushed Alex into a surgical room. A few of the staff raised their eyes at Dr. Fedorcenko's new look, but he was chief of cardiology, so who were they to question his whims? Anytime someone began to call him by name in the presence of the MVD agents, he adroitly cut them off, maintaining his disguise without alarming his staff. Seeing that everything appeared to be flowing according to plan, Cameron, with great reluctance to leave Alex even for a minute, slipped into the background and went to her appointed place.

Anatoly and Podolsk were pacing in a waiting room when, an hour later, Dr. Fedorcenko appeared.

"I am sorry, gentlemen," the doctor said gravely, "but the patient has expired. I did everything I could, but we simply did not catch it in time."

"I want to see the body," Podolsk said. Anatoly had feared this but had counted on the fact that Podolsk had never been very thorough in his work. The man would choose now to improve himself?

Anatoly flicked a covert glance toward the doctor, who merely shrugged and said, "Come this way."

Anatoly felt like one nerve stretched to its limit. He didn't understand enough about medicine to know if all was going as planned or not. For all he knew the patient *had* died. Certainly Aleksei had looked near death.

The patient had been moved from the operating table back to a gurney in the corridor of the operating rooms. A sheet was pulled up over his face. Anatoly looked closely to see if he detected a telltale rise and fall of the man's chest. He saw no movement. He did see that the doctor was engaging Podolsk in conversation as they progressed toward the gurney, telling him all about the surgery and what went wrong. The account the doctor gave was quite graphic, dwelling on gruesome details about pus, fecal contaminants, and blood—lots and lots of blood, enough to make even a man with an iron stomach recoil. Podolsk was looking green and pointedly not looking closely at the body. He had his duty to perform in confirming the death of his prisoner, but duty only went so far.

The doctor lifted aside the sheet to reveal Aleksei's deathly pale face.

"You may feel his pulse," said Fedorcenko.

When Podolsk hesitated, Fedorcenko took the man's hand

and pulled it toward the patient's neck. Podolsk's hand trembled as the doctor pressed it against Aleksei's neck in the vicinity of the carotid artery.

Anatoly smiled in spite of himself. He was sure all Podolsk would feel was his own shaking fingers, as Anatoly thought the artery was an inch or so to the left of the fellow's fingers.

Finally Podolsk jerked his hand away. "All right." He turned toward Anatoly. "Well, that's it. But don't think I'm going to Siberia alone, Anatoly."

"We did all we could, Sergei." Anatoly threw a consoling arm around his comrade's shoulders. "Let's go get drunk before we tell the general, yes?"

Podolsk nodded eagerly.

As they walked away, Anatoly ventured a quick look back. Fedorcenko gave him a reassuring smile, the only tangible evidence that this crazy escape plan might truly have worked.

PART V

*"Victory and defeat are each
of the same price."*

<small>Thomas Jefferson</small>

41

THE SIGN ON the door read "Quarantine—No Unauthorized Personnel Admitted."

Inside that room Cameron prayed that the sign would do its job and keep the curious away. The room was located at the end of one of the more quiet sections of the hospital, and few ever passed by. It actually had been a stroke of genius to hide Alex in his own hospital! Thank Bogorodsk for that. In the flurry of carrying out the rescue plan, Cameron realized she hadn't had the opportunity to thank him. He had taken the greatest risk and made everything possible. How could she properly thank the burly MVD agent? She hoped she would see him again to do so, but such a reunion might not be wise and certainly would be risky.

A stirring from the bed interrupted her thoughts, though her contemplation had only been a brief distraction from what had been dominating her every thought for the last few days—sleepless days for her, as her heart clenched with constant fear.

"Alex . . ." she murmured.

He was still in a semiconscious state that bordered on delirium. Yuri was keeping him heavily sedated, trying to allow the IVs of glucose and vitamins to restore some of his strength. The awful gray hue had left his skin, but he was still pale. He was

415

also feverish, which Yuri had said was probably from residue of the drug they had given him to induce vomiting.

Cameron was Alex's sole "nurse." Yuri had given her a quick course in basic nursing so that she could give injections and administer other necessary treatments. She was at Alex's side twenty-four hours a day. The only time she had left the room was to apply for an extension on her visa, ostensibly because of her sister's illness—the reason she'd given for needing to extend her stay. Miraculously the visa had been granted quickly, and she wondered how much the indispensable Colonel Bogorodsk had had to do with that.

The only other person to enter Alex's room was Yuri, but the last time he was in he'd warned Cameron that he would have to cut back on his visits. It would look suspicious for him to focus too much on the quarantined patient, especially if it resulted in the neglect of his other duties. But he felt Alex was out of danger, though he had added with a gravely arched brow, "For now."

Cameron didn't have to ask what he'd meant by that ominous phrase. She knew as well as he that as soon as Alex was stabilized, his real ordeal would begin. Though Alex had only been addicted to heroin for no more than three weeks—according to Bogorodsk—the doses given him had been frequent and heavy. He would no doubt have as difficult a time shaking off the effects of the drug as someone who had been addicted for years. They could not wait until his health was fully recovered to start withdrawing him from the drug. The longer they hid him in the hospital, the greater the chance of discovery. It would take only one staff-person-turned-informant to destroy Alex's hope for freedom.

There was no possibility of trying to get him out of the country while still addicted. She hated to admit it, but he would be far too unreliable. Someone would have to accompany him, and false papers would have to be procured for that person. Unfortunately, the sources for obtaining papers had dried up with Marquet's departure, not to mention that one of the names Alex had given in his interrogation had been the fellow he had used for that purpose. Perhaps Bogorodsk could produce papers, but he had no doubt jeopardized himself to the limit. Cameron hated to ask more of him unless absolutely necessary.

Cameron uttered another prayer that they would be given the time they needed.

Alex mumbled something. Cameron leaned closer to discern his unconscious ravings. Then she turned, picked up the cool, damp cloth, and gently swabbed his forehead.

His eyes suddenly opened. They were clearer than they had been for days.

"Camrushka . . ." he breathed, barely audible.

"Yes, Alex, it's me." She touched her lips to his hot, pale cheek.

"I am not dreaming. . . ." He reached out his hand, and she grasped it firmly. "To feel you, to truly feel you!"

She knew what he meant. Though she had been nursing him, swabbing the forehead of an unconscious man wasn't the same as touching her husband, awake and coherent. Tucking her arms as far under him as she could, she bent close and touched her lips to his. His response was weak but fervent, then the hand he had tried to lift to her shoulder fell back to the bed. The effort seemed to have drained him.

He murmured in Russian, "I'm so sorry . . . Camrushka . . . so sorry . . ."

"Don't worry, my love," she replied, also in Russian. "You've nothing to be sorry about."

He began to mumble again, indecipherable words to which she responded with untiring words of love. His passion faded, and he seemed to slip away from her once again. The moment of lucidity was gone.

Having heard that comatose patients had the capacity of hearing, she took up her Bible, which she had packed along with the other things she'd brought to the hospital, and opened it to Psalm Twenty-three, the most comforting passage she knew of.

"'The Lord is my shepherd; I shall not want. He maketh me to lie down in green pastures: he leadeth me beside the still waters. He restoreth my soul: he leadeth me in the paths of righteousness for his name's sake. Yea, though I walk through the valley—'" Her voice choked.

She knew Alex was in God's hands no matter what, that he had the hope of life eternal. Yet to think of losing him, especially when she had finally found him after so long, was crushing to her. Nevertheless, she made herself read on.

"'Yea, though I walk through the valley of the shadow of death, I will fear no evil.'"

She hadn't realized before, but the verse spoke of the *shadow* of death, not death itself. Of course, if you were actually dead, you wouldn't need God. If Alex was anything, he was in that valley now. That shadow was upon him. But he wasn't alone, nor was she.

"'. . . for thou art with me; thy rod and thy staff they comfort me. Thou preparest a table before me in the presence of mine enemies: thou anointest my head with oil; my cup runneth over.'"

She had begun reading to comfort Alex, but the oil of the words coming from her lips ran over her head, as well, filling her and running over the brim.

"'Surely goodness and mercy shall follow me all the days of my life: and I will dwell in the house of the Lord for ever.'"

Cameron kept reading several more Psalms, feeling truly at peace for the first time in a long while. Soon, because she'd been awake for nearly forty hours straight, her eyes drooped shut, and the Bible slipped from her hands onto her lap.

A sound woke her a couple of hours later. Her gaze went immediately to Alex, but he, too, was sleeping, and it seemed real sleep this time, not the restless writhing of semiconsciousness.

The sound came again. A knock on the door. Who could it be? Yuri would not knock. Well, she wasn't dressed in this nurse's garb for nothing. Her Russian was at least good enough to fend off a curious interloper. She rose and went to the door, making sure the surgical mask was in place over her face to support the ruse she was attending an infectious patient.

Opening the door a crack, she was greeted by a familiar voice.

"It's me, Cameron," said Jackie.

Cameron realized how much she had missed her sisters' company—both of her sisters.

"You've got to put on a gown and mask before you can come in," Cameron instructed quietly, "in case someone is watching."

Jackie found both items on the small supply trolley next to the door. Properly garbed, Cameron let her in. Once inside, Jackie paused to set down an item she was carrying before giving her sister a warm embrace. When they tried to kiss each other's cheeks, they realized they had forgotten the masks. Laughing quietly, they removed these, then finished their greetings.

"You've brought my typewriter," Cameron said, indicating the item Jackie had set on the floor. They spoke in hushed voices.

"I thought you might want it."

"I suppose I might, but for now I'm afraid the noise might disturb Alex. Though at the same time I am desperate for him to wake up."

Jackie glanced toward the bed. "He's unconscious?"

"Sort of, but partly because Yuri is keeping him sedated." With a shrug she added, "Maybe that's for the best now. He would hate to be in this state for his first meeting with one of his sisters-in-law."

Quietly Cameron moved the vinyl-upholstered chair, which she had been using for both sleeping and sitting, away from the bedside. Then she moved the only other chair in the room, an old straight-backed wooden chair, close to it. The women sat down.

"I want to assure you," Jackie said, "that I wasn't followed here. Robert came with me and showed me some pretty nifty tricks for eluding the police. Maybe I'll take up cat burglary if teaching doesn't pan out."

Cameron chuckled quietly, then grasped her sister's hands as sudden emotion claimed her. "Jackie, I'm so glad you came. I'm . . . okay." Her lip trembled a little. "I've felt God's peace, especially lately, but it does get lonely."

"I wish I could stay longer to keep you company. Perhaps Blair—"

"It's too risky."

"I know, and I wouldn't have come except . . ." Pausing, Jackie gazed down at their clasped hands. "I had to come and say good-bye. My exit visa arrived, and I have to leave tomorrow."

"Well, it is time you got back to Emi," Cameron said more bravely than she felt. "We'll see each other soon."

Jackie nodded, moisture filling her eyes. "What an experience we've had! I am so happy it is turning out successfully. But I never doubted that for a minute—" A sheepish expression crept over her face. "Well, I've got to admit when we were waiting in that interrogation room, I had serious visions of spending the rest of my life in Siberia. At least Blair looks good in those fur hats. I look ridiculous."

"Me too!" Cameron smiled, but a wistful, distant look briefly supplanted the smile.

"You're going to miss Russia, aren't you?" Jackie asked.

"Miss this stupid country?" But Cameron's derisive snort couldn't hide her real feelings. "Yes, I suppose I will." She shot a glance over her shoulder toward the bed. "He will miss it, too. Though it was nearly the death of us, we'll probably always love it."

"Robert says Russia isn't the government, it's the people."

"Yes, that's what we'll really miss—the people." Wanting a cheerier subject, she asked, "Is Robert leaving Russia, too?" She arched her brow coyly.

"As soon as his replacement arrives."

"Will he be living in Boston or Los Angeles when he gets back to the States?"

Jackie turned pink. "Cameron!" Then she added despite her embarrassment, "I have a feeling he will be visiting Los Angeles in the near future."

"How about that, Jackie? You and I both had to come all the way to Russia to meet the men we will spend our lives with."

"Well, in my case that might be premature—"

"My money is on a wedding in a year."

"Robert and I will get married when you and Alex have a baby." Jackie grinned gamely.

"Oh, the pressure is on!" Laughing, Cameron enjoyed and appreciated the levity. But she couldn't avoid the more serious implications of the discussion. "It will happen . . ." she murmured. "Sometimes it is hard to believe, even now when we have come this far. But it will happen . . . won't it?"

"I know it will, sis!"

They talked for a while longer, then Jackie rose to leave. "Well, I better go. I still haven't started packing. Robert wanted me to tell you that he would have come up, but he thought it might draw too much attention."

"I understand. Thank you for coming."

She put her arms around Jackie again and didn't want to let go. She had always been the big sister, the strong one, but she knew that was as much a ruse as the nurse's uniform she now wore. Inside she was as needy as anyone.

"Cameron, you are not alone in this room," Jackie said. "Just keep telling yourself that. I almost *feel* God's presence here, like His arms are wrapped around this room and around you and Alex. When you feel a little lost, just close your eyes and conjure up that image. A father holding his children—you know, like we always wanted."

Those words were to carry Cameron through the days that followed when she and Alex seemed to be truly in the "valley of the shadow of death."

42

ANATOLY CONTEMPLATED his future and found within him some very mixed feelings indeed. Without a doubt he was anxious to join his family. Yet a part of him was melancholy. When he departed Russia, he would cross to the other side of the entity that the capitalist rogue Winston Churchill had dubbed the "iron curtain."

Anatoly chuckled dryly. Once in the West, he would definitely have to curb his tendency to use such phrases as "capitalist rogue." There, Churchill was no doubt something of a hero, as were other western dignitaries he'd learned to denigrate.

"I may have to become a capitalist myself!" This time his chuckle held more amusement. Might not be so bad. Having fancy automobiles, radios, clothes to my heart's desire. My Vera dressed in the latest fashions. She deserved all the things they had lacked in the Soviet Union.

Still, he had never despised his life in Russia. He was a Communist and had grown up learning to revere the Glorious Party. A child of twelve at the time of the Revolution, he'd been submerged in politics by his revolutionary parents. Lenin was venerated, almost deified, in his home. When he was old enough to serve his country in the army, he did so proudly, fighting in the waning days of the civil war. When he had been offered a position with the secret police, he'd taken it with a zealous desire to purge his beloved motherland of traitors and malcontents.

Only gradually had the sheen worn off his zeal. Yet even now, when he clearly saw the corruption of what had once been truly inspired, he did not hate the system. But he had come to be a more pragmatic man than a zealot. He could and he would live in the West. He would work for a bourgeois boss, perhaps even become a bourgeois entrepreneur himself. Still, it saddened him to leave the country he loved.

But leave he must.

So far he had dodged the wrath of his superiors in the loss of a prime prisoner. He'd argued that he had come on the case only three days before it fell apart and could hardly be blamed for a failure that no one could be expected to fix in so short of a time. His excuse had been accepted, while poor Podolsk was even now on his way to a post in Omsk, where the chill of approaching winter could already be felt in the air. Anatoly had retained his rank and his Moscow post. Nevertheless the authorities were still investigating the debacle, and a few discrepancies were being discovered. For one, the doctor who had operated on Rostovscikov was nowhere to be found. The body was missing, as well. One or the other of these inconsistencies might well occur in the disorder that was Soviet bureaucracy, but both? Very suspect. It wouldn't be long before Anatoly was scrutinized more thoroughly.

He was ready to go, physically if not mentally. He would take the morning train to Leningrad and there board the train for Finland. Unlocking the top drawer in his desk, he pulled it open to ensure that his travel papers were in order. He had two sets. One was completely legitimate, in his name and granting travel to Helsinki. But just in case the so-called boom had fallen and Anatoly Bogorodsk could not travel safely, he had another set under an assumed name.

Shoving aside papers he'd had covering the documents, he sucked in a sharp breath. They were gone!

Could he have removed them earlier and in the stress of the

escape forgotten? He racked his brain trying to think of a time when he might have done so but was positive he hadn't. Only he had the key. And Pavel!

No, that couldn't be! Why?

He was about to call in his assistant when the man himself entered.

"Colonel Bogorodsk—"

"I was just about to call you. Were you in my desk?"

"Colonel, I am so sorry!"

Somehow Anatoly didn't think the man was apologizing merely for taking the papers but for something far more heinous. "What is it, Pavel?"

"I . . . you . . . they . . . I—" Pavel stammered, visibly shaken.

"Out with it, Pavel! What have you done?" Even as he spoke, Anatoly felt panic rise inside and a compelling desire to flee in that very instant.

"Your family is safe!" Pavel burst out. "But mine . . . mine! Oh, God, forgive me."

Anatoly jumped up, ready to run, yet still regarding his trusted assistant in disbelief. "What have you done?"

"They are on their way up—"

"The police?" His colleagues, his associates, his comrades.

"I found the papers. I knew you were planning to leave." The words began spewing from Pavel now like a poisonous flood. "I suspected what you were planning to do for the doctor. They questioned me! They threatened my wife . . . my children! I had to tell them my suspicions. You would have done the same!"

As if the iron inside had suddenly melted, Anatoly sank back into his chair. In the outside corridor he already heard the tramping of approaching doom.

"Yes . . ." he murmured, "yes, my friend, I would have done the same." They were all prisoners, weren't they? No one was really free. Perhaps they would even find Aleksei now, though there was no way Pavel could know any of the details of the escape.

"Do you forgive me, Anatoly?" Pavel pleaded as the outer office door burst open.

Part of Anatoly wanted to tell him to go to blazes. Yet there was a larger part that simply could not find the motivation for hatred. "Of course I forgive you, my friend."

The MVD agents, at least a dozen of them, stormed into Anatoly's office. Quickly, he was handcuffed and led away.

Anatoly's interrogation was brief. His captors knew he would never break—they had no ready threat to hold over his head with his family safely out of Russia. Moreover, they knew of his reputation in the force as one of their best agents. They knew it was useless to even try to break such a man. Actually, it was only Anatoly who gleaned any useful information from the session. By the time they finished, he was fairly certain they were assuming that Aleksei had long since fled the country. In fact he helped along that conjecture by hinting that he'd had similar travel documents to those found in his desk made for Rostovscikov.

They would not launch a serious manhunt for Aleksei. That was something at least.

In his cold, bare cell the hour after his interrogation, Anatoly sat quietly thinking of the what-might-have-beens in life. There was probably not a man in this vile prison who had more regrets than Anatoly Bogorodsk. The greatest was that he would never see his beloved son grow to manhood, perhaps become a doctor, doing good with his life instead of evil. He found comfort in knowing that his son would leave a better legacy than he had.

When his cell door finally opened and the guards led him away, he hoped that this, the end of his life, would somehow make up for all that had gone before.

After walking down a long corridor, they came to a room Anatoly knew well. How many had he sent to this room?

He was taken inside and placed before a wall where the stains of those who had come before would never be completely washed away. They put a blindfold over his eyes.

He felt no fear.

He'd always known in his heart that he was ready to make

this sacrifice. Words came to his mind—even an atheist reprobate such as himself knew some religious words, though only thanks to Aleksei.

"Greater love hath no man than this, that a man lay down his life for his friends."

I love you, my dear son! I love you, my dear friend, Aleksei! I hope you have both redeemed me. For at the end I do desire redemption more than I thought I would. I desire forgiveness for my sins. I do not deserve heaven but only hope that God will not despise me too much.

The sounds of gunfire reverberated in the room, taking a man's life, but perhaps opening a gateway for him, as well.

———

In his office Semyon looked over the photographs in his portfolio. These were the best of his career, all from the war. He hoped one day to put them together into a book honoring the Great Patriotic War. He had thought he'd gathered enough to present to a publisher, but the folder didn't seem complete. Then he remembered some he had removed a few months ago to use in propaganda leaflets. He went to a file cabinet, opened a drawer, and shuffled through the files. Absorbed in this task, he didn't hear his door open.

"Semyon."

He froze where he stood, thinking perhaps he was suddenly hallucinating. A waking dream—a good dream, not a nightmare. He was afraid to turn, fearing he'd only find emptiness.

"Semyon, you were not really angry at me, were you?"

Then he did turn, and it wasn't an apparition he'd heard. "Father!"

Tveritinov nodded and strode to within a few inches of his son. There he stopped. Both seemed at a loss for what to do next. Tveritinov had never fostered the habit of fond embraces. Did he, like Semyon, now regret that fact?

It was easier for Semyon to shake off the stoicism he'd

learned. "Oh, Father!" He threw his arms around the man and wept.

Tveritinov responded by lifting his own arms, a bit leaden at first, but once they clasped his son to him, they relaxed, though at the same time, they gripped the young man for dear life.

"I thought I'd never see you again," said the elder Tveritinov.

"And I feared the last words you'd ever hear from me would be those horrid things I said in your cell."

"I believe we are experiencing a miracle, eh?"

"I'm sure of it. You are completely free of those false charges?"

"It would appear so," said Tveritinov. "Zharenov was discredited to the extent that Khrushchev couldn't distance himself from the fellow fast enough."

"Amazing." Semyon wondered how it had come about and immediately thought of Bogorodsk. He'd have to find a way to thank the MVD agent.

"Can you spare time from your work long enough to come home with me, to the dacha? Your mother is anxiously expecting us."

Semyon grabbed his coat and hat. As he and his father exited the office, he felt compelled to say, "Father, I must tell you—I met my half sisters recently."

"Did you?" He seemed surprised but not dismayed. "I'm glad of it. It has been a heavy burden on me these last few years."

"I understand why you didn't tell me. I don't mind."

"Well, what were they like?"

Semyon arched a brow and smiled wryly. "Very interesting, I must say! All are quite beautiful, but in my opinion a bit too independent. Too obviously bourgeois. But I can't hold against them the fact of their deprived upbringing." His words were part jest, yet despite his father's misfortune, Semyon still believed in the way of life he'd been taught to love.

"Any chance of converting them to the socialist way of life?"

"If I see them again, I will try. It can only do them good." As they stepped outside into the crisp air of a late summer day,

Semyon added, "You need not fear them converting me, Father."

"I never did fear that, son."

Both men exchanged a meaningful look, knowing they spoke of more than a political conversion. They would always remain father and son. But again Semyon felt compelled to take the exchange beyond the reserved bounds they were accustomed to.

"I love you, Father," he said.

Tveritinov swallowed, his natural reserve in check except around his eyes, now glistening with affection. "I know," he breathed.

43

"Please give me something!"

"You know I can't, Alex."

"Don't you see? It's no use. Please, I beg you!" Alex all but dropped to his knees before her. "Give it up, woman! I'm lost!"

"I won't accept that!" she replied, but her voice was shaky. Two days of this had begun to wear her stamina thin. As if even the shadowed light of the room oppressed her, she walked to the window and pulled open the drape. She'd nearly forgotten there was a world out there. Bathed in the light of the afternoon sun, she wanted to forget the struggle of wills she was fighting. It took all her own will to turn back to face her husband.

"I tell you, I've got to have something or I'll die! Please . . . please . . . I beg you!" Alex cried.

"Stop whining!" she shot back, the dam of her frustration breaking, not for the first time.

Cameron had always known she wasn't the nurturing type. It had been relatively easy to feign such a character quality while Alex had been sick, helpless, near death. But Yuri had deemed him fit enough to cease his maintenance dose of narcotics two days ago, and since then it had been pure torture for both patient and quasi nurse. Yuri had tried to prepare her for what to expect, not wanting her to be shocked. He'd warned her that their patient would seem an entirely different person from the man they once knew. All his advising hadn't helped her cope. She could hardly bear this weak, tortured man who had tried nearly everything to get some drugs. Fear that he might actually attempt to escape the hospital room had prompted Yuri to put a lock on the outside of the door. Now Cameron and Alex were like prisoners locked together in combat. There were moments when she did indeed regret ever finding Alex, when that lock kept *her* in, denying her any means of escape.

"You don't like whining?" Alex was railing back at her. "You don't like weakness, either—I know that about you. Well, you've got both. Accept it and get out while you can."

"I'm not going anywhere," she said, though in truth all she wanted to do was escape. "The door is locked! I couldn't get out if I wanted to."

He'd been standing shakily, but suddenly he crumbled back on the bed. "Can't you see? I'm too weak. I'll die. I'll truly die."

"Maybe that would be better than living your life as a slave."

He laughed, the sound like an old boot scraping over broken glass. "At least we agree on something!"

"I'm not going to let you die," she retorted, "nor am I going to let you live a slave to drugs."

"I'll always be a slave to them. I know that now. I'm hopeless."

"You beat it once. You will do it again."

Dismally he shook his head. "No, not now that I know what I am really made of."

"Alex, you didn't do this to yourself this time," she implored. "They did it to you. You had no choice. I'll tell you what you are made of. You withstood their torture for weeks. You are strong!"

"And all they had to do was wave one small carrot in my face, and I was theirs! I can't even remember how many friends and innocent people I betrayed."

"Anatoly said you didn't reveal anything that brought too much harm to anyone. An American who was only deported, a few others who had already been arrested. Even when your mind was muddled, you were strong enough to protect your friends."

"If you hadn't gotten me out, I would have given them all up!" he yelled. "Yuri would have been next!" he sneered. "Then your name! I would have given my own mother's name if it would have kept that sweet nectar flowing in my veins."

"But you didn't!"

"I wish you would just accept the truth, Cameron. I am no longer the man I was. You know what I think of, what I've prayed for every minute of every miserable day since you rescued me? To be back in that prison. I curse you for taking me away from there!"

"Stop it, Alex!" It was getting harder and harder for her to tell herself that this was the addiction talking, not the man she loved and had married.

As if he read her thoughts, as if he knew exactly how to twist the knife in her gut, he said, "I know how you despise weakness, Cameron. You'll soon despise me, and I will deserve it. For your sake, leave before that happens."

"You are right, Alex, I used to have a hard time with weakness, but that was before I came face to face with my own weaknesses. We're all weak." She stepped close to him and reached a hand to his shoulder, thinking that if she could just touch him, that might succeed where words were failing. But he winced and drew away.

As if he had struck her, she dropped her hand and her shoulders slumped in defeat. The next time Yuri came, she would leave and never come back. She'd done all she could. She was so tired of fighting for both of them.

She dropped down onto the chair while Alex lay on the bed, curled up and moaning softly.

By the time Yuri came about a half hour later, she had forgotten all about leaving. She had spent some time in silent prayer, and though still tired and confused, her commitment to Alex had been restored. She knew now why they had married. In Germany she had told Alex that she believed there was a power in the marriage vows, a power that would bring them together. What she hadn't realized then was that the same power would also *keep* them together.

When she heard the sound of the lock being turned, she rose. Alex heard it, as well.

Alex rolled over. "Cameron, if you love me, please make Yuri get me something!"

Sighing, she had no ready response. She wanted to tell him that she did love him and for that reason she would never ask such a thing of Yuri. But she'd already said those words so many times, she knew they meant nothing to Alex in his present state.

Yuri opened the door and came inside.

He'd barely shut the door when Alex demanded, "Yuri, give me something, please! I can't stand it another minute!"

Yuri looked at Cameron, and she shrugged helplessly.

"Don't look at her!" Alex screamed. "She doesn't care if I die!"

Calmly Yuri replied, "I've brought you something to eat, Alex."

"I don't want to eat!" Alex retorted like a spoiled child.

Ignoring that, Yuri said to Cameron, "Would you talk to me outside for a moment?"

Out in the corridor with the door shut, Cameron felt as if she had been reprieved from a death sentence. Even the antiseptic hospital air of the corridor felt sweet and free.

"Yuri, I don't think I can take much more of this," she admitted miserably.

"The next couple of days will be the worst," he said. "He's not violent, is he?"

"No." She couldn't help being shocked at such a suggestion. Alex, so gentle and patient and kind. If he were to change that much, she knew she'd despair altogether.

"I told you anything might happen," said Yuri. "That's why I am worried about locking the door from the outside. You have to be able to get out if he—"

"He would never harm me!"

"Probably not, but I wish we could have a lock inside that

you'd have the key for. But that would mean trusting a workman to come into the room."

"Yuri, I know I'm safe."

"Maybe we should just keep the door unlocked. If he gets out, so be it."

"If he is recaptured, I don't think he will be as strong as he was before. He will give them all our names."

"Well, right now that seems the least of our problems," Yuri said.

"Now what?"

Always there had been the fear of discovery lurking over them. Already once, Yuri had barely deflected a curious doctor from entering the quarantined room. And a janitor who couldn't read had come into the room before the lock had been installed. Cameron's Russian had been good enough to scare the fellow away, but there remained the worry that the man would suspect something amiss and report them. It never happened, but that didn't alleviate the fear.

"Cameron, Anatoly Bogorodsk was arrested yesterday," Yuri said. He paused when she gasped and seemed reluctant to finish. "He was executed," he said with great difficulty.

"No . . . no . . ." she moaned.

"He was a good man."

She nodded, tears and emotion choking back any other response.

"This means the police probably discovered that Alex didn't die in surgery and has escaped."

She simply could not process that at the moment. Only one thought plagued her. "This will kill Alex."

"We mustn't tell him, at least not until he is out of the woods."

"Yes . . ." She forced herself to consider the hard practicalities of this news. "We may not have much time now."

"The police have come to the hospital and are trying to find the elusive doctor who operated on Alex," he said. "So far, any of my people who might have recognized my disguise are keeping it to themselves."

"Yuri, you're in danger, too, then!"

"I'll be fine," he said. "I have many friends here. And I've weathered worse storms than this. For now, I think Alex is safe, too. There have been no questions raised about this room, and I don't see how any connection can be made to the escape."

"But what if Bogorodsk talked?"

Yuri smiled grimly, and even before he spoke she realized it had been a dumb question. "I am sure they executed him quickly because they knew he would never talk. They also must assume their quarry is long gone. The only loose end is the doctor, and it is likely they will just consider him an innocent dupe. It might all simply fade away with Bogorodsk's execution. With that the police will have their pound of flesh for the debacle."

"We owe everything to him," Cameron said. "I'm not sure I ever thanked him."

"I am sure he knew how you felt."

They stood there in silence for a few moments, Cameron trying to gather back her tattered emotions so there would be no chance that Alex would suspect something was wrong.

"Here's some food for you both." Yuri gestured toward a tray on the supply trolley where he usually left their meals. He then handed her something wrapped in a clean white cloth. "This is a sedative and a syringe should he get too out of hand."

She looked at the packet with horror. "Won't that just make things worse?"

"No, it won't undo the strides made in breaking his addiction. It's fairly mild, not a narcotic. You remember how I showed you to give an injection?"

She nodded with a shudder. Plunging a needle into an orange was a far cry from putting it into human flesh, and as many times as she had already done it to Alex, she would never get used to the procedure.

"I'm going to spend the next two nights here at the hospital," he said. "I'll be able to come up more often that way. Just until we get him over this bad time."

Nodding, she went back into the room carrying the tray, the white packet tucked in her pocket. The click of the lock made her cringe.

She put the food on the bedside table. Alex was still curled up on the bed groaning.

"Alex, here's something to eat."

"I said—"

"You'll be leaving here in a couple of days," she cut in smoothly. "You will need your strength. You must eat."

Rolling over, he faced her. His countenance was drawn together, taut with pain. She knew the agony he was feeling was real, that he wasn't just a weakling raving for drugs. The withdrawal was physically torturing him. He could well die.

"Please eat, Alex." She smiled gently. Seeing his pain helped to renew her patience.

He picked up the bowl of soup and flung it against the wall. It hit with a loud crash, the red broth of borscht dripping down the plaster like blood, bits of cabbage and meat making it more repulsive yet.

All patience, thin though it was in the first place, fled from Cameron. "You spoiled brat! That was my dinner, too!"

"I told you I don't want food!" He reached for the teapot.

Cameron grabbed his hand, restraining him. "Don't you dare!"

But he wrenched the teapot from her, and it quickly joined the soup.

"Okay! If you want to bring down the whole police force on us, fine!" Then she had an idea. She took the white cloth from her pocket. "Here, this is what you want." Her hand trembling, she unwrapped the items in the cloth. Uncapping the syringe, she plunged the needle into the small vial of sedative.

But she forgot that Alex was a doctor, and his mind apparently was not as despoiled with drugs as it appeared.

"That's not what I want!" He obviously recognized the label

on the vial. He grabbed it and the syringe from her and flung those toward the broken crockery.

"You selfish beast!" she cried. Moisture spilled from her eyes, tears of grief she'd barely held back a few minutes ago. "He died for nothing then, didn't he?" She gasped as the words spilled out with the tears.

It took a moment for the words to penetrate Alex's self-absorption. For an instant she thought and hoped they would go unnoticed.

"What are you talking about?"

"Nothing," she said quickly.

"Who died?" he demanded.

"I'm not going to tell you."

He jumped from the bed, grasped her arm, and harshly pushed her back against the wall, their feet crunching over the broken dishes. For a moment all she could think of were Yuri's warnings about violence. Had she so misjudged the man she loved? His hand pinched her arm painfully. He was stronger than she thought. She looked down at his hand, now bruising her arm, then up into his eyes, where she saw more fear than violence. She wasn't afraid, but something she couldn't explain made her answer the question in his piercing gaze.

"Anatoly Bogorodsk . . ." she uttered in a strangled voice. "They discovered he helped you escape and executed him."

For a moment that didn't seem to penetrate, either. When it did, the fire inside him was doused as with icy water. The hand gripping her fell limply to his side.

"Oh, no . . ." he groaned.

He stumbled back away from her. She thought he might fall, and she grasped his arm, but he shook her away and stumbled to the bed. Dropping onto it, he curled up again as he had before, but this time he made no sound. He drew himself up into a taut ball and didn't move.

"Alex . . ." Cameron entreated as gently as she could.

He didn't respond. She put her hand on his shoulder. He didn't move away but again did not respond. She repeated his name but could think of no other words of comfort. He still did not move or make a sound. Even as she tended the cuts on his bare feet from the broken crockery, he lay there like a corpse.

Watching him helplessly for several minutes, she finally did the only thing she could think to do. She crawled onto the bed with him and put her arm around him. He made no response, not even after an hour had passed. How could she have been such an irresponsible fool? Yuri said not to tell him. Was she so selfish she had wanted to hurt him for hurting her? Was she that stupid and shallow?

Had she sent him over the edge mentally? She'd heard of people becoming catatonic. Had she done that to Alex?

In this turmoil of mind, it was a miracle she could sleep, but sheer mental and physical exhaustion finally overcame her shattered thoughts.

44

WHEN SHE AWOKE, moonlight was streaming in through the drapes she'd opened earlier. But that wasn't what caused her to wake. She turned and saw Alex sitting up in the bed leaning against the headboard. In the small confines of the hospital bed any movement would have been difficult to ignore, not that she wanted to. Even in the depths of her sleep she had feared he would never move again, and her dreams had been of despair and desperation.

"You're awake," she said, unable to say anything else beyond stating the obvious.

"I didn't want to wake you." His voice was rough with strain, the hands resting on the blanket shaking.

"Are you . . . okay?"

He shook his head. "I was thinking about someone dying for me . . . *dying*, Cameron! It's incomprehensible."

"Like Christ dying for us."

"Maybe, but—I am ashamed to admit it—that often is little more than an idea to me. Anatoly . . . dear God! That is so real. I . . . don't think I can bear it."

"But you must, Alex."

"Yes, I must." He sounded more resigned than convinced. "I didn't want him to do this. I didn't expect it of him. And what makes it worse is that I never had the depth of feeling for him that he obviously had for me. Sometimes I felt more fear than friendship toward him, that if I wasn't friendly to him I'd get into trouble. There were times when I even used his friendship for the protection it often offered. Would I have died for him? No, I'm sure I wouldn't have. I gave no more to saving his son's life than I would have given to any patient."

His head flopped back against the metal headboard with a thud. He struck his head against it a couple more times. "Why did he do such a stupid thing?" Alex cried, tears oozing from his eyes.

"You don't really mean that, do you, Alex?"

"Now I owe him my life, but I can't do something as easy as taking an executioner's bullet for him. Now I have to live. I have to be a better man." His tone was full of scorn rather than promise.

In spite of herself she smiled at the irony of his words. "It shouldn't be so hard for you," she said tenderly. "You've been doing that all your life."

She scooted up to sit next to him and placed an arm around him. For the first time in days, he didn't reject her touch. Instead, he draped his arms around her, laid his head on her shoulder, and wept, perhaps as much for the man who had died as for the one who must go on living.

———

The next days were by no means made easier by Alex's epiphany. The physical withdrawal was as agonizing as ever, but he never again begged or even asked for the relief of drugs. He welcomed the physical and mental torture. In a small way it helped him feel more worthy of his friend's sacrifice, though in his heart he knew that would never be possible. He would try to bear his sufferings. He would live each day knowing it had been bought with a heavy price. Maybe that *would* make him a better man.

Finally, the time came when Yuri pronounced Alex ready to take the next step in the difficult journey that still lay ahead of him. Leaving Russia would be one of the most painful things he would face. He had come to love this country, for all its many faults. It had taken him in when all else had rejected him. It had given him back the vocation he loved. And friends he dearly loved would be left behind. Once across the Soviet border, he would never be able to come back. He would never see Yuri and his family again. He thought of that parting just before his capture. At least through that he'd been able to say good-bye to dear Anna, who he knew would pass away to heaven before he saw her again on this earth. Would he ever see sweet little Sophia again or her fiery husband? It seemed unlikely. And so he tried to keep focused on the new life that awaited him. The life with the woman he loved, the one he had also feared he would never see again.

Yet those thoughts forced him to face the most difficult parting of all. Before he could have that new life, he must part with Cameron once more. This would be torment for both of them, now that they were so close to grasping the future they had promised each other they would one day have together.

Alex, more than anyone, knew how much could still go wrong. The papers Marquet had procured for him were not of the best quality. Close scrutiny would likely reveal them to be fake. On the trip he must make across the Iron Curtain, there were any number of places where he would be required under normal circumstances to show them. Then there were all the possibilities of *abnormal* circumstances. There no doubt would be warnings posted at checkpoints to look out for a man of his description. Or he might be waylaid simply for *looking* suspicious. No number of disguises would completely hide his pale, gaunt appearance, his weak gait, and the tremor in his hands.

His system was cleaned out of the drugs for the most part, but that gnawing need was still too fresh. Physically the drugs were gone, but mentally . . . He didn't admit to Cameron or to Yuri that there were times when he thought of those injections. Not only thought of them, but thought of them fondly. He remembered the warmth of the narcotics flowing in his veins and the heady euphoria they gave him. He cursed himself whenever such thoughts entered his mind. Experience from his last addiction had taught him that if he persevered, those thoughts would diminish. But when they came now, fighting them, especially in his weakened physical condition, nearly brought him to his knees.

Cameron had asked Yuri if they shouldn't perhaps wait another few days. Alex probably hadn't hidden his thoughts from her as well as he had hoped. But Alex had insisted on going. He knew the only way to be completely free of his addiction was to plunge into his new life.

Yet to do that, he must temporarily leave the reason for that new life.

Inside the hospital room that had been their prison, Cameron clung to him tearfully.

"I didn't think this would be so hard," she said.

"It won't be long." He tried to comfort her, though he knew how lame his words sounded.

She still hadn't received her exit visa. She had been counting on Anatoly to expedite it. Now there was no telling what might become of it. The Soviet Immigration Ministry could be so inconsistent about such matters.

"You have the name of the hotel in Stockholm?" she asked, trying to be brave.

"Yes, and I will wait there until you come."

"Let's see if you are ready." She stood back and surveyed him.

He was wearing clothes borrowed from his brother-in-law, Gary. The men were about the same size, though the clothes hung a bit on Alex's now thin frame. Yuri had offered something from his wardrobe, but the clothes were all Russian-made. Alex was traveling as a Swede on business in Moscow, and it would be highly unlikely he'd wear any substandard Russian fashions. The nondescript brown wool suit, one of Gary's few civilian garments, was something a midlevel businessman would wear. The brown fedora helped shadow the pallor of Alex's face. He'd had a hard time taking the overcoat, which was rather expensive and would be difficult for Gary to replace in Russia. Alex said he could do without it, since the weather was still fairly mild, but the rain beating against the window didn't help his argument. Cameron insisted that it would appear strange for a businessman to be traveling without a coat.

"You look quite handsome," Cameron said with a loving smile.

"It's been a long time since I have worn American-made clothes. I got rid of mine when I came to Russia. I wanted to be a good Communist, you know."

She picked a piece of lint from his lapel. "They fit you well."

"Do they?" He chewed his lip. As much as he was anticipating his new life with Cameron, there were things to fear. How well would *he* fit back in with the American way of life? Disuse had made his English atrocious. Had his medical skills deteriorated, as well? If indeed he would even be able to practice medicine in America. Larry Marquet had made promises, but after all that had happened, could he be held to them? What would Alex do then? Allow himself to be supported by his wife's rich family?

She must have guessed what he was thinking. "One step at a time, Alex. First, Stockholm. That's all that matters right now."

He touched her soft cheek, then bent and kissed her lips. "First, Stockholm," he breathed.

Yuri came in then to see if they were ready. "The coast is clear," he said.

Alex embraced his friend one last time, then picked up the valise, also borrowed, but this from Robert Wood. Cameron had recently told him some interesting things about the embassy official who had played such a peculiar part in Alex's life. He might possibly one day even be Alex's brother-in-law, according to Cameron. What a world this was! Perhaps Alex really could fit in to it once again.

He and Cameron grasped hands once more, intoning that word they now clung to, "Stockholm!"

He left the room feeling very alone, more so even than when he had been in prison and feeling hopeless.

The empty hospital corridor seemed a thousand miles long as Alex traversed its length. He had practically lived in this hospital for years and in the most real sense was leaving behind blood, sweat, and tears. As much as he tried to look ahead, he knew each step was taking him farther and farther away from an important piece of himself. He felt drained as he reached the front doors of the hospital, as though he were leaving some of his strength behind. He reminded himself firmly that he wasn't. His real strength was in his heart, in the abiding love of his Lord. He was in no way alone.

He took that first step out the door with renewed hope. All that was left behind was a memory, not a millstone. Many of those memories were to be cherished, but there was a lifetime of cherished memories beckoning him.

A week later he arrived at the hotel in Stockholm. As much as he had trusted God to be with him on his journey, he was still a bit amazed he had made it unscathed. Never had his papers been questioned, though more than once they had been scrutinized. It could only have been the hand of God that kept him safe.

This was the first time in eight years he had breathed free air. Still, he had a tendency to look over his shoulder. And he felt strange when he spoke to the desk clerk, reticent to give too much information. But he had to inform him that he was expecting someone to arrive later.

"Who might that be, sir?" asked the clerk.

Alex hesitated a long while until it finally dawned on him that he need not be secretive.

"My wife," he said, for the first time since their marriage uttering those words to anyone. So fearful had he been of discovery, he hadn't even told Yuri.

The clerk glanced at Alex's passport, then said, "Mrs. Swenson?"

Alex blinked, almost forgetting he was traveling under an

assumed identity that he would have to maintain rather than make tedious explanations to the clerk. Would Cameron remember? She was better at these things than he.

"Yes," Alex said.

In the next days Alex tried to amuse and distract himself by visiting some of the tourist sites of the city. He spent time at the museums and went to bookstores, enjoying buying books he would have been arrested for reading in Russia. He bought a few English textbooks to help him brush up on the language. A week passed, then two.

He began to worry. When he had departed Russia, they had been so concerned about his safe passage, they hadn't given thought to the perils of Cameron's. Was there a minuscule chance she might be linked to him by the MVD? If so, they would haul her in for questioning. They would detain her for as long as they wanted because she had no diplomatic immunity. He told himself over and over that she had powerful friends and an even more powerful God. She would get out of the country.

By the sixteenth day after his departure from Russia, he was beginning to despair. He was in his room, unable to make himself take up any of his petty distractions. He paced the small area, his mind in a torment. If Cameron did not show up, he knew what he would do. He would find a way to feed that tiny hunger left in him from his addiction. He would feed it until he was senseless—

No! He gave his head a hard shake, then squeezed it between his hands as if attempting to obliterate the detested idea. She was his life, yet she could not be the end or the beginning of his life. Neither of them could live like that. It was enough that he bore the burden of Anatoly's life. He would not place a similar burden on her. He would stand or he would fall, but not because of her.

Yet, dear Lord, how can I bear life without her? Help me to trust you.

Still, he paced. And as evening came on, he knew he'd never be able to sleep. He was considering going out, finding something, a movie, anything, to keep him from going crazy with worry.

He barely heard the light knock on his door.

"Alex, are you there?" Her voice finally penetrated his tumultuous thoughts.

Racing to the door, he flung it open. She grinned at him, and as he lifted her in his arms, he couldn't tell if he was laughing or crying.

He kissed her over and over, vaguely aware of her heel catching the door and kicking it shut.

Finally he took a breath. "Camrushka!" he whispered. "You are here."

"I'm sorry it took so long." They kept holding each other as they talked. "I started to despair it would ever happen."

"Not you, my love!"

"Forgive me."

"I don't feel so bad now for the terrible, fearful thoughts I had." He kissed her silky hair, unable to get enough of her. "We must both work on our faith."

"Together."

Nodding, he breathed in her sweet fragrance. "Camrushka, we are truly free now, yes?"

"Finally, Alex, we are free." She then lifted the chain that was around her neck. On it was the old key he had given her during the war. "I don't know if we'll ever get to use this, as we once promised each other."

"In this moment I believe anything can happen," he said. "We will keep this key, and as it once reminded us of hope, let it now remind us of miracles and possibilities."

45

CECILIA TRIED to be calm. Seated in a chintz chair in the hotel suite, she glanced across the small sitting area to where Cameron and Alex sat on the sofa. Alex had come to act as translator, and of course Cameron would not be separated from him so soon after their homecoming. Indeed, Alex had insisted she come. Cecilia appreciated their willingness to accompany her back to Europe when they had been in America for only a few months. She needed them now, especially Cameron, for more than their knowledge of Russian.

Cameron smiled at her mother, a soothing gesture as she obviously noted Cecilia's tension. "He'll be here soon," she said.

But he was late. Only a few minutes, but still it wasn't a good sign. Cecilia glanced at her wristwatch for the tenth time in the last fifteen minutes. With a gentle smile she touched the watch. Keagan had given it to her this last Christmas. That thought occupied her scattered mind for a while.

It still amazed her that he had given her such a nice gift after all they had been through. A mere four months before Christmas she had feared all she would ever get from him was the boot. How she had struggled in the months after her surgery over telling him about Semyon! And how many times had she come to the point of telling him, then backed out. What a coward she was!

449

She still wasn't certain how she had finally overcome her fear. But one warm summer night they had gone to bed early and neither could sleep. Keagan thought it was the muggy heat. Cecilia thought it was because all the girls were off on a risky mission in Russia and it had been some time since they had heard from them. The last word had however been momentous, a secure note sent by Blair in the diplomatic pouch: "We found him!" But there had been nothing since.

Whatever the reason for their sleeplessness, Cecilia suggested some warm milk, so they padded down to the kitchen in lightweight robes in the middle of the night. Cecilia took milk from the icebox and poured some into a pan while Keagan rooted about in the cupboards for mugs. She had to smile that after twenty years in this house, he was still totally in the dark about the arrangement of the kitchen.

"How are these?" he said, putting two hot-chocolate mugs on the table. She hadn't seen them in years. They had Christmas designs on them and had been used years ago during the holidays.

"They'll be fine," she said, giving the pan a stir.

He opened the icebox. "Is there any of that pot roast left from dinner? We need a little something to snack on with the milk."

"Are you sure you want something that heavy this late?"

"You take the fun out of everything, wife!" He shut the icebox door, then ambled to the cookie jar. "Any arguments against a couple of cookies?"

"I don't see the harm."

He filled a plate with the chocolate chip cookies, then sat at the table, not waiting for the milk to try one.

"You know," he said between bites, "the girls are fine. No news is good news, and that is from a newspaper man!"

"Yes, I'm sure you are right." Suddenly she knew it wasn't the girls that had kept her awake. She knew the moment she had been dreading had come. "Keagan, I have something to tell you." Yes, this was like a bandage that must be ripped off quickly before one thought too much about it.

"Don't tell me we've lost another cook?"

She lifted the pan from the burner. "No, that's not it." With deliberately refined motions, she brought the pan to the table and poured the milk into the mugs. She knew she was procrastinating again. She had to remove the bandage now or never.

Setting the pan on the table with no thought to the hot surface burning the wood, she slipped into the chair adjacent to Keagan's. "Keagan, what I have to say is difficult. I ask that you let me finish before you say anything."

"Okay, but get on with it before the milk gets cold."

She licked her lips. "This happened thirty-one years ago. I should have told you then. I was a fool to hide it—"

"Stop, Cecilia!"

"Please, Keagan, you promised to let me finish."

"I don't want you to finish."

"But—"

"I know!"

She stared, uncomprehending. "What do you know?"

"I know what happened thirty-one years ago." He leveled a gaze at her that she could not define. Was it a look of pleading? He went on, "Don't say anymore. We'll forget it ever happened."

Comprehension washed slowly over her. "How . . . long have you known?"

"I've suspected for years, but I only knew for sure a few months ago, after your surgery."

"How?"

"That's not important."

Unexpected anger welled up as the full import of his words struck her. "You knew!" she railed. "You knew all these months and you said nothing? Letting me suffer in torment over it?"

"I thought it for the best," he offered lamely.

As quickly as the anger gripped her, it dissipated with a new realization. More gently she repeated, "You knew . . . and you said nothing?"

Absently he stirred his milk. She knew how he hated scum to form on his hot milk. She waited, watching him. Did she really know this man she had been married to for thirty-four years? Yes, she knew about things like the scum, that he hated pulp in his orange juice, and no starch in his shirts. But what of his heart? She had tried to get into that part of him over the years, but maybe not hard enough because she had feared what she might find there. There had always been a part of her that knew he did not really love her and that she did not deserve his love anyway.

Now she didn't know what to make of any of it. Had he remained silent out of love or fear?

"Why, Keagan? Why didn't you say anything?" she entreated.

"I'm sorry," he said. "I didn't know you were suffering so over it. But . . ." He paused. "We have *both* made mistakes, and I have made far more than you. I guess I thought you deserved your secret. Or I deserved for you to have a secret. I can't explain it any better."

"This is no trifling secret," she said. "I betrayed you."

"And you know very well I have betrayed you, as well. Can't we just call it even? Can't we go on with our lives as they were?"

How very tempting his words were! But a quick perusal of their past made her wonder if that was really what they wanted. The last year had been a great improvement, but how easy would it be for them to lapse backward? Especially if they brushed such a huge problem under the carpet.

"Keagan, I want our lives to be better, don't you?"

"Haven't I been good lately?"

"Yes, but that is not what I meant. I want us to live without fear, without barriers. And it will never be this way if we ignore our problems."

He rolled his eyes. "Women! You always want to *talk*."

"Because it is good for a marriage."

He let out a resigned sigh. "Can you spare me the gory details?"

"Thank you, Keagan." She reached over and laid her hand over his. "There is a reason why we can't just ignore these things. You see, Cameron has found him."

His brow knitted. "And?"

"If it is possible, I will want to go see him."

"It would be too difficult for you to go to Russia."

"I understand that, but we might be able to meet outside of Russia somewhere."

He pondered this for a long moment, his expression taut, his green eyes hooded and unreadable. "This is what I feared. You would find your lover and—"

"My lover?"

"That's what this is about, isn't it? You want to go see your . . . him?"

His eyes flashed and were quite readable, but what she read in them rather shocked her. "Keagan, are you jealous?" she asked, unable to hide the pleasure in her tone.

"Wouldn't you be if I dredged up some old lover and wanted to see her?"

She rubbed his hand gently. "Keagan . . . Keagan . . ." A tender smile curved her lips. "This has nothing to do with a lover. And just so you know, I never loved him. We were lonely, needy, that's all. There was never love."

"Would you tell me clearly, then, what this is all about?"

"You were the one who didn't want me to be clear," she said defensively but added quickly, "I wouldn't want to see him in any case. That is far in the past, and he is dead anyway. I am talking about our child. Keagan, I am talking about my son. Cameron has found him."

"Oh," he said flatly.

"If there is a chance, I would like to see him."

After a long pause he nodded. "I couldn't begrudge you that." With slight hesitation he added, "You wouldn't ask me to go with you, would you? I mean, I could accept a lot of things, but that— I don't think I could bear meeting your . . . son."

"Keagan, my love—" His brow raised at that word *love,* a word spoken so seldom between them. "Yes, Keagan, I love you, and I would never ask such a thing of you."

He seemed truly relieved.

She could not keep from adding, "I am sorry I never gave you a son. If I could somehow make Semyon be your son, I would. But, dear, please hear me when I say that if I had given you ten sons, I could never have done better than I did with our daughters. They are a treasure, if only you could believe that."

He didn't respond, but she knew he had heard her. She could see his mind taking in the words and, she could only hope, embracing them.

Her thoughts now returning to the hotel room in Stockholm, Cecilia looked at her watch again. What was keeping him? She knew he had arrived in Stockholm, but he was still a Soviet citizen and no doubt under scrutiny, despite his family's prominence, perhaps even because of it. Maybe he hadn't been able to slip away on his own.

When a knock came to the door, Cameron jumped up and answered it. It was just the waiter with the tea cart they had ordered. He wheeled it into the room, Cameron tipped him, and he left. Cameron smiled encouragingly at her mother.

Then another knock. If this wasn't him, Cecilia thought she might scream.

Cameron, who had not resumed her seat, answered it. Cecilia hurried to her feet. It was Semyon.

"Please come in," Cameron said.

"I am sorry to be late," he said in very practiced English.

Cecilia came to him. "Hello, Semyon, I am . . . Cecilia Hayes." How she wanted to say, "Your mother." But Cameron had hinted that he might have a difficult time with those words.

"I am happy to meet you," Semyon said.

"I didn't realize you spoke English," Cecilia said. "It will be wonderful to converse without the need of an interpreter. Do come in and sit down."

Semyon tossed a befuddled look at Cameron and said something in Russian. Cameron apparently had trouble deciphering the words spoken so quickly. She looked to Alex, who rose and joined them.

"He said he only learned a few English phrases for the meeting," Alex interpreted. "I think he memorized these by rote. He really doesn't speak much English and comprehends less."

This disappointed Cecilia, for she had hoped to speak directly to him. They all seated themselves, and with Alex interpreting, they finally began the meeting she had been hoping and praying for, for thirty-one years.

They talked for over an hour, she having more questions than he. He answered them all openly and willingly. Most of his questions were about his father. Cecilia showed him the pictures and the letters she had. As he read the letters from his birth father to Cecilia, all focusing entirely on Semyon and on Yakov's love for his son, Semyon's eyes grew misty. But he kept a firm hand on his emotions. Cecilia thought he must have learned his stoicism from his adopted father, because Yakov had been a far more passionate man. Nevertheless, she sensed that Semyon's passions, though imbedded deep within, were there, and he was a sensitive and thoughtful young man. Intuitively she knew he was a son to be proud of, in spite of the fact that he was a Communist, and a loyal one at that.

Cecelia offered the photos and letters to Semyon, but he took only one photo of him and his father together, saying too many photos and especially the letters would be too incriminating for him to keep.

Finally the time came when he had to depart. He rose and she did, as well.

"I don't know if it will be possible for another meeting," he said.

When the words had been interpreted, she replied, "I understand. I am just so happy we could at least have this time together."

"I am glad, too. I know so much I didn't know before, and I now feel more complete. Do you understand? I know you didn't leave me because you didn't care."

"Semyon, for all these years, I have lived with regret. But please be sure of this, I have always loved you."

He swallowed. She could see he was fighting hard to control

his emotions. She hesitated over her next words, not wanting to push him over the edge, but she knew she could not watch him leave without uttering them.

"Semyon, would you mind . . . would it be all right if I . . . hugged you?"

He nodded, but quickly she wished she had just acted on her words rather than speaking them, because awkward moments followed. They stepped closer to each other, their arms reaching clumsily. For a moment she feared it might become just a quick brush. But after all these years of waiting she could not let that happen. So with determination she reached her arms all the way around him. At first he seemed a bit wooden, then slowly he lifted his arms, as well. That was all it took for the brush to become a true embrace. Mother and son held each other as had always been intended.

Before he left, he picked up a package he had laid on the table earlier. "I brought you a present," he said, holding out the gold foil-covered box.

"Oh," she uttered. "I brought you nothing. Cameron said it might not be a good idea to give you anything foreign."

"You have given me the photo of my father. That is enough." He pushed the box toward her once more.

She took it and lifted the lid. Inside was a beautiful fringed shawl, made in a traditional Russian style she remembered. It was of a fine wool, a black background with a design of vivid red flowers.

"It's lovely!" she exclaimed. She took it from the box and wrapped it around her shoulders.

"My mother said you would enjoy it. I wanted you to have something to remember me with."

"I shall treasure it, Semyon." Fingering the wool of the shawl, she wondered if he had known what it would mean to her to have a gift from her son.

With her heart clenched inside her, she watched him go. She tried not to dwell on the harsh fact that this might well be the only time she would ever see him. Yet she thanked God she'd had this time, a meeting against all possibilities.

46

CAMERON SURVEYED the scene in the kitchen with poignant amusement. Blair, of all people, had taken charge of the cooking, with Jackie as her competent assistant. Cecilia hadn't been certain she'd be up to cooking the huge meal for nine and had suggested a caterer because they had recently lost another cook. But Blair had insisted on cooking. From the delicious fragrances floating about the room, there was no doubt she had done a marvelous job.

This would be a special meal for more reasons than the holiday that provided an excuse for it. First, Blair and Gary were home on a short sabbatical from his post in Russia. There were still a few months left to his tour, but he had announced that an embassy position in Rome had opened, and they would be going there next. They had actually taken well to the life of international diplomats. They both still longed for children, and for the first time Blair was actually talking seriously about adoption.

But the main reason they had come home was so that Blair, along with Cameron, could be bridesmaids, or matrons, in Jackie's wedding, which was going to take place on Saturday. Yes, she was finally going to become Mrs. Robert Grunwald. For much of the last year she and Robert had carried on a long-distance love affair while he dealt with family duties in Boston, which he sometimes referred to as a mop-up. But actually the Wood/Grunwald clan was bouncing back fairly well after Robert had forced them all to claim their Jewish heritage. A month ago he had moved permanently to Los Angeles, where he was setting up a law practice. Never very close to his family, he was happy to settle in Jackie's hometown so that she and his soon-to-be step-daughter would not have to leave those who were so dear to them.

All of their lives seemed to be working out well. Cameron had wondered when she and Alex had first arrived home after the escape from Russia if things might regress to the turmoil of the past—with their father, at least. Keagan had never accepted Cameron's marriage to Alex, and now with the reality of it unavoidable, he had balked once more.

"I don't care how good a man he is, Cameron," Keagan had declared. "Do you realize how this could destroy your career, being married to a Commie—"

"An *ex*-Communist, Dad!" she retorted.

"That doesn't matter. To be closely associated to anyone with past or present ties to Communism—I don't even want to think of the repercussions."

"That's just your imagination, Dad."

"You've been out of the country most of the time since the war. You are not in touch with things. Fear of Communism is growing."

"Alex and I have dealt with far worse. We'll deal with that, too."

It had taken time and getting to know his son-in-law before Keagan was able to mellow enough to accept him. It had been the same story with Robert. Keagan swore up and down he wasn't a bigot, yet to him, having a Jew in the family was almost as bad as having a Japanese. Yes, he had come to love and accept Emi, but in his mind that was something totally different, though he had never been able to define that difference. Only when he saw how happy Jackie was with Robert and how well Robert treated both his daughter and granddaughter did Keagan soften his attitude toward his future son-in-law.

Now sitting at the kitchen table with her mother, Cameron was getting a bit restless.

"Are you sure I can't help?" she asked her busy sisters.

"You just take it easy, sis," said Blair. "We've got it all under control." She was opening the oven door and removing the beautifully roasted turkey.

Cameron doubted she could be of much help anyway. She still could barely boil water. But that wasn't all. She simply wasn't comfortable being on her feet for too long. Her ankles had a tendency to swell, her back often hurt, and she was just plain clumsy. But she supposed that was normal when one was eight months pregnant. She still couldn't believe it. Around Christmastime, she and Alex would be parents! She was going to be a mother! The idea scared her to the tips of her shoes—if, indeed, she could *see* the tips of her shoes!

At least she knew she would have wise and experienced help from her mother and Jackie. And she was married to a doctor, for heaven's sake—that should mean something. Except Alex had confided that the last time he had delivered a baby had been in medical school, and he had cared for very few after that. Well, help wouldn't be far away, since she and Alex had decided to settle in Los Angeles. She was working for the *Journal,* having been promoted to the position of city editor. Alex had taken a post as a surgeon at Los Angeles General Hospital. Larry Marquet had been true to his word—after Cameron had leaned on him a bit—and Alex had been made a U.S. citizen and had received his license to practice medicine. All their dreams were coming true, but neither of them would ever forget the price that had been paid for their happiness.

Blair pronounced that everything was ready, and the family was called to the dining room, where the table was laid out with Cecilia's finest settings. After the appropriate oohs and aahs were made over the perfect turkey, Keagan rose and lifted his glass of sparkling cider into the air.

Almost-six-year-old Emi was squirming a bit in her chair and eyeing the food hungrily.

Keagan laughed. "I see you got your share of the notorious Hayes impatience, little girl! But I don't often get the whole family around like this, so I have to give a speech. Don't worry, I hate long speeches, too."

Everyone laughed and Jackie put an arm around her daughter to soothe her.

"Well," Keagan went on, "I just have to say that looking out on this family, I can hardly believe what we have become. A Japanese, a Ruskie, a Jew—"

"Dad!" Cameron intoned warningly.

"Pipe down, girl, and let me finish," he admonished, an amused glint in his green eyes. "Where was I? Jew, Japanese, Ruskie . . . and of course us Micks . . ." He turned a smug grin toward Cameron.

With a half-apologetic shrug, she smiled back.

He continued, "Why, we're a regular American melting pot right at one table. And you know what? It's a nice feeling. Not half bad, really. Makes us rather interesting. But that's not all I want to say." He paused and glanced at Emi, who had started wiggling again. "Just one more minute, kiddo. All this reminds me of how we got this way. You young fellows out there, that's how. And I have to tell you honestly, if I had done the choosing, I would not have chosen any of you as husbands for my daughters. Which only goes to show, it's a good thing I didn't! I'm going to say right now before God and my wife that my girls made pretty fine choices. I'm looking forward to welcoming yet another son-in-law into the family. I have one more thing to say, and this last has been a long time coming. I am proud of my daughters! Not in spite of them being females, but because of it. You young gentlemen have to agree with me when I say they are truly better than sons!"

Everyone stood and toasted heartily to Keagan's words. Cameron felt a little dizzy and had no doubt that Blair and Jackie were feeling the same. If they never heard such words from their father again, those were enough to last a lifetime.

History Written With
Passion & Faith

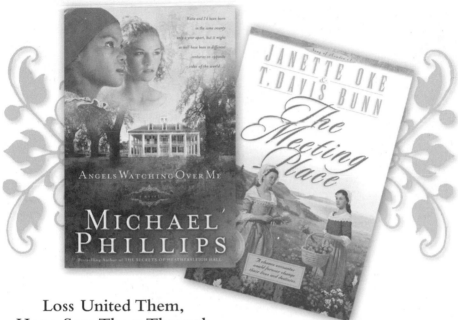

Loss United Them, Hope Sees Them Through

Brought together when their families were lost in the Civil War, two Southern girls must rely on each other to stay safe. One the daughter of a plantation owner, one the daughter of a slave, they fight against everything they'd been taught about the other in order to trust, survive, and see better days ahead. A dramatic historical series from bestselling author Michael Phillips.

Angels Watching Over Me
A Day to Pick Your Own Cotton
The Color of Your Skin Ain't the Color of Your Heart
Together Is All We Need

A Chance Encounter Will Forever Change Their Lives

The year was 1753, and the lines of separation between the French and British in Acadia were firmly drawn. But then a chance encounter of Catherine Price and Louise Belleveau leads to an unexpected friendship in this heartwarming tale of devotion and loss, of bonds stronger than blood and faith stronger than tragedy.

The Meeting Place
The Sacred Shore
The Birthright
The Distant Beacon
The Beloved Land

 BETHANYHOUSE